To Helen,
with the best
of wishes —

Geo Carl
5/30/03

THE CHERRY TREE

From Northern Liberties Press a new novel...

THE CHERRY TREE

THE CHERRY TREE

BY

LEE CARL

northern liberties press

Philadelphia, Paris
Kuala Lumpur, London

Published by
Northern Liberties Press
Old City Publishing Inc.
628 North 2nd Street
Philadelphia, PA 19123, USA

Visit our web site at: **oldcitypublishing.com**

This book is a work of fiction. Names, characters, places and incidents either are products of the author's imagination or are used fictitiously. Any resemblance to actual events or locales or persons, living or dead, is entirely coincidental.

ISBN 0-9704143-4-X (hardcover)

Library of Congress Cataloging-in-Publication Data

Carl, Lee, 1929-
    The Cherry Tree / by Lee Carl.
        p. cm.
    ISBN 0-9704143-4-X (hardcover)
    1. Philadelphia--Fiction. 2. Aged men--Fiction. 3. Arson--Fiction. I. Title.

PS3603 A75 C48 2003
813'.6--dc21

                                        2002070191

To Gordon and Joan,
for 50 years of friendship

and

To Jackie,
my teacher, my colleague, my friend.

Previous books by Lee Carl:

The White Squirrel

Under The Burdock Weed

Acknowledgements

The author gives special thanks to his astute editor, Fred Maher, and to Guy, Ian, Susan, Donna, Diane, Gus and the entire staff at Northern Liberties Press.

Chapter One

Sultry. The stink of smog.
Mid-July.
After midnight.

A small, greasy man moved around in the rear of his bookstore straightening magazines and turning off lights. He pushed his sweaty fingers through his thin, black hair, sighed, and dug for his keys.

Minutes later, Eddie Sharp's bulbous nose and scarlet rosacea glistened in the glare of neon as he stood on the sidewalk pulling on his padlock. He glanced at the steel mesh that guarded his window, then walked east, past another Arch Street porno shop that still flashed its gaudy lights to beckon lusty old men and glassy-eyed young studs.

The year was 1978, long before the rebirth of this strip of Center City Philadelphia, years before the first brick in the new Convention Center that would rise some 15 years later to convert dinginess to glisten and gleam, attract throngs, and change a few blocks of Arch Street forever. These were the seedy days of murk and grim.

Dark, slight and bent, Eddie hurried under the rusty Reading Terminal overpass, toward the old Trocadero Theater, a burlesque house during decades long gone. He roomed near there, on the edge of Philadelphia's Chinatown. A grizzly drunk lay curled in a doorway, and the warm night breeze carried trash paper along the sidewalk. A blue-and-white police car crossed Arch, speeding south on 10th, as paper flew across the street from gutter to gutter. Fire sirens obscured the distant, mournful call of a ship on the Delaware River.

Parts of the Delaware Valley fell asleep as Philadelphia quieted. Although night lights burned in shops and department stores, the Market Street East district was nearly deserted by the time the moon-faced clock on the ornate tower of City Hall struck 1:30. Several pedestrians hurried, scurried or staggered, and one brave soul stepped down into a subway entrance where summer heat mixed with the smell of urine.

South on Walnut and Spruce streets, a few prostitutes scanned the light traffic for interested johns. Male hustlers had staked out territories on Spruce near 15th. Loitering under the picturesque gaslamps-of-old, a skinny, pimply faced kid tarnished the steps of the Academy of Music at Broad and Locust Streets. In the narrow alleys, where artisans had toiled in the days of Ben Franklin, gays and straights shifted from bar to bar.

Police called Eddie Sharp back to his Arch Street porno shop shortly after 2 a.m. The padlock had been jimmied and pornographic magazines had been pushed from the shelves and scattered about wildly. In the rear, 10 of 14 peep-show booths had been smashed, leaving broken glass and splintered wood scattered about. The greatest fury had been unleashed against the west wall racks of gay porno. Scores of magazines had been ripped and tossed, surely in violent anger.

"You got enemies, Eddie," said a lean, blond cop who stood in the doorway. He couldn't have cared less.

* * *

Eight days later.
Early evening.
Hotter. More sultry.
Jeffrey Broomell kicked off his shoes, stretched out on the hotel bed, closed his eyes and relaxed his muscles, but he could still feel pulsation in his biceps. His heavy briefcase full of textbooks still seemed to tug on his arm.

An hour later he slipped back into his well-polished shoes, then wet his face in the bathroom and dried it on a thick, white towel. He rode the elevator to the ornate lobby of the Ben Franklin Hotel where he circled a cluster of patio tables and umbrellas. His intent was to find seafood at one of Philadelphia's finest restaurants and pamper himself with lobster in drawn butter—compensation for eating alone. He hated to eat alone.

Jeff was a textbook salesman out of Chicago. He had arrived at Philadelphia International Airport on a morning flight and had visited the Penn, Temple and Villanova campuses before kicking off his shoes at the Ben Franklin.

A tall, sandy-haired, blue-eyed traveler, he was a trim 35-year-old who looked the part of an out-of-town salesman, well-fitted in his tan suit. He stood apart from others and was quickly eyed by more than the common streetwalker. But Jeff passed up the hungry stares and his own fleeting temptations. He ate in a deep corner of Bookbinder's restaurant on 15th Street, taking his time, enjoying the air conditioning as well as his martini and lobster.

Thoughts were of his wife—a small, bubbling blonde—and of his two towheaded daughters, ages 5 and 7. He looked at his wristwatch. Martha was probably in the kitchen. Janie surely had her hands into everything, and Martie undoubtedly was in a streak of never-ending questions.

Hours later Jeff kicked off his shoes again and stretched out on his hotel bed. He sighed, then gave a whispery shout: "Shit!" His lobster dinner had filled him with guilt, especially since he couldn't pass it all off on his meager expense account. The Broomells paid too much mortgage on a small house in a treeless development outside of Chicago. He turned his mind to stuffed animals and pretty little things for pretty little girls.

At 10:30 Jeff clicked on the television, switched from channel to channel to channel, and then turned it off. Minutes later he slipped into his shoes and left his room, with no set purpose. Under the lights of Chestnut Street he decided: Maybe one drink at one bar.

Philadelphia's arty alleys offered him an assortment of taverns and clubs, but he wasn't choosy. A brick archway under pink neon was the first entrance to beckon. The tavern was dark inside, but Jeff's eyes couldn't miss the giant pink elephant hanging in the center of the large square bar—a bar crowded with males whose eyes turned on him. He knew at a glance that he was in the wrong place, and almost tripped over his feet as indecision rattled him. Although he wanted to leave, the stares prevented a quick turnabout. One fast drink, perhaps. Then he would leave. No. No, he'd be too uncomfortable. No. He spun around, and a tingle raced up his backbone as he reached for the golden oak door.

Just as Jeff pulled open the door, a dark figure in the alley tossed a flashing object that smashed on the concrete entryway. Bottle-glass flew in all directions as flames roared through the gasoline vapors. Jeff screamed as splattering fire burned his face. The doorway was ablaze and he was engulfed as tongues of flame lapped at his body.

Chapter Two

The old house reached toward the sky, seemingly stretching, narrowing to its single attic window. Its porch had been shaded for years by a wide-spreading oak that was long gone, a gnarled tree whose stump still rotted near the raised and cracked sidewalk. The house was putty and gray, the shades of mourning doves and city pigeons. It was lightened by rain, wind and sun, darkened by streaks of soot, hardly a color at all when merged with evening. Gone was all but blue, deep in the ridges of crooked shutters that distorted the shape of every window. The Victorian curlicues that trimmed the high gables were bare but for crusts of bird waste. A trumpet vine, its orange-red horns tooting the glory of summer, had a stranglehold on the porch, lifting the railing and bending the rain spout, separating the tin roof from the fancy curls of wood trim.

An old cherry tree at the south-side-rear was as aged as the old man who lived alone in the house. It still bore fruit, but its fat limbs were cracked and bleeding with sticky sap. Like the old man, it had been hurt by the cuts and bruises of life. Unlike him, it felt the warmth of the sun.

Mason House, as the tall ghost of the 19th century was known to residents of this Philadelphia suburb, stood near the town marker, alone, announcing the township line to motorists who knew local landmarks. It took a corner slice from the north end of an old cemetery—a sprawling park of tombstones, shrubs and trees. A rock wall turned along the south side of Henry Mason's property and turned again to mark the rear of his yard. The wall dipped low as the earth sloped up, making the deep, southwest corner of Mason's backyard the only easy mark for youngsters who wanted to climb into the graveyard. A cluster of old privet, more tree-like than hedge, helped climbers hide their awkward struggles at heaving, pulling, lifting and jumping. A hedgerow of firethorn along the back wall shielded the approach and escape route from the gaping rear windows of Mason House.

The young adventurers were sure the old man didn't like their trespassing, but it was the only way, especially in evening when the high iron gates were locked. Besides, the nearest gate was a mile walk. Anyway, it was more fun to intrude where unwanted, to sneak onto that bedeviled land that was under the spell of the old man. Billy Bannon had first traveled his secret path when exploring at age 11. His schoolmate, Clarence Scott, had suffered two kicked chins while boosting him over the wall. But the job had become easier as years passed. By age 13, each had learned to hoist himself.

Not until this summer, at age 16, had Billy taken Lori into the cemetery. Without a car, he found no better place to cuddle. So, in late June, he and Lori staked out a grassy patch behind a large tombstone of pink granite marking the Smythe family plot. Spreading yews, old azaleas and a blue spruce joined the tombstone in building a barrier that concealed Billy's hideaway from the cemetery road—a curving roadway seldom used at night.

Billy was a slender youth with big eyes of warm brown. His thick, curly, black hair contrasted strongly with his fair, wax-like skin. His features were clearly cut, almost chiseled—straight nose, high cheekbones above deep hollows, heavy brows above large eye sockets.

Lori was a high-school cheerleader—trim, blue-eyed and blonde. She was a hyperactive girl easily excited by the wonderments of life. She wiggled in passion and widened her eyes, not only for Billy, but for chipmunks, touchdowns, snowstorms and big red roses. Her cute turned-up nose would poke itself into any mischief.

This was an evening in early August. Warm at dusk. The fragrance of newly mown grass, the perfume of love. Crickets and tree toads had begun the chorus of night sounds that Billy and Lori associated with their special place on the ground behind the tombstone. The sounds and scents were linked with moist lips and beating hearts, with feeling, touching and breathing together.

The 16-year-olds rolled closer to that heavy slab of pink granite. He pushed hair from her eyes, then lay his cheek on hers. Teasingly he hissed into her ear. She giggled.

The moon shone brightly between the branches of giant elms and hemlocks, flickering as breezes tossed the boughs. Billy and Lori suddenly realized that they had stayed too late. They tightened the belts around their jeans and then raced toward the corner of the cemetery and Old Man Mason's house. Hand in hand they ran, dodging bushes and trees. In a thicket of mock orange, he boosted her to the top of the wall. She jumped as he hoisted himself.

On the other side of the wall, Billy squinted at his wristwatch. His father was a police lieutenant who set rules. Lori's mother was a worrier who fretted and fussed because her daughter was "too pretty for her own good." The teenagers stayed crouched behind Mason's bushy privet, peeking at the house between clusters of the tall woody shrubs.

"There!" Billy exclaimed in hushed words. "Those windows! Look. See what I mean? They have boards over them. Now do you understand?"

A rear window and two side windows, shrouded by the limbs of the old cherry tree, were nailed shut, flat strips of wood crisscrossing over the shutters. Obviously the boards were intended to seal one particular room from the outdoors—a second-floor room on the southwest corner. Lori stared hard. She watched as speckles of moonlight raced across the boarded windows. Wind tossed cherry branches that screeched as they scratched old clapboard and a shabby rainspout. Lori's eyes widened and her lips parted.

"Clarence says the old fart keeps something up there in that room," Billy said. "Something strange. You know, like something real weird. Clarence is sure of it. He climbed the tree. Said he heard sounds in there."

"What kind of sounds?"

"Somebody yelling and crying. And like some thumping and scraping. Weird stuff. Like I said."

7

"Clarence makes up stories."

"Not this time."

"He's always making up stories."

"I'm telling you, he heard something. I could tell by his look. He was all excited. His face was all sweaty and pale. Honest to God. I could tell he heard something strange."

"It was probably just the old man talking to himself." Lori really wanted to believe it was more.

"Maybe. But somebody was yelling at something that wasn't answering. And why close up those windows?"

"Maybe they broke." She didn't really believe that.

"Three windows in one room? Yeah, just like that, three windows blow open in one room. No way."

"I got to go." Lori started along the wall, crouching as she hurried. "Ouch!" She scratched her arm on the damnable spines of the firethorn.

"You okay?"

"Let's hurry."

Billy took one last look at Mason House, its high upper stories reaching well above the tangle of growth, an unkempt thicket of sassafras, grape and cedar that smothered the lower back of the house, nearly hiding the rear porch and pantry. In the moonlight, the narrowing third story and fourth-floor attic appeared almost stately, the blemishes erased by the blue-white hue. A reflection of days long gone.

* * *

The two teenagers climbed the wall earlier than usual the following night and scampered around the cemetery for almost an hour, teasing each other and talking a lot about little or nothing, delaying, anticipating.

"Did you ever eat dandelions?" he asked.

"The flowers?"

"No, the leaves. Dad calls them greens. He likes them, so Mom fixes them. I don't like 'em."

"I didn't know you could eat them."

"How about mushrooms? You like mushrooms?"

"I love them," she answered. "How about you?"

He gave her a clumsy kiss, and she shoved him into a cluster of prickly arborvitae.

"Hey, cut that out!" He lifted himself from the bush, brushed himself off, snorted like a pig, and ran after her.

Lori giggled as she dashed this way and that, then laughed as he grabbed her around the waist and kissed her on the nape of the neck.

On their way back to their special place, they zigzagged among beds of red and pink geraniums, then detoured to the cats. The caretakers encouraged cats to breed in a secluded grove where thick evergreens hid a plywood shelter and several tin bowls.

"Meow!" Billy called.

None of the cats answered.

The large pink stone of Smythe lay not far from where the boy and girl had entered the cemetery via Old Man Mason's backyard. Billy ran toward it, racing ahead of Lori.

"Come on!"

He squatted behind the gravestone, waited, then pulled Lori down into his arms. They rolled over, then stretched out their legs.

The day had been gray, the evening grayer. This night would bring no moonlight. But that would not take away the magic. The summer of summers—that's what it had been and still was for Billy and Lori. Neither had held so tightly before. Neither had experienced such feelings. They saw beauty in a finger, a nose, a chin, an ear lobe. How it felt to have cheek on cheek, to feel the smoothness of 16-year-old skin, the firmness of 16-year-old flesh.

They could not pull away until after darkness—darkness that came more quickly than before and seemed to fall more heavily upon them. No stars. The teenagers held hands as they hurried toward the near corner of the cemetery. They could barely see their way as they climbed the wall and then leaped into Mason's yard.

Lori peered between clumps of privet and hushed herself as she called out in surprise, "There's light there! See it?" Lowering her voice even more, she whispered, "Just a thin line of light between those shutters, where the boards don't cross. See? Somebody's in that room."

"Let me see." Billy crouched. In the dark, moonless night, the house was a tower of blackness, dim lights hardly visible through the shrouded windows of the first floor.

"See?"

"Yeah. And that other window, too. Look. Just a little thread of light between the boards."

"Climb the cherry tree."

"No."

"Please?"

"No. I don't want to."

"Oh, come on, Billy. Climb it. See if you hear anything."

"No. Let's go."

"Don't you want to find out?"

"Lori!"

"If you won't climb the tree, I will."

"Y'know what my old man would do if we got caught? Can't you see it? A cop's kid climbing Old Man Mason's cherry tree and trying to peek into his windows. The thought makes me shiver. Holy crap."

"We won't get caught. Nobody'll ever know. It's black as pitch. Besides, Clarence did it. If Clarence could do it, we can."

"No way! Clarence is Clarence. I'm not Clarence."

Lori pushed her way between the clumps of privet and sneaked toward the cherry tree. Billy watched for a few seconds, sighed, mumbled, and then followed as he shook his head. He tripped on a root, but caught himself as he muttered a curse. Here and there his feet sunk into spongy sod, raised and softened by moles.

"Wait," he whispered as Lori made a feeble effort to reach for a branch. "Let me." He glanced from side to side as if fearful that someone had heard him.

Billy grasped a low, fat limb and lifted his feet off the ground to where his sneakers took hold of the trunk. The rough bark burned his hands as he grunted while pulling himself up to the first crotch. Turning, he looked down at Lori, then up into the tree. Seconds later he hoisted himself to the next crotch, then began to work his way out on a large limb that reached upward toward one of the boarded windows. Suddenly he felt the limb give, sending a shockwave through his body. He stayed frozen until he heard the cracking of the brittle branch as it began to bend and break under his weight.

Lori gave a hushed cry: "Billy!"

Realizing that he had crawled out on a dying limb, the boy grabbed for a higher, healthier branch, lifting his weight as he struggled to maneuver back toward the trunk. With each tug-and-shift his knees weakened and sweat bubbled on his forehead. Once again in the safety of the crotch, he breathed deeply, felt the beat of his heart, and questioned the reasonableness of his mission.

"Are you okay?" Lori called in a strained whisper.

"Yeah," he answered quietly. "But this tree is dying."

"What are you going to do? Maybe you should come down."

"Shush."

"I'm sorry. I shouldn't have..."

"Shush!"

Billy began again, this time crawling out on a higher, stronger limb whose offshoots were abundant with leaves. He stretched himself out and squirmed forward like a lizard, inches at a time. As the branch thinned, he held more tightly with hands, arms and legs. When about 10 feet from the house, he stopped as the bough began to bend. He thought he heard movement in the room, but no matter how hard he strained he wasn't sure. Then it came—a shadow, momentarily blocking that thin line of light, as if someone or something had passed close to the window. Then again. And again. A man or beast, perhaps? Some mumbling? He wasn't sure. Then he was certain, because the voice grew loud, but was muffled into nonsense for Billy. It was heavy and rumbling, perhaps the ravings of the old man. Louder still it came, until it was shout upon shout.

Lori walked closer to the house and looked up. Billy was but a dark mass in the foliage. He didn't move, and she questioned her perception. Surely that was Billy. But she wasn't certain.

"Billy?"

"Shush!"

A moment later the voice softened, only to grow loud again. Billy squirmed closer to the house. The bough bent, and he held tightly, his muscles taut. He was within seven feet of the window when he distinguished a few words from a long, loud, rambling tirade. "…and Lord damn them with fire…" Billy flinched. "…burn them with blazing sulfur…" The teenager edged backward, his legs bent like a frog's. No way could he turn around safely, so he kept inching rearward until the limb was fat enough to permit quicker moves. He maneuvered fast and within minutes jumped from the tree's lowest limb, grabbed Lori by the hand and pulled her toward the firethorn hedge.

"What is it?" she asked, her eyes wide as her emotions peaked.

* * *

Rain fell the next night. Then it drizzled for two days more. The weather stayed hot and humid, and within a week mosquito wrigglers were in their glory, twisting and squirming toward adulthood in scores of water-filled cavities in the cemetery—tree hollows, concrete urns, gutters, sink holes, vases of dying flowers, and other nooks and basins.

To Billy and Lori it seemed that all the buzzing mosquitoes had split from their pupae on the same night—that muggy Tuesday night of swatting and scratching. No necking could stand the test too long, and when the teenagers fled toward Mason's property, the western sky was still streaked with sunlight. As they climbed the wall they vowed never again to wear shorts. Next time they would soak themselves in insect repellent.

Mason House loomed sharply against the fading light of the late evening sky. A hazy yellow moon was barely visible, and all seemed stilled by the heavy, humid air. Billy and Lori scratched their legs as they peered again between those clumps of privet. It had become a ritual.

"Mom told me his wife got killed in a car crash," Lori whispered. "A long time ago. Mom said she was real pretty. Long, blonde hair."

"I've only seen him once." The boy's words were hushed. "Maybe... maybe twice." He was thoughtful. Puzzlement lowered his brows.

"I've never seen him."

"One night in Jake's Deli. He bought something and left.

Clarence poked me and said, 'That's the old geezer. That's Old Man Mason.' Outside, we sat on the curb, sucked on our Coke bottles, and watched him walk away. He turned and looked back at us. Just stood there. And I felt stupid for staring."

"What did he look like?"

"Tall and thin. Kind of bushy hair. Gray. I don't remember much. But there was another time, I think. I must have been very young. He was standing there, on his big porch. My father grabbed me and pulled me away. It was weird. I remember a funny look on Dad's face. Strange. Real strange."

"Mom said he has a son who went to Korea, came back from the war, and then disappeared. Nobody knows where he went." Lori pushed her way through the privet. "Come on. Climb the tree again."

"You don't give up, do you?"

"Come on."

"Hell, no. Anyway, it's too light out. Let's get out of here. Man-oh-man, I'm itching like crazy."

Lori stepped back between the tall clusters of hedge, grasped the boy's hand, and pulled. "It's getting dark. Dark enough, anyway. We'll just do a quicky, a fast up-and-down. Then we'll go."

"I like this 'we' stuff. I'm the one who does the climbing."

"Please?"

"I'm not going up that tree," Billy insisted as he pushed through the privet and began sneaking over the mole hills toward the house.

"Let's head for the tree, then go over there, into those bushes." Somehow Lori felt that if she got close enough to the house, some sort of hidden meaning would rub off. Maybe she would learn the mysteries through osmosis or feel the pumping pulse of the enigma.

"I can't take the mosquitoes."

"They're not bad here," Lori said as she pushed her fingers between Billy's, gripping his hand tightly.

"Like hell they aren't! And just wait until you hit those freakin' bushes."

"Shush."

They stood under the cherry tree, lifting their eyes skyward. No

13

light came from the boarded windows, but that didn't dampen Lori's curiosity. For the moment, she gave up her idea of snooping through the bushes around the edge of the house.

"It's all dark up there," Billy said.

"That's when we should get close to those windows and listen. If we hear sounds when there's no light in that room, then we know for sure he keeps something locked up in there. Don't you see?"

"I'm ready for a hot bath." Billy scratched his elbow. "Let's get out of here."

"Boost me up the tree. I can climb."

"No way."

Again and again Lori tried to leap for a low branch. Billy couldn't help but smile at her futile efforts. Each of her attempts pricked his manliness. His macho virility refused to allow him to stand there while his girlfriend tried to climb the tree. So, after a few false starts, he stepped forward and pulled her back. He grasped that low, fat limb and began his struggle. More sure of himself this time, he used the same grips, pulls and pushes, and aimed for that sturdy limb above the second crotch. The rough bark chafed his bare legs, but felt somewhat good at first as it scratched and scraped his bug bites. He tried his best to ignore the intensified itch as he reached for that strong, helpful branch.

Billy slipped and his feet came down hard on the dying limb that had frightened him before. The brittle bough creaked and cracked and gave way under his weight. It scraped the house, giving off a harsh grating sound as it tore at the clapboard and dislodged a piece of rusty rainspout. The boy grunted and held fast to the bending bough above.

"Oh God!" Lori exclaimed. "Are you all right?" She bit her bottom lip. "Billy! Talk to me, Billy!" She kept staring up into the tree until too much dirt fell into her eyes. She squinted, bent her neck and shoulders, and looked at the ground as she tried to remove tiny bits of bark. Her eyes watered as she blinked, giving some relief. Billy was safe in the second crotch by the time Lori lifted her head and stared right into the face of Old Man Mason.

To say Henry Mason's expression showed ill temper would be an understatement. He stood about six feet from Lori, ready to lash out angrily. The tall, lean man, just topping six-foot-two, had appeared from around the shrub-shrouded back corner of his house. Slightly bent by age, he no longer struggled to lift his shoulders. And he had given up other wearisome efforts, such as shaving every day and combing his hair. A gray mop topped his long, gaunt face. He had failed to button and zip everything, and his wrinkled pants stayed up without a belt, thanks to a safety pin.

Lori might have run if not for Billy's hanging in the tree. Her mouth open, she kept staring at the old man as a confusing mixture of impulses and thoughts raced through her mind.

Mason had expected a boy, but was taken aback only for seconds before yelling, "What the hell do you think you're doing?"

"Just... Just looking."

"Looking? Looking at what?"

"It's not her fault," Billy said from above.

Startled, Mason looked up into the tree. His anger grew to rage. "Get the hell down from there! You hear me? Get out of there! Not in that tree! You hear me! Never there! No, no, never!" The ferocity of his tone seemed beyond that demanded by Billy's naughty deed. His entire body began to shake. "You can't... Not the cherry tree."

Lori's eyes couldn't grow any wider. She meekly explained, "We just wanted to pick a few cherries."

Mason breathed deeply. He kept his eyes on Lori as he sucked in air again and again, wheezing each time he exhaled. Recovering from his outburst, he finally said, "It's long past cherry season in these parts, girl." Although somewhat subdued, his tone was still harsh enough to send another shiver through Lori.

Billy ripped his T-shirt, scraped his back, knocked his elbow, leaped to the ground and twisted his ankle. He was still struggling to balance himself when the old man spun him around and grabbed him by the back of the neck. Holding a wad of T-shirt, Mason pushed Billy toward the back of the house while the boy choked and coughed from the pressure of the neck band against his Adam's apple. Lori was suddenly yanked by the wrist. She found herself being pulled along by Mason as he shoved Billy.

"You're trespassing," Mason scolded gruffly. "You're smart enough to know that, aren't you?"

They skirted the thicket of sassafras, grape and cedar as Mason pushed and yanked the teenagers toward the shrub-covered, weather-worn porch and pantry door. Though amazed at the old man's strength, Billy was certain that he could escape if he so wished, but he didn't dare try. He tripped up the steps without falling, being held upright by Mason's grasp. Lori's feet moved fast as she was almost dragged and forced to quicken her pace. The crooked screen door was ajar, and Mason forced it open with his foot and elbow, then shoved the boy inside.

A dingy, overhead lamp lighted the pantry—a small room lined with shelves of dusty jars containing food preserved many years ago by Mason's wife. The huge kitchen held a massive, black-iron coal stove whose fat pipe took an L-turn into the wall. Next to it was a gas range purchased in the late forties—wide and white with a double oven, soiled and streaked with grease. The green linoleum floor-covering was worn to a reddish brown in front of the porcelain sink. A large, hooded light hung above the broad, wooden table that had been painted ivory over dark green that showed at chips around the edges.

Billy hit his hip on the doorjamb as Mason pushed him into the dining room where a mahogany table stretched from east to west. A huge china closet loomed in the darkness, its dusty glass hiding Anna Mason's blue willowware. Sparkle and shine were gone from the 19th century punch bowl that adorned the sideboard.

Henry Mason had not neglected everything, as the living room proved. Anna's house plants lived on, crowding every window, bending and reaching, crawling to get light. They had become the flesh and blood of a memory. In Henry's mind, each plant was part of the woman who had nurtured them in years of good times. Leaves and succulent stems darkened the room more than Anna's curtains and draperies had darkened it in days long gone, days before Henry pulled down all the hangings and heaped them in the cellar to rot.

Lori and Billy were told to sit in straight-back chairs—the boy on one side of the fireplace near an overgrown fiddleleaf fig, the girl on the other side amidst palms and jade plants. Between them was the once white woodwork and tile, darkened and smudged by decades of soot.

Mason sat opposite the teenagers in an intricately carved Victorian love seat, upholstered in pale blue satin, now soiled and worn. He scowled at his captives, who, for the first time, got a clear view of his face, its deep lines and hazel eyes, puffy and red around the edges. Fear quickened the heartbeats and quivered the muscles of Billy and Lori, prisoners in a house that had always filled them with awe. The surroundings—old Queen Anne chairs, the reaching and twisting plants, the high ceiling and tarnished red-rose wallpaper, a dusty harpsichord—stirred up a strange, haunting, mysterious, storybook feeling in the boy and girl.

Billy's cheeks twitched when he timidly said, "We're really sorry, Mr. Mason. Honest. We're sorry."

The old man kept staring, but said nothing. A far-off gaze and a troubled brow marred his face. It was not a look that sprang from the moment's agitation, but surely one that had grown through the years, deepening the sorrow in his eyes and sucking his flesh into deep ridges.

The boy tried again: "Can we go now?"

"No." Mason's response was quick and stabbing.

Billy glanced at Lori, who eyes were transfixed on the old man. He then looked down at the floor while unconsciously linking his fingers and squeezing them tightly.

"So, I'm waiting," Mason said.

Billy looked at him. He and Lori parted their lips, but said nothing.

"What were you doing out there?" Mason's voice was harsh, but not simply from anger. His was a rasping, gravelly throat, scorched by years of cigarette smoke.

"I just wanted to climb your tree," Billy said as he scratched the mosquito bites on his legs and tried to avoid Mason's stare.

Spurting words suddenly, Lori said, "We were in the cemetery. It's our favorite place. We go there often." She kept rattling on, nervously. "Maybe we shouldn't, but we use your yard. It's the only easy way to get in and out."

The old man looked hard at the girl for nearly 30 seconds before asking, "What's your name?"

"Lori... Lori Lippincott."

From somewhere deep in Mason's thoughtful, sad eyes came a slight glimmer. He studied her for a moment as he rubbed his cheek with his gnarled fingers. "Of the Aaron Lippincotts?"

"My grandfather."

Mason looked at the boy and was about to ask his name when he was suddenly engulfed by a wave of melancholy. Billy reminded the old man of his son. The smooth, fair, radiant flesh of youth burned Mason's heart and paralyzed his tongue. Stomach acids began to gnaw at his ulcer. Fearful of his emotions, Mason rose quickly, turned away from the teenagers and walked to the adjoining hallway where a handsomely carved newel spun into a banister that followed the steps to the second floor. He lit a cigarette as he glanced up the stairs. Troubled by his reactions, he stood still, then glanced this way and that before fighting off a nervous shiver and forcing control. "Come on," he called. "Get out of here. You hear me? Get out." With apparent command of himself, he opened the inner door of the vestibule—a heavy oak door of leaded glass— and then drew deeply on his cigarette as he pushed the outer door and stepped onto the front porch. "Come on. Move. Before I change my mind."

The teenagers hurried past him and didn't slow until they reached the sidewalk. Billy hesitated, then looked back. He watched the old man turn slowly toward the door. "Good night, Mr. Mason," he called.

Henry let loose a cloud of smoke as he stepped into the house. He could stifle some impulses and hold back for those moments of revengeful relief. Then again, he sometimes deliberately yielded, allowing himself to wallow in self-pity and torturous memories.

He walked slowly to the bay window and fingered a fiddleleaf, but his eyes focused on nothing. His taut lips pinched his cigarette. A moment later he forced himself from troublesome reverie, from thoughts of past pleasure that brought pain today. He pushed his finger in one pot after another to judge the amount of moisture in the soil. But escapes seldom lasted. He slipped back to the 1940s when he turned and felt the presence of Anna at the harpsichord. She played and sang, "Ah, sweet mystery of life at last I found thee; I know at last the secret of it all..." He saw her long yellow hair, her rosy cheeks. His eyes wanted to tear, but they stayed dry.

Henry bit his little finger, hard. He counted: one, two, three, four... But nothing helped.

Thoughts of Anna's touch, the brightness of her eyes, her bosom against his, a run through the rain, warm sun on the grass, the beach, laughter, love—they all piled one atop the other until he fled from them suddenly, hurried to the kitchen, and doused his cigarette in the sink. A belly pang told him not to smoke.

Henry grabbed a pot, struggled to hold it firmly, and shoved it under a stream of spigot water. With gas at full flow, he watched the blue flames wrap around the pot as he waited for the water to boil. He poured in the oatmeal little by little, and when it was time he spooned the pasty globs into an earthenware bowl.

How handsome Andrew looked in his uniform, but how woeful his expression when he boarded that train. Again Henry watched him in his mind's eye—watched him toss that duffel bag over his shoulder, turn away, and not look back.

The old man gritted his teeth as he poured milk into his bowl of oatmeal. He stirred the mixture mechanically, barely aware of his actions as he repeated his nightly ritual.

Little Andy was spooning sand into his bucket. A wave broke, and the seawater surged onto the beach, wetting his bottom and washing away his castle, a mound of sand topped with a shell. Andy started, but then looked up at his dad and smiled broadly. His laughter filled his father's heart.

"Damn them with sulfur fire." Henry's gruff mumble was barely audible as he carried the oatmeal up the back stairs that twisted from a narrow, kitchen door to the second floor. The upstairs hallway was long and dark, lighted by a small flame-shaped bulb that gave an orange glow to the high walls and ceiling. Henry walked the length of the hall, stopping in front of the only closed door—a walnut stained door to the room with the boarded-up windows. A key projected from the keyhole.

Henry stood motionless before the door, his shoulders bent, pain gnawing at the lining of his stomach, sadness and anger pulling on the flesh of his face. He held the bowl of oatmeal in both hands and felt the throbbing of his heart.

Chapter Three

Hubert Pugg was homely and fat. His belly fell over his belt and his thighs rubbed each other. Nearly buried, his weak chin was a tiny button amidst flesh. He was a compulsive eater, "Because my wife won't stop her fuckin' naggin'." Thirty-seven, but looking 50, he didn't help his appearance by letting his sparse red hair grow straggly, forming a circle of red-orange strands around a shiny crown. His job as a steamfitter at the shipyards was in jeopardy, and he drowned his misery most nights by flopping in front of the tube and sucking on bottles of beer. Now and again he would take a break to scream at one or more of his six kids, ages 3, 5, 6, 8, 9 and 11.

Hubert's wife, a skinny little thing who fretted all the time, had just about closed him out of the bedroom because, "His belly hides his widget. The truth is, I can't stand the fat slob!"

Little fights over nothing always grew into big fights over something. "All right! All right! I'll get the hell out of here!" Another excuse for Hubert to slam the door and leave their narrow row house in the Olney section of Philadelphia. He had recently taken to watching peep shows in Center City, and could think of a thousand reasons to justify his dropping threescore or more quarters a visit. "Serves her right, the naggin' bitch!"

He bobbed and swayed south on the Broad Street subway and got off at City Hall where Billy Penn's clock struck the hour of 10. Tuesday nights were quiet in downtown Philly—especially after 9 o'clock.

A breeze cooled the sweat on Hubert's forehead as he crossed the square and headed for Cherry Street, near Arch and only a couple short blocks north of Market. Cherry was a narrow street of shabby shops buried in a drab district of wholesalers. Flashing neon drew Hubert toward a squatty storefront simply marked Adult Books. He waddled across Cherry and then struggled to step down and open a door that was screened with heavy, crisscrossing steel mesh. He entered sideways, scraping his belly and buttocks.

Inside, he casually shuffled from paperback to paperback and magazine to magazine, all lined up on racks against the walls and down the middle. He never raised his head to look at the proprietor, a mousy man who leaned back in a swivel chair behind a cash register and a glass counter that enclosed an assortment of dildoes and other tools of the sex trade.

Hubert intended to cash a five into quarters, but as usual he first devoured the covers of several sealed magazines—sealed mainly to keep browsers from soiling the pages. A few were unsealed as teasers, and he found them.

The shop's only other "customer" was a slim, freckled, 18-year-old, sandy-haired male who sheepishly gazed at the boy/boy magazines after nonchalantly working his way slowly to the gay racks on the east wall.

Hubert tugged to get his wallet from his tightly stretched pants pocket. "Uh... gimme five in quarters," he mumbled as he tossed the bill on the glass.

Seconds later, with a fist full of quarters, he pushed aside a dirty green curtain and shuffled into a dark backroom where stalls lined two walls and the air smelled of stale semen. None of the red lights glowed, meaning all stalls were empty. He made his way to Stall 6, simply because it had not disappointed him on previous visits. He opened the flimsy door and squeezed between the plywood walls. A quarter in the slot, and—plop, rattle, buzz—suddenly, in "glorious" spotted and speckled color, on a four-by-four inch screen behind dirty glass, came a close-up of oversized breasts.

Hubert stayed in Stall 6 until he ran out of quarters, then returned to the dildo counter for a refill.

Two hours later he was in Stall 8, having spent the entire time in four booths. Sweating from the heat of the poorly ventilated room, plus that generated by his own lust, the fat man unbuttoned his shirt and tugged on soaked underwear that stuck to his body. His sparse hair was pasted to his temples.

The 18-year-old was long gone, and no other browsers, voyeurs or loiterers had entered the shop, so Wally Wurtz could safely pick his nose. The thin, buck-toothed, 30-year-old ran his hand through his greasy hair and looked at his Mickey Mouse watch. After midnight. He yawned and the swivel chair screeched as he spun. Rising slowly, he stretched, then scratched his crotch. Wally hated to ask anyone to leave, but it was time. The red light above Stall 8 led him to Hubert. He hesitated, then knocked. "Hey in there. I'm closin' up."

"Give me a second."

"I can't, man. I gotta get outta here an' lock up the joint."

"Be right out after this quarter."

Wally walked down the row, checking each booth. He was in a far, dark corner when racks came crashing down in the display room up front. He stood still as if struck stupid with fear as the rumbling, bursting, thundering destruction continued. His hesitation was no pointless reaction, for he had been robbed at gun-point twice. The smashing, banging, and a streak of cursing brought Hubert flying from his cubicle, trousers still unzipped. He poked his head around the curtain just in time to get hit in the face by porno magazines. Ducking too late, he came up with a sore nose, then stood with the curtain draped over his shoulder and gazed in disbelief. An old man was pulling and pushing over entire racks of paperbacks. He was ripping up magazines and tossing them about furiously, as if driven by frustration and anger. Cursing and shouting about fire and brimstone, the violent intruder smashed the glass case and scattered the dildoes and other sex toys.

Seconds later, just as the porno-raider left, Wally nudged Hubert and peeked from behind the curtain.

"Holy shit!" Hubert said, finally finding words.

"My God," Wally whispered in response.

"Did you see that guy?"

"No, man. I didn't want any part of it."

"Nuts. Fuckin' nuts. Old guy, he was. In a freakin' frenzy. You shoulda seen 'im. God almighty."

With delayed but sudden courage, Wally shoved the fat man and leaped into the room screaming for help and shouting for the police. He raced about in circles, then aimed toward the door, still yelling.

The word "police" sent Hubert into a dither. All he could think about was getting away from the place before the police arrived. "Oh God," he mumbled, fearful of the publicity and terrified that his wife would find out about his depraved adventures. Sweating and trembling, he hurried to the open door and saw Wally outside in the street shouting for the police. He squeezed through the doorway, stepped up onto the sidewalk and began to waddle away as fast as he could—sort of a fat man's jog, accompanied by huffing and puffing.

"No you don't, fatso!" Wally shouted as he sprang toward Hubert. "I need you, damn it! Get the hell back here! You're a witness! You saw the fuckin' creep who smashed up my place!"

Hubert kept moving, his mind filled with horrifying thoughts of being questioned by the police, maybe even by newsmen. His wife would find out. So would his neighbors. And his boss at the shipyards. Oh God—the kids! Please, please, no. He said a quick prayer and tried to make his fat legs move faster.

Wally kept chasing him and easily grabbed him by his shirttail just as a blue-and-white patrol car turned the corner flashing its lights.

Hubert began to cry.

Chapter Four

Billy Bannon lived in a row house made of red brick on a base of schist, a metamorphic rock common to the area and just as boring as brick after brick after brick. The gray slabs, speckled with mica, not only trimmed but built the walls of thousands of Philadelphia-area houses—especially those look-alike row homes with sloped front lawns, often converted to rock gardens.

Mary Bannon, Billy's mother, had decked her slope with clumps of "life everlasting" (a name handed down from her grandmother), a succulent sedum of thickly clustered, gray-green leaves and fuzzy, pink flowers. The sedum clumps were interspersed with white begonias and jagged chunks of schist. The front garden was a needed outlet for Mary since none of the houses on Sunset Place had backyards to speak of—only squares of concrete with holes for umbrella clotheslines.

Morning sun was shining on the flowers when Billy rolled from bed at 8:30 and began his usual quick-scramble to ready himself for his summer job at Pizuto Produce. He knew he'd be uncrating cauliflower within the hour. He stumbled around his blue, white and maple room—a boyish room of model boats, rock collections, jars of insects and pictures of sports heroes.

"Urrrr," he grunted as he stretched.

In and out of the bathroom fast, Billy was quickly back in his room pulling on sweat socks and sneakers, cut-off jeans, and a cherry-and-white pullover with TEMPLE spelled out on the front,

FIGHTING OWLS on the back. The shirt was from his brother Bob, a 20-year-old physical education major at Temple University who was spending his summer flipping burgers in Atlantic City.

Thumping leaps took Billy downstairs and through the modestly furnished house to the kitchen where his father was drinking coffee and reading the newspaper at the table while his mother was rinsing dishes at the sink.

"Slow down," his father ordered as Billy pounced on a stool and shook the table, spilling a bit of his dad's coffee. "What did I tell you about rushing?" Charley Bannon scolded without looking up from his newspaper.

"What do you want for breakfast, Billy?" asked his mother, a trim, 42-year-old, fair-skinned woman with warm brown eyes and dark wavy hair. Mary Bannon's age was showing around her neck and under her eyes, but her youthful sparkle had yet to fade. Her built-in happiness had seen her through the ups and downs of life.

"A couple eggs," the boy said. "Once over lightly."

"I see where somebody ripped up another porno shop last night," Charley said as he continued to read the newspaper. "This one's not far from us. Over around Sixty-Ninth Street." Billy's father was a big man—handsome, but much chunkier than Billy would ever be. He had even features, but they were broader than Billy's would ever spread. His dark hair had receded slightly and was touched with gray—very little gray, but then he was only 45. Anyway, baldness worried him more than grayness, for his father was nearly bald at 50. Charley looked like a cop, talked like a cop, acted like a cop, although he hadn't worn a uniform in six years. For some reason—perhaps a dozen reasons—his plain clothes had a difficult time hiding the truth. Sometimes he tried the tweedy look, other times the navy blue suit, and still others, the rugged lumberjack look. Right now he was sporting a summertime yellow shirt, open at the neck.

"Maybe it's good that somebody's attacking that filth," Mary said.

"Not when innocent people get blown up." Charley looked up from his paper.

"Well, maybe it'll keep people away from those places." Mary dried her hands, turned and faced her husband.

"Damn it, Mary, you're not talking sense. You know that's not the way to solve the problem. What if Billy here just happened to be walking by? What if I had been checking out the place? Hell, Harvey Brooks picks up porno flicks and he's a family man with three kids."

"Well, Harvey has a problem."

"Says that's the way he turns his wife on."

"They're both weird, and you know it. Don't listen to your father, Billy." Mary turned away and stepped to the refrigerator. "Anyway, I'm glad they didn't call you in," she added while reaching for eggs.

"It's not our case. It's on the Philadelphia side." Charley folded the newspaper, sopped up spilled coffee from his saucer with a paper napkin, then drank from his cup. He grimaced because the coffee had cooled. "Just over the Upper Darby line. Not far from that appliance store where we bought the washing machine."

Billy wasn't listening. His mind was on Mason House and the old man. He toyed with the salt and pepper shakers—glass shakers that sparkled and flashed rainbow colors as he pushed them in and out of a patch of sunlight on the table.

The eggs sizzled when Mary flipped them.

"Dad," the boy began, cautiously, his tone serious. "Dad... what do you know about Mr. Mason in the big house over by the cemetery?"

"What do you mean?" A strange expression spread across Charley's face. For an instant his eyes revealed alarm. Billy felt tension radiate from his father as he picked up curious messages from silent vibes. Again he remembered that moment of a day gone by: an old man on his porch, looking at them, searching; the sudden yank, the tight squeeze that hurt.

"Well, he's a weird old coot, don't you think?" Billy's words were weaker than he had expected because of what he saw in his dad's eyes—something he had never seen before. That something filled him with wonder, yet bewilderment and odd feelings of shame that made him look away. It was as if he shouldn't intrude.

But it was all so fast. Gone. Charley had control of himself and played the cop's role. He leaned back, frowned, and stared coolly—first questioningly, then knowingly at his 16-year-old son. "You been snooping around the old man's house?"

This wasn't the first time Billy had pricked the cop in his father. As usual, he was put on the defensive. "Sort of, but not really."

"And what's that supposed to mean?"

"When you're there, you can't help but look."

"At what? Exactly what do you look at?"

"I don't know. Lori and I walk there a lot." He looked down and toyed with the shakers.

"You mean you walk in the cemetery and neck behind the tombstones." Charley wore his interrogation expression, the same distrustful look he used on shoplifters, even murderers.

"Jesus, Dad!" It seemed that Billy could seldom chat with his father without the cop oozing out of Charley.

Mary shot a cutting stare at her husband as she slid a plate of eggs and toast in front of her son. "Your father used to chase young lovers out of the cemetery, Billy. In the days when he cruised around in uniform he got a strange delight out of popping out of the bushes and surprising them. But he did little more than chase, because of his own track record. A hypocrite, he's not." She returned to the stove and kept her back to Charley and Billy as she said, "Ask your father how come he knew all the favorite places." Not wanting to reveal her flushing face, she fiddled with the teakettle and the coffeepot as she tightened her lips.

Billy didn't grasp his mother's meaning—at least, not right away. But as his father's embarrassment grew, the boy's eyes brightened. "You mean... you mean you used to go there?"

"Evening after evening he'd help me over the wall," Mary said while still facing the stove.

"Well, I'll be!" Billy had never thought of his father that way.

Aware of his blush, Charley smiled weakly before lowering his eyes. He was quick to make a partial recovery, but not before Billy devoured his father's sheepish look. The boy loved it. How he wished his dad were human more often. Truth was, Charley was plenty soft deep inside his elephant's hide. Years ago, when Billy and Bob were tots, young Charley-the-Cop had often allowed warmth to melt him. The boy didn't fully realize, but it was that warmth from the Big Man—back in the days when strings were tied and tightened—that gave Billy his love for his dad now. How he wished his father's hard shell would crack more often. Although he had tried to fight off cynicism, Charley had toughened his hide through the years to help rebuff the sad and the ugly.

"The old man's a recluse," Charley said as he straightened up and regained his composure. "He only comes out at night to get food at the deli, or whatever. But he's a good, honest soul. When I was a kid he used to let me pick cherries from his tree."

Billy started at his dad's mention of the cherry tree.

Charley pinched his lip, and the hard shell began to crack again. "I can still see him all dressed up on Sunday morning, walking his pretty wife under the blossoms along the cemetery wall. He was full of life then, would laugh when he played catch with his boy, always kept his house all fresh with paint."

Again Billy saw something he had never seen before in his father's face—a softening of muscles, a giving in, a slight flush, a deep far-off stare, a cleft in the facade, a story untold.

Looking down at his cup, Charley continued: "He just broke apart after his wife died. Especially after his son came home from Korea and then disappeared. Something bad must have happened between them, and Mason closed himself in and grew old. Everybody leaves him alone, and you should, too. He may be odd, but people around here who know, they kind of respect him."

Mary stood with her hands on her hips, looking at her husband. She hadn't heard him rattle on about anyone or anything with such compassion since little Tommy Harris saved an old lady from drowning in Ridley Reservoir—and that was 15 years ago.

"But he's got a room all boarded up," Billy explained, a touch of excitement raising his voice and speeding his words. "Around the back corner. It's real weird, Dad!"

Charley was about to interrogate again, not only because of Billy's obvious snooping at Mason House, but to help shake off his own emotional dilemma. Mary sensed the shift. Years had taught her to read him well, although his deep-rooted retreat of seconds ago had tossed her a bouncing ball that she couldn't quite field. She poured fresh coffee into his cup as his mind slipped back to cherries. He remembered stealing them, even after Mason had treated him and his young friends to all they could pick.

"It's not the same today, walking in that cemetery at night." Charley was in control. "It's just not the same. So many weirdos around." His words were tempered. Not harsh. Simply thoughts said aloud. Seconds later the cop in Charley vanished again: "Who cares why he has a room boarded up?"

Mary was more than puzzled by her husband's quick changes in mood. Each shift seemed to be an effort to counter the previous shift. Never before had she observed such behavior.

Grabbing and folding his newspaper, Charley feigned a sudden need for the toilet, left the table, and hurried to a half-bathroom sandwiched between the dining room and kitchen. The closet-sized room barely allowed him to spread his knees and read the paper while he sat on the lid, his pants still belted. He hated the feelings of painful youth that surged into his middle-aged gut, those squirmy feelings that came from guilty thoughts of embarrassing deeds. He really didn't want to think about Henry Mason.

Mary washed a cup and saucer, her thoughts afar.

Billy was hardly aware of the eggs he forked slowly into his mouth.

When the bathroom door flew open, Charley kept his face buried in the newspaper and tried to force all thoughts in new directions: "That textbook salesman from Chicago—the guy hit by that Molotov cocktail—he's still in Jefferson, critical. Burns over half his body, poor sucker. Damn, he's got a wife and kids!" Charley continued to read as he stepped to the table and sat, keeping his eyes from Mary and Billy. "What the hell was he doing in that kinda place anyway. Goddamn, anymore you never know about people, do you? Pity his wife."

Mary turned from the sink. She wanted to say something, but Charley was apparently engrossed, so she chose not to interrupt his concentration, real or unreal. Anyway, she wasn't sure how to express the perplexity that was gnawing at her. Thoughts creased her brow as she stepped to the window and looked into the yard without really seeing.

Billy, who had begun the day with a rush, was suddenly aware that he had been slowed by a web of thoughts. He glanced at the clock, then leaped to his feet. "Oh man, I'm in trouble! Man oh man, I'm really late! Pizuto's got a load of cauliflower due in early."

* * *

Out of breath, Billy Bannon was 20 minutes late arriving at Pizuto Produce, a square, wooden building, just off busy Route 3, West Chester Pike, and popular among residents on the eastern end of the county. Already women were pawing over kale and cucumbers. Billy went to work at once, stacking cauliflower and cabbage at the same time, while ignoring glances from Joe Pizuto, a small, hollow-cheeked man with steel gray curls, who was at the checkout counter weighing bananas.

A vivid imagination helped carry Billy through the tedium of his work hours. His mind was often elsewhere, building all sorts of dream castles. As his thoughts traveled in and out of adventures, he built a pyramid of cabbage heads, somewhat higher than safe. But the heads were not really cabbages at all. They were big, green roses of jade, first forming a Byzantine dome, then a Cambodian palace.

Before noon he was stacking rutabagas, surely one of the world's most unpleasant vegetables—big roots, yellow and purple, the colors of black eyes and other bruises of the human flesh. He was in an evil land, turning warts of the earth into a heap of staring eyes with purple irises—a mound of turnips, each bulbous root staring at the customers to draw them near with hypnotic magic.

But it was a shipment of out-of-state, late season cherries that again sent Billy's thoughts back to Old Man Mason—never long from his other escapes. Mason House was growing into his chief adventure, erasing other journeys-of-the-mind at the slightest suggestion. Billy no longer needed Lori to prod him. He was now far beyond her in traveling dark hallways of the unknown.

Suddenly Lori was squeezing the Jersey tomatoes. She often came by to talk about this or that, all pretty much in pretense. She really wanted to see Billy's young muscles at work, lifting crates of lettuce or whatever. Any excuse to be near him. Billy saw her from the corner of his eye, but pretended he didn't. He was well aware that her little white sunsuit left her bare at the midriff. As usual, he put on a show, hands and fingers in constant motion, first among the pea pods, then the potatoes.

"Hi," she whispered, tugging on his arm. She liked the feel of his biceps in action.

"Oh, hi." His eyes said more, twinkling sheepishly as he tossed her a silly, crooked smile. "What's up?"

"Nothing much." She rubbed his shoulder. "Well, that's not exactly true. There is something."

"What?"

She put her arm around his waist. "Mom wants me to go to the shore with her tomorrow."

"Oh?"

"And stay."

"How long?"

"Maybe a week. Maybe more."

"You got to be kidding!" He lost all traces of his smile.

"Aunt Tilly has a place at Stone Harbor for a couple weeks. She invited Mom, and that means me, too."

"Why don't you stay home. Let your mom go alone." Billy's eyes lighted. "Hey, we could use your house."

"No way, and you know it. That's exactly why she wouldn't go without me."

"Man oh man."

"You could come down for the weekend." She tickled his ribs. "Please?"

"Nah. I told Pizuto I'd work Saturday. Anyway, I couldn't get a ride. Besides, it wouldn't work. No way. Not with your mother."

"Well, she wants to go, and I can't do anything about it." Lori twisted a piece of his hair, then moved her finger up and down and around his back. "Did you have your lunch break yet?"

"I can leave in a few minutes. I got enough for a couple Big Macs and fries. Then we can walk over by the railroad tracks."

* * *

Weeds and grass grew high along the spur line. Billy kicked a can as he and Lori walked the ties. He took her hand.

"Do you want a house on a hill, or down in a valley?" he asked.

"I don't care. Either. As long as it has roses. The kind that crawl up."

"Ramblers?"

"Yes. Red rambling roses."

"If we lived in a valley, maybe there'd be a stream nearby. We could sit along the edge and wet our feet."

"But if we're on a hill we can look down into the valley."

"You'd like that?"

"A white house with blue shutters. It would look nice on a hill. But with big trees, and a gate. And red rambling roses all about." Lori squeezed Bill's hand. "Mom says we're too young to talk about things like that."

"What else does she say?"

"You know. Stuff about waiting. Puppy love doesn't last. It's not the real thing. Stuff like that."

"That's what parents say. They don't understand. I don't tell anybody how I feel." He pulled her off the ties and onto the cinders. "Come on. We gotta move, or I'll be late again."

"No one can understand how another person feels. You know?" Lori slowed his pace by pulling back. She put her arm around his waist, and rubbed her cheek on his shoulder.

Chapter Five

Henry Mason slept late—not just on this, a gray morning, but on most sunny mornings, too. Depression tied him to his bed. Wretched thoughts followed wretched dreams.

His bedroom was a faded reflection of a bright and shiny past. Window curtains were gone, but the valances still hung, their ball fringe, once pink, now bleached by sunlight and grayed by dust. Henry slept under a yellowed and wrinkled sheet. A Martha Washington bedspread, discolored by age, was bunched on the floor at the foot of the bed where it remained day and night during summer. Handsome mahogany chests and lamp tables, like the bed's high posters, had not been polished since touched by the hands of his wife. Anna had made beautiful all that she touched, in Henry's perception. He saw her built-in happiness as having affected all objects of her life, animate and inanimate. Henry's vision of her was always with him. But each apparition added depressing weight and tightened the ropes that held him down. He could neither escape the dreams and thoughts that spawned wretchedness nor the ghosts of beauty and happiness that wrought pain and sorrow.

It was noon before Henry struggled from under the sheet and sat on the edge of the bed, still clad in yesterday's underwear— wrinkled, baggy shorts that were too large for his shrinking waist and thighs. He looked down at his bony knees while trying to suck energy into his body. Minutes piled onto minutes before he pushed himself to his feet.

An old, white porcelain, pedestal sink—standing like a giant mushroom—greeted him boldly and coldly in a bathroom that had lost its softness. Long gone was Anna's way of blending porcelain with soft frills, pastels and warm light. Starkness reigned. Though his eyes focused on little, Henry stared down at the claw feet of the old tub while he struggled with constipation, his wrinkled shorts bunched about his feet, his knees spread wide.

Later, in the hallway, Henry walked slowly toward the boarded-up room. He hesitated in front of the closed door, then reached out as if to touch that door, but pulled back his hand.

"No," he muttered, shaking his head.

Henry's chin stiffened as his lips tightened. His lower teeth pushed against his uppers until his gums ached. He stood motionless, his eyes fixed on the grim portrait of Grandmother Mason, framed in a heavy oval of walnut behind dusty glass. The face was almost his, but topped with braids and a bun. Never was there a morning that he failed to look into her face and hear her words: "Henry, mind your mother and your father, and don't question the ways of the Lord."

Still undressed, except for his undershorts, Henry started down the steps, his mind set on watering Anna's plants, always his first major chore of the new day. A long-spouted, green watering can— the two-gallon size—rested at the foot of the stairs, already filled with water. Anna had taught him to let the water sit overnight "to filter out the bad chemicals."

From window to window he watered plant after plant, always testing the soil first with his finger. He pulled a dry leaf from a dieffenbachia, crumpled it, and buried it in the potting soil. "Give it back to the earth," Anna had said so often that the words were deeply etched in his brain.

Finished. He could go back to bed. How easy that would be. But, no. He wouldn't do that.

Henry sat in one of those uncomfortable, living room chairs—the ones with the straight backs. He lifted his eyes, then lowered them, stared at the harpsichord, and breathed in a little more pain. Something happened to a man who lived alone for years among so many memories. The memories tried to take over and run his life. They occupied time, stopped action, started action, closed eyes, opened eyes, pushed from room to room.

Anna in blue. Frothy blue. On the boardwalk at Atlantic City. Touched by the sun and the wind.

How much she liked dining at nice restaurants—those steeped in warm and cozy ambience. Candlelight cast a glow on her cheeks. Across the table. Soft. A sparkling wine glass lifted to her lips. Radiance. A little idle talk about shop windows on Chestnut Street, Martha Haskins' trip to Europe, a baby elephant at the Philadelphia Zoo. How strange. The things that come to mind. Assorted and scattered. Nothings and somethings.

Henry felt Anna in his arms. Tears moistened his eyes. He could barely tolerate the feeling. When it nearly strangled him, he pushed himself up, gasped for breath, and sought escape in the kitchen.

One egg. Cracked open and plopped into a glass of milk. As Henry stirred, he studied the streaks of yolk as they blended and vanished. He beat the mixture far longer than necessary in a strange effort to occupy his mind and bury his thoughts in the creamy yellow milk. After adding sugar and vanilla, he paced from sink to stove to table and back to sink again, stirring the entire time. He sipped while standing. Then sat to drink in earnest. But he guzzled too fast, choked and gasped. Now he was angry. So few minutes had elapsed, yet his drink was gone. He stared into the glass. Breakfast was over. Totally swallowed. Gone.

The smell of bacon, of coffee, of toast. Anna was inside his head again. He felt the glow of her breakfast table. Rainy or gray, it mattered not. Her table was bright and warm.

Young Andy was so handsome. Fair skin. Hair and eyes of warm brown. Lashes too long and thick for a boy. He spilled his orange juice, and he was sorry. Almost too sorry. That look on his face—it was the same look of shame that unfolded years later. After Korea.

Henry struck the table hard with his fist, but the blow did not erase the pain or anger. He picked up the empty glass and struck the table again, smashing the glass and sending the pieces flying across the table and onto the floor.

"Damn you, Andy!"

Henry had slashed his hand badly, puncturing his palm and cutting gashes in three fingers. Without a wince, he stepped to the sink and held his hand under gushing water for several seconds.

Slowly, deliberately, he turned off the faucet, examined his wounds, and then wrapped a towel around his hand. Leaning on his arms, he hung his head as haunting recollections continued to plague him.

He remembered when 12-year-old Andrew cut his foot on a tin can while walking barefoot along the railroad spur track near Naylor's Run. "Stupid! Why were you so stupid? Why?"

Holding his wounded hand high, he hunted in drawer after drawer for a pencil and paper. He finally tossed an old calendar on the table and threw aside the towel. As blood ran from his cuts, he printed in bold letters with a black crayon: "I don't have a son."

Weakened by his words, he slouched, slid into a chair, closed his eyes, and cradled his head in his arms on the table.

Later, when he opened his eyes, his gaze moved slowly around the room until it fell upon the cabinet doors under the sink. Within seconds he lifted himself, moved slowly, opened those doors and grasped his bottle of rye.

Whiskey had never quelled his anger. But it often permitted him to act on his fury.

Chapter Six

Evening, past sunset, and Billy without Lori was a rare sight indeed. But there he was, alone, sitting on a curbstone, swatting mosquitoes and drinking cola from a bottle in front of Jake's Deli. Restless, he extended his legs, wiggled his feet, then pulled them back to the gutter. He could hunt for Clarence. "Nah," he said under his breath, unsure of his reasoning. Something kept intruding from the back of his mind, and little by little it was turning into a compulsion.

Now it was dark, and Billy took his last swallow, rolled the bottle between his hands several times and left it in the gutter. Pushed by a deep-seated urge, he began strolling toward the cemetery and Mason House. He passed Broder's Tailor Shop, the Hair Fashion Salon, Joe's Pizzeria, and then a row of houses. Soon row homes gave way to singles, then to an open field.

There was Mason House, more formidable than ever, rising into the darkness of the humid night, set against the sky and trees that rustled. The swishing murmurs of the trees joined a chorus of crickets and tree toads. Billy stood across the street, under a sycamore and away from the lights of an occasional car. He suffered the exhilaration of awe—more awe than he had ever felt. His craving grew because of fascination and bewitchment that turned Mason House into a fear-inspiring obsession.

Light moved from room to room, and Billy's eyes followed. The second-floor front stayed aglow briefly, followed by the stairwell and living room. Then a dull light flashed on in the kitchen. It was at that moment that Billy ventured across the street, trepidation not withstanding. Despite the push of adrenaline and a quick heartbeat, he held back the urge to hurry, attempting a nonchalant pace. He casually side-stepped into a dense patch of rhododendron. Seconds later he began sneaking along the side of the house.

The kitchen windows were high above the ground, their sills brushed by thick clusters of bush honeysuckle and spirea, so entwined with wild morning glory as to be unrecognizable. The window shades, turned brownish yellow and split at their brittle edges, had been pulled down most of the way. They picked up shadows of someone moving about, heightening Billy's fearful fascination. He scratched his arms and ankles, then tried to ignore the bug bites as he pulled at the morning-glory weeds in an effort to separate bound-up sprays of spirea. Breathing hard, he stood on his toes, but couldn't see into the kitchen. He jumped, got stabbed by a twig, and decided not to jump again, fearful of being heard. Immobilized, he barely breathed as he waited and watched.

The windows turned dark. Billy thought he heard a door open and shut inside the house. He continued to stand still for several seconds more, then started when light flashed through the bushes and vines from a cellar window. It cast a dull, mottled glow on his jeans below his knees. He quickly stepped aside, turning his ankle on a protruding root. Stumbling sideways, he caught himself and muffled a grunt. To appease his anxiety, he backed off quickly, then stood motionless under an old elm tree that was half dead of blight. He was not about to be defeated by his own emotions, however, and little by little he tightened his guts and readied himself for another onset.

The moon—big, yellow and hazy—rose from behind distant tree tops and cast a glow on Mason House as Billy shook off a shiver and stepped toward the cellar light. The boy lay on his belly and quietly pushed himself inch by inch into the thick bushes and vines where he was assaulted by jabbing sticks and twigs, tickled by tendrils, and poked in the ribs by old stubs. He nosed himself slowly toward the window.

Surely he would find the old man digging a huge hole in the cellar floor, or moving a slab of concrete to conceal something, or opening a vault, or closing a wall, or kneeling over a long, pine box. Schoolbook assignments of Poe's *Cast of Amontillado* and *Tell-Tale Heart* stirred in his brain, mixing with late-night video re-runs of horror films.

Henry Mason was a blurred figure, not only because of dirt on the old panes of glass, but because of a large, bare bulb that hung between him and the window. At times, the glow nearly eclipsed him from Billy's view. When Henry moved from side to side, the boy caught his best glimpses of him, but even they were hazy. The light erased his head and torso much of the time, but Billy managed to see him bend over a table or workbench and obviously toil with something. That something surely had to be strange, in Billy's way of thinking. At one point the teenager thought he saw a bottle in the old man's quivering hand. Whatever it was, it reflected light from the hanging bulb, giving off flashes of amber.

Suddenly Mason moved from Billy's sight. The light went out. But the boy stayed on his belly, his heart still thumping, his legs protruding from the thicket, lying still in the moonlight.

Whiter and somewhat smaller, the moon was now high above the treetops, painting a cooler luster on old Mason House. Darkness and a clearing breeze allowed the shimmering, blue-white spark of the North Star to cut through the thinning haze. Wispy puffs of mist scattered and faded. Billy stepped quickly and quietly from the thick patch of rhododendron and walked toward home to begin his nighttime dreams.

In Mason House, 78-year-old Henry, weary and weathered beyond his years, stood at the kitchen sink, smelled his hands, then washed them with yellow soap. Again he lifted his fingers to his nose, and again he washed his hands, vigorously, building up as much lather as possible before rinsing.

Later, he bent his body at the stove and stirred oatmeal. When it was pasty enough, he spooned it into a bowl, added milk, and began to carry it to the second floor.

Chapter Seven

Lori was still at Stone Harbor.

Billy sought Clarence. It would be like old times, before Lori stepped between them and captured so much of Billy's time. Clarence had felt put out at first, and he tried to hold his own by wooing one girl after another, always rebuffed, partly because of his clumsy come-on efforts. Anyway, his mind was still mainly on baseball, basketball and street hockey. He had yet to experience Billy's kind of overriding feeling for the one-and-only, the kind that reeled the head and conjured up desires day and night.

The teenagers sat side-by-side on their favorite curbstone in front of Jake's Deli, each gripping a bottle of cola. Both stared down between widespread, jeans-covered knees into the gutter where their well-worn, discolored sneakers scuffed and grated now and then on street grit as their feet squirmed. Conversation leaped from the Phillies' slump and the price of running shoes to Clarence's hidden copies of porno magazines to TV late-shows and Mason House. Each time their thoughts ran dry, they swigged from their bottles or wiggled their feet.

Clarence Scott was a lanky blond with a long face, a beak for a nose, and deep-set eyes under heavy brows. He was generally a likable 16-year-old, and a "cool dude" among his buddies. His ways and manners were folksy and his movements gangling. Born with big hands, he had the habit of tucking his thumbs under his belt and hanging his long fingers over his pants pockets. His bony shoulders appeared to shrug constantly, and his limber limbs seemed loosely joined, but were put into action smoothly on the ball field or basketball court. Clarence's faults, at least in the eyes of his teachers, were his lackadaisical attitude, poor study habits, and mischief-making—sometimes an almost malevolent mischievousness. He had once let loose a potent, sulfur "stink bomb," filling a classroom with the smell of rotten eggs and causing a short-term evacuation. In ninth grade, he had locked his science teacher, Miss Pruitt, in her classroom closet where she had been searching for test tubes and litmus paper. Expelled, he suffered angry stares from his mother for 10 days after her visit to the principal's office. This year's summer work for Clarence was again at Lowry Lumber, where he sawed, stacked, loaded and unloaded.

Having finished dinner, the Scott's only son had been perched on the front steps of his house, a row home much like the Bannons', for almost an hour before Billy bounced up the street, struck a casual pose, and then called, "Hey, what's up?" A slap-of-the-hands later, and following tradition, the boys had strolled up the hill and around the block to Jake's Deli, where they now pondered the "truth" about Old Man Mason.

"He probably has something strange in the attic, too," Billy suggested, unloading but a tiny touch of his vivid imagination.

"Yeah," Clarence responded, expressing total agreement by nodding his head rigorously.

"And I'd sure like to know what he does in that cellar. I'm telling you, man, he's got something strange going on down there. Like I said, he was mixing up some kind of brew."

"We gotta find out."

To mix Billy's adventurous flights-to-fancy with Clarence's compelling lust-for-mischief was to stir up a stew more powerful than any witch's brew. The deadly combination had often led to trouble—as when Billy's imagination had sent them searching about a "suspicious" truck of chickens parked near a shopping mall. Surely a front for smuggling. Clarence's mischief-making, of course, led to opening the gates so the chickens could walk, flutter and cluck through the busy mall.

Now, on this night of Masonry, after the colas were long gone, and when darkness had closed in, the spinning thoughts of the two 16-year-olds were linked in a curious chain that took Billy back to that sycamore tree with Clarence at his side. Mason House was dark, not a light from attic to cellar.

"The old fart must be out," Clarence said.

"Or doing something in the dark," Billy added.

"Like what?"

"I don't know. Something weird."

The moon was high and the breeze less sultry by the time the stealthy twosome slipped into that patch of rhododendron, bent their shoulders, shushed each other, and began to wind their way among the thickets along the north side of the house. They became more daring in their movements and louder with their whispers as they gained more sureness that Henry wasn't home. Soon they were almost brazen as they darted from window to window and door to door—bending, stretching, touching. They raced through the back yard, zigzagging about the overgrown shrubs and pushing through the pesky vines. At the southwest corner they stopped in unison as if suddenly struck by a force that froze their muscles. Together they lifted their heads and stared between the branches of the cherry tree at the boarded-up windows. Dark. Not a thread of light.

"This is a good time to throw rocks," Clarence urged. "If anybody's in there, maybe they'll yell or something."

Billy kept staring up as his friend searched for a stone, a rock, or any loose missile. His imagination ran wild, and for a moment he paid no attention to Clarence's demand for help.

"Damn it, Billy, help me, will you!"

Billy's fanciful musing still kept him gazing upward.

Clarence found a piece of broken brick near the tall privet hedge. Seconds later he tossed it at one of the boarded-up windows where it banged, rattled the shutters and bounced back against a limb of the cherry tree before it fell to the ground. The boys stood quietly, listened, but heard nothing. Again Clarence searched, this time joined by Billy. When the twosome had gathered a few pebbles and stones, one fist-sized rock, another hunk of brick, a jagged piece of broken terra cotta, a black walnut and a rusty two-inch bolt, they sent a rat-a-tat-bang-bang-boom barrage at the boarded windows. Their hearts pounded as they waited in silence. Nothing happened. Disappointed—in fact, feeling downright thwarted—they shuffled and kicked their way into the back yard.

"Hey! Look! Over there!" Clarence pointed to a vine-shrouded, wooden, one-car garage that leaned against an old oak. Most of its paint had peeled away long ago, blending it into the foliage and making it even more difficult to see in the moonlight.

"I've seen it before. Lori and I—we've cut behind it lots of times."

"Ever look inside?"

"Nah."

"Let's go!"

After a quick jog, the boys were peering through dirty, cracked windowpanes in old doors that hung on rusty hinges. Billy wiped away grit and cobwebs to help the moonlight enter.

"I think there's a car in there," he said.

"Y'mean the old man's got a car? Let's see."

"See it?"

"Yeah, I see it," Clarence added.

"It's some old kind of car."

"What kind?"

"I'm not sure."

The teenagers pulled the latch from the rotting wood, forced opened the creaky doors and fixed their eyes on the rear of a silver-blue sedan, its bumper shining with moonglow.

"It's a Packard!" Billy exclaimed.

"A Packard?"

"Yeah, a Packard!"

"Wow!"

"Must be from the forties. Hey, it sure is something, isn't it?" Billy touched the right-back fender. "Wow!" His eyes gazed on silver spokes on the wheel hub. "And look, it's got running boards."

"Running what?"

"Running boards." Billy could just about see as he moved along the side of the car. Feeling his way, he touched the door handle, then put his foot up on the step-board. "This. It's a running board, stupid."

The boys crawled all over the car, struggling to see in the dark, touching headlights, grill, trim, the fancy decorative statuette on the hood. They climbed inside, bounced on the seats, squeezed the upholstery, and took turns behind the steering wheel.

"It's in great shape," Clarence said.

"Yeah. But I bet it hasn't been used in years. I mean, lot's of years. Decades maybe."

"Let's see if we can roll it out of the garage."

"Hell no! Are you crazy or something? Why would you want to do a dumb thing like that?"

"We can get a better look at it, then leave it out there to shake up the old bastard. He'll find it sitting in the middle of his back yard."

"That's stupid. Besides, the tires are flat as hell. Look. We'd never be able to move it."

Still euphoric over their discovery, the boys jostled each other as they pushed in and out of the car a few more times. Then, as they both sat on the front seats, Billy at the steering wheel, Clarence turned, looked about and saw light in the kitchen of Mason House.

"Oh my God!" he exclaimed. Let's get the hell out of here! The old bastard must be home!"

Light not only streamed from the kitchen windows; it came from the open backdoor, reflecting on the weatherworn porch, overgrown foliage, and a patch of grass. Jumping and twitching, Clarence poked his friend in the ribs with his elbow. Billy turned and saw more than light. Silhouetted in the moonglow and kitchen light, standing in front of the garage, was the figure of a man—old, bent and baggy—surely Henry Mason.

"Oh shit, we've had it," Billy mumbled while sliding down in his seat. "Oh man, oh man."

"What are we gonna do?"

"I don't know. Oh man, oh man."

"Jeeze, oh jeeze. We're done for, man."

Mason turned on his flashlight, sending its beam into the rear window of the Packard. Seconds later he was opening the driver-side door and practically shoving the flashlight down the throats of the boys. Low in their seats, Billy and Clarence looked up, their wide and fearful eyes blinded by the shaking light.

Chapter Eight

The subway train rose from a gaping hole in the ground and kept on climbing until it was an elevated train above tight rows of tarnished houses that stretched out from the soot-covered trestle that followed Market Street through West Philadelphia. The hour was late, and darkness hid the city's blemishes.

Passengers were scattered here and there. Few if any were in each car. Henry Mason sat alone in the rear, over the wheels, swaying rapidly in a train that jounced its travelers. Bitterly angry, he was feeling guilty and sorry for himself. Anxiety tightened his stomach—a stomach that ached because his emotions were out of control. Unable to solve a dilemma wrought through many a year, he could not prevent the churning of his gastric juices. Unable to control his rage or curb his frustration, he could not stop the acids from inflaming his stomach, bringing his ulcer near the bleeding point.

Henry had found it maddening enough to commit this night's dastardly deed, let alone be nearly caught in the act. The exploit itself had built his anxiety to an unbearable level, as did other hostile acts in days past. But his frenzied high was suddenly throttled. His needed relief—his release from anger—was not forthcoming. In its place were the fear and guilt of being seen, cursed and chased—emotions that stirred his guts too fast for his aging heart.

The brakes screeched on the final curve as the train moved toward Upper Darby and the end of the line.

Henry stood on the platform at the 69th Street Terminal after stepping from the subway-elevated car that had sped him from Center City Philadelphia. Leaning against a pole, he waited until the other passengers were gone. Then, alone on the deserted platform, he walked slowly along a graffiti-stained wall to a flight of stairs.

The sprawling terminal was an octopus whose tentacles led to buses, trolleys and trains that fed municipalities to the west and south. With its maze of tracks, the old brick structure was an entryway for suburbanites who worked in Philadelphia and fled to their township and borough homes each night. Its glory days were long gone, and its rebirth was yet to come. Storefronts along the concourses were shabby during this low point in terminal history, a far cry from the prosperous days of early and mid century when 69th Street's shopping district was aglow and humming. And now, at this late hour, when the restrooms were locked to chase the perverts, the terminal was a lonely place where derelicts were hustled off by cops.

Henry huffed up the stairway, clinging to a railing. He pushed through swinging doors into the terminal's main concourse—wide and high, tarnished, dark and gloomy, with a newsstand at center. A few stragglers milled about. Shades were drawn in the change-and-token booths, and only night-lights burned in the Horn & Hardart bakery shop, closed like the other shops and food stands.

About the time that Billy Bannon and Clarence Scott were standing under that sycamore tree, Henry Mason was boarding his bus at the terminal. And when the boys were sneaking along the north side of Mason House, the old man was riding in the bus. One of only five passengers aboard, he sat in the rear holding his stomach, doubled over in pain.

Later, when Billy and Clarence sighted the garage, raced to its doors and saw the Packard for the first time, Mason was walking along the cemetery wall, bent and grimacing, yet slightly relieved, having belched and expelled gas several times. He breathed heavily and relished an occasional breeze that dried the sweat on his forehead.

Mason House was an oasis for Henry. His yearning for it pulled him almost too fast for his weakening legs. As the house grew nearer, he craved its refuge more and more, so anxious was he to cradle himself in its bosom. On the porch, he nervously fished for his key and impatiently struggled to slip it into the keyhole.

A sense of relief and safety came to him as he turned on a dim light in the hallway, but the comfort was diminished by concern for tomorrow's suffering wrought by tonight's transgression. His distorted morality gave far less solace than usual because of fear of discovery.

Henry hurried through the dark house, anxious to reach his bottle of antacid in the cabinet above the sink. Switching on the kitchen light, he grabbed for the bottle and quickly poured himself a jigger of the milky-white liquid. His trembling hand lifted the shot glass to his lips, and with one quick jerk of the hand, in the same way he often belted whiskey, he gulped the antacid. After breathing deeply, he licked the chalky white from his lips as drivel ran down his chin. He leaned on the sink for a moment before downing another shot and wiping his chin on his arm.

After hanging his head over the sink for several seconds, he began to clear eggshells, banana skins and other day-old garbage from the drain board. He pushed the refuse into a paper bag and carried it to the pantry where he opened the backdoor, intending to toss the bag onto the porch. Immediately he saw the open garage doors and alarm surged through his body. He dropped the trash and grabbed a flashlight from a pantry hook.

Henry seldom opened the garage. The car carried too many memories. In his thoughts it was Anna's car—her style, her color, her trips to the Pocanos or Atlantic City. On occasion he was drawn to it, but only when he craved more self-destruction than the harpsichord could give, only when he wanted his heart to ache more than his stomach.

The flashlight off and held at his side, he stepped slowly from the porch, hesitating on each step, and cautiously approached the garage, detouring in a wide arc through the yard.

Were they searching?

Did they know?

Had they followed?

How could they have come so quickly?

Stop thinking foolish thoughts!

Nonsense!

Damnation! Why this on top of that? And on top of that? And that? How many times was he to be clobbered in one day? Anna would have found a message in it all, as she always did when the milk turned sour. "Someone's trying to tell you something, Henry." Annoying words then. But coveted now just as much as her touch or smile. "You're not living right, Henry." Bothersome words then, so welcome now—as welcome as her sigh, her fragrance, her hair tossed by the wind.

Standing behind the car, Henry turned on the flashlight and aimed its beam through the back window. He saw two heads slide down. Thieves? Lovers? Kids? Vandals? Maybe that Lippincott girl and her boyfriend? Anger raged in him, fueled by the stress and frustration of the past hours. All trepidation was wiped away as fury pushed him into the garage. He grabbed the driver-side door handle so hard that he stubbed his fingers, sending pain up this arm. With unusual force, he opened the door, slamming it against old, rusty, garden tools that hung on the garage wall.

The frightened faces of Billy and Clarence, wide eyes flashing fearfully in the beam of light, disturbed Henry far more than they should have. Seeing the two boys together conjured up a memory so painful as to almost destroy his senses. His reaction was abnormal in the extreme, blotting out time, place, events of the day. Suddenly the matter was more than an intrusion onto his sacred domain, more than trespassing on his private property or defilement of his memories. It was boy-with-boy. And that ghost of the past— composed of Andrew's fair skin, brown eyes and even features, all seen in Billy's face—was about to bring Henry's wrath down hard on another fancied foe, unholy and immoral.

Henry grabbed Billy at the throat and held a wad of T-shirt so tightly in his trembling hand that it nearly strangled the boy. Choking and coughing, Billy was yanked from the car, his shirt ripping across his back and shoulders. Rakes, spades, hoes and a pitchfork rattled, banged and fell as the youth was pulled and dragged from the garage by a sickly old man who surely should not possess such strength, an old man obviously driven by an inner force—a force that was overworking glands that secreted powerful propellants.

Clarence clattered and knocked his way out of the garage, felt the urge to run and hide, but caught himself after a quick lunge forward and turned back. His loyalty kept him at Billy's side.

Henry shook Billy violently, with strength far greater than normal. He kept shaking until the boy cried out, "Stop it! Please!" Perhaps it was the pain in Henry's stomach that kept him in touch with reality. Maybe it was the yearning underlying the hate that tempered his rage just enough to keep it from blinding him completely. Each minute that passed lessened his fury but a trifle.

Finally, there came a moment when Billy could have pulled away and run. But he didn't.

Billy's return to the inner sanctum was much like that of his first visit. He allowed himself to be pushed, pulled and deposited on that same straight-back chair in the living room of the plants. Clarence took the seat on the other side of the fireplace, the chair on which Lori had sat on that fearful night when she was chilled by awe, her eyes transfixed on the old man. His presence instead of hers prompted an unexpected question from the quivering lips of Henry, obviously agitated as he paced back and forth before his prisoners.

"Where's the girl?" Henry stopped pacing and glowered at Billy. "Why aren't you with her?"

"She's away," Billy began. "She's..."

"That's not what I mean," Henry interrupted. Breathing heavily, he stared from Billy to Clarence and back again as he searched his own mind. His unsettled eyes and weighty brow revealed confusion that gradually slipped away as he changed from a possessed man haunted by aberrations to a more logical thinker angered by real and present transgressions. Suddenly he was ready to explode with a tirade about sneaking, snooping, trespassing, breaking-and-entering, and a host of irate thoughts that flooded his brain. But he struggled to hold back.

"What is it you want?" Henry finally asked, his anger tempered. A pleading look said more than his words. His eyes were begging Billy and Clarence to leave him alone. "Why do you come to my house? Why do you climb my tree, enter my garage?" Although his words remained harsh, they failed to hide the plea that oozed from his gut. The boys could feel it.

Henry paced again, but this time his steps, posture and expression were devoid of obsession. He said nothing for minute after minute, then sat on the Victorian love seat and scowled at his captives. But his intent to converse was stymied by Billy's eyes, flesh and features. Only the hair was different—much darker than the light brown locks of his son.

As the vibes from Billy increased his pain, Henry began to feel that Clarence was in his way. He saw the gawky teenager's eyes and ears as impediments to whatever was about to happen, perhaps because he feared exposing himself in some way. He had no full understanding of his reaction, but could feel the interference as he sensed ensuing trauma.

Henry rose from the love seat and aimed his eyes and words at Clarence. "Get out of here!"

Stunned, Clarence folded in his gangling arms and legs, stood with a sudden bounce, and then gawked.

"And stay away," Henry added. "If I ever see you near my property again, I'll slit open your goddamn gizzard."

Clarence knew he didn't have a gizzard, but that failed to weaken the threat. Yet he didn't move. His head hung on hunched shoulders, suspended in confusion. Not that he didn't want to free his feet and leap into hasty flight. But they stayed glued to the floor. He was sure, at least at that moment, that he could not bring himself to leave Billy behind to suffer whatever evils lurked in Mason or his house.

"Get out!" Henry yelled. His chin trembled until he locked his teeth and tightened his lips.

"Go on, Clarence," Billy said.

Clarence stared at his friend.

"Go on," Billy insisted. "I mean it. Get going. I'll be okay. Really."

Billy's words and tone were enough. Clarence found his way out through the front door with little trouble.

If anything ugly was supposed to happen next, it didn't, although boy and man waited in fearful expectation. Billy's reflection of young Andrew failed to plunge Henry into a bitter brew of past deeds or remorse. On the other hand, it didn't enable him to reach across the abyss.

Eyes could not lock on eyes too long. In time, Billy looked down and Henry turned away. Only when Henry's beating pulses subsided did events take an unexpected turn.

"What's your name?" Henry asked.

"Billy Bannon."

"Any relation to Charley Bannon, the cop?"

Billy looked up in surprise. He hesitated, then said, "My father."

"Your father?"

Billy looked down again and his distress doubled. Here it comes, he thought—a policeman's son, caught trespassing. His body and mind had yet to recover from the old man's fury, and now this. He couldn't quell the shakes. His throat still hurt from the stranglehold. Raw, red skin burned his neck. He reached over his shoulder and tugged on his torn shirt, not just to cover the gaping hole that bared his back, but in some subliminal way to protect the vulnerable flesh of a cop's son from the exposure of his lawbreaking.

The wheel-of-chance had come up with an unexpected number. A sudden change came over Henry Mason, and when Billy lifted his head, he became well aware of that change. It showed in the old man's questioning eyes and parted lips. For a long moment Henry said nothing. In time his lips tightened. He frowned and shifted his stare from Billy's awe-struck expression to the boy's restless feet. He examined thoroughly, filling the teenager with a new and different discomfort.

"So you're Charley Bannon's son," Henry began, slowly, softly. His eyes said much more, betraying a mind jammed with thoughts and images that craved freedom, but could not escape.

"Can I go now?"

"No. Not yet."

"It's late. I gotta get home before..."

"No wonder you climbed my cherry tree," Henry interrupted. "No wonder you broke into my garage."

Billy was perplexed to the point of bewilderment. He gawked

for several seconds, then scowled. His thumping heart was so acutely felt and intrusive that it interfered with his thoughts.

"Has your father ever said anything about me?"

"Not much. I mean, nothing really." Billy looked down and tried to keep his feet from bouncing in a nervous jiggle.

"Look at me."

The boy looked up again.

"Do you steal?" Henry asked.

"What?"

"I said, do you steal?"

"I don't know what you mean."

"Are you a thief? Do you take things that don't belong to you?"

"No! Never! We were just looking at your car. It's a Packard."

"I know it's a Packard." Mention of the car caused Henry to tense up. Again he examined Billy from head to foot. "What kind of justice do you believe in?"

The question only muddled Billy's thinking a bit more. Since no answer was forthcoming, Henry stood and walked to the hallway where he opened the vestibule door.

"You father's an officer of the law," Henry said matter-of-factly. "Why don't you ask him about Henry Mason's kind of justice?"

Slow to stand, Billy then hurried to the hallway, brushed by the old man, and pushed quickly onto the porch. He had no intention of asking his father about justice, or in any other way revealing his unhappy visit to Mason House. Without looking back, he leaped from the porch and raced down the pathway into the darkness. Henry followed him with his eyes. He wanted to know the boy, yet feared him.

* * *

That night Billy lay awake for hours, puzzling over Mason's words and actions, not able to shake off a sharp vision of that sudden, surprising look on the old man's face. But more than that, he wondered about his father.

Chapter Nine

Evening.

But it had been gray all day. The air was still and heavy, the tree leaves motionless. A cluster of white toadstools had pushed up into Mary Bannon's rock garden.

"They say the weather's going to change tonight," Mary said after swatting a fly that had been crawling up her kitchen cabinet.

Charley only grunted as he went on reading the newspaper.

"The weather man on Channel Six says the heat's going to break," Mary added, just in case her husband hadn't heard her first comment.

Charley offered another grunt, then said, "Gasoline prices are going up again." *The Evening Bulletin* was limp from moisture, so he stretched it out on the table, next to his cup of coffee. "I'll be damned. Look at this. That fire-bomber hit another porno shop. Some woman turned the corner and got a look at him. Says he's an old guy. The owner took off after him. Almost nabbed him."

"Want more coffee?" Mary dried her hands on a towel before stepping toward her husband, pot in hand.

He looked up as she poured, then blew into his cup.

"You know, Charley, I've been thinking." Mary sat opposite him, put her elbows on the table and interlocked her fingers. "Billy's getting away from us just like Bobby."

"What do you mean?" He glared at her.

"Bobby's been at the shore all summer and he's only called home twice."

"He sent us saltwater taffy."

53

"But it's Billy I'm worried about. His thoughts are way off somewhere most of the time. Haven't you noticed?"

Charley felt uncomfortable. He scanned the newspaper, but didn't read.

"We don't really know him."

"That's nonsense."

"Charley!"

He looked up. "We talk! I talk to him!"

"About what? The Phillies? Come on, now, Charley. Billy's a serious kid. He's imaginative. His mind's popping with all sorts of things. But I don't know what's inside him. And I'm sure you don't know, either."

"You worry too much."

"No. That's not it at all. You don't get it, do you? Charley, you set rules, plenty of rules. Be in at eleven. Do your homework. Don't run down the stairs. But when do you really talk with him?"

"Okay, okay! So what do you want me to do?"

"You could open up to him. More than you did with Bobby when he was in high school. He might see you as human. He might even talk about himself."

"You're upset because he got in so late last night."

"You didn't even talk to him about it."

"What do you mean?" Charley glowered at his wife. "I gave him hell!"

"Hell? Yes, you gave him hell, and that was about it. But you didn't talk. You didn't really talk. Anyway, I'm not just thinking of last night. What does he do any night? Do you know?"

"Seems to me you're the one who shut me up about the cemetery."

"You weren't handling it right."

"Damn it, Mary, you really got a bug up your... whatever."

"You should let him open up because he wants to. He's not able to bare himself because you don't share with him."

"What kid can bare himself to his old man? I know I didn't."

"And that's part of the problem."

"Now what's that supposed to mean?"

"I think you know."

Charley turned away, stared out the window, and tried to ignore the remark. His chin stiffened. "Look, he knows better than to get into trouble. So, he hangs with Lori. She's a good kid." He looked down at his newspaper.

"Tell me, Charley, what do you think Billy's doing right now? Huh? What do you think?"

* * *

"Ouch!" Lori's sunburnt flesh was painful to the touch, especially about the neck and shoulders. It inhibited Billy.

"Damn!" He sat up.

"Sorry."

Billy was quick to smile. In fact, his face was blissfully radiant as he hung his head over hers, and looked down into her big blue eyes. "It's okay. It's just so great to have you back." Only hours had passed since Lori's return from Stone Harbor, and already she and Billy were behind that pink slab of granite on the Smythe family plot.

After a few more hugs and kisses—all gentle because of Lori's bright pink, tender skin—Billy began to rattle off more about his adventure with Clarence at Mason House, a subject never far from his thoughts. Lori lifted herself and sat against the tombstone as he unloaded more details, some with slight embellishment.

"...So I got away and ran right out onto the porch and jumped. He stayed there staring at me as I went up the street."

"Did you look back?" Lori asked.

"No. I just kept going."

"How do you know he was looking at you?"

"I could feel him in that doorway, watching me. I couldn't sleep when I got home. I kept thinking about what he said. I kept seeing him. Every time I closed my eyes I saw him staring at me."

Lori shivered, maybe because of the images in her mind, or because of her sunburn or the sudden breeze that was pushing away the heat and humidity. "Hold me, Billy. Please."

Billy was gentle, his touch soft. "My folks know we come here," he whispered.

"What?" Her body tensed.

"It's okay. Dad couldn't say much, because he used to come here. With my mom. Can you believe that?"

"You're kidding?"

"No."

"He told you?"

"They told me. She kinda pushed him into it."

"Do you think maybe they think... you know... that we..."

"No. I don't think so. Dad, he's so sure of everything and everybody. To him, Mom is one way, I'm another, and Bobby's this and that, and everyone fits into a certain mold. He makes things conform to his view. As long as I live by his rules, I'm okay. Same for Mom and Bobby. So, then the world is all right. Nothing's out of line. You get it?"

"Not really. I mean, your being here with me, that can't be according to the rules."

"As long as I live by his curfew..." Billy smiled and kissed Lori on her sunburned nose. "But he's an okay guy, really. He's just got this crazy kind of brain that organizes and plans things one way and that way only. And he doesn't really open up and let it all hang out."

"He frightens me a little."

"That's the cop thing. You know, the big cop act. He's so used to playing the role he can't turn it off. But Mom's on some kind of a crusade. She wants to change him, and she's about to launch a family togetherness campaign. According to her, the three of us are going to do this, that and something else together. Dad doesn't know it yet, but we're about to visit the zoo. Mom read about the new Wolf Woods. Never knew she was into wolves, but all of a sudden she's flying high because they're out of their cages."

Boughs bent as whispery rustling breezes swept the cemetery and the first cool winds of August stirred the leaves and branches. Soon the clouds separated. They moved quickly— swirling puffs in a dark sky racing across the face of the moon. An owl screeched in the distance.

* * *

Mary stared at her husband. "A good cop doesn't always make a good father."

Charley pushed the newspaper aside. "So I'm not a good father? If that's what you're saying, I really resent it."

"You're an okay father. No, you're more than okay. But why not better? Look at me, Charley." Mary rolled her eyes, aimed them at his frowning countenance, pulled her thoughts together, forced a smile and allowed it to fade, then said, "I know how you feel inside. I know what's underneath those rules and regulations. I know how you feel about your kids. But do they? Maybe. Maybe not."

"I don't see Harry Flood or Sam Smiley with their kids at the ball field."

"Does Billy—or Bobby, for that matter—know about the time we got caught in that abandoned house?"

Charley shot daggers at his wife. "You gotta be kidding? What kinda thing is that to tell your boy? You're not making any sense. Besides, that's a private thing. That's not the kind of thing you talk about. Not with your kids."

"Maybe not. But then find something else to tell him— something that will bring you closer. Let him know you've made mistakes. Maybe then certain things won't happen."

"What the hell is that supposed to mean? What in God's name is going to happen?"

"He'll move away some day. And he'll remember his dad, the policeman. But he'll never really know you."

Charley's face reddened. "Damn it, Mary, when he was a little boy, we did all sorts of..."

"When he was little!" she interrupted. "But this is now, and now is different. Don't you understand? It's the curious teenage mind that dreams up ideas, gets restless and seeks answers." She leaned forward and fixed her eyes firmly on him. "Charley, I've been bothered ever since..." She hesitated.

"Go on. Ever since what?"

"Well, I've been dwelling on disturbing thoughts ever since we talked with Billy about the cemetery and Henry Mason."

"So that's it! I'll be damned. I should have known. You haven't been the same since."

"I've just been thinking, that's all. Can't seem to shake off thoughts that keep going around and around."

"Well, your mind is playing crazy tricks."

"Did you see the way Billy looked at you that morning?"

"What morning?"

"When we talked about Mr. Mason and the cemetery and all that. It was like he saw something he'd never seen before. It was a revelation to him. It's been eating at me ever since."

Charley stared at his wife in puzzlement. "Honest to God, Mary, I don't know what you're talking about."

"He saw your softness. And he saw something else, something deeper, something untold."

"What the hell is all this?" Charley looked sheepish and turned back to his newspaper. "Let's drop it, okay?"

"I love you Charley, and I always will. But maybe I liked you better when you didn't play the all-perfect cop. Why do you need to play policeman with Billy and Bobby?"

Charley's eyes flashed in anger. "I am what I am. Okay?"

Mary rose from the table, turned her back on Charley and began to walk from the kitchen. She stopped in the doorway and grasped the doorjamb as her thoughts raced. Suddenly she spun around, looked at her husband and said, "There really is something, isn't there?" Her expression asked questions. A slight twinkle of wonder brightened her searching eyes.

After a quick glance at Mary, Charley looked down at the newspaper again and mumbled, "Forget it."

"I never asked, did I? And I never intended to ask. But I always knew there was something that was yours, and not mine to know. So, you don't have to tell me. I can live with that. But maybe you can share it with Billy. You might be surprised. He might even respect you more."

"How can I be a cop and do that?" Charley snapped. "How can I criticize others after I've admitted screwing up myself?"

"Ah!"

"Okay, okay. So I'm not perfect."

"Ann Landers would say that whatever it was that happened before we married is none of my business. So would Dear Abby.

Believe me, I'm not asking. I'm just wondering if you could build a bridge with Billy by baring your soul or spilling your guts."

Charley turned sad eyes but a warm smile on Mary. It was an expression that said he didn't know, he wasn't sure.

She smiled back, stepped toward him, reached out and squeezed his shoulder. "Show him that you can make mistakes. I think it would be a good thing." Leaning down, she kissed his cheek. "Whatever your deep, dark secret—and believe me, I've always known it was there—I know you've changed your ways. That gives you all the right in the world to criticize others."

Mary had always been intuitive, and Charley was sometimes in awe of her insight. Somewhere deep in her past she had honed special skills in sensing the shape of events and then changing that shape. Charley knew she could manipulate, but with good intent. Shrewd, business-like at times, she didn't always expose her deepest feelings. But love and caring were there, and they were the underpinnings of her decisions and her efforts to mold.

The product of a large family, Mary had learned to survive with six brothers who had been given too much freedom by a father who favored males. She had been tied tightly to home and to a mother who needed help around the house. No child of hers would become such a prisoner, she had told herself long ago. Yet she realized that her spoiled brothers had made little of themselves. Surely there was a middle road. That's what she wanted for her boys.

Charley had a deep respect for his wife. More than that, he loved her profoundly with emotions that stirred under his tough facade.

"I remember when you picked buttercups and daisies for me," Mary said. Her smile not only turned her lips; it brought sparkle to her eyes.

* * *

The clouds were gone. Stars shown brightly in a clear, black sky, and a stiff breeze rustled the sycamores as Billy neared home after leaving Lori. He found Clarence sitting on the curb under a streetlamp.

"What are you doing here?" Billy asked as he stood before his house. He leaned against the lamppost and looked down on his friend.

"Y'see the Phillies game?" Clarence toyed with a piece of sycamore bark, tossed it, and then stretched his legs. "Can't believe they walked in the Cubs' winning run."

"Nah, I was out."

"Yeah, I know. She's back, isn't she?" Clarence picked up pebbles and tossed them into the street.

"Who?"

"You know."

"Lori? Yeah, she's back."

Clarence tossed more pebbles. "I've been thinking."

Billy waited, shifted his weight, then kicked Clarence's leg. "So? What about?"

"That we should go over to Mason House and pry open the old fart's shutters."

"Now? Y'gotta be kidding! Hey, look, it's late. I gotta go in."

"I can get my old man's hammer and chisel."

"Get out of here, will you!" Billy showed his annoyance, first with tone of voice, then with another kick.

"Looked for you earlier. Been back and forth." He glance up at Billy. "I'm not talkin' hot air. We don't have to do it now. But maybe sometime when the old fart's out. But we can plan it now, can't we?"

"I don't know, man." Billy's tone was negative.

"What's the matter? Y' chicken?"

Chapter Ten

Visions of Andrew.

And Henry suffered. Up and down the cellar steps he went, until he had gathered nails, screws, hammers, screwdrivers, pliers, an auger and two old boards that were rotted at the ends, once part of Anna's washing platform. He stood in the kitchen, staring at his gatherings while he gasped for breath. Surely these devices, he told himself, would help close out Andrew.

Later, Henry climbed the stairs twice and dumped the tools in the upstairs hallway, then descended into the room of plants where he placed the boards under a split-leaf philodendron near the south windows. As he bent, he was startled, catching a glimpse of a face in one of the windows—a face obscured by the darkness of night and the philodendron leaves. At least he thought it was a face. Now fear tried to stymie him, but he fought well, gathered his wits, and casually side-stepped out-of-sight, into the shadows of giant palms near the fireplace. He stood motionless while his thoughts stewed.

Why don't they leave me alone? Or, are they there at all?

Shadows and mirages had loomed often in his lifetime. He knew how to fight them. He had won many a battle.

His thoughts talked to one another: Window, window in the wall, was there such a face at all? Spies? Yes, spies. Shut up! Shut, shut, shut up!

Henry peeked, and the face was there—fleetingly, gone so fast that he still questioned its existence. He grabbed a double-pronged fire iron. Gripping it too hard with old fingers, he slipped into the hallway and sneaked up the stairs, then hurried down the back steps to the kitchen and out into the yard. Minutes later he was on the south side of the house, screaming at the thick cedars that hid the windows of his living room.

"Come out! Come out from there you blood-sucking varmints!"

Clarence kneeled behind the bushes, between his friends— Pete Lewis, a slim, freckle-faced redhead, and Skip Lanning, skinny and swarthy.

"Come out or I'll whip your asses 'til they bleed!" Gripping the handle with a force that made his arm quake, Henry held the two-pronged poker well above his head.

Nothing.

Then a slight rustle.

"Do you know what I can do to you?" Henry's voice was more threatening than ever. "I'll break your puny legs with this! You hear me? I'll break your bones!" The old man brought the fire iron down heavily on the cedars, then poked among the thickly entangled evergreen switches.

Suddenly Pete took off, flying toward the street, his shirttail flapping. Skip followed, crouched, his hands atop his head. The teenagers leaped and ran up the street like wounded gazelles in flight.

"Scat, you little bastards!" Henry yelled. "I catch you here again I'll skin you alive! You hear me? Skin you alive!"

Clarence was frightened, but didn't flee. Hoping that the attack was over, he squeezed himself into a ball, wrapping his arms around his legs and burying his head between them. But Henry sensed that someone remained. He stayed there, quietly waiting. Seconds later he began to beat the bushes furiously, striking again and again until the fire iron came down hard on Clarence's arm.

"Stop!" the boy screamed. "You hurt me!"

The blow had momentarily paralyzed his arm, sending excruciating pain down to his fingers and up into his shoulder.

"Please stop," Clarence said as he stepped from between thick branches of cedar. He held his arm, gritted his teeth and stared with fear into the face of the old man. "We weren't doing anything."

Henry held the poker high, as if he were about to bring it down on the boy's head. His jaw trembled in fury. He couldn't speak.

Clarence began to back away slowly, step by step, fearful for his life. The ferocious look in the old man's eyes terrified him. Suddenly he turned and ran, still clutching his wounded arm.

When Clarence was far gone, Henry lowered the fire iron and remained standing and trembling and gazing toward the street. Within seconds the tool fell from his quivering hand. Tears welled in his eyes. "I didn't mean to hurt you," he mumbled. "Why don't you leave me alone?"

* * *

Clarence didn't fully understand his annoyance with Billy and resentment of Lori. In fact, he couldn't admit such feelings, even to himself. He was unable to separate the sources of his frustration, and it became easier for him to abuse Henry than pick on his long-time friend. When the old man struck back, Clarence found the excuse he needed to avenge his hurts, no matter from where they came.

It had not been difficult to recruit mischief-makers such as Pete and Skip from among his so-called friends. And they were full of sympathy for Clarence the day following their cedar-bush spying, after seeing the large purple and yellow welt on his right arm—an ugly bruise that still thumped. That night it was perfectly logical to hang Old Man Mason in effigy from a low, sappy limb of his cherry tree.

* * *

Lori was giggling and Billy was tickling as he helped her over the cemetery wall and into Mason's yard. It didn't take a double-look to spot the dark image of a body hanging in the cherry tree and swinging in the night breeze among the rustling leaves. Eerie, to say the least. Billy broke toward the effigy, despite Lori's attempt to hold him back.

"Don't, Billy! He'll see you! It's too light out."

Dusk hung over Mason House, enticing bats to leave the high gables, silhouette themselves against the fading light, dart, turn, zigzag and always avoid the reaching branches of the cherry tree.

"What the hell!" Billy suspected the worst.

"Please, Billy!"

The boy faced the feet of the swinging effigy and looked up. The dummy's head was an ugly muskmelon, carved with gashes, dripping with juice. It's hair was a spaghetti mop, straggling down around the melon. Well-worn, stained and wrinkled pants hung low, baring a waist of twisted newspaper below a frayed, moth-eaten, black sweat shirt streaked in white paint that spelled out: DEATH TO THE FUCKING OLD CREEP!

"You idiot, Clarence!" Billy whispered with vehement disdain. "You freakin' idiot!"

Billy leaped at the effigy, grabbed it with both hands, yanked and broke the cord, and squeezed the dummy as he pulled it into his arms. He stood there squeezing in anger as Lori neared and gazed into his crazed eyes.

"Let's get out of here, Billy!"

"Stupid! So stupid!"

"Let's go! He'll see you and think you did it."

Too late.

Old Man Mason appeared like an apparition in the darkening dusk. Lori could tell by the look in Billy's eyes. She watched the boy tighten his hold on the effigy, watched him squeeze until its melon-head fell to the ground and split open. Then she turned. There was the old man, like everthing else, blending with nightfall, almost lost in the reaching vines and shrubs that tangled about his house.

"You don't learn, do you, boy?" Henry's words seemed to still the air.

"I was taking it away," Billy said with an urgent plea for belief. "Honest. It's just some old junk."

Henry moved toward the boy as Lori backed away. Not until he was nose-to-nose with Billy and tugging at the effigy did the boy step backwards and repeat, "I was taking it away."

"Let me see what you're trying to hide."

"It's nothing. Just some old stuff."

"Let me see."

"It's just rags and junk and stuff. Somebody hung it up there."

Henry took a firm hold and pulled, but Billy refused to give up the headless effigy. Suddenly the old man shoved, hoping the teenager would lose his balance and drop the deformed image.

Lori yelled, "Stop it!" as Billy skidded and tripped, caught himself and clung to a branch while still holding fast to the stuffed dummy. His sneakers were tangled in the spaghetti mop. Kicking to free himself, he planted his feet firmly on the ground among the roots of the cherry tree.

Henry grabbed as fast as a frog takes a fly, snatching the effigy. Billy wanted to explain, but just stood there, dumbfounded by the old man's quickness—an agility that seemed to belie his infirmity.

"What have we here?" Henry muttered.

Billy wanted to tell the old man not to read the message on the shirt. But he only parted his lips.

Lori came to his aid: "Billy didn't do it, Mr. Mason. He didn't. Honest. He just wanted to get it out of the tree."

Henry's reaction was not exactly what the boy had expected. As the old man read the words, his anger appeared to fade. It was replaced by sadness and an enfeebling hurt. His eyes seemed to ask: Do you really see me this way? Do you want me dead?

"Let's go, Billy," Lori whispered.

As Billy backed away he kept staring at Henry. He took Lori's hand, turned suddenly, pulled and hurried off. As they neared the sidewalk, they hesitated, looked back and vaguely saw the old man hunched under his cherry tree.

Only then did Henry yell: "Go away! Stay away! How many times must I tell you to stay off my property?"

But he did not fully mean his words, and he carried an image of Billy into his house—an image of a scared boy who tried to hide something from him. He could not shake off the vision as he stood in the middle of his dark living room, seeing nothing around him. Then he knew. It was more than Billy. It was Andy. He saw Andy, a fearful teenage Andy holding a broken smoking pipe—a pipe that was never to be touched, the priceless meerschaum pipe handed down from Grandfather. It was in two pieces, squeezed into young Andrew's tight fists.

"I hurt you, didn't I, Andy?"

In time, Henry focused on the moment and picked up the old, rotting, washing platform boards from under the big, split leaves of the philodendron and carried them upstairs to his pile of tools. After letting the boards fall, he stood looking at the tools in confused contemplation. Maybe, he thought. But then, maybe not. After all, he just might want to open that door again. He might want to see the butterflies or touch the cherry picker.

* * *

Billy caught up with Clarence the next night, after the baseball game in Naylor's Run Park. He held back until Clarence had a chance to slip off his fielder's glove, wipe sweat from his brow, and guzzle a pint of water. Then he pulled him aside and let loose with an angry whisper: "What the fuck's wrong with you, man? That was a real shitty trick."

"What the hell y'talkin' about?"

"Stickin' it to Old Man Mason like that! Puttin' up that stupid melon head! Don't tell me it wasn't you, pisshead!"

Clarence smirked.

"Hey! Wipe off the grin, you freakin' jerk!"

Quickly losing his sneering smile, Clarence moved with haste, away from the field and the dispersing crowd. Right on his heels, red-faced Billy followed him to the rocky creek, across the footbridge, and along the narrow, wooded path on the other side.

"Put on your brakes, man!" Billy yelled.

Clarence slowed his pace as his friend grabbed him by the back of his belt. After some heavy words and a few shoves, Clarence tried to play buddy-buddy patch-up and confessed to another plot: "Some of the guys agreed to hold back their piss from noon 'til dark, then meet along the tracks and piss into a plastic bag. They're gonna tie it to a gutter hook so when the old man opens his backdoor it'll bust in his face."

"That's stupid, man! That's really stupid! Shit, man, that's the stupidest thing I ever heard of!

"Not my idea."

"So, whose stupid idea?"

"Those other guys." Clarence looked down at his feet, then spun away from Billy to hide his sheepish expression. After hearing a sigh of disgust from his long-time chum, he turned a sad-eyed, hound-dog look on Billy, forced a pleading smile, and then said, "So, what do y'say, buddyo?" He lifted his hand in search of a high-five slap. "You wanna hit the deli for a couple of Cokes?"

* * *

It took guts beyond guts for Billy to sneak into Mason's yard again, especially carrying a long stick with a penknife taped to its tip. Moving slowly from bush to bush, he stayed out of the moonlight, skulked along the back wall, then among the shrubs and trees along the garage.

It was to be a quick strike.

In and out.

Zip-zap, and then gone.

One.

Two.

Three.

Four.

Five.

A deep breath.

Billy crouched near the back porch, then attacked like a venomous snake, his six-foot fang jabbing quickly, hitting its mark and puncturing the hanging bag so that the urine poured onto the porch. He was gone before the final dribble.

Henry Mason didn't open his backdoor that night. In fact, he didn't open it for nearly a week. The remains of the plastic bag hung like a strip of flypaper, gathering insects during the heat of each day.

Chapter Eleven

Near the end of summer. Golden fields. Cool nights. Wild morning glory vines had grown thick in Mary Bannon's rock garden, choking the begonias.

Jeffrey Broomell, the textbook salesman, was off the critical list. He had been shipped to a Chicago hospital where he could be near his family while undergoing additional skin grafting.

Goldenrod and wild asters bloomed along the highways. Weeds were high against the outside of the cemetery wall.

Hubert Pugg had refused to give police a description of the old man who ravaged the Cherry Street porno shop, despite weeks of prodding. His wife had not spoken to him since her initial outburst: "You fat pervert, you!"

Billy was still stacking local corn and Jersey tomatoes. Late summer squash was abundant now, and the first load of butternut, Hubbard and other winter varieties had arrived. On chilly nights, he and Lori carried blankets into the cemetery where they rolled up and snuggled. They still spied on Mason House, but always from a distance.

Buttonballs were at full size on the sycamores. Large, woolly, silver-green leaves of the mulleins were in thick clusters along the railroad spur, many of their tall spikes bearing yellow flowers.

Mary Bannon had increased her efforts at family reform, promoting dessert-and-coffee discussions at the dinner table, togetherness at concerts and museums, and fun-and-games at picnics. She had arranged a Sunday afternoon get-together with Bob at the shore, and had even joined Charley and Billy for a Phillies game at Veterans Stadium.

The tools and boards remained undisturbed on the hallway floor in the second story of Mason House, just where Henry had dumped them. Occasionally he stopped to reflect on them, but more often simply stepped over the pile.

Henry had climbed to his attic twice since the night of Billy and the effigy. Both times he opened the same chest and looked at the same toys—touching them and lifting several to his bosom. Each time he had tossed the toys back into the chest, slammed the lid, and angrily condemned himself. His attic visits were followed by speedy descents into the cellar for gulps of whiskey that sent his ulcer on a painful rampage.

On this, the fifth day of September, Henry slept late, watered Anna's plants at noontime, and dressed himself in a stained undershirt and a paint-spotted pair of pants. Although he glanced out the windows, he didn't sample the fresh outside air that had blown down from Canada to cover the Northeast. He stood at the kitchen sink and drank milk from the carton to soothe his stomach, then climbed steps to the third floor where unused rooms were closed off and thick dust lined the hallway floor and baseboards. At his left was a dark, narrow flight of stairs that led to a trap door.

Henry climbed the steps and pushed up the door—a trap operated by pulley and weight. He coughed as dust flew, and then crawled into the stuffy attic where old boxes and crates, picture frames, broken lamps, discolored books and Christmas trimmings were scattered among a host of other items. Working his way to the toy chest, he reached out and touched the lid and moved his thumb along its lip. Although chipped and blotched, the paint that Henry had so intricately brushed on the lid still portrayed smiling faces of chipmunks and raccoons. Barely smiling, he studied the lid, then pulled back his hand and sat quietly on the floor, gazing reflectively toward the only window that gave light to the crowded attic—a place he had not visited in many years, until this summer.

Today, and in recent days, the thoughts had come again and again. They had begun to occur with the first intrusion of Billy. Little by little they became more frequent, these painful pieces of the past. And the barriers, in place for so many years, were falling despite Henry's efforts to strengthen them and purge the invading images. With each yielding, with each giving-in, with each failure to thwart long-suppressed memories, Henry was hammered by the hurts. But it was more than the reflection of Andrew in Billy that evoked yearnings and opened wounds. Henry was growing old, and time was racing toward the finish line.

Poignant and pensive, the old man opened the chest as if, for some reason, he was compelled to lift the lid. A smile touched his lips as he picked up a tattered puppy—once white and fluffy, now soiled, a leg missing. He pushed stuffing back inside the sad-eyed pup. Gently, he fingered its soft fur. Putting the dog aside, he reached into the chest for a pair of cigar boxes tied together with brown cord. The twine fell apart when he pulled. He fumbled the boxes, spilling their contents on the floor. Dropping here and there and clanking atop each other were lead soldiers of many lands and eras—British redcoats and American rough-and-readies of the Revolution, Ethiopians and Italians armed for battle, Japanese and Chinese holding guns of the mid-1930s, American Indians on horseback. One by one Henry stood the soldiers on their feet, lining them up in a lengthy column.

Sousa's martial music drummed and trumpeted in Henry's head, and the soldiers marched as they had often marched in Andy's imagination. Christmas morning. Long winter nights. The living room floor. Marching, marching and going off to war. Andy lining them up for battle. Here, there. Behind pillows and potted plants. Storming the fireplace, climbing the stairs. Drum-adum-dum, drum-adum-dum. Handsome little Andy, grinning with adventure.

Andy lay asleep, his head on the pillow next to his puppy, his fingers clutching a soldier boy, his face smiling with dreams of tomorrow.

The No. 6 trolley took them to Willow Grove amusement park, through the woods, the wind blowing Anna's hair. Andy was anxious and bubbling. "When will we get there, Dad?"

Little Andy had no fear of roller coasters. "Come on, Dad! Hurry up, Dad."

Long before Andrew's birth, Henry and Anna would sail in a pedal-boat in the park pond before settling on a bench for a concert at the band shell. Anna would wear a pretty summer hat—yellow or pink.

Anna was rounded with child, beauty in the fullness of her face. Evening colors were soft. Words were hushed. Slowly, back and forth, back and forth they swayed in the wicker rocker on the porch.

"He's gone, Anna," Henry muttered. "Andy's gone."

Hearing himself, Henry suddenly knocked over the soldiers, first with an angry swing of his right hand, then with an angry swing of his left. He breathed heavily as he surveyed the scene. Why not destroy the toys? Why not rid his house of all bits and pieces of him? Why the torments, the reminders, the little parts of Andrew scattered here and there? To play hurtful games? To punish himself? No. His calling was to punish, not to be punished.

Henry felt vindictive when he crawled from the attic and struggled awkwardly down the stairs. He kept his eyes down. Even when he reached the second level he stared at the floor to avoid doors and pictures on the wall. He saw the pile of tools, but not the door to *The Room*. Not in many days had he gone to *The Room*.

It was the cellar again that called him to the whiskey bottle despite Anna's chastising efforts to stop him. No memories were about to get in his way. He would feed on the need to punish and muster strength to battle Sodom.

Chapter Twelve

Philadelphia streets were wet and shiny from a drizzle that had settled over the Delaware Valley at nightfall. The sky was dark and heavy and mist was thick when two fat women struggled to squeeze under one umbrella while walking awkwardly through the City Hall courtyard. As they passed a subway entrance at about 11:15, a man in a long, black raincoat and a turned-down rain hat came up from the underground concourse into the rain-soaked square. He carried a bulging paper bag in his right hand and tightened the collar around his neck with his left. Bent forward and walking like an old man, he cut through the drizzle unnoticed by the hurrying women. He took shelter for a moment under the east arch of City Hall, then crossed the street toward the John Wanamaker department store.

The wet streets reflected the city lights. Traffic was light. A yellow cab sped around the corner, spraying water. The bent man kept a steady pace. He shuffled along Market Street, then turned on 13th while holding the bulging bag against his bosom to protect it from the rain.

Not far away, on narrow Sansom Street, music echoed from a bar each time the door opened. Neon gave bright reflections and a pinkish glow to brick and stone up and down the tightly packed street where cars parked with wheels on the curb.

Two young men, laughing and chattering loudly, bounded up the street and entered the bar as the dark figure turned from 13th onto Sansom and slipped into the shadow of a doorway, clutching his bag-covered object. Minutes later the man moved stealthily toward the bar, only to pull back when the door flew open and two high-spirited men staggered arm-in-arm into the heavy mist. When they were out of sight, the skulking man stepped into the street, lit a fuel-soaked wick with his cigarette lighter and tossed a missile into the doorway of the bar. The flaming bottle crashed and burst into a roaring blaze.

Chapter Thirteen

Henry Mason looked out his side and rear windows more and more with each passing day. He kept telling himself that he was surveying his property to help protect it. Outwardly, he refused to admit that he wanted Billy Bannon to trespass on his land. The desire was hidden among complex emotions and masked by rationalizations. Henry was afraid to want, but the hunger was increasing.

He stood in his bedroom that Thursday evening in early September, his back against a bed post, and gazed out into the jungle of growth that filled much of his yard. He squinted at the orange-red sun that was broken into shimmering rays by the moving branches.

* * *

Billy carried a blanket as he hurried along a narrow street of row houses, Lori holding onto his belt, sometimes pushing, sometimes being pulled. At an open intersection, the last of the orange-red sun flashed into their eyes.

Township schools would open on Monday, so Billy and Lori had little time left before their schedules tightened. They became almost frantic in their desire to grasp each other whenever possible.

The shadows of dusk had spread over the cemetery by the time they stretched out on the blanket behind that pink granite tombstone.

"Look! See?" Billy pointed to a fleck of red among the maple leaves. "It's a cardinal."

"Where?"

"Over there!"

"I don't see it." Lori snuggled close to Billy, her eyes searching the trees. "Oh, yes! Now I do!" She watched as the bright red bird took flight and joined his mate on the branch of a birch.

Billy blew his warm breath into Lori's ear and whispered, "Do you like birds?"

"Of course I like birds. What a silly question. Doesn't everyone like birds?"

Billy pulled away, looked into her eyes, then pushed his nose against hers. The coming of school touched him with melancholy. "I feel like I want to say all the things I didn't say but wanted to say all summer."

Lori giggled. "About birds?"

"No, about you. You're a real person, Lori."

"What's that supposed to mean?"

"You're real flesh and blood."

"I hope so."

"And you're here with me."

Lori giggled again.

"You're so pretty," Billy said, "but it's what you really are that counts."

"What exactly am I?" She fixed her eyes on his, played with his hair, toyed with his ear.

"You like birds."

She laughed.

He chuckled, then blew into her ear and whispered, "You're good to me. You like pizza. You're smart. You like to talk about birds and bees and me, about the moon and stars and me, about Keats and Shelley and me. I think maybe you like me. Maybe you like me for what I am."

"Oh? And what are you?"

Billy couldn't find the words. He grinned comically, shrugged his shoulders, and finally said, "I'm a guy on the hunt."

Lori looked puzzled.

"You know," Billy said. "What's the word? I'm... I'm curious. Better yet, inquisitive. That's the favorite word of Mr. Faber, my chemistry teacher. Inquisitive. That's me. I want to find out about things. All sorts of things."

"Like what?"

"Like... Like what happens to earthworms when the ground freezes in winter."

Lori snickered.

"I guess I imagine things when I don't have the answers," Billy said. "Mr. Faber says it's good to be imaginative. Imaginative and inquisitive. That's me."

"Now you're boasting."

"No. You asked me." A solemn expression sucked in Billy's cheeks and took the sparkle from his eyes. "Besides, I want you to know who I am, what I am."

"Why so serious?"

"Maybe it's time to talk serious."

"My mother gets embarrassed when I talk about serious things."

"What like?" He ran his fingers through her hair and looked at her with care.

"It seems I'm too young for everything. I think that's when she misses my father the most, when I get serious and ask questions and all. It's always, 'That time will come,' or 'Not now, Lori,' or 'You're only sixteen.' She doesn't like to talk about feelings and stuff like that. Some girls have mothers that are more like sisters and they can talk about anything. I wish my mom was like that."

"You can talk to me," he whispered.

"Not about everything."

"Yes you can. Try me."

Lori smiled weakly, ran her finger down Billy's nose and across his lips. "I worry about things."

"What kind of things?"

"Oh, things. Like us. I worry about us."

"Why?"

"Because of the way I feel."

"What do you mean? How do you feel?"

"You know."

"Tell me."

"I want you so much." She touched his lips again. "It scares me.

Aren't you ever scared? I wake up scared sometimes. Scared that I'll lose you. If I didn't have these feelings inside, I guess I wouldn't be scared."

Billy gave Lori a comforting squeeze.

"I lie in bed worrying about it," she said. "My mother doesn't believe that kids our age can be in love. It's frustrating. She says whatever we feel, it won't last. She's not right, is she? She can't be, can she?" Lori kissed him on the lips. "Tell me how you feel, Billy. Please."

"You know how I feel. Each of us knows how the other feels. It's just there, and we know it. That's all."

"It's scary."

Billy brushed hair from Lori's face, kept gazing into her eyes, then wrapped his arms around her. "What's the matter with my happy little cheerleader?"

"Is that the way you see me? This... This happy little cheerleader?"

"That's just part of you."

"When I'm with you, I'm not always that way. I'm not always the way other people see me."

"I know."

"Hold me."

"I want to take care of you." Billy held tightly. "I want a good job, so I can take care of you. Maybe some kind of scientific research or something." He pulled away and smiled. "Then I can find out about those worms. Mr. Faber says I'll be looking for answers all my life. He says I have that kind of mind." Lowering himself, Billy hovered over her and stared deeply into her eyes.

A sudden breeze chilled Lori, and she reached over Billy to grab a corner of the blanket. She screamed in fright, and Billy sprang up as shivers of shock raced through his body. Eyes wide and mouths open, both hurried to their feet and then stood motionless, staring at the old man who stood but a few feet away.

Henry Mason said nothing. He just stayed there in the shadows, in his wrinkled shirt and pants, his eyes aimed at the teenagers.

Lori trembled while Billy strove to shake off the sudden scare. Finally gaining enough control to organize his thoughts, he wrapped his arm protectively around Lori and asked, "What do you want?" His voice quivered as he said, "We're not on your property. We're not trespassing on your land."

Henry tried to find words to explain himself, but they failed to form, maybe because he wasn't sure why he was there.

Billy had no way of understanding the undercurrent that was pulling and tugging at Henry. He spurted words with little thought: "You're a crazy old man! What've you been doing, standing there watching and listening?"

Henry said nothing.

Lori stayed at Billy's side, shaking and breathing heavily. She sought words, then asked, "Why don't you leave us alone?"

"What do you want?" Billy asked as the old man continued to gape at them.

"I saw you," Henry muttered in a barely audible, raspish voice. "I saw you come here."

"So?" Billy's stare grew intense.

"I came looking for you."

"And now I suppose you want to take us as prisoners." Billy's tone was sharp and cutting. "Maybe you want to lock us up in that boarded-up room of yours."

Stunned by Billy's words, Henry was speechless until the teenagers began to back away. Then he pulled his thoughts together and simply said, "I guess I came because I like you."

Billy and Lori stared in disbelief.

Chapter Fourteen

F riday.

The beginning of the end. The final weekday. The start of the last weekend before the opening of school.

Few tourists at the Betsy Ross House.

More butternut squash for Pizuto Produce.

Chrysanthemums, clusters of orange-red berries on the firethorn bushes, touches of yellow among the Norway maples, rust on the oaks and bronze on the beeches.

Billy had yet to tell anyone about his latest encounter with Old Man Mason. Maybe he would tell no one, and swear Lori to secrecy. But why? To protect himself? From what? He hadn't done anything wrong in the cemetery. To protect Mason? From whom? From ridicule, perhaps? Something told Billy to wait and think—something in the old man's eyes, something in his words, "I like you." The boy had dwelled on those words since yesterday's dusk. Now, Friday, at Pizuto Produce, cucumbers or big Spanish onions made little difference. No matter what he unloaded, stacked or sorted, his thoughts slipped back to that strange figure of a man, standing in the cemetery, cloaked in the shadows of evening. His perplexity tied him to the image. Although resentful of Mason's intrusion, he felt compassion for the old man, for he had heard pathos in his voice. Through a facade of embitterment, he had seen a glimpse of yearning. Whatever its meaning, he sensed that it was not solely of this time, but of times past.

* * *

Mary Bannon's hands were wet when the doorbell rang. She looked at the digital clock in the electric-stove timer. Two past four. Neither Billy nor Charley was due home yet. She dried her hands, tossed the towel on the drain board, fluffed her hair, and wondered how frowzy she looked after a half day in the kitchen preparing for Bobby's homecoming. The beads of sweat on her forehead stemmed from a hot oven laden with Bob's favorite cookies and cakes. Atlantic City's boardwalk burger-flipping season was over for Billy's brother, who would arrive in time for Temple's opening football game against Penn State.

"Yes?" she asked after opening the front door, and before grasping the occasion—a rare one, indeed, for it was seldom that Henry Mason ventured into the sunshine.

Henry didn't smile. He just stood there with a heavy, two-foot-high microscope held tightly to his side, cradled in his right arm, supported by his left hand, and braced against his hip. Dressed a shade neater than usual, he had put on a blue cardigan sweater that sported shiny silver buttons—a sweater stored for decades in its gift box, until today.

"May I help you?" Mary did not recognized the old man, not having seen him for years, really never knowing him, and remembering him only as the gentleman with the pretty wife in the sixth pew of Bethany Presbyterian Church.

"Where can I put this? It's for the kid."

"The kid?"

"This is Bannon's, isn't it?"

"Yes." A serious, questioning expression controlled Mary's face until she saw better-days-of-the-past behind the 79-year-old mask. "Why, Mr. Mason! It's you, isn't it? Please come in."

"Can't stay. This is for the boy."

"Billy?"

"He hangs with that Lippincott girl?"

"Yes."

"That's the one. Here." Henry lowered the microscope to the floor inside the door. "It belonged to my..." Unable to finished his sentence, he shifted thoughts. "I shined it up. You see that he gets it."

"I don't understand."

"You tell 'im it's to help him find things out. He'll know what I mean."

Chapter Fifteen

Lori deliberately didn't defrost the fish. Strengthening her will, she decided this would be another night of dining out with her mother—not at McDonald's or Burger King, but at a real restaurant with at least a smidgen of ambiance, perhaps one of her favorites. So she closed the refrigerator, returned the dinner plates to the cabinet above the sink, and escaped from the kitchen.

She would wait outside on the front steps, next to the potted, pink geraniums that had grown leggy during the hot, humid summer.

As Lori waited, she prepared her vivacious act, the one that would buoy up her weary mother and persuade her to eat out. She had a multifarious relationship with her mom—one that ranged from total frustration to respect and love. But Lori's teenage years had tipped the scales toward tension. Puberty had stimulated probes that Evelyn Lippincott attempted to avoid.

Evelyn was a working woman who tried hard—almost too hard—to stay young, because she believed her life depended on it. Her hair had become a shade lighter each year since she divorced Gordy Lippincott. Now it was almost platinum. From nighttime mudpacks to daytime sunscreens, she fought against her fears with stubborn determination. Living was difficult for Evelyn, mostly because she struggled to look the part that her job required—a pleasant, cheery sort-of-soul, smooth in movement, charming in speech, attractive from morning's first hello to evening's "Good night, Mr. Tobin. Have a pleasant dinner. Your first appointment tomorrow is with Mr. Downing at nine."

Each morning frightened Evelyn, for it was the start of another day, another eight hours as a never-let-the-chin-sag professional woman who was pushing 50 and trying to hide it. Her position as administrative assistant to Murray K. Tobin, vice president for corporate relations at Allied Electric, required not only secretarial management, word-processing skills and the compiling of research data, but also a large order of PR-gladhanding and a thousand smiles a day.

Besides all this, she tried to be both mother and father to Lori. The parent role filled the weary hours—early, late and weekend. Lori recognized her mother's efforts, but grew tired of standard rules and pat answers. She sensed the pressure and strain on Evelyn, yet failed to curb her growing impatience.

Again and again Evelyn reminded her daughter that life was difficult. "I haven't had it easy since your father walked out on us."

Suddenly Evelyn found herself adrift in quickly moving time. After all, the little girl was supposed to stay little. A working mother didn't need new complications. Disruption of the status quo would upset a tenuous schedule of living.

"Time will come for that, Lori, so don't..."

"We'll talk about it sometime when..."

"You're too young to..."

"He's a nice boy, but don't get serious. You're both too young to..."

"I have enough problems without that sort of..."

Evelyn wanted the best for her daughter, and said so often. That's why she worked so hard. That's why she set rules.

"Sweetheart, be good now and help your mother with..."

"Don't ever disappoint me, Lori, after all I've..."

"I can't stand over you every minute of the..."

"Do your homework first, be in on time, and..."

"I have to trust you, Lori."

The Lippincott's modest home was not far from the Aronimink Red-Arrow trolley station, a convenience that Evelyn needed. Its overgrown evergreens troubled the mailman, who cursed their spreading branches. Thanks be to providence, the house was brick and needed little paint. Lori shared household chores with her mother, seldom shirking her duties. She often cooked, but just as frequently convinced her mother to eat out, most often at fast-food outlets. But dinner at Springhouse Gardens or the Copper Kettle was more to her liking. Little by little she was engineering the schedule by ducking the rebuffs, waiting, then using finesse.

"I can't, dear, maybe another time, when..."

"I have a headache. I'll just have to rest or I won't..."

"Not now, Lori, please try to understand..."

"Why don't you just scramble some eggs while I rest my..."

* * *

Thirty-three years ago at age 16, Evelyn had been the image of Lori today—same expressive eyes, trim figure, turned-up nose, buoyant spirit. Her figure still caught glances, and despite a full day's work she looked trim and well groomed as she sat across from Lori in the Green Room of Springhouse Gardens. She was still wearing the smartly fitted business suit that had seen her through eight corporate hours, including a two-hour quiche-and-martini lunch with account executives from Haskin & Haskin. Arriving home late, she had been disappointed that Lori had not defrosted the turbot and washed the spinach. But Lori had planned with skill, and her well-rehearsed lines praised Mama's sacrifices and offered comfort at Springhouse. Quiet music and lighted candles behind red glass set the mood. The restaurant was a blend of rock, pine, water, greenery, low lights and ever-so-proper waiters.

Lori was slow to order, maybe because she wasn't hungry. Evelyn chose sauteed scallops with mushrooms a la Springhouse, then began a long, whispery discourse on office politics and Murray Tobin's pigheadedness.

"I'll have the Chef's Special salad," Lori said. She smiled sheepishly at the waiter, expecting her mother's outcry.

"Is that all! Oh, darling, you must eat!"

"It's a big bowl of salad, Mother, and really all I want."

"You have no need to worry, Lori. Not with your figure."

Lori ignored the remark and asked, "What do you think of me, Mother? I mean, what kind of a person do you think I am?"

When the waiter was out-of-sight, Evelyn leaned forward and said, "Why, you're a lovely, young girl."

"A lovely girl?"

"Yes, and a very lively and pretty one, too."

"Oh, Mom."

"Are you going to start one of your strange discussions again? Really, dear, not tonight. It's been such an exhausting day. You can't imagine."

"I don't want to be just lively and pretty. I know what they say. 'Oh, that Lippincott girl. She's that cute, little cheerleader.' That's how they all see me."

"They all?"

"Yes, everybody, it seems. Mom, I want to be a complete person."

"Why, you are."

"I mean complete. A complete, feeling woman, with significant ideas. I want to be me, what I feel inside, and not just what people see. Not just some cute kid that people like to look at."

"You are a full person, honey."

"I have ideas, like... like what I want to be, what I want to do. I want a house with a special room in it, just for Billy. Where he can experiment, study his rocks, cut up his toadstools, or whatever."

"For Billy? Aren't you jumping the gun again?"

"Did you ever wonder what happens to earthworms in the winter when the ground is frozen?"

"Lori! What kind of nonsense is that? And stop this stuff about Billy!"

"I know how I feel. You don't want to listen."

"You're only sixteen. You have time." Evelyn glanced nervously about the room. "I don't know why we have to go through this all the time."

"What if I told you I was pregnant?"

"Oh, good God!"

"I'm not. But I could be."

"What do you mean, you could be. Have you and Billy..."

"You don't understand what I'm trying to tell you. I know girls who got themselves pregnant and caused their parents all kinds of other problems, too. I'm not one of them. All I'm asking for is some talk and some answers. But you always push me aside."

"I'm sorry, honey, but you know how hard it is to..."

"Mom, I don't want to hear it. I don't want to hear about how busy you are, how difficult it is to be mother and father. I just want you to listen for a change."

Evelyn said nothing, as if she suddenly realized something about herself that she didn't like.

Lori caught a rare look of self-doubt in her mother's expression. She leaned forward and smiled warmly, as if to comfort.

"Oh, Lori, I'm so sorry."

"I love him, Mom. I really love him."

"But, honey, it's..."

"Don't."

"Oh. I did it again."

"Mom, I'm ready to explode. He's all I think about. I just want to be with him all the time. I doodle his initials and write his name over and over in school, when I should be taking notes." Lori looked down and toyed with her fork. "You should be glad I'm telling you. Most girls don't. So instead of wait, wait, wait and don't, don't, don't, please just say you understand. Please."

"I am glad you want to share with me. Really. And yes, I think I do understand."

"That's what I want."

"But where does that leave us, honey?"

Lori glanced about the room, toyed with her fork again, and with hesitance said, "I don't know. But I guess if you understand, you'll... you'll... well, you'll understand."

Evelyn studied her daughter's expression, then said, "Just in case?"

"In case of what?"

"I don't know. You tell me."

"Oh, Mom!"

"Look, Lori, I'll admit I've probably been wrong. I haven't wanted to face your growing up. More than that, maybe I'm afraid."

"Afraid?"

"Yes. It's a pretty crazy world out there. And the thought of you being tossed into it scares me to hell! I guess I haven't wanted to face up to it."

"Mom, just because you and Dad messed up your marriage..."

"We didn't just mess it up. It wasn't as simple as that. And we both felt a lot of pain. But it's so much more. It's the mistakes, the hurts, the days you wish you could relive and change. You say you love Billy. Okay. I'll try to accept that, although I know something about teenage crushes."

"How many times do I have to tell you it isn't just a crash?"

"Okay, okay. You're in love. So what does this mean? You want to get married? Is that what you want? Or are you asking for permission to sleep with him."

"That's uncalled for, Mother."

"What about college? Your father said he'd pay your way, and you crawled all over him with thanks, ran around in dizzy circles, laughed and cried all at once. And what about Billy? He's going to college, just like his brother. The Bannons wouldn't have it any other way. You want him to, don't you? What about all those things he wants to learn? I've seen many a guy who married too soon and missed out on law school or med school or something else he'd always dreamed about. Everything's gone. All gone. And there's no more chance, because he's held down with family problems and ends up with a lousy job. Then who does he blame? And what does it do to his marriage? Too fast, too eager, and then, oh so sorry. Strapped to a routine of crying kids, overdue payments, medical bills, a leaky roof, and a frustrated wife. And how does love hold up then?"

"Some people marry and put each other through college."

"Some people, maybe. With good jobs. Try that and you'll be packing a heavy load. You might never get out from under."

"So you're saying we couldn't do it."

"I'm telling you to look at naked reality."

"Mom, are you sexually frustrated?"

Evelyn was taken aback. Her face flushed and she groped for words. Just then the waiter returned with scallops, mushrooms and salad. She excused herself and walked briskly toward the restrooms.

Lori was hurting inside. She was confused and angry, mainly because she didn't have the answers. Although she wanted college, especially for Billy, she couldn't face the immediate years ahead without his touch. How often she had dreamed of sharing his pillow.

Returning to the table, Evelyn stood and looked down on her

daughter resolutely, holding emotions in check. In unfaltering words she said, "I was about to tell you that my sexual needs are none of your business. Then I saw the catch. There is one, isn't there?"

"What do you mean?"

"If I were to say that, then it would follow, I suppose, that your sexual concerns would no longer be my business. A faulty premise, of course, since a daughter is a mother's charge, and not the other way around. The relationship is not reversible."

"I'm sorry, Mother. I shouldn't have."

"Frankly, I couldn't answer your question. I wouldn't know how. I presume you think my attitude has revealed some sort of frustration. Maybe so. Too often I'm exhausted when we're together. But to be so bold as to..."

"Forget it, Mom. Please."

Evelyn seated herself and looked down at the scallops and mushrooms. Then with unflinching directness, stared at her daughter and asked, "What is it you want to know, Lori? Whether I ever went to bed with Murray Tobin?"

"No! Stop it, Mother!"

"Eat your salad."

Chapter Sixteen

Andrew had become John more then two decades ago when he was 25 years old. He was now 48 and respected by horticulturists and other Cornell University plant scientists who used his skillful hands.

Thousands of years before Andrew became John, great glaciers of the Ice Age had pushed into New York State, scooping up earth and rock, hollowing out valleys. Northward flowing streams, widened and deepened by the ice as it gouged its way south, later became long, narrow, picturesque lakes—the Finger Lakes.

The resulting beauty gave John what he wanted. It helped cleanse his mind. Among the lakes that quelled his pain was that nearest to his home and his work—Cayuga, 40 miles long, 435 feet deep.

A few hundred years ago the Finger Lakes had provided abundant fish for the Iroquois who lived on the slopes and in the valleys, who hunted in the woods, on the hills and in the fields between ribbons of water. The Cayuga tribe, a member of the Five Nations of Iroquois, had made its home around Cayuga Lake. Before the white man cut his roads and built his villages among the lakes, many a brave of the Cayuga tribe had stood upon the slopes and watched the sun rise over that lake.

Now it was John who often wandered to Cayuga's banks, watched the sun and marveled at the glistening water.

It was 1954 when young John Smith (no middle name or initial) drove his 10-year-old Ford, faded yellow and spotted with rust, up the newly built northern extension of the Pennsylvania Turnpike to

Scranton, then up U.S. 11 through Binghamton, N.Y. Winding north through small towns, he then turned west on a country road, continuing through wooded land and tiny villages until he coasted down into the City of Ithaca at the southern tip of Cayuga Lake.

Here he was to stay—here on the slopes of the valley once revered by the Cayuga Iroquois and carved into Ithaca by white men. Home to about 30,000 residents when Cornell was in session, Ithaca dwindled in summer to about 20,000 despite vacationers who came to see its streams and waterfalls.

Cornell had spread itself over East Hill. Some of its buildings looked down on rocky waterfalls and deep gorges that carried streams through the campus toward the valley and the lake. The university covered miles of rolling land from the endowed campus of ivy halls to apple orchards and pastures of grazing sheep and cattle. John cherished the Cornell Plantations, an Eden of winding roadways, paths, gardens, woods and streams. Time escaped him there, whether he simply walked among the flowers and trees or toiled in the garden beds.

Horticultural care of the campus required a team of specialists, not only to tend the rose and iris plots, but to nurture tropical plants in greenhouses, cultivate herbs, prune trees and shrubs, and protect ferns clinging to the steep sides of rocky gorges where winding walkways led students down to roaring water, bathing pools and flat rocks for sunning. The specialists hired helping hands to dig, trim, plant, weed and carry out a host of chores.

John Smith had been lucky when he arrived in Ithaca and found Cornell in need of an extra hand to tend the gardens. He had been seeking escape, and the job freed his mind. The pay was poor and the labor far afield from the political science he had studied at college. But he cared little. When he allowed his thoughts to slip to the past, he channeled them to his mother, giving her thanks for cultivating his passion for plants.

More than 20 years at Cornell had taught him much. "I could start my own nursery and landscaping business," he had told his wife again and again in recent years. He knew how to prune, slip and graft to thicken foliage and double blooms. He knew when to separate iris tubers, how deep to plant lily bulbs, where to cut a rose stem.

On the fifth day of September, as Henry Mason was lining up Andy's toy soldiers in his attic nearly 300 miles south, John Smith was standing among his flowers in front of Cornell's Plant Science Building. Pink snapdragons and spikes of light blue larkspur stood high among clusters of white petunias, yellow zinnias and deep red cockscombs. The annuals were at their peak of brilliance, having grown all summer. As he did each September, John marveled at the success of winter planning and springtime planting. The payoff sparked euphoria in him. His garden was ready to greet the students about to return for the fall semester.

John knelt and pinched off a dead blossom, then checked the back of nasturtium leaves for aphids. Minutes later he rose and again proudly surveyed his handiwork.

Six-foot-one and slender, John was muscle toned from garden work. Fair-skinned, he appeared more burnt than tanned, his face casting a reddish sheen. The sun had bleached his light brown hair. As for his features, they were not unlike those of young Billy Bannon, but aged by time, sun, wind and worry.

At mid-afternoon John climbed into his pickup truck and drove to the Plantations to spade the rose gardens until the shadows told him to quit.

John headed home at dinner time, walking from the Cornell garages to Buffalo Street, a sharp slope that plunged toward center city from a small shopping district just outside the campus gates. He and his wife shared a tall, three-story, frame house that, like others on the street, stood proud and erect, holding tightly onto the steep incline. Halfway up the hill, the gray-green clapboard house reached high into the elms. Scalloped trim edged its tall windows and porch. Like many a house on Buffalo Street, it had been cut into apartments. John and Beth rented the third floor and attic.

John's spirits continued to float high as he walked down Buffalo hill, the momentum forcing him to hold back and tighten his calf muscles. Although he walked up and down the street day after day, his insteps always ached from the acute bending of his feet.

"I'm home!" he called after mounting three flights of stairs—stone steps outside, two double flights inside, broken by landings. Still euphoric, he took a deep breath, leaned against the doorjamb, continued to visualize his brilliant garden beds, and smiled in pleasure. "Yo Beth! I'm home!"

The living and dining rooms of the apartment were almost one—divided by a waist-high set of bookshelves, topped, of course, by a pitcher of flesh flowers. Three flower-filled landscapes, brushed in oil by Beth, decked walls of oyster white. Wide sills were deep enough for Beth's blue-gray pottery pieces. A hanging copper pot of cascading Boston fern gave green life and feathery movement to a pair of open windows overlooking Buffalo Street. White wicker chairs, donated by Beth's mother, lightened the load of heavy upholstered chairs clustered about a coffee table.

Beth had been an art student at Cornell, a talented painter who had often set up her easel on the Plantations. She had painted the roses that John had nurtured, the trees that he had pruned, the walkways that he had pebbled. They had talked and shared and appreciated. "You're not going to marry a gardener!" her mother had protested. "Mom, he's more than a gardener! He's a creative genius with flowers, a beautiful person, and I love him!"

"Beth?" John called.

"I'm in the kitchen."

John looked down at his fingernails, slipped his hands into his pockets, and walked to the kitchen, a bright room of pine, stainless steel and cafe curtains. Still feeling his rush, he was ready to kiss his wife and proclaim floral bliss, but suddenly stood still and frightened after entering the kitchen. From the high he so welcomed, his mood dropped far below his subdued norm, far below his generally soft, quiet, pensive self. Color drained from his face when he saw the steel strongbox on the table in front of Beth.

"Look what I found," said the thin, dark-haired brunette, whose hair was severely fashioned into a knot. Beth was attractive, but not beautiful, except to John. Her spoon nose turned up too much, but her expressive eyes sparkled with delight. She was about to say more, but the look on her husband's face shocked her, leaving her momentarily speechless.

"Where did you get that?" John knew where. But no other words would come.

Beth stared curiously, searching his face. "Oh, I see. It's yours, isn't it? Here I thought I had found a treasure of some sort left by previous tenants. What else, I asked myself, would be tucked under attic floorboards?"

John looked away, then down at the floor.

"It's something personal, I see," Beth said. "None of my business, right?" She hadn't seen such a look on John's face since that letter came, the one from Timothy Wood. "Well, here then, take it." Her expression began to change as she pushed the strongbox toward John. Sadness mixed with puzzlement.

Beth had begun to realize that certain things could not be shared, that certain questions could not to be asked. She had tried to overlook a gaping hole in his past and shrug off contradictions about his early life. Again and again she had pushed discrepancies far back into the recesses of her mind to be uncomfortably ignored.

"Go on, take it away," Beth said, turning from him to gaze out the window. "I was stacking shoe boxes in the attic," she related quietly, pensively. "The boards were loose." This was the second time she had been confronted with something tangible, some proof of secrecy. It hurt. She was sorry it happened. "There's a yellow bird perched on the maple. Just a little bird. I'm not sure what it is." Beth didn't want to know his secrets. But they existed, and she knew it. She wished they didn't. So often she had not permitted herself to think logically, fearing truth that might haunt her and build a gulf between them.

Turning toward her husband, Beth instinctively put her hands on her belly as if to protect her unborn child, not to remind him that she was pregnant. She and John were only too aware. Forty was a dangerous age for a woman's first pregnancy. He worried more than she.

The silence hurt. John wanted to explain, but couldn't. He wanted to hold Beth in his arms. Instead, he picked up the strongbox without looking into her eyes, turned, and walked from the kitchen.

* * *

Only the sounds of birds echoed through Cornell's Fall Creek Gorge. From the sweet mournful pee-a-wee of the wood pewee to the loud caw of the crow, the morning calls, songs and chatter of countless birds reverberated between the walls of the narrow canyon as the first of Saturday's sunlight touched the treetops. A flock of Canada geese, heading south, paused for breakfast and rippled the water of Beebe Lake on the north side of campus, their trumpeting heronk resounding in the deep hollow of the gorge.

John Smith stood on the narrow footbridge, high above Fall Creek. Far below him, the rushing waters swirled and tumbled over rocks into a deep pool, then flowed on toward Ithaca Falls. Trees and shrubs clung to the sides of the gorge, except where steep walls of rock were too vertical to hold soil.

This was not a working day for John. But he had awakened before dawn nonetheless. Fitful feelings so plagued him that he staggered from bed early, weary of fighting with his twisted sheets. Unable to curb his restlessness, he fled from the house, hiked up the hill, and trudged across campus to the suspension bridge, reaching it in time to see the sun rise and splatter the rocky cliffs with an orange-pink glow.

John could not erase thoughts of Beth's reaching out to him without a question about the locked strongbox. Speaking not a word to each other, they had readied themselves for bed. He had lain stiffly. She had pulled him to her. He worshiped her for it, but was saddened by his inability to open up, free his thoughts, bare his soul. How cruel, to love so, to crave the fullness of two as one, yet offer nothing to give logic to the present. How unfair to Beth not to respond to her quiet overture.

When the sun's brightness fell upon him, John turned west as if the warm rays of light were not meant to grace his face. The glare of the new day, he feared, opened a wound for all to see. But only the birds were there.

John leaned on the bridge rail and tried to free his mind by tossing his thoughts into the abyss. He told his alter ego again and again that he had no reason to dislike Andrew any more than John. As he had so often, he tried to convince himself with step by step logical thinking. Anyway, this was today, not yesterday. This was John Smith's life among the zinnias and marigolds. So why must he be reminded? Why the strongbox? Was he somehow incomplete without the link? Was he unable to destroy everything that was?

Never expecting to father a child at 48, John looked on the baby as a belated gift, held back until he had proven himself. For months, now, he had been building new dreams, envisioning pink or blue, tiny fingers around his thumb, first steps, first words, bedtime stories, toys, stuffed animals. A stuffed dog, perhaps. White and fluffy.

John remembered the day that Fluffy lost his leg, caught in the chest latch and ripped off in haste. "Can't you put it back on, Mama?" Although an amputee, Fluffy continued to protect Andy and sleep at his side.

Since the news of Beth's pregnancy, John had envisioned the rest of his life, conjuring up dreams of each year, knowing that his son or daughter would be but 20 when he turned 68. He saw his daughter carrying her books to school. He saw his son on the baseball diamond. He guided one or the other along nature trails. He explained the wind, the sun, the moon.

And now, as John stood on the footbridge—a span tagged Suicide Bridge by Cornell students—he could not properly order his thinking. Thoughts of years to come flashed quickly, one piling on the other. Frustrated, he tried to shake off the visions. He realized that he had disgorged all he could into the canyon, so he walked toward home, not prepared for Beth, not hungry for breakfast, not recovered.

Beth was in her white housecoat, standing at the front window, watching for her husband. He had gone out early many a morning to see the gardens wet with dew, fresh from the night air. But this was different, and she knew it.

John walked slowly. Beth watched him hold back on the steep sidewalk. She turned from the window, annoyed with herself for being unable to conquer her resentful feelings. After all, it was just a small thing, wasn't it? A box. Perhaps of private papers penned with intimate thoughts. Maybe too beautiful to impart, too sad to share, or too foolish to admit. She knew better, really, because John had told her too much with his eyes.

Beth busied herself with nonentities, now and again staring pensively at the door. When it opened she simply said, "Hi. Out for a walk?"

"Yes," John answered flatly. He stepped inside, glanced at her, then looked away.

"Are you okay?"

"Yes."

"You sure?"

He glanced at her. "I'm sorry."

"For what?"

"You know."

"Not really."

Although they both wanted to reach out, the uncomfortable distance between them was too great.

Chapter Seventeen

Henry's gift to Billy and Mary's push for a closer father-son relationship had spun heavy thoughts in Charley's head, ending any hope of his sleeping late. Idea churned into idea until Charley was on his feet grabbing for his terry robe and tiptoeing away from his sleeping wife. He closed the door quietly. Seconds later he was tightening the cord around his robe as he stood in the doorway to Billy's room, gazing at his sleeping son and taking in every slight movement, every breath.

Billy lay on his side, the sheet pulled to mid-rib of his bare chest. His nose was pushed into his pillow, so he sucked in air between his parted lips. Nearby on his cross-legged worktable stood the microscope, surrounded by beech leaves, tree fungi, weed seeds, a jar of insects, a tube of clay soil, and other specimens. Until bleary-eyed and then some, the boy had focused his microscope again and again, well into the night.

This was a day to sleep late—Saturday, two days before the start of school, no Pizuto Produce. Bob was coming home, and Mom was planning family fun at a special dinner.

Charley argued with himself as he struggled to put his thoughts together. The result was no organized approach, but no backing off. He was resolute, and would simply have to chance it. Whatever would come, would come.

Billy stirred as his father stepped to his bed. Waking the boy seemed wrong. But Charley knew that the day would soon close in around him and choke off his chances. The morning was fresh and quiet and conducive to the sharing of secrets. Besides, Charley reasoned that if he stumbled he might have time to pick himself up.

He wanted to touch the boy, squeeze his shoulders, rumple his hair. But instead he sat gently on the bed and whispered, "Hey there, Billy. It's morning. You hear me?"

Billy started, maybe because of the quiet words. He was accustomed to the buzz of his alarm clock, or a loud shout from the hallway. His eyes opened as his body twitched.

"Dad! What's wrong?"

"Nothing. I thought we'd talk. Do you mind?"

Billy rubbed his eyes and sat up. "No. I guess not." He pushed hair from his forehead, then glanced about the room. "What time is it?"

"It's early."

"You sure nothing's wrong?"

"Only that maybe we haven't talked like we should have."

"You okay, Dad?"

"Summer's over, and you'll be going back to school Monday."

"Yeah, I know."

"And I've let the days slip by. Mom says I'm letting the years slip by, and maybe she's right."

"Mom's been funny lately. I don't know what all she's up to. Trying to tie us together, or something."

"She's a pretty smart lady, you know?"

Barely awake and ill at ease, Billy searched for words. Seconds of silence finally pushed him into saying, "Hey, this is Saturday. Bob's coming home." He immediately realized that the comment was not germane.

Also uneasy, Charley picked up Billy's drift. "Yeah, Bob's coming home today." He glanced about. "Nice microscope."

"You should see what it does."

"Did you thank Mr. Mason?"

"Not yet." Billy looked down. "He's strange, Dad. I'm not sure how to go about thanking him."

"I'm sure you'll find a way." Charley was thoughtful. "I was wondering why he gave it to you?" The big-boned policeman was more than surprised; he was astonished, not only by Henry's choice of Billy, but by the old man's re-entry into daylight.

"He knows I want to find out things," the teenager blurted.

Charley was deeply puzzled. "What do you mean?"

"About what makes things happen. How things grow and fly and swim. He heard me tell Lori."

"How did he hear you?"

"I told you. He's weird!" Billy was defensive and annoyed. He didn't want to talk about the cemetery and his sharing of thoughts with Lori.

"I wouldn't call him weird. When people get old, they sometimes seem that way, especially to young guys like you. They get set in their ways."

"Weird ways."

"Well, sometimes they withdraw, particularly if they've been hurt. And they think about better days and their loved-ones, long gone. We can't say it's right that Mr. Mason closed himself in, but we can try to understand why. He has his memories and some of them hurt, I'm sure." Charley's tone revealed even more compassion than his words. "Whatever happened in his life, it changed him in many ways."

Billy was dumbfounded. He didn't even try to hide the astonishment that dropped his jaw, widened his eyes and sharpened his gaze. Never had he heard such heart in his father's words. He felt the urge to tell his dad about being grabbed, shaken and held by Old Man Mason, but he couldn't do it.

"You know, Billy..." Charley hesitated and rubbed the stubble on his chin. "You know, maybe you've done something for Mr. Mason. I don't know how, and you don't have to explain it. But the very fact that he came here and gave you the microscope... well, that might be more of a gift for him than for you."

Billy conquered a touch of guilt and looked into his father's eyes. "How do you mean?"

"Maybe you resurrected him. Brought him into the daylight. Gave him something new to think about." Charley smiled, grabbed Billy's blanket-covered foot and shook it. "He must like you."

"He said he does."

"He did?" Charley could barely control his curiosity, but he held back, remembering his promise to himself—no interrogation. He recalled Mary's words about letting Billy open up on his on. But hammering his brain was her suggestion that he build a bridge by sharing his own mistakes.

Billy's number-one question—the one that had kept him unsettled since he was grabbed in Mason's garage—was about to burst from his lips. The time was right, because Charley was struggling with the very first steps of bridge-building.

The boy looked down as his body tensed. "What does he have on you, Dad?"

The big cop didn't flinch. But no impetus could have been greater than Billy's blunt question. Charley swallowed hard, then said, "Can you share if I share?"

Billy looked at his father, but said nothing.

"I'm not so good at so-called heart-to-heart talks or spilling guts." Charley glanced around the room while trying to focus his thoughts. "It's just not my way, you know? But I... well... things happened to me. A long time ago. I didn't think I needed anyone. Truth is, I guess I really wanted somebody to..." His words choked off.

Billy felt uncomfortable. He looked toward the window and chewed on his lip.

"You didn't answer me, son. Can you share if I do?" Charley realized that such a deal would be unfair, so he didn't hesitate, letting his words fall quickly and matter-of-factly: "I was a thief, and Mason caught me, forced me to atone, and then set my course as a cop." Charley looked down at his intertwining fingers. He had never said such things aloud before, and the sound of his own words shook him.

Billy didn't feel the full impact of Charley's confession until he looked into his father's eyes and saw a deep, moist, troubled message that pled for understanding.

"And I'm not talking about shoplifting a candy bar," Charley added.

Suddenly Billy didn't want to hear anymore, despite questions abounding in his head. "You don't have to..."

"It's okay. Really."

Billy looked embarrassed as he glanced here and there. He knew his father to be a strong, honest, demanding cop, never out-of-line.

Admitting to any sort of weakness, let alone a felony, was completely out of character, in Billy's way of thinking, so he was quick to realize his dad's trauma. Suddenly he wanted to help. He forced a weak smile and said, "Hey, you got guts!"

Charley searched Billy's eyes, then tested him with words: "What kind of guts? It doesn't take guts to steal."

"Hell, no, Dad, I don't mean that!" Billy was stunned that his words could be misinterpreted. "I mean to unload. To tell me. It's cool."

Charley wanted to hold his son to his bosom, but couldn't. He was quiet for seconds, then said, "I was a bad kid. I was heavy with a girl named Babs Finney. And I was willing to pay for her by stealing."

Charley looked at Billy for reassurance. The boy's eyes told him it was okay to go on.

"She pushed me into getting her this, then that, until it got way out of hand," explained Charley, who knew that his need to unload stemmed from more than Mary's initiative. In fact, it stemmed from more than his need to bare his soul, or to grasp a fast-growing chunk of his flesh and blood. Pushing harder than Mary or anything was fear—his fear that his son would learn the truth from Henry Mason. No matter how painful it was for him to tell his story, he could not allow his son to hear the woeful details from anyone but himself.

Billy was intuitive. "Dad, I don't think Mr. Mason would ever tell." The boy wasn't sure why he said that, having little knowledge of the old man. It was just something he felt, something from that night when Mason intruded on his special place in the cemetery.

Charley was taken aback. He glanced around the room, pulled together some thoughts, and then said, "I always let Mom believe that our shady spot in the cemetery was only for her and me, together."

"You took Babs there?"

"That's where Mason found us, with a necklace from his jewelry shop." Charley skipped the details. But he remembered them: Babs Finney stretched on the ground, her red hair fanning out like the spreading tail of a tom turkey, the diamond necklace wrapped around her plump breasts.

"You okay, Dad?"

"Yeah. Sure." Charley's thoughts had wondered again. With

every break in the conversation the big cop pondered Billy's relationship with Mason—its extent, its reasons, its eventual outcome. "I'm sorry. Where was I. Oh, yes. Mason was a prosperous, middle-aged shopkeeper in those days. He owned a chain of jewelry and watch-repair shops—one in the Northeast, two in downtown Philly, one at Sixty-Ninth Street. He was sharp. You didn't pull things over on him. He watched me. He knew what we were doing in the cemetery, knew what we were doing hanging around Sixty-Ninth Street. He was just waiting. Cool as a cucumber, he was. Standing there in the cemetery. 'No sense running,' he said. 'Either we work out a deal, or I go to the cops.'"

"A deal?"

"I don't know why, but for some reason he decided that I was worth saving. As for Babs, last time I heard of her, she was working the streets, down around Tenth and Walnut."

"What do you mean, 'worth saving'? What did he do?"

"I had to work it all off."

"How's that?" Billy was wide-eyed, trying to grasp everything and put the parts together.

"Well, first I had to return the stolen goods or pay back in cash. All the time he held the threat of telling over my head. He made me work for him. Even had me carry cash back and forth from the bank, while he watched. He kept records, even a scrapbook of old crime clippings. He would deliberately accuse me of thefts I didn't commit, then watch me struggle to get out from under. He'd tighten the screws, then let up a little, only to tighten again."

"Jeese!"

"He had me doing yard work around his house, too. Cut the grass, trim the hedge..."

"And pick cherries?"

"Yeah, and pick cherry's from his tree."

"Man oh man."

"It's not over, Billy There's never been an end. And never will be. Every day I'm paying my debt. That's why I'm a cop. He told me that the only way I could make amends was to select a job that would..." Charley sought the right words.

Billy came to his aid: "Serve mankind?"

"That sounds so pompous. But, yeah. Something like that." Charley looked at Billy, awaiting his next comment.

The teenager said nothing. But, within seconds, he put his arms around his father and held tightly.

Chapter Eighteen

orry I got so angry when you kept me waiting at the Wanamaker eagle. I spoiled your lunch. You just kept picking at your patty shell. I wish we could do it all over again. I wish we could eat in the Crystal Room, then walk along Chestnut Street. You could look in the shop windows. You always liked that.

Henry sat and gazed at the harpsichord. Anna was there, as she used to be. And it wasn't wrong to talk to her now. It wasn't wrong to explain, so she'd understand.

That time we argued about fluoride in the water. You were right. I was wrong. I'm sorry.

And that time you wanted to see 'Johnny Belinda' and I wanted to see 'Snake Pit.' I'm sorry. I wish I could take you to see 'Johnny Belinda' now. I'd sit through it two, three times. You always liked the movies. I'd take you to any movie. If I only could.

Remember your favorite walk? By the tidal marsh? You'd watch the water birds and pick tassels from the reeds. I wish I could take you there.

Henry was startled by a knock. But it wasn't the sound alone that jarred him. It was the sudden interruption of his thoughts. He was abruptly returned to the present, and made too aware of self and circumstance. His nature was one of cycles—times to remember and times to forget, a process that allowed mood to give way to mood, without the jolt of any external force.

Shifting nervously, Henry tensed, then glanced about the room, acutely conscious of himself in time and space. No one sat at the harpsichord.

The old man chose not to answer the knock. Then it came again—a hesitant tap, tap, tap. He walked to the bay window, looked out between potted palms, and saw Billy Bannon, dressed in his first-day school clothes. The boy backed away from the door, turned and hurried down the porch steps.

Billy was almost glad that Mason had not answered. Now he could put off until tomorrow what he should have done yesterday. As he stood at the street corner, ready to cross the intersection, he heard a gruff voice call, "Bannon! Come back here!"

The teenager spun around to see Mason standing on his porch in an undershirt and baggy pants. Billy hesitated, glanced here and there, then started to retrace his steps. When he found courage to stare, he watched the old man light a cigarette, puff a few times, then cough convulsively.

"Are you okay, Mr. Mason?" Billy asked as he mounted the porch.

Henry simply choked until the coughing stopped, then turned and walked into the house, leaving the door open. Billy suspected that he was supposed to follow, but he stayed on the porch, off balance, his legs unsure of which way to go.

"What's keeping you, Bannon?"

Billy managed to move his feet while struggling to put his thoughts in order. His logical side pled with his irrational side: *What the hell's wrong with you? He's just an old man. Just a single, solitary soul. You came to say thank you, so get on with it. Just say it and leave.*

The hallway was dark, as was the living room of crawling plants and crowded windows. A damp mustiness closed in around Billy as he tried to adjust his eyes. Old Chippendale and Queen Anne chairs loomed in the shadows, and he stumbled over a misplaced footstool while aiming for the fireplace, remembering well where he had been told to sit before.

"No, sit over there," Henry instructed, pointing to a more comfortable chair—an old leather armchair near the south wall.

"I can't stay, Mr. Mason. I just wanted to thank you for the wonderful microscope. It was generous of you. I certainly don't deserve it after climbing your tree and entering your garage."

There, he had said it. And much better than he had expected, although his words sounded a wee bit practiced.

"Have you used it?"

"Oh, yes! For so many things."

"Sit down."

Billy's eyes were adjusting, and he saw a touch of excitement and eagerness in the old man's expression.

"Well, okay. But for just a minute. I'm on my way home from school. My folks don't know I stopped here."

The leather chair, well worn at the edges, was deeply hollowed by years of use. It could have swallowed Billy. But, unable to fall into its comfort, he remained stiff and tense, leaning forward. Looking about, he forced words: "Did Mrs. Mason play the piano?"

"That's not a piano. It's a harpsichord."

"Oh. I didn't know. I thought it looked like..."

"It's a harpsichord. And yes, Mrs. Mason played it."

"Oh."

"It was handed down from her mother's mother."

Henry sat on the soiled love seat, much too far from Billy for comfortable conversation, if such were possible at all. It was as if he wanted, but didn't want. As if he yearned to know, yet forced distance.

"What do you like?" Henry asked.

Billy was at a loss. "What do you mean?"

"I know you want to find out things."

"My science teacher says I'm curious, and that that's a good sign."

"Do you know nature well?"

"I know most trees. I know a mushroom from a poisonous toadstool."

"But what do you know about rocks?"

"Rocks?"

"Yes, rocks. I used to work with rocks. Very precious ones. Diamonds, emeralds, rubies."

"I have a rock collection. Some quartz and agate. Even some petrified wood from Arizona."

"What do you do with that Lippincott girl?"

Billy was taken aback by the abrupt question, so out of context.

He stuttered. "Wh... wh... what do you mean?" He edged forward in the chair to a more uncomfortable position.

"Do you really want her?"

"Yes. I love her." *I wonder what he's getting at? Maybe he's a dirty old man who wants to know what we do in the cemetery.*

"What do you do together when you're not in the cemetery?"

"Mostly talk." *What the hell! It's none of his business. Why is he so interested in Lori?*

"No one believes you're really in love, do they?"

"I don't know." *He said something there. It's not supposed to be the real thing when you're only sixteen. It doesn't matter that Grandma was only that age when she married.*

"Girls were meant for boys." Henry's hand shook as he tried to light another cigarette.

"Right." *What the hell's he talking about?*

"A man must be a man."

"Right."

"My standards of justice are based on strong moral principles."

"Right." *I have to get out of here.*

"They give me uncommon strength. Physical as well as mental."

"I really have to go." *Why's he telling me this stuff?* Quickly on his feet, Billy stepped away from the chair.

"Wait a minute. I have something for you." Henry inhaled smoke and coughed it out as he walked to the stairs in the hallway.

Billy fidgeted while the old man climbed the steps. He looked about the room until his eyes were held by a set of four gold frames on the wall across the room, above the harpsichord. He stepped close to them. Nothing was in the frames but jagged pieces of broken glass.

Just then Henry returned with a book. "Here."

Billy spun toward him. "For me?"

"Yes. Take it."

Billy took the reddish brown volume and fingered the gold embossment on the richly embellished binding. He flipped the front cover and glanced at words written in smoothly flowing cursive: "To Andy on Christmas, 1938." Then he turned the pages, opening the book here and there, flipping from chapter to chapter. He saw pictures of an almond tree in bloom, an orchid of the vanilla plant, enlarged needles of the stinging nettle, a bulbous ovary of a pumpkin, and a deadly amanita, the most poisonous of fleshy fungus.

"I can't take this book, Mr. Mason."

"Why not?"

"You've already given me that microscope. Why are you giving me these things? You hardly know me."

"Do you like the book?"

"Oh, yes! I mean, wow, it's really cool!"

"Then keep it. I don't give recklessly. And you should learn to receive, young man."

The boy flipped more pages, casting his eyes on an enlarged photo of a ginseng root, a male flower of the hazelnut, a giant breadfruit in the hands of a Fijian native. Billy's radiant expression showed that he was captured. "It's great! It's a wonderful book." He fingered the binding. "It's really... Well, thank you very much, Mr. Mason."

Henry turned away from the boy, reached around a potted rubber tree for an ashtray on the windowsill, snuffed his cigarette among other butts, and walked into the hallway. His back to Billy, he stood still for a moment, and then said, "Good day, Bannon."

Billy was quick to leave, saying "Thanks" twice as he hurried through the vestibule and onto the porch.

Henry's jaw was rigid, his lips tight. His eyes appeared to focus on nothing as he walked stoically into the living room. Tight control over his emotions slipped only fleetingly as he glanced at the harpsichord. For a brief moment his eyes seemed to plead for help.

Seconds later he lowered himself into the leather chair and gazed on the harpsichord.

Anna played soft music: *Ah, sweet mystery of life at last I found thee; I know at last the secret of it all; 'Tis the...*

When the words and the music faded, Henry was unable to keep Andrew from his silent discourse with Anna: *Remember the time he made the weather vane? Shaped like a rooster, it was. He fastened it to the garage, but it wouldn't swing with the wind. He tried and tried, but it wouldn't turn. I sneaked out at night and fixed it, oiled it, and when he saw it pointing north with the wind in the morning he was so happy. Remember, Anna?*

Until now, Henry had never shared thoughts about Andrew with Anna to avoid any contamination of the fair and the beautiful. In fact, most of his interplay with Andrew was confined to the upstairs hallway and *The Room*, where the windows were boarded up. Any solitary, unshared thoughts about Andrew that slipped into his closed mind, outside of the second-floor hall or *The Room*, were quickly killed with anger—before Billy Bannon. But now such thoughts stayed longer. They included flashing images of Andy's childhood fun, smiles of pride, school days. And they were even being shared with Anna. *We did what we could, didn't we Anna? It wasn't always easy, but you were a good mother. We gave him college, and so much more. Why did he...? Why do you think... ?*

Henry scowled and turned his head suddenly as if damning himself, or maybe even damning Billy Bannon for opening holes in the dike. Freeing himself from the chair and the harpsichord, he hurried toward the kitchen with ritualistic purpose.

Oatmeal was in order first. He poured, stirred, heated and carried a steaming bowlful up the twisting back staircase. The second-floor hallway was dark, lighted only by a flame-shaped bulb that gave an orange glow to the high walls and ceiling. He walked the length of the hall, stopping in front of the only closed door—that walnut-stained door to *The Room*. As always, the key projected from the keyhole.

With effort, Henry sat on the hardwood floor, stretched his legs into a V, placed the bowl between them, and leaned back against the wall opposite the door. He breathed deeply. This was the ritual of every-so-often. It came only when the train of thought carried it here, only when the mood was such. Often the talk would begin outside the door and end there, with never a hand put upon the key. Seldom did he enter *The Room*. Only when the tug-of-war between father and son grew to rage. Only when Henry could damn all parts and pieces.

The old man reached for his bowl of oatmeal. He spooned it and swallowed hard as he saw six-year-old Andy at the seashore, 12-year-old Andy nursing a wounded bird, 18-year-old Andy waving from his dormitory window.

Chapter Nineteen

Dressed in a trench coat and pulled-down rain hat, the old man staggered as he trudged along a commercial district of West Chester Pike in the darkness of a clear night. His large pockets bulged with bottles that rubbed his thighs. He smelled of whiskey and gasoline.

* * *

Not many miles away, Julia Evans was about to finish her chores and close up Madame Laporte's boutique.

Julia was a 24-year-old graduate of Bryn Mawr College who had made all the right moves and followed all the right paths for a Main Line offspring of a prominent family. On top of all that, Julia was pretty—a blue-eyed classic with long amber hair, highlighted by luster captured from every surrounding glow. Her profile was almost Grecian, yet softened just enough to make her very touchable. Men liked her, enjoyed dating her, but seldom got beyond the first few kisses. Relatives and family friends saw her as prime choice among eligible females.

Julia was certain she would never marry, saw little practical use for her liberal arts education, and was beginning to spend money to pamper herself. A year ago she had decided to work, even though her father made it unnecessary. "Selling clothes!" her mother had exclaimed. "That's absurd!" Ella Evans was an attractive, well-groomed, 47-year-old WASP who played tennis and rode horses.

She would have liked her daughter to join all the right societies and social sets, and marry the successful son of a Main Line family. But Julia had a way of getting what she wanted. In deference to her parents, however, she had chosen an exclusive shop—a Main Line boutique of high-priced women's apparel, located on a quiet avenue in Ardmore, just off the main shopping district. It catered to all shapes and sizes, from blue-blood dowagers to young Bryn Mawr College students.

Suspicious of her nature since mid-teens, Julia had finally learned the truth several years ago at age 20, thanks to an aggressive roommate at Bryn Mawr. Her attachments to women, however, had been brief in those days, and still were today, especially when the affinity was strong. Frightened and guilty, she would retreat to her parents' world of high-fashion parties and trips abroad, and to dating the Main Line's most eligible young men.

Julia's secret belonged only to her and a few passing acquaintances. Feminine in walk and talk, she didn't like contact sports or man-tailored clothes, caught the eyes of men from 16 to 60, and never overtly sought the company of women who attracted her.

Each year had become more difficult for Julia. For some time now she had been withdrawing from social fun as she sublimated. She toiled long hours at the boutique, often staying past closing time. The pain of retreat and suppression was beginning to show in her appearance and disposition. She smiled less. The fitting of women and the dressing of mannequins, however, never allowed her to repress completely. She tried to fight the feelings, and often cried herself to sleep at night. Self analysis was convincing her that she had been unconsciously drawn to selling women's apparel.

Only twice had she met customers who sensed her sexuality. In one case, return after return had led to touching, then a brief relationship. From that time on, Julia had fought her feelings just a bit less, allowing herself to finger the mannequins. She dressed them with particular care.

Soon to turn 25, Julia was beginning to wonder if she were destined to sublimate until she became an old bitch of a spinster like some other closet lesbians. She was pretty, she had feelings, and she wanted to love.

It was Wednesday night. Julia stayed late at the boutique. Madame Laporte had closed her shop at 9 o'clock, leaving it in Julia's charge. The troubled young woman sat alone in the back workroom, surrounded by clothes on hangers and racks. She stared at a naked mannequin, reached out and touched the breasts, then turned and hurried into the showroom.

After moments of anxious thought, Julia tossed a blue cashmere sweater over her shoulders, covering the top of her pale blue dress, and then hurried outside where she nervously locked the white colonial door and tossed the keys into her purse. One last glance through the windows showed her that the night light burned. She walked toward busy Lancaster Avenue, not to go home to her parents' estate in Radnor, but to find the place that Wendy Seabury had described more than a year ago. The name and directions were still on a slip of paper in Julia's purse, folded small, soiled, fragile from wear. How often she had unfolded the note, only to fold it again. How often she had decided to throw it away, only to bury it deeper in her purse. Once she had retrieved it from a trash can.

Julia was not the kind to frequent bars alone. She had sipped daiquiris in many a club, but always with a date or a group of friends. Not that she couldn't hold her own alone anywhere. She was quick, bright, poised, and sharp at figuring out any situation.

As for unwittingly exposing her secret tendencies, she never really gave it a thought. It just wouldn't happen. She had no need to pretend anything, because she had always lived in a straight world. Julia had strength for much, had suffered without giving in. Even now, she couldn't conceive of hurting her parents. In her view, they were never to know the truth.

Julia had parked her black sports car just off Lancaster Avenue, in a lot behind the Ardmore Theater. She gunned it a few times, raced the motor to a roar, pulled from between parked cars and sped onto the avenue.

It was nearly 11 o'clock by the time Julia located The Black Tulip, once a modest wooden house, now an arty gay bar, painted black and trimmed with yellow window boxes and shutters. The door also was yellow, but for a huge black tulip, painted in stylized design, a la the Pennsylvania Dutch. The place was set back from

West Chester Pike on a narrow street—mixed commercial and residential—in Upper Darby Township, not far from the 69th Street Terminal. Unlike many of Philadelphia's gay bars, it attracted women as well as men.

Julia parked her car on the street, a block beyond The Black Tulip, in front of a vacant lot bushy with wild locust trees that were beginning to hide the remains of a service station. Between her and the bar stood a few storefronts and poorly kept twin houses. Lamplights reflected on parked cars that crowded both sides of the street. Julia stayed in her car for a moment, then with a burst of certainty stepped to the sidewalk and began marching toward the bar. Her quick pace soon gave out, however, and she was actually sauntering as she neared The Black Tulip. After all, this was a big first step for Julia. But her leisurely stroll failed to curb the fast beat of her heart. Her anxiety raged as she closed in on the doorway and stood before the stylized tulip. She vacillated briefly, then spun and headed toward her car. It was unlike her to panic, and she cursed herself, almost aloud. She turned just in time to see four young men, chattering and laughing as they entered the bar. They looked happy, but she wondered. No way would she be comfortable, she decided, until she saw a woman enter. Wendy might have been wrong. More than that, the clientele could have changed.

Standing near her car in the shadow of a bushy locust, Julia worried about looking like a pickup, a loiterer, or a burglar casing a nearby junk shop. She was startled when two woman, a heavy blonde of about 25 and a long-legged brunette of about 30, suddenly hurried around a corner and met her from behind, scaring her almost to a scream. Highly keyed, Julia had been ready to jump.

"What are you waiting for, honey?" the brunette asked. "It's okay. Don't be afraid. Go on in. It's a nice place to make friends."

The blonde tugged at the brunette and scowled with annoyance. "Come on, Til, let her be."

When the two women were in The Black Tulip, Julia made her move, slowly at first, then with a steady, deliberate pace. She held her head high, added a touch of confident smile, and pulled open the Tulip door with authority. Eyes turned on her as she pushed into the crowd.

Inside, The Black Tulip was decorated like a fairy-tale tearoom, something out of Alice in Wonderland. Huge, eye-catching cutouts of the Mad Hatter and the Queen of Hearts decked the walls, and Julia wondered about the meaning. Ribbons and streamers of colorful crepe paper stemmed from a cluster of pink and blue balloons above the bar. They fanned out across the ceiling to all walls and corners of the barroom, then fell as curls all the way to the floor. Not only was the crowd heavy at the bar; it filled most open space deep to the corner booths. Julia pardoned and excused her way among the men and women until she barely reached the bar where she motioned to one of the bartenders—a clean-shaven, sandy-haired male of college age. The push of customers kept her waiting long, but she didn't use the time to look around and study the clientele. That would come after a few drinks.

As it turned out, Julia downed five daiquiris before she found herself in a somewhat comfortable relationship with another woman. She had fended off a few pushy come-ons, and had spent almost an hour chatting with two men: one a lanky, effeminate male, the other a handsome, deep-voiced gymnast who could have fooled anyone.

* * *

Outside, the old man in the trench coat slipped in and out of the shadows. He passed The Black Tulip several times, hesitating often. Once he stood among the bushy locusts on the plot vacated by the service station, ducking out of the way of passers-by. Three times he walked blocks away from the Tulip, only to approach it again. Twice he hid in an alley between houses before circling the block.

* * *

Nel was a gentle and pretty woman, but somewhat sad-eyed and timid. She had cut her soft brown hair short only weeks ago, seldom used makeup, spoke quietly, and had often come to The Black Tulip, usually leaving alone. Julia had sought her out, being attracted by her fair skin, dark eyes, and the yearning that molded her expression. Julia and Nel had made their way to a booth in a far corner where, in time, they tried to share secrets despite the noisy crowd. Although a stranger in a new world, Julia eventually opened up with surprising ease. The daiquiris helped, but so did Julia's desperate need to unload, and her recognition of a knowing sort of kindness in Nel's eyes. Nel had been reticent at first, despite her obvious compassion. That was her way.

Small talk had helped build comfort, which increased affinity and eventually led to open dialogue.

"I lived a lie for a long time, too," Nel said in an effort to console.

"You don't anymore?"

"No. But then I don't see my family, either."

"Oh."

"It hurts."

"I couldn't do it that way. I think I'll always have to live the big lie." Julia grabbed her drink and gulped.

"Then you're not being true to yourself."

"Maybe not."

"You'll never really be yourself. You'll never be free."

"Are you really free? I mean, which is worse, being open about it, or giving up your family? Maybe by opening one door you close a lot of others."

Nel pondered the point.

"Anyway, there's no other way for me," Julia said. "Except maybe to live two separate lives like some."

"I tried that, but I couldn't shake off the guilt. I couldn't look my father in the face."

Neither woman spoke for a moment. But each kept looking at the other. Finally Julia whispered, "You're nice to be with, Nel. I'm glad I came."

"I have a place. Want to go there?"

No one within the noisy barroom heard the crash of the bottle on the concrete walkway outside the door, but they were quick to see fire as the gasoline ran right under the door to form a flaming puddle inside. Unlike the other fire bombings, this one roared quickly out of control. The gasoline-fed flames leaped up the inside of the door, scorching the heavily varnished wooden panels that had been highly polished. On all other attacks against gay bars, the flames had raged high outside, only to burn themselves out on the concrete or brick without causing serious damage, except, of course, for the burning of Jeffrey Broomell, the Chicago book salesman. The Black Tulip's streamers and ribbons carried the flames high to the center of the bar where the balloons popped as patrons screamed and panicked. Fire fanned out across the ceiling, following the streamers to all parts of the barroom, while the blaze engulfed the doorway where old wood, highly oiled, offered quick combustion, sucking in oxygen as flaming jets shot from the panels, leaping higher and higher. In seconds, the front of the barroom was a flaming inferno. The cutouts of the Mad Hatter and the Queen of Hearts only added fuel. Quickly they turned brown and shriveled, their painted expressions becoming distorted until they burst into roaring fire. With the front wall and the ceiling ablaze, the customers pushed ruthlessly toward the small back exit, a door not nearly large enough for the pressing crowd. Men and women shoved in panic and began to climb and crawl over each other, screaming as the smoke choked them, as the heat closed about them.

Outside, the fire blazed through the roof, orange tongues lapping at the night sky, a yellow-red glow and thick smoke high above the trees. Nearby residents poured from their homes, and crowds gathered in clusters on the street, between the buildings, in the open lots and beyond. Upper Darby and Llanerch fire companies were the first to arrive, followed by Manoa, Haverford and Garrettford-Drexel Hill.

Noise of the screeching sirens echoed through the Delaware County communities, but was barely heard inside The Black Tulip where panic became ugly, frenzied, violent. Men and women tore at each other, reached and grabbed and pulled. They stepped on the unconscious, the suffocating, the weak. They ripped at each other's clothing and hair as they pulled to reach air. Shoes, fingernails and jewelry dug and scraped the flesh of screaming patrons, drawing blood before the fire singed, then blistered their bodies. The stench of burning hair and flesh began to fill air already dense with smoke.

Ambulances from nearby hospitals, rescue squads and the local police began to carry away the injured who managed to escape. Some ran out screaming, their clothes afire.

The walls collapsed under the pressure of water from the hoses as firefighters began to control the blaze. Soon, smoldering embers and scorched wood lay upon a pile of bodies. Julia Evans was burned beyond recognition, as was her new friend, Nel.

Weeks passed before police identified Julia's body as that of the missing daughter of Mr. and Mrs. Frederick J. Evans III of Ivy Hollow, Radnor.

Chapter Twenty

The afternoon had grown gray from clouds that blew in from Cayuga and the other Finger Lakes. September felt more like October, and the dark mist that covered the sun offered a mood for thought. Beth wallowed in that mood as she sat at the window near the Boston fern, again watching for John. Without speaking aloud, she talked to the unborn child who had yet to swell her belly more than a trifle. *Your daddy is a moody man, but very special. He hides parts of himself, but he's kind and unselfish, and he'll be a good daddy. You'll see. You're going to be special, just like him.*

Beth pictured the lake country and knew that someday her child would smell the grapes in the vineyards. Such a full, rich aroma. Little fingers would touch, maybe pick and squeeze, and get red and purple stains all over. But that would be okay.

Your daddy plants seeds and grows things—splendid things. He gives us roses and tulips. And he gave you to me. And you will be splendid, too.

Beth thought more about little fingers and how she wanted her baby to touch and feel and explore as much as possible. Touch the flowers. Dig in the soil and squeeze the warm earth. Push deeper and feel the cool earth.

And Daddy will scold you when you pull petals from his daisies. She smiled.

So late in life to start. But that made the baby all the more special. Not that he or she wouldn't be special anyway, being born of John Smith. Daddy was quiet and thoughtful, but strong and firm.

Beth remembered the first time she had seen John, standing there, shaping a stubborn firethorn, training it to climb a brick wall, lost in his thoughts, intent on his purpose. Right then and there she had felt his virility.

"Firethorn oh firethorn," she said, startled by the sound of her voice as it broke the silence. For years that firethorn had told Beth much about the time of day, month or season through its shadows, size, colors, blooms and berries. But when it covered the wall, it told her less. She had begged him to cut it back, so she could watch it grow, remember when, and see him now as then.

Touch, little baby. Touch.

How curious it had seemed at first that John was always here or there as expected. Always at the right place at the right time. But soon she knew why. Irises early. Roses later. Herbs on Friday. Greenhouses, Monday.

Feel the smooth stone, little baby. Feel the rough rock.

Why had she liked older men? Why John? Maybe his solitude gave him some sort of strength. How she liked to watch him bend and stretch. Bare top. Muscles. Red skin. Moist shoulders, glistening in the sunlight.

Painting him on canvas had become a habit in those early days. Sometimes just a tiny figure in the distance. But he was there—reaching, bending, kneeling. So perfect for every field of clover, hill of ivy, walkway edged with jonquils.

So proper and gentle. So embarrassed when flattered.

Beth had praised the heavens time and time again for giving her the eye of the artist and the craving to create. And she still gave kudos to herself for choosing art school. Without the oils and brush she might never have met John, let alone reaped the joy of putting him and his gardens on canvas.

Little baby, grow to be like your daddy in whole or any part. Perhaps a movement, a look in the eyes, a smile, a firm hand.

Beth puzzled over strange feelings of sadness that lay under her peaks of pleasure. Surely they didn't come from the womb, her cradle of joy. Hormonal changes? She thought not. John? Maybe. When he comes home, she told herself, hold him tightly and let yesterday go, even if he can't.

An impulse sent Beth dashing from the window to her bedroom. She was back in minutes dressed in a flowing negligee of pale blue. "Like one of your heavenly blue morning glories," she proclaimed, spinning about and blossoming with anxiety. She wanted to please him—so much.

Big drops of rain—those well-separated drops that often preceded a heavy downpour—began to splash against the window panes. Within minutes a cloudburst dropped a torrent of rain on Buffalo Street, obscuring Beth's view. He'll be soaked, she thought, frowning as she squinted.

There he was, hunched in the heavy downpour, walking in the street along the rushing gutter, holding back as best he could on the steep slope.

Beth turned excitedly, hurried to the bathroom for a towel, then to the door, anxious as a newlywed. John's long climb seemed to take forever, but in minutes he stood in the doorway, overalls soaked and dripping, hair plastered to his forehead, shoes oozing.

"I'd better kick these off."

"Don't. Come on."

"Hey, look at you!"

"I've been waiting."

Beth tossed the towel around his neck, then moved it up to blot his forehead and help dry his hair. Then she stepped away and gazed at him.

John looked at his hands. "At least the rain washed away some of the garden dirt."

"Come on." Beth pulled him toward their blue, white and pine bedroom. "We'll worry about supper later." She stripped the spread from the bed in one quick pull, then began to undress John. "Let's get you out of these things. Damn. Everything's stuck to you!" Together they pushed his overalls to the floor.

When John stretched naked across the bed, Beth used the towel again, soaking up moisture from his chest, his belly, his thighs. Then she lay next to him and kissed his ear, his neck, his cheek.

He smiled, turned and kissed her on the lips—soft at first, then hard as he pushed his body against hers. "Let's get rid of this," he said as he unsnapped her negligee. "It's pretty, but you're much prettier." He cupped his hands around her breasts, kissed them, buried his nose between them, and then moved his hands about her shoulders. Her skin was as soft as the petals of roses in his gardens. Her scent was the fragrance of the lilies he nurtured in the shaded valleys.

Her sigh heightened his pleasure.

* * *

The next afternoon, and for the seventh time in seven days, Beth stood among the pine furnishings and took a look at her profile in the full-length mirror on her closet door. Her belly barely showed change. She noticed a slight rounded swell. Perhaps distention since yesterday? Perhaps not. John had told her to wait weeks before looking. "Maybe then you'll see a difference." He was probably right, but that called for impossible restraint.

She examined herself overall and decided that her breasts hung just a bit too much to the sides, but were far firmer than many, and that her buttocks were smaller than countless others, but certainly not boyish. Generally she retained a good figure with suitable curves to most parts. Surely nothing to displease John. At least not yet. She turned and looked straight into the mirror. Her face was a touch fuller, but that made her look healthy. Just so her cheeks didn't get puffy. She filled them with air until her ears popped, then laughed at herself as she let go with a blast. After tipping her head one way, then another, she took a moment to act silly before the mirror—a couple wiggles, an S-curve pose, and a Marilyn Monroe smile and eye flutter.

Suddenly aware of time, Beth darted to the bureau, pulled open a drawer and rummaged for her panties and bra. John would soon be home. He had promised to take her to dinner. They would drive up the west side of Cayuga Lake to Taughannock Falls, stand on the overlook, and watch the water cascade over the sheer cliff. She would wait for John to break the hypnotic spell, take her hand and lead her to the inn where they would dine, overlooking the lake.

She felt good—her body so fresh and clean, her mind bubbling with thoughts of her baby, of John, of dinner at the falls. She was still so much in love. But suddenly that peculiar feeling returned, moving up from her stomach to her throat. She froze for an instant, and told herself she didn't care about that strongbox. But where had he put it? Why did he have to hide it? If it were right here, somewhere in the open, on the shelf, she wouldn't touch it. Not if he didn't want her to. He could even leave it unlocked and she wouldn't open it.

Who are you kidding, Beth? It would haunt you day and night. It would tempt you. It would have the lure of the forbidden. She brushed off the thoughts, spun about and grabbed for her clothes.

John's moods had never troubled Beth, for they made him what he was. What did it matter if he drifted into pensive thought? That was John. The reasons really didn't matter. The causes were irrelevant so long as she delighted in the results. His sensitivity gave her pleasure, because she never puzzled over the pain that engendered it.

Beth had such hopes for the future—a house someday, with a garden built by John. And oh what a garden it would be—with rocks and driftwood, shaded dells of ferns, a lily pond, and stepping stones into patches of white impatiens and blue iris.

His first gift to her had been a tulip bulb.

"I want you to have this."

"What is it?"

"A tulip bulb, silly woman!"

"Oh?"

A rare hybrid, it had bloomed each spring since, in shades of vermilion and white, outside of Beth's window in her mother's yard where Beth had planted her gift from the Cornell gardener who had captured her with his kind words and strong muscles. She saw him then as she saw him now—a perfect blend of physical strength and sensitivity. And these were the traits she had infused into her portrait of him, a painting he still refused to allow her to hang because of his modesty.

Suddenly she was fearful that something might happen to her dreams. She sat on the edge of the bed and stared toward the window. Perhaps he had been married before and didn't want to say. But why? That made no sense. Maybe he had a bastard child hidden somewhere. She wouldn't care. Perhaps he had been a thief, a felon. She would forgive him that, and he knew it.

Chapter Twenty-One

The burning of Jeffrey Broomell, the textbook salesman from Chicago, had upset Henry to the point of over-drinking whiskey and churning his stomach into piercing pain. But it hadn't distressed him nearly so much as the burning of The Black Tulip. For the first time, he had actually seen devastating results, because The Black Tulip was a tinderbox that had burst into flame before Henry was out of sight. For a few minutes he had stood on West Chester Pike and looked back. When the first whiffs of smoke glowed orange he had become paralyzed with fear, motionless despite the wish to run. When the flames suddenly roared high, terror had held him for a few seconds before he fled.

Each day since, he had drunk whiskey and cursed Andrew.

Now he was in his cellar again, standing before a workbench that held an assortment of hammers and saws, a steel vise, a monkey wrench, assorted screwdrivers and putty knives, jars of nails and screws, a collection of empty bottles of all shapes and sizes, five two-gallon containers of gasoline, and several fifths of whiskey. The bare bulb behind his head swung slowly to and fro on its chain, moving Henry's shadow back and forth across the workbench as he poured whiskey into a jelly glass and gulped it down. This was his third visit to the workbench since noon.

Forgetting to close the bottle, Henry turned and tripped on an old spaghetti mop that lay next to a box of candlewick. He leaned on a pole that supported the floor above, then pushed his left hand tightly into his painful stomach before reaching for the railing at the stairs. Slowly climbing toward the kitchen, he slipped twice, swatted at a hanging broom that tickled his face, gagged and drew phlegm into his mouth.

"Eat your oatmeal, Andy, or I'll spread it all over your body and stick you to the wall, and you won't hang out the windows anymore. Keep worrying your mother, and you can't have any more cherries."

Henry leaned against the kitchen sink.

"Damn you, Andy!"

He struggled awkwardly in wiping drivel from his lips and nose.

"How dare you torment your mother's soul?"

Henry cried, his body shaking as he held his head over the sink.

"I miss you, Anna. I know what God knows. That you're the purest woman He ever blessed. And I need you. Oh, God, how I need you."

Henry was losing his certainty about his son, and he feared the turnabout—a drift initiated by Andrew's reflection in Billy Bannon. "He's changing, Anna. Andy's changing." If the son could no longer be the receptacle, no longer take in and absorb the full fury, then the father was cursed. "No. I will not be damned. I am the one who damns."

Again Henry turned to Anna for help, for his vision of her had always enabled him to direct his anger. After all, he destroyed evil to protect goodness, and Anna was goodness. Conflict between morality and immorality generated his fury, and he needed fury to give him energy. Yet energy driven by fury needed steady legs, for without them it steered him wildly out of control. A wobbly burst pushed him from the sink, through the dining room and into the living room where he veered too far to the right and rammed into the plants at the bay window, knocking over potted palms, damaging a huge fiddleleaf fig, and separating a host of succulent leaves from a giant jade.

The old man knelt and worked feverishly to put the pieces together. "I'm sorry, Anna. I'm so sorry." Hindered by alcohol, pain and grief, he worked awkwardly, tipping this way and that as he scraped soil from the floor with his fingers and fingernails, pushed roots back into pots, and tried to straighten stems. He wept while mumbling curses.

"You're no son of mine!"

Again, it was Andrew's fault. But Andrew's image kept blurring and reshaping. No longer was it the well-defined reflection from that fateful day that forever plagued his father.

A broken branch of fiddleleaf fig frustrated Henry. He tried to fix it with trembling hands as his stomach burned with pain. He finally backed away in anguish because his unsteady hands could do nothing but worsen the break. Dazed and doubled over, he stumbled into the hallway, then gripped the newel and tugged at the banister as he pulled himself toward the second floor.

Upstairs, he leaned against the wall and lifted his eyes as if seeking strength from God, who he saw as a vengeful force and champion of his retribution. Hyperventilating, he did not move toward *The Room*, seemingly trapped by his visions. It was little Andy—Andy of boyhood—who was getting in his way. Anger had always increased on the way to *The Room*, even when the surge came late, peaking in front of the door, often with the oatmeal nearly gone. It had led him to scourge and purify.

"I'm not wrong!" he yelled at himself as Andy-the-Good continued to blur Andrew-the-Bad. "The Lord rained brimstone and fire upon Sodom and Gomorrah!"

Outside, the crickets began to rub their forewings together to chirp the night's first sounds, harbingers of an oncoming chorus. Henry's poorly attended thickets of bush and vine were at full thickness of summer's end, giving night creatures a September feast. In a tall hemlock across the cemetery wall, a barred owl announced the start of his night-hunt with an eerie series of hoots.

Henry knew the night sounds well, for they had often called him from Mason House for deeply reflective walks along the cemetery wall—walks that sent him to dark streets and alleys. The calls and cries fixed images of the winged and wingless in his mind. But each creature's features changed and became part of the old man's fixation as the night sounds began to beat tormenting messages through their incessant rhythms.

In the upstairs hallway, where the night sounds were muffled, nothing freed Henry from the arguments in his mind.

When he finally put his hand on the key, his mood and pace differed from those of past approaches. His sudden decisions, those that had always been evoked by wrath, had been replaced by a more conscious judgment. Diluted anger and a new curiosity supplanted the blind rage that, in the past, had been the only force to provoke his unlocking of the fateful portal.

Henry opened the door and slowly stepped inside, unlike his previous shoving of the door to a crash against the cracked plaster wall, unlike his frenzied rush to the fossils of torment. Maybe he would still chastise the ghosts. Maybe he would still quote scripture. Maybe he would still condemn the lust of mankind. But not until he touched the clay figures that even his blind rage had not destroyed.

Chapter Twenty-Two

Again and again unreasonable fury had pushed Henry into a strange dimension, making his rantings and ravings almost nightmares outside of his conscious self. And now, no matter how poignant his Billy-born recollections of young Andy, he still slipped into vengeful compulsions from that consuming malignancy incurred one crushing day. Whiskey, of course, helped pull him down into the maelstrom.

Wearing baggy pants and a soiled sweatshirt, Henry carried a sack-covered bottle as he walked the downtown Philadelphia streets at nighttime.

* * *

Two blocks away, Mabel Beesley sat in her third-floor apartment window, still spying on the street below as she had done since morning.

Mabel wore her frilly, lavender, Monday dress—the one with the scallops around the neck and the puffy sleeves. It differed from her Tuesday dress in color rather than style. Tuesday was peach. Wednesday, pale chartreuse. Each day was an adventure for Mabel, even though she seldom left her Spruce Street apartment. Every morning she primped before her vanity mirror. She actually felt excitement as she readied herself for hours of watching Spruce Street, hours on the telephone with Martha Horton, hours describing every detail of her daily routine, including her fancy little tea parties, always on time, and only for herself.

Each morning she tilted her head this way and that as she powdered her face—a round, puffy face, not the kind that wrinkled easily. She didn't look her 75 years, despite pure white hair. Every night she tightly turned that hair into a score of pink curlers, and every morning she freed a score of ringlets.

Mabel's small bedroom was overfilled with pink ruffles and hundreds of trinkets—glass elephants, porcelain birds and an assortment of souvenirs from places she had never been.

Her kitchenette displayed a colorful array of potholders and plastic flowers. It was there, each morning, that she sliced two honey-cinnamon crullers into six pieces, put them on a small cake plate and covered them with a glass dome decorated with twin butterflies. Right on schedule she would carry the plate to a small lace-covered table in her dining alcove and place it next to a china teapot trimmed with pink rosebuds. Then she would sit on her gold bentwood chair, wait until the wooden bird sprang from her cuckoo clock, unfold her embroidered napkin, smile at nonexistent guests, and pour tea.

Mabel's morning call to Martha Horton was always shorter than her evening call, because Spruce Street had yet to tell its major stories. Each day Mabel maneuvered about her blue silk settee and chairs and her three goldfish bowls before reaching the front windows where a pair of opera glasses hung on a purple stretch-band suspended among organdy curtains. A gift from Martha, they had seen heavy use for seven years. The ornate French telephone rested on a three-legged stand near the windows, not far from a coffee table crowded with apothecary jars filled with lemon drops, butterscotch squares and cinnamon hearts.

Today, as usual, Mabel had seated herself early in her gilded window chair and peered between the curtains. At mid-afternoon she had watched a pregnant woman scold and yank a screaming child. "Humph!" she had uttered in disgust as she took a closer look through her binoculars, then instinctively lifted the glasses and, for the seventh time since mid-morning, scanned a couple of third-floor windows where she had once seen erotic lip service above the Yellow Bird Cafe—something she and Martha had talked, tittered and gasped about for years.

Now it was nighttime, and Mabel held the telephone in one hand, the opera glasses in the other.

"Guess who's back again, right on time. Baldy Cigar. He just went into the Smoke Shop. But he'll be right out, you wait and see. I'll bet he goes off with that same woman."

Baldy Cigar was Mabel Beesley's name for a little, round cigar-chewing man who appeared every Monday night at about 10 o'clock. He was one of many familiar "friends" whom she had never met.

Mabel kept her opera glasses aimed at the Smoke Shop as she told Martha Horton about her supermarket boy: "So as I was saying, when he finally arrived with my groceries, he brought me those big sardines in tomato sauce. I wanted the little ones in mustard. You know, the ones in the little..."

"Hello? Mabel, you there?"

"What a minute."

"Mabel?"

"I'm here. I'm looking at some poor old fellow in baggy pants. He keeps ducking in and out of doorways. I think he's drunk. He's carrying a paper bag. Let me focus, now." Mabel squeezed the telephone headset between her ear and shoulder as she adjusted the opera glasses. "I think he's got a bottle. Why do these old drunks always carry their bottles in paper bags?"

"What's he doing?"

"I can't see him now. He ducked up the alley. Anyway, like I was saying. I wanted the little sardines. Oh, wait a minute. Wait. Here comes Baldy Cigar, just on time. He's walking toward the corner. So, as I was saying, he brought me those big sardines. I was going to send them back, but decided to keep them, after I told him what I thought. Anyway, I kept them, and you know what I did? I heated them in a little extra tomato sauce. Oh, oh! Here she comes. I knew it. Old Frizzy Hair herself. She's wearing black silk, no less. Can you imagine? I suppose his wife's busy every Monday night."

"What makes you think he's married?"

"Because he only comes on Monday nights. Probably his wife's night out or something. Maybe she plays Bingo on Monday nights. Poor dear. I wonder if they have children. Anyway, like I was saying, I split open the sardines and took out those little bones. Not that you have to, but I don't like them."

"Are they gone?"

"What's that?"

"Baldy Cigar and his girlfriend. Have they left?"

Mabel grabbed the dangling binoculars and took another look. "They're going up the street. But here comes that old guy again. The one in the baggy pants."

"What's he doing?"

"He's crossing to this side of the street, but he keeps looking back toward the Yellow Bird." Mabel found traffic to and from the Yellow Bird Cafe by far the most exciting. "Now he's standing by the trash container. Keeps looking across the street."

"What's he look like?"

"I'll have to stand up. He's too close to the building. Wait a minute. No, now I can see him from my chair. He's near the street again. He's sort of tall. Kind of round-shouldered. Bent. He's sideways now, and I'm focusing on his face. Long face. Gaunt looking. A shaggy crop of hair."

"Is he still looking at the Yellow Bird?"

"Yes. A couple of those young men are going into the Yellow Bird."

"What's the old man doing?"

"Why, he's... Wait. I don't see him. He's gone!"

"Oh?"

"A light just went on in the Griswold Hotel. Fourth floor. Must be Mr. Undershirt. Yes, he's home. Now he's flexing his muscles in the window. She's not home yet, though. He won't like that."

"You think they'll have another fight?"

"I'll bet my goldfish on it."

"Can you still see him?"

"No. He pulled down the shade." Mabel lowered her opera glasses. "That old man's back again. He's standing in the doorway of the hotel, looking toward the Yellow Bird. Strange."

"What do you mean?"

"Well, he's so sneaky. Moves into the shadows of the doorways, then peeks out. Now he's walking toward the Yellow Bird. He's right under the street light. I can see him well. Oh, here comes that pretty boy who always wears the dark glasses. The old man saw him and turned back."

"I wonder what he's up to?"

"Here he comes again. He slipped into the next doorway. I think the car traffic stopped him."

"Stopped him from what?"

"Now he's crossing over here again. He tripped up the curb. I'm sure he's drunk."

"What's he doing now?"

"Just standing. Looking at the Yellow Bird. Now he's between parked cars, just waiting."

"For what?"

"He's in the street. He lit a match. I think he's going to throw that thing!"

"What thing? Mabel! What's he going to throw?"

"No, he pulled back." Mabel was standing at the window, her heart beating faster than on the night she watched a handsome disco dancer in toreador clothes pee in the street.

"Mabel!"

"I think he's that person!"

"What person?"

"You know, that person. The one who throws fire bombs."

"Oh, my God, Mabel!"

"He's standing on the curb right below me."

"Well, do something!"

"What can I do?"

"Well, you can't just sit there and let him throw it!"

"I'm not sitting. I'm standing. Oh, my!"

"What is it?"

"Oh!"

"Call the police!"

"But he might come after me."

"He'll never know. I'll hang up, and then you call the police. You don't have to give your name."

"They'll never get here on time."

"Mabel! Now, I'll hang up, and you call the police. Then phone me right back."

"Oh!"

"Mabel, do you hear me?"

"I'm scared, Martha!"

"Don't just stand there, Mabel! I'm going to hang up now."

Mabel didn't move. She stood motionless, watching the old man step into the street again and light another match. With sudden impulse, she dropped the phone, let the opera glasses swing loose, pushed up her window and yelled, "Don't do that! Don't you dare do that! I'm watching you!"

The old man turned, lost his balance, but managed to look up. Seconds later he disappeared into the shadows.

Chapter Twenty-Three

Saturday morning. Billy could have slept late. But he awoke before the morning sun splashed across his bed. He lay there, staring at the ceiling, a torrent of thoughts keeping him immobilized. Never before had rapture and remorse mixed to spin a whirlwind in his brain. Nirvana, unequaled in his young life, was being stabbed again and again by anguish. His anxiety about last night's episode in the cemetery stemmed more from fear of looking into Lori's eyes on Monday morning than anything else. It was heightened by the maddening fact that he couldn't see her before then. Gritting his teeth, he cursed her mother for insisting on a weekend visit to Grandma Wilson, her maternal grandmother in Hoboken. How he wanted to run to her, study her face, reassure himself, and hopefully absolve himself of any guilt. His regret had more to do with Lori and her reaction than with the occurrence itself.

Although he had lain awake for hours, it was still early when he leaped from bed and hurried to Bobby's room—a masculine room heavy with trophies and sports posters. Closing the door behind him, he stepped to the bed and shook his brother.

"Get out of here," Bobby muttered, his lips barely parted, his eyes closed. He pulled a pillow over his ear.

Billy yanked the pillow away. "Bob, wake up!"

"What do you want?"

"I want to talk."

"Not now." Bobby opened his eyes halfway. "It's Saturday, isn't it?"

"I gotta ask you something."

Slowly, Bobby sat up and rubbed his eyes. Bigger than Billy, he resembled his father, the big cop, and owned a well-developed body turned bronze by the summer sun. "Damn it, dude. Can't it wait?" He stretched, grunted, and then looked up at Billy. "What the hell is so important?"

Billy sat on the edge of the bed, stared intently at his brother and asked, "When did you first do it? You know what I mean. With a girl. When? What was it like?" He had always been comfortable talking frankly with Bobby, but had never gotten around to that all-important question.

"What?"

"You know, your first time? When was it? How was it?"

"What kind of question is that?"

"Come on, Bobby!"

"Shit, dude, what are you up to anyway? What's going on?"

"Just tell me, okay? Just tell me."

"Man. That's really kind of a personal thing. You know?"

"Bobby!"

"I don't know, man. Let's see. About your age, I guess. Why?"

"I want to know. That's all. What was it like?"

"Maybe you better tell me what you're up to. You still latched onto that Lippincott girl?"

"Yeah."

"Is that what this is all about?"

"Maybe."

A crazy smile played around Bob's mouth and danced in his eyes.

Billy felt a strange sort of embarrassment. Never before had he been embarrassed talking with his big brother. "It's been rough, you know? Y'hear what I'm saying? So many times, just about making it, but never quite. You know?"

"So what do you want me to say, that you should? Hell, Bill, I'm not going to say that."

"You said you did it at my age."

"That was me. Hey, man, if you're looking for some sort of approval, you're not getting it from me."

"What was it like the first time? How did you feel afterwards?"

"Afterwards?"

"Yeah."

"Come off it, dude!"

Billy showed vexation. He blurted, "I know you jocks. A girl on every floor of the dorm."

"You don't know this jock. I don't screw around that way." Bob was annoyed and stiffened his jaw, but quickly pulled himself into a brotherly smile. "So, look. I'll tell you. It was that little blonde from over Landsdowne. And it shouldn't have happened. Not with her, anyway. Okay?"

"Her? The cross-eyed one?"

"Her."

"Purple lipstick?"

"That's the one. Over in the cemetery."

"The cemetery? You too?"

"What's that supposed to mean?"

"Nothing."

Billy saw the cemetery in his mind's eye. Last night. Quickly erect with 16-year-old stiffness. Pulsating. Ready too soon.

"Are you okay?" Bobby asked.

Billy stood, turned away from his brother, hesitated, then darted into the hallway. Seconds later he locked his bedroom door, pounced on his bed and stared at the ceiling again.

Within minutes, Bobby was knocking on his brother's door. "Open up, Billy. Let's talk."

"I'm okay."

"Look, I didn't realize how serious you were. Are you in trouble?"

"No. Shush. Don't wake Mom and Dad. I'm all right. Honest. We'll talk later."

"You sure?"

"Yeah, I'm sure."

Bobby waited, then backed away slowly.

Again Billy envisioned that mid-September moon behind gently moving boughs of pine, giving little light to the cemetery where the air was fresh and dry from a Canadian high that had drifted south. So easy to breathe. Cool enough to add to desire. Not chilly enough to add one bit of restraint.

"Does it hurt?" he had asked Lori between quick breaths.

"It's okay. Go ahead."

The sounds of the night creatures, somewhat fewer since August, stole little from the silence. In the distance a whippoorwill repeated a whistling rendition of its name.

"I'm hurting you."

"Don't stop."

"Oh God."

"It's okay. Go on."

"You all right?"

"Yes. Hold me."

Gone was the sound of the whippoorwill. The moon was above the pines, casting its cool light on the low limbs of maples, patches of grass, tombstones. Soon the moonlight fell across the plot of Smythe, spreading a glow upon Billy's bouncing buttocks.

A breeze rustled nearby maples and hickories, freeing leaves that whirled in circles and fluttered to earth. From across the rolling cemetery came the cries of cats, their screeching yowls muffled by the north breeze and a barrier of evergreens.

Billy had finished, but Lori's tremors would not cease. He stayed there, holding firmly, confused by her tears.

"You okay?"

She couldn't answer. Her wet eyes gazed up into his and seemed to ask a million questions. She breathed through parted lips, drawing deeply from her bosom.

"It was okay, wasn't it? You wanted to, didn't you?"

She still said nothing, and kept gripping his shoulders almost too tightly. Her moist eyes continued to stare into his.

"Lori?" His expression pleaded for an answer.

"Don't talk. Please. Just hold me."

* * *

Stretched out on his bed, Billy breathed almost as quickly and deeply as he had in the cemetery. He waited for Bobby to rap on the door again, but the knock never came.

It was his mother who finally tapped and called: "Billy! What are you doing in there? Why is your door locked? Come to breakfast."

"I'll be down in a minute."

"I made French toast. It's getting cold. Is something wrong?"
"No. You go ahead down. I'll be right there."

* * *

Billy was quiet at the breakfast table. He winked at Bobby as his brother donned a cherry-and-white cap and hurried off for a tailgate party and the Temple-Pitt football game. He tried to talk with his parents after Charley finished reading his newspaper. Fishing for something to say, he blurted, "I'm going to show Mr. Mason some of my rocks."

"That's nice," his mother said.

* * *

Later, after Charley had reluctantly driven Mary to Springfield Mall, Billy busied himself in his room putting rocks into a dark green canvas bag. He had decided to follow-up on his impromptu idea born at the breakfast table.

His heavy jumps down the stairs, with the bag over his shoulder, were carefree and deliberate because the big cop wasn't home to scold. A slam of the door and a few more leaps and he was on his way under the shedding sycamores. The bag swayed with the swing of his bouncy gait, up the hill and around the corner, as he attempted to cover his misgivings with a facade of bravado. After all, he had reached an essential level of manhood. Hadn't he?

* * *

A few lazy flies buzzed about Henry Mason's porch as Billy knocked. The old man didn't answer, so the boy tried again, this time without timidity. Billy's earlier visit had turned out less intimidating than he had expected, despite the strange conversation, so today's approach was not so difficult. Besides, Henry's words had blurred and faded more each day and now seemed less peculiar. On top of all that, the book of plants had been exciting Billy with every chapter, giving him a steadily increasing regard for the old man.

The boy fidgeted, pulled the sack of rocks from one shoulder and tossed it over the other, then knocked again. He would not have been so bold if he had not spent days trying to convince himself that a visit was in order. The sudden idea of showing his rocks had given him a reason to call and a chance to share an interest. Billy was well aware that the old man had been trying to reach out, and he was beginning to realize what it must be like when loved-ones are long-gone.

It was a disappointed Billy who stepped from the big porch and strolled down the front pathway. He suspected that Henry was closed-in behind those doors, refusing to answer. Actually the old man had ventured from his house only twice since the burning of The Black Tulip.

Billy sauntered toward the cemetery wall, the canvas bag still over his shoulder. He sat on the ground along the sidewalk, in the shade of an old beech tree. Tossing the bag aside, he leaned back against the wall. His thoughts wandered as he watched an occasional car speed by.

The wall, the cemetery and Billy's drifting thoughts conjured up last night's feelings of desire that were followed by consternation and doubt. Now he saw none of the cars that passed. In fact he was aware of little until time moved sunlight into his eyes. Then he gritted his teeth and captured that moment again—that moment when he first tossed the bag over his shoulder, leaped down the stairs, slammed the door and bounced up the street. With renewed energy, he grabbed the canvas sack.

Back on Mason's porch, the teenager wasn't going to give up—not this time. He knocked again and again, forcing himself into sureness and determination. But he still jumped when the door opened and Old Man Mason stood there, staring, red-eyed and rumpled.

"Hello, Mr. Mason."

Henry didn't smile. He kept looking at Billy, and the more he gazed the more he weakened his impulse to close the door in the boy's face. He snorted and breathed out the smell of whiskey and tobacco.

"I brought some rocks," the boy explained. "Thought you might like to see them. Maybe you can tell me things I don't know."

It had been an eternity since anyone had come to Henry to share and ask his opinion. That a 16-year-old should do so was overwhelming and it showed in his eyes, despite his resistance. Yet, because it was this particular boy, Henry's emotions were divided. His heart-breaking fear and his impulse to push away fought with his desire to know and the pull of affinity. Finally, the old man grunted something, then motioned, and Billy followed him into the musty hallway.

The living room seemed darker than before, though it was mid-afternoon. Anna's plants had grown, their stems and tendrils carrying broad leaves and feathery fronds to the corners of every window. Billy stopped short and waited for his eyes to adjust.

"No," Henry barked. "This way." He led the boy to his kitchen, somewhat surprising himself. Pulling an intruder through his house was one thing. But inviting someone into it was quite another.

Billy was pleased, not simply because he wanted to share his rocks, but because the gesture indicated that he might be right about Mason's needs. Not only gifted with insight beyond his years, the teenager held perceptions of Mason instilled in him by his father. Keenly aware of the dynamics at work, he saw the microscope, the plant book and now the rocks as supports in a bridge being built by some underlying force—a potent force, yet perhaps disruptive, even fragile.

The spacious kitchen was much brighter than the living room, but the big wooden table was crowded with cans, bottles, cartons and jars. Henry often ate directly from containers, clearing a space on the table only when necessary. His widely scattered meals were becoming less frequent as his drinking increased.

Using his forearm, Henry began to clear space for the rocks, but stopped abruptly when he realized that an open bottle of gasoline teetered at the table's edge. The odor of gasoline had alerted Billy, who glanced from the old coal stove to the grease-stained gas range.

"Is something leaking, Mr. Mason?"

Without looking at Billy, Henry simply screwed the top on the bottle and set it deep between canisters on the counter, then returned to clearing space on the table. Finally, he glanced at the teenager and ordered him to "Sit down."

Billy sat, opened his bag and spread some of his specimens on the table. Hunched over the table, the old man rooted among the rocks and picked up a translucent chunk of pinkish stone and said, "Rose quartz. Not a bad piece." Henry sat next to Billy as his eyes darted from rock to rock. "Azurite and malachite. See these circular bandings? If this were polished you'd see brilliant colors."

Henry's enthusiasm, while restrained, was still more than Billy had expected. The boy quickly emptied his bag and spread out more chunks of stone. Maybe it was Billy's movements, the push of his hand, his eagerness, or a look in his eyes that kindled something in the old man. Whatever the impetus, Henry caught a glimpse of Andy and felt an urge to embrace the boy. But he turned away.

"Mr. Mason, are you okay?" Billy's expression sobered as he gazed on his thin, gray host. He saw Henry's neck muscles twitch as a shiver ran up and down the old man's spine.

Henry was in control when he looked back at the table. Avoiding Billy's eyes, he picked up a rock and said, "This is feldspar."

Billy knew feldspar, but said nothing as he listened and watched. In time, Mason's interest seemed firmly fixed, and the boy relaxed as he absorbed one detail after another.

"Do you know, Bannon, that an emerald is a green variety of beryl?" Henry was being carried back to another era of his life. As long as the boundaries were tight, as long as his thoughts stayed with gems, it was safe for him to reminisce.

Billy became more relaxed. Twice he turned to Henry and smiled. As the comfort level increased he fished for questions outside the realm of rocks and gems. "You like to grow things, too, don't you, Mr. Mason? I mean, all those plants..."

"They were my wife's," Henry said matter-of-factly.

"Oh." Billy wanted to say more, but words wouldn't come. Again he searched his mind, then made an effort: "That's some cherry tree you got outside."

The old man's mind began to move in and about events that had written good and bad chapters in his life. Then his thoughts closed in on persons and objects that had given pain.

Billy was unaware that he was dangerously close to stepping on a land mine. And he picked the worst possible time to comment, ever so gently, "I notice you have a room upstairs all closed up. Why is...?" He never finished the question, becoming suddenly aware of its impropriety. His better sense scolded him for stupidity even before he saw the look on Mason's face.

Henry stiffened and bristled. His face reddened while his chin hardened. His eyes glared, melting Billy into a weak and shameful glob of flesh. Severe discomfort plagued the boy as sweat ran from his armpits. Slowly he pushed his rocks into his bag without looking up.

Henry said nothing as his redness faded to pasty white. He simply stood and walked away.

The sack over his shoulder, Billy found his way to the open front door. Henry was standing on the porch, facing the street, his sore, red eyes burning in the September breeze. The boy walked past him, stepped down, and then looked back.

Henry fixed his eyes on him.

Billy smiled weakly, then parted his lips as if trying to say something.

Turning away, Henry stepped toward the door.

"Mr. Mason, I..."

The old man stood still, but kept his back toward the teenager.

"I really..." Billy struggled. "I really like you, sir." His stilted words were not his best and he knew it, but he couldn't leave without expressing his feelings, no matter how awkward his words. "You're an okay guy, Mr. Mason."

Henry entered his house and closed the door.

Billy stood there, wounded. After a moment's delay, he turned and walked away. Two blocks north he sat on a fireplug, let his bag of rocks fall to the ground, and gazed into the gutter. He felt he had lived a lifetime in the last two days.

Chapter Twenty-Four

"Another freakin' oil spill. Prices keep going up, and they keep spilling it." As usual, Charley drank his coffee without looking at his cup, his eyes fixed on the *Inquirer*. "And look at this, vandals turned over a statue in Fairmount Park. I'd like to get my hands on them."

Mary carried a carton from the refrigerator to the sink, then poured herself a glass of orange juice.

"Some old lady on Spruce Street says she saw the fire-bomber," Charley continued. "Says she scared him away by yelling out the window. Can you imagine? Almost two weeks ago. What the hell has she been waiting for? Burns me to hell! These stupid asses that don't go to the police right away."

Mary seated herself across from her husband as Billy sauntered into the kitchen, dressed for school and carrying his chemistry book.

"Would you believe this? She says she saw him through binoculars from her third floor apartment window. Third floor? Says she can describe him perfectly. What the hell was she doing with binoculars? Probably some old nag who needs some voot-voot in her life and fantasizes all to hell."

"You want eggs, Billy?" Mary asked. "Or cereal?"

"Scrambled, I guess, Mom." The boy seated himself between his mother and father.

"They have this sketch here," Charley added. "An old goat with bushy hair. Looks a little like a long-faced Albert Einstein."

Billy paid little attention to his father's utterances, having heard such rambling reports of news morning after morning. His thoughts were of reaching school in time to meet Lori at his locker before first period. As he fretted over his approaches to Lori, his mother busied herself pouring his orange juice and preparing his eggs.

It was later, after Charley had left for work, that Billy glanced down at the front page and saw the sketch under the words, "Have you seen this man?" The drawing reminded him of Henry Mason, so much so that he couldn't take his eyes off of it and couldn't swallow another forkful of eggs. He wondered why his father hadn't seen the likeness. His mother would have been startled by his expression if she had glanced his way. But she was busy at the sink. He didn't want to talk to her, tried to gather his wits, forgot about his Lori-induced anxiety, picked up his books and said, "I'm late, Mom. Gotta run."

On his way to school he dropped coins into a newspaper vending machine, grabbed an *Inquirer* with a quick and nervous hand, and slipped it under his arm.

"Wait up, Billy!"

It was Clarence and two friends—a skinny redhead and a chubby, pimply faced blond. Billy, his mind afire with troubling thoughts, did not want to walk with them, and he surely didn't want to talk with them. He felt the urge to sprint ahead, but controlled himself and slowed his pace until they caught up.

"Wait'll y'hear what George got himself into," said Clarence, a silly grin on his face.

Billy could not have cared less. He said nothing and heard little of the teenage chatter and boasts as the pack-of-four made its way down a shady street lined with single houses.

As they mingled with other students on the wide stretch of concrete in front of the high school, Clarence punched Billy's arm and asked, "What the hell's with you, anyway?"

"What do you mean?"

"You're like out of it, or something."

"Just thinking."

"About Lori? You're getting to be a love-sick creep, you know that?"

Billy raced toward one of many glass doors in the textured concrete walls of the sprawling school. Inside, he dodged students as he ran past the auditorium, turned a corner, and hurried down a long corridor. He looked neither left nor right as he sped to his locker. Lori was already there and quickly responded with a radiant smile that faded fast when it wasn't returned. Billy's somber face deepened her troubling thoughts about Friday night's episode in the cemetery. Badly in need of reassurance, she had hoped and prayed for a warm and comforting greeting.

"Look at this!" Billy shoved the newspaper at her.

Lori struggled to gather her senses. Her mind was so preoccupied that she could barely focus on the headlines.

"Look!" Billy insisted.

"At what?"

"Don't you see?"

"An oil spill?"

"No. Down here. This picture. Who does it look like?"

"Well... Let's see. To tell you the truth, I don't know. At least, I don't think I do. Should I?"

"Keep looking."

"You mean, Mr. Mason?"

"I knew it! Yes, I mean Mr. Mason."

"I'm not sure, though." Lori was somewhat relieved that Billy's expression purported no pox upon her.

"Damn it! It looks just like him. And I don't want you to say a thing about this. Understand? You got to promise. Not a thing!"

"What are you talking about?"

"I want to find out. On my own. Understand?"

"You want to find out if he's the fire-bomber?"

"Yes. And I don't want anyone to know. So you have to swear. I mean it, Lori, you have to swear."

"What about us?"

"What do you mean?"

"You know. Friday night."

"Oh. Oh, jeeze, Lori. I'm sorry. I got carried away. Are you okay?"

"Yes. Are you?"

"Oh, yeah." Billy pulled her to him and whispered into her ear: "Everything's okay with me, if it's okay with you. It happened. It doesn't change things. Honest."

Chapter Twenty-Five

Since Billy's summertime freedom had gone the way of the school bell, his nighttime snooping had become restricted. He was allowed out until 11 o'clock—sometimes midnight—on Friday and Saturday nights only. On Wednesdays, if he had a date, he was permitted to stay out until 10:30 if his homework had been completed. All this was on a give-and-take-a-little basis, with Billy taking as much as he could.

Spying on Mason House was confined to two or three nights a week and always cut into Billy's time with Lori, who had come to expect all of his free nighttime hours. Billy's current scheme was to take Lori home early on date nights, then run along the trolley tracks behind Drexel Hill homes, race through backyards, climb a fence or two and head for Mason House where he'd spy for an hour or less. Lori didn't like it, but her mother was pleased by her early hours and started to say nice things about Billy. As for Charley and Mary Bannon, they were getting annoyed by the lateness of Billy's dates and had threatened to tighten the rules.

Billy was possessed in his drive to learn the truth. His entire purpose differed from the summertime poking around that had led him up the cherry tree and into Mason's garage. Clarence was not part of this, and Lori was to stay away and keep quiet. Billy's curiosity often kept him awake nights and interfered with his concentration on homework. So much more was involved than a strange old man, unknown but as the recluse in the big house near the cemetery. Now Henry Mason was someone who talked and walked and showed feelings, someone who had suffered and had tried to reach out. More than that, he was the man who had touched the life of Billy's father, who had affected Charley Bannon's sense of justice, even if he had blinded the big cop to Henry's faults. The boy wanted to protect his father somehow from whatever it was. More than that, Billy felt affinity for the old man, in and of itself. Despite the fact that Henry had turned his back on Billy, the boy was certain that he and the old man had built a bridge between each other.

The boy's restlessness and preoccupation were showing more each day to the annoyance and concern of his parents, Lori, and his high-school teachers.

Ever since he had seen the police sketch of the fire-bomber and had read the report of Mabel Beesley's sighting, Billy had fretted over Henry's rambling remarks about justice and punishment. One night he suddenly remembered the gasoline in Mason's kitchen. He sprang up in bed, his heart pounding as though he had awakened from a terrifying nightmare.

Weeks passed, nights grew cooler and the sycamores bared their limbs as the maples turned red and yellow. But Henry never left home on Billy's snooping nights—Wednesdays, Fridays or Saturdays. The newspapers reported no fire-bombings, no attacks on porno shops or gay bars.

Now it was early October, and time for another Friday night embrace on the stoop of Lori's house, between the big spreading yews.

"I'd better hurry."

"Please wait."

"I don't have much time."

"Billy!"

He kissed her again, but pulled away quickly. "Really, I better get moving."

"All evening, and you didn't ask."

"Ask what?"

"Whether I got my period."

"Did you?"

Lori nodded.

"Oh, wow! That's good. Why didn't you tell me? What were you waiting for?"

"I wanted you to ask."

"That's stupid. I don't get it."

"Haven't you wondered? Didn't it bother you? Didn't you care? Is Mr. Mason so important that you forget about... well, you know? Did you stop worrying about what could have happened? Don't you care about me?"

"What is this? Were you testing me?"

"I guess I wanted to know that you shared my concerns. That it was our worry, not just mine."

"Of course I care. I mean, wow, that's great news."

"I don't think you understand. The truth is, my body and mind wanted to have part of you growing inside of me. Every time I thought about it, it felt so good. But I knew it couldn't be. My mother would have killed me. And, oh my God, your father... I hate to think of it. It would've messed up everything, I know that. What with college and all."

Billy wrapped his arms around her and whispered, "I'm sorry."

"Hey, it's okay. I just wanted you to care."

"And I do. Honest."

"Even that night. Right after it happened. It felt so good to know that part of you was inside me. I guess that's because I love you so much."

"So, we know what we can look forward to."

"Tell me you love me. Please?"

Billy held her even more tightly. "Oh, I do. God, I do. I love you so much, Lori."

Within moments, Lori pushed him away and said, "So, go on. Go snoop on your Mr. Mason." She touched his nose with her finger, smiled and blew him a kiss. "I'm scared to death you're going to get yourself in trouble."

"I'll be careful."

"You might get hurt somehow."

"No. That won't happen."

"You keep saying that, but I think it's all crazy and scary."

"I have to go." He kissed her again, then backed off.

"You're going to get in serious trouble!"

"Don't forget to take the phone off the hook again when your mother goes to bed. I'll see you tomorrow." He turned and ran.

As Billy began jogging along the tracks, Henry Mason was pushing aside his oatmeal for more whiskey. The steaming bowl rested on the counter next to an open carton of milk while Henry returned to the cellar for two more swigs.

The whiskey added pain to his belly and stopped his climb up the stairs midway, where he bent over and cursed Andrew as well as a force-of-evil named Timothy Wood, a haunting figure that tormented him. Never had he blamed himself for the ache—a piercing pang that, to him, was still the cutting dagger of years past.

Angered by the pain and staggered by the whiskey, Henry backed down a few steps, turned and gazed on the box of candlewick, then on the bottles and cans of gasoline. Those intruders of long ago had no right to keep hurting him.

"Get out! Get out of my house!"

October. Just as now. But until then a favorite time, with children rustling and romping through piles of leaves. A drive through the country with Anna. Fall colors—scarlet, russet and yellow touched by the warmth of autumn's evening sunlight. Pumpkins in the fields around bundles of cornstalks. Since then a cursed time when melancholy sucked strength that only anger could replenish.

Billy was crouched in the thick foliage on the north side of Mason House when Henry walked onto his front porch carrying a bottle in a paper bag. The old man leaned on the railing for a moment, breathed hard, then watched his steps as he made his way to the sidewalk and began walking south. The boy stepped out of the bushes, but stayed in the dark and watched Henry stagger along the cemetery wall. He was about to follow when the old man turned around and started back toward him, wavering, almost stumbling. The boy froze. Gathering his wits, he backed up slowly into the bushes, but didn't dare make a sudden move to hide himself. He was certain he was about to be discovered as the old man swayed close to him while nearing the porch. His heart pounded, and at one point he swore that Mason's eyes stared directly at him. But Henry passed by, gripping his bag-covered bottle with one hand, the railing with the other, as he awkwardly climbed to the porch and entered the house.

Breathing more freely, Billy wondered if Henry had changed his mind, forgotten something, or found himself too sick or drunk.

Billy sneaked back into the thick foliage and waited. Something rustled the leaves. Perhaps an opossum. The boy started. He felt the beat of his heart as electricity lifted his hair.

Minutes later the door rattled and banged. Henry was on the porch, checking his pockets. Again he leaned on the railing, breathed laboriously, slowly made his way to the sidewalk and began staggering south. Billy stepped from the darkness, more hesitant this time. Stretching his neck and straining his eyes, he waited until the old man was well along the wall before moving toward the sidewalk.

Farther along the wall, Henry slowed his pace, then leaned against a pole at a bus stop. Billy watched from under the beech branches and suddenly realized that he had not planned well. "Damn it!" he muttered under his breath. He quickly toyed with ideas, but could figure no way to follow, no way to board the same bus. His frustration surged when the headlights of an oncoming bus flashed into his eyes and brightened the cemetery wall. He crouched, closed his eyes, lifted his arms across his face, and stayed paralyzed for seconds. Once more in the shadows, he breathed again and realized what he should have done: run swiftly through the cemetery in hopes of catching the trolley that always bettered the bus by minutes.

* * *

Frustration kept Billy awake that night. When he finally slept, his emotions plunged him into a frightening dream in which he pounded on a locked door with both fists and tried to call for help, but couldn't.

Whimpering, Billy fought to escape and awoke to find his mother standing over him. "Are you okay?" she asked.

"I was dreaming." Again he could feel the beating of his heart.

"I know." She wiped sweat from his forehead with her handkerchief. "I heard you moaning. I was about to wake you."

"It was just a stupid dream."

"I'm worried about you."

"It's nothing, Mom."

She sat on the edge of his bed. "You want to talk about anything?"

"No, Mom. Really. I'm okay."

She wiped his temples.

Chapter Twenty-Six

Nighttime at Mason House. The same hour, one week later. Cooler winds tossed more leaves as autumn deepened. Time ticked off slowly, building impatience within Billy-the-Spy. Each sound—a creak, a crack, a rustle—interrupted the moment.

Then: the piercing jab, the electricity, the shot of adrenaline.

The unsteady steps of Henry Mason were as before, and Billy relived the moment. Looking down at his feet, the old man walked from porch to walkway to sidewalk, then south along the wall. The boy watched from a dense thicket. But this time he darted across the street to the shadow of a bushy cedar from where his eyes followed Henry's wavering walk.

Again, midway along the wall, Henry stopped and leaned against that pole.

Billy stayed up the street on the far side until he saw Henry shift his bag-covered bottle from right hand to left in an effort to dig for coins. That was the boy's clue to run, knowing the old man was about to board a bus for the terminal. With a burst of energy, Billy raced across the street and tried to scale the cemetery wall, but found it too high. He scraped his elbows and scuffed his sneakers before giving up and running north about 100 feet to where a low-limbed crabapple tree beckoned him. Determination, hard pulls, grunts and quick-and-tricky footwork lifted Billy high enough for a leap to the other side. He dropped far and heavy, bending his knees to the ground. His pulse rapid, he struggled to get his knees working for the long run ahead.

The cemetery was dark and replete with obstacles. Billy dodged gravestones, shrubs and trees as he scrambled on a zigzag run. He dashed across open stretches as if chased by the worst of beasts, then darted this way and that like a bolting jack rabbit. He jumped over hedges, and at one point came to an abrupt stop after pushing his way through evergreens to face a looming mausoleum. In the deep darkness under trees he kicked through leaves, then circled a cluster of cedars as a hissing scream sent a shivery shockwave up his spine. A cat leaped from the bushes and raced into the night.

When Billy reached the far wall he ran back and forth searching for a low point. He began to panic, knowing he would never reach the terminal in time, unless he hailed a trolley within minutes. Near the east gate stood a shortleaf pine with a broken limb, split where it joined the trunk. Its wide fan of needled branches lay on the ground. Billy grabbed and yanked, pricking his hands and arms. He pulled again, but to no avail. Frustrated, the boy stepped back and surveyed the scene, then tried harder. His hands burned and his muscles ached as he tugged, twisted and strained. Sticky sap oozed into hands. "Sonofabitch!" he muttered. Stepping back again, he inhaled the smell of pine oil, then threw his entire body into the prickly limb, scratching his arms and face. Standing and retreating, he breathed hard, tightened his muscles, and attacked again. This time the limb gave way under the forceful thrust of his body weight.

With renewed hope, Billy scrambled to his feet and began tugging at the limb. Little by little he inched it toward the wall. Then, with a burst of energy, he hoisted the heavy end, only to drop it as jagged bark scraped his arm, leaving a five-inch brush-burn. For a moment he stood there, holding back tears of frustration. But seconds later he tried again, raising the heavy end to the top of the wall with a sudden heave. Using hands and feet, he crawled up the limb to the top of the wall, dropped to the sidewalk, staggered until steady, brushed himself off, and ran down the street.

Billy cut through a few backyards, hopped a picket fence, and brushed up against a cage of rabbits. Two houses later he was chased by a German shepherd. The barking dog was chained, but scared Billy enough to send him running out of a driveway. From there, he ran in the street until he reached the Red Arrow line. No

bells, no blinking lights, no trolley in sight. All he could do was
wait and hope that the bus was late.

After minutes of fidgeting, he saw the light of an approaching
trolley, nervously twiddled his dirty fingers, then quickly dug for
carfare. Blotched with gummy pinesap, his fingers kept sticking
together and adhering to his pockets.

The Red Arrow trolley followed a beeline to the 69th Street
Terminal, unlike the bus that traveled with traffic, turned this way
and that, stopped at intersections, and waited for lights. Billy was
among few passengers in the car as it swayed along the rails, over a
bed of cinders, up a slope, across a trestle and down. Soon it ding-
ding-dinged its way into the terminal.

Moving with deliberate purpose, Billy stepped from the car and
pushed through swinging doors. He hurried along the concourse as if
chasing and searching. Turning at a juncture, he raced even faster
down another concourse, for no one was there to impede him. Ahead
he saw a single soul—a soldier on a bench, leaning on his duffel bag.
Glancing about nervously, Billy pushed through a glass door onto an
empty platform, hurried to the west end, and stationed himself in the
shadows next to a support pole. He knew that incoming buses would
pass him before discharging.

The boy's nervous system was charged to react when the first
bus rolled in. As bright headlights cut the darkness, tingles raced
through his body as his muscles quaked. Instinctively he swung
from one side of the pole to the other, partially hiding himself.
Marked with the West Chester route number, the bus was not
Mason's after all. Hot air from the grinding motor blew into Billy's
face as the bus lumbered past. A sinking feeling sucked little juice
from his highly charged anxiety.

Billy tried to regain at least a modicum of composure while the
passengers stepped from the bus. He moved to the other side of the
pole and nervously rolled sticky pinesap into tiny gumballs and
picked them from his hands.

...a good, honest soul.
When I was a kid he used to let us take cherries from his tree.
...a good, honest soul.
...honest soul.

I can still see him all dressed up on Sunday mornings...

This was not the first time that Billy's mind had repeated his father's words. It had happened again and again during many a late night hour and many a quiet daylight moment.

... walking with his pretty wife under the blossoms along the cemetery wall.

He was full of life then, would laugh when he played catch with his boy, always had his house all fresh with paint.

...broke apart when his wife died.

...broke apart...

Beams of light from another bus struck Billy's face, jolting him from his thoughts. Again he swung around the pole and stiffened. And again he felt hot air when the big machine rumbled past. He thought he saw the old man as the windows flashed by, so he stepped back and watched. Henry was among the last to reach the platform and push through the swinging doors. Faltering slightly, he still carried the bag-covered bottle.

Billy followed, at first not too close, not too far. But the concourse curved and Mason slipped quickly from view, so Billy quick-stepped and gained on the old man. In the expanse of the main waiting room, the boy slowed his pace and watched as Henry dropped coins and pushed through a turnstile leading down to the Market Street elevated/subway line. He waited until a few others paid their fares, then followed, hoping a train would not pull out before he reached the platform. Seeing no train below, he stopped at the top of the stairs and decided to wait until a train rumbled beneath him. He picked nervously at the pine gum, fearing a long wait, for he knew that few trains left the terminal during late night hours.

...his son came home from Korea and then disappeared.

Something bad must have happened...

...closed himself in and grew old.

...people around here who know, they kind of respect him.

Who cares why he has a room boarded up?

Billy heard a train and started down the steps, too fast. He miscalculated. Henry had not walked far from the stairs, and Billy was almost upon him before realizing. The boy stopped short, backed up a few steps and stood still, petrified. Much too close, he barely breathed as he hoped the old man would keep staring at the train as it slowed to a halt.

"What are you up to, boy?"

Billy spun around at the sound of the gruff voice, nearly lost his balance on the stairs, and came face to face with a uniformed policeman. "What?"

"What are you doing?"

"Nothing." Billy's stomach tightened. A feeling of hopelessness mixed with his anxiety.

"Nothing?"

"This is my train. I gotta go." Billy's desperation was increased by his fear that the train would pull out as soon as it loaded passengers.

"Backing up the wrong way, weren't you?" The broad-shouldered, strong-jawed cop fixed a steady stare on the boy. His dark, intense eyes asked questions and seemed to demand more than his heavy voice.

"Well, not exactly."

"Either you were or you weren't. I've been watching you. Seems to me you're hiding from someone."

"No, not really."

"Or maybe following somebody?"

"No. It's just that there's this old guy down there who talks too much. I didn't want to get stuck riding with him." Billy surprised himself with his quick-flowing fib, but made the mistake of breaking eye contact and looking away.

The officer studied the teenager's expression. "Is that right? Well, maybe we should go upstairs and talk."

"I don't want to miss the train if I can help it."

"There's always another."

"Pretty scarce this time of night."

The policeman gave Billy another once-over. "Where do you live, son?"

Billy's desperation pushed him to no-no land: "Do you know Lieutenant Bannon?"

"You mean Charley Bannon?"

"Yeah."

"Sure, I know Charley."

"He's my father." Billy took out his wallet and showed his Social Security and YMCA cards. "I'm meeting my brother downtown. He goes to Temple. He's treating me to pizza and than taking me back to his dorm for the night." Billy was certain his face showed all sorts of revealing signals. While lying didn't come easy to him at any time, it was particularly onerous when he knew the lie might get back to his father. He would simply have to own up to everything before his dad learned the truth elsewhere.

"Your dad's a good man, son." The officer's tone said much more than his words.

Billy cringed, then glanced down toward the waiting cars, still standing only because this was the end of the line, the hour was late, and the train was early.

"Okay, get out of here," said the patrolman. "Go ahead. Catch your train."

Billy bounded nervously down the steps and raced west on the platform as he tried to guess Henry's car, not wanting a head-on confrontation. "Well, here goes," he mumbled, relating his choice to Russian roulette. He leaped aboard, hoping he was a car or two behind the old man. Taking a seat above the wheels, he finally allowed himself to sigh, then tried to put his thoughts in order.

The doors closed with a hiss, and then Billy and three others in the car were jostled as the train moved. Visions of Henry flashed in the teenager's mind with every jerk and sway.

...because I like you.

Billy envisioned Henry standing in the cemetery, looking down at him and Lori.

...because I like you.

...I like you.

...like you.

The train rattled on at ground level until after the next stop, then gradually climbed onto the steel girders of the elevated line, above the shabby shops of West Philadelphia. Thrusting and rocking, the cars reached their peak of oscillation when the train hit its high-point of speed between stops. Billy's stomach churned as his head bobbed.

...Charley Bannon's son.
No wonder you climbed my cherry tree.
What kind of justice do you believe in?
...ask him about Henry Mason's kind of justice.

Although the train was moving rapidly, Billy worked his way to the front of the car and tried to gaze through the smeared glass. The swaying unnerved him as he pulled on the handle of the sliding door and was hit by a blast of wind. Peering through the second door, he counted about a half dozen passengers. He struggled but managed to keep his footing while the cars swayed in opposite directions and the stiff breeze billowed his zipper-jacket. Before the train began its plunge into the earth, Billy was safe in another seat over another set of wheels.

...Mr. Mason closed himself in...we can try to understand why.
...might be more of a gift for him than for you.
I was a thief, and Mason caught me...
...he decided that I was worth saving.

A shrill blare of the horn announced descent into the ground. Sounds that had flowed freely into the open air suddenly became trapped in the subway tunnel. Clatter was loud, yet muffled by the walls. Screeches echoed along the steel and concrete.

After the 34th Street stop, Billy moved forward, holding onto one seat after another. Ignoring the warning signs, he struggled again to pass between cars while the train sped ahead. But he retreated when he sighted the back of Henry's head, quickly closed one door and panicked as he tried to reopen the other. Before the train screeched into the 30th Street Station, he managed to slide the door and slip back into the car where all eyes were upon him. He looked from person to person, smiled weakly, and mumbled, "Bad idea."

Billy moved to the side doors in the forward half of the car and readied himself for the 15th Street stop. When the doors opened he stepped out halfway, watched for Henry, then pulled himself in as the door closed. He did the same at 13th, and again at 11th. No Mason in sight. Fear that he had somehow missed the old man sent his anxiety soaring.

Barely able to contain himself, Billy stretched his neck at the

8th Street stop and immediately sighted that crop of mussed hair, those bent shoulders, that awkward walk. Henry was there on the subway platform, moving slowly toward a turnstile, the bag-covered bottle still in his hand. Billy leaped from the train, just clearing himself from the closing doors. For a moment it seemed as though Henry saw him, and Billy froze as the pounding in his chest quickened. But the old man went on his way.

Billy waited as Henry climbed to the street, then followed. As he peeked from the subway exit, he saw Henry jaywalking toward the former Gimbel's store, now vacant and dark. He stayed back until the old man turned onto Chestnut Street, then ran, stopped, and glanced around the corner. As Henry passed the Benjamin Franklin Hotel on the south side, Billy began a slow and stealthy walk on the north side, hugging the buildings. But when Henry disappeared from Chestnut Street, the teenager darted again.

Old Man Mason found his way to the scene of one of his earlier attacks, perhaps to reenact, or to punish himself while punishing others, to hurt again by painful reliving. Just off Walnut Street, he walked up that arty alley of assorted taverns and clubs, that pathway paved with Belgian blocks, that same narrow street that had attracted the Chicago textbook salesman. He stood across from that brick archway marked by pink neon, that golden oak door that had led Jeffrey Broomell to a crowd of men around a pink elephant.

"Andrew! Damn you, Andrew!"

Tears streamed down Henry's face as he lifted the bottle from the bag. He looked left and right, then raised the bottle higher, as if to toast. "To you, Timothy Wood! May you rest in hell!" Henry lowered the bottle, squinted at it closely with whiskey-blurred eyes. Clumsily, he placed it on the curb, then fished about in his pockets for his matches.

"Happy birthday to you. Happy birthday to you. Happy birthday Dear Andy. Happy birthday to..."

The old man sat on the curb next to the bottle of gasoline just as the tavern door opened and laughter echoed up and down the alley. Two men glared at him, scoffed and giggled and hurried toward Walnut Street. Henry struck a match and watched the flame. He held it close to his face and stared at it until it burned his fingers. He tossed the burnt match to the Belgian blocks and lit another, took the bottle in his hand, and stood.

"No, Mr. Mason, please!" Billy stepped from a dark doorway and walked up to Henry. "Don't do it. Please don't do it."

Chapter Twenty-Seven

Mary Bannon seldom drank coffee after 9 p.m. But here she was, after midnight, pacing from room to room in her housecoat, a mug of steaming brew in her hands. Again she settled at the kitchen table, fretting. A moment later she stood and grabbed the wall phone for the fifth time and attempted another call to Evelyn Lippincott. And again she heard the buzz-buzz-buzz of a busy signal.

Charley had gone to bed early, weary after a full-day investigation of a convenience store holdup. At about 12:20 he was shaken from deep sleep by his wife, who not only grabbed his leg, but rattled off disturbing words: "Get up, Charley. Billy's still not home, and I swear the Lippincott phone must be off the hook. Something's not right. I'm sure of it."

Mary was back at the kitchen table drinking coffee when Bobby arrived home after the Temple-Delaware night football game and a few beers at Dr. Watson's Pub. Too much beer usually sent him back to his dormitory on Fridays, but not this night. He was home for the weekend.

After a few frenzied words, Mary sent him onto the streets to hunt for his brother, just as bleary-eyed Charley made his way down the steps, carelessly dressed in a red-plaid shirt, its tail hanging over his jeans.

Pacing again, Mary stopped short and shot a worried stare at her husband. "You'd better get over to the Lippincott house. Wake somebody up if you have to."

Charley grunted as he opened the door and stepped out. When he reached the sidewalk, Mary called after him: "Phone me if you can. Let me know if..." She switched thoughts. "Billy might pop in any second. I don't want Lori running over here all worked up."

* * *

It was 12:50 when Bobby finally found Billy near a bus stop along the pike. "Stick with me, Bobby, please, just for tonight. I'll tell you everything, later. Don't worry, I'll explain it all to Mom and Dad. But for now, let's just say I got carried away and I'm late. Okay?"

"You look terrible. What happened to your arms? They're all scratched. What's that on your hands?"

"I'll hide them in my pockets."

"From Dad? You gotta be kidding! Level with me, will you?"

"I'll come to your room and talk. Later. Okay?"

"I'm afraid you'll be talking right away. You're not getting away with anything. They're up waiting for you. And you know damn well that Dad'll pump the guts out of you. Now what the hell's going on?"

* * *

Mary stood rigid, her muscles tense, as she talked on the wall phone. "He's here, Mrs. Lippincott. I mean, Evelyn. Yes. Call me Mary, please. Okay. I will. Please tell Lori to go back to bed." Twisting the telephone cord around her finger, Mary kept a steady stare on Billy, who sat with his father and brother at the kitchen table. "I'm sorry. I apologize for everything." After hanging up, she shook her head and continued to look at Billy. "You talk to her tomorrow. Express your regrets in no uncertain terms. You hear me? She's not an easy woman to appease."

After Mary rejoined her husband and sons at the table, Billy continued to detail everything he could recall—from his first encounter with Henry Mason to his last. In return, he suffered stares of incredulity, anger and alarm, along with words of disbelief. At times, Mary turned away to compose herself. She rose from the table at 2:30, backed off and stood in the doorway. All eyes were on her.

"I've heard enough. No doubt you men have things to say to each other, without me. I'm going to bed, but I probably won't sleep." She stepped away, only to turn back. "You father's right, Billy. You should have come to us long ago." As she gazed on Billy's sad eyes, she wanted to comfort him, but couldn't find the words in front of Charley and Bobby. She blew a kiss and walked away.

Billy looked at his father. "Is it wrong to like a man who..."

"Throws fire bombs and kills people!" interrupted Bobby.

"But maybe he's not right in the head all the time."

"That's called crazy!" Bobby exclaimed. "The old goat's a murderer. You get it, Billy? Murderer. Do I have to spell it for you?"

"A person can be good and bad at the same time, can't he?" Billy looked from Bobby to his father.

"Ah, a good murderer!" Bobby said mockingly. Abruptly, he pushed his chair back as if to punctuate his words. He went to the refrigerator, grabbed a piece of bologna, rolled it up and shoved it in his mouth.

"Can't he?" Billy asked again.

Bobby glowered at his father. "What shut you up, Dad?"

Suddenly Billy realized that his brother knew nothing of his father's history with Henry Mason. He tried to read his father's expression.

Charley ignored Bobby's remark, looked at Billy and said, "Sometimes things happen to a good man, and he ends up doing bad things. It can work the other way around, too."

Billy was quick to grasp the significance of his father's words. "But when a man turns bad can he still be good?"

"That's crazy, dude!" Bobby interjected.

"Go to bed, Bobby," Charley said. He looked at his younger son. "You mean, can a man be both things at the same time? Can he have a good side and a bad side? Like Dr. Jekyll and Mr. Hyde?"

"Right! Like Jekyll and Hyde!"

"I can see where this is leading," said Bobby. "To a deep and profound analysis of Old Man Mason's schizophrenic brain by my father, the cop, and my brother, the high school student. I don't need to hear any more of this. I'm going to bed." After stepping from the room he added, "That old buzzard is just plain crazy, man."

Billy sat quietly for a moment, then looked up at his father and said, "I know I'm not supposed to like a murderer, if that's what he is. And I guess he is, 'cause he sure enough threw those fire-bombs that killed people. But I can't help it, Dad. I like the part of him that's good."

Charley saw something in Billy that he had never before seen. Seldom at a loss for words, he was stymied in his effort to respond.

"But I was frightened by the look in his eyes tonight," Billy said. "He looked so angry."

"Full of hate?"

"Yeah, I guess. Why do you think he hates so much? I mean, I guess lots of people don't like those kind of places. Especially porno shops. But they don't throw Molotov cocktails."

"I don't know for sure. But maybe I can find out."

"Really?"

"Maybe I owe you that."

"What do you mean?"

"Oh, just something your mother said. Besides, maybe I want to know for myself, too."

Billy looked puzzled, then said, "No one should hate that much. But you know, as soon as he realized who I was, he looked so dazed and confused, then kind of sad. He didn't say anything. He just dropped the match and walked away."

* * *

Three o'clock had come and gone by the time Charley entered his dark bedroom and sat on the bed. "Are you still awake?" he whispered to Mary.

"Yes. How is he?"

"He'll be fine. More of a man than I ever gave him credit for. A bit foolish. But maybe that's okay. You were right, Mary."

"About what?"

"About me and Billy and our relationship and all that stuff. And I'm going to do something about it. For him. And for me."

* * *

Long before the soft orange sun of morning peeked between the blinds of his bedroom window, Billy lay awake troubled and anxious after only three hours of sleep disturbed by a nightmare—a cemetery obstacle course of terror. Now, as he stared at the ceiling, he was haunted by images of tombstones, subway stations and dark streets. But the most troubling vision of all was that of Henry with his bottle and lighted match. Billy turned his head and looked at his microscope. He drew solace from it.

Whether it was because of the microscope, the chirping sparrows outside his window, or the warm patch of October sun upon his pillow—Billy suddenly leaped from bed and dressed quickly. He resolved to leave the house before his parents or Bobby awoke, for he wanted no confrontation in the light of the new day— surely a day that would bring revised and troubling questions. He wanted no more words, no more analysis. Morning had already mixed the real and the unreal into a devilish brew. Now he struggled in vain to clear his head while hunting for a special rock imprinted with plant life—a rock that he thought might be a key to Mason's house. He found it in a cigar box, slipped it into the pocket of his zipper-jacket, and, with Andrew Mason's plant book under his arm, tiptoed down the stairs and out the front door.

Billy knew the hour was too early for knocking on anyone's door, let alone Mason's. So he wandered on a roundabout route, eventually following Cobbs Creek to a wooded area where some trees stood naked among others ablaze in autumn colors. He sat on a stump near a thicket of laurel and opened his book to a treatise on locoweed. "Yeah, loco," he muttered before reading about horses and cows turned manic by munching. Unable to concentrate, he closed the book and watched a gray squirrel circle a hickory trunk, scamper through the laurel and bury a nut in the moist earth. Anxious energy forced him to his feet. He kicked leaves as he left the stump and walked among shimmering flashes of sunlight that filtered through the trees.

Time moved slowly and the hour was still early when Billy strolled along the cemetery wall toward Mason House. He decided to delay knocking by sitting on Henry's back steps and trying to read again.

At the back of the house, Billy pushed aside vines and sat on the splintery wood. He glanced at the garage and thought about the Packard, then looked down at his book, opened it, and read: *After acquiring a taste for locoweed, the animal refuses all other food.*

Billy lifted his head, gazed into the distance, and thought about Henry. Seconds later, he looked down and tried to focus on the words: *During the period of hallucination or mania the animal performs all sorts of crazy antics.*

Again Billy glanced at the crooked, vine-covered garage and remembered the bouncing glow of Henry's flashlight and the look in his eyes.

Lusterless hair, feeble movements and sunken eyeballs characterize the second stage, a period of lingering emaciation. Later, the animal dies as if from starvation.

Billy wondered about the effect of too much whiskey on a tormented brain. He closed his book and questioned his rationality. He urged himself to leave, felt the impulse, but stayed, deciding to wait until he heard movement in the kitchen.

Henry awoke earlier than usual because of pains in his stomach. He tried to lift himself from bed, only to have an overwhelming weakness throw him back on his pillow—a strange weakness that sucked energy from every part of his body. With little reason to rise, he would have stayed in bed if not for the pressure of his bowels. In desperation, he tried to roll from the bed and finally managed to place his feet on the floor. He held onto the chest of drawers while gathering enough strength to guide himself to the bathroom.

His head between his knees, Henry stayed on the toilet for nearly 20 minutes, long after passing black, odorous, pasty stool. In time, he maneuvered down the back stairs and into the kitchen, only because his stomach cried out for milk and antacid.

Billy thought he heard movement. His head sprang up and his heart pounded. He stood, put his ear against the door, and listened as a cabinet door slammed. He froze for seconds, then knocked lightly. "It's Billy Bannon, Mr. Mason, are you in there?" He tapped again. "Mr. Mason, please let me in. It's Billy. Billy Bannon. Mr. Mason!"

Inside, Henry was seated at the kitchen table drinking milk between swigs of antacid. He was aware of Billy, but ignored him, having no strength or desire to see him.

"Please, Mr. Mason! I'm not going to leave. I brought something for you. A rock. It's a fossil. I think it's from the Mesozoic era. Really. Y'gotta see it."

When Henry finally opened the pantry door, the boy knew at once that he faced a sick man. Billy's lips parted, but his words evaporated. Henry's face was a pallid shade of green. His hollow eyes stared at the teenager, but expressed nothing.

"Leave me alone, boy," Henry whispered in a rasping voice.

The book under his left arm, Billy held out the rock in his right hand. "Look, Mr. Mason. It's a fossil. See?"

"Go away." Henry stepped back toward his kitchen.

"Here, feel it." Billy pushed into the pantry. "You can see the impression of fern-like leaves."

"Where's your father? Isn't he going to arrest me?"

Billy thought he smelled gasoline again. He stepped toward the kitchen as Henry stumbled backwards, caught himself, and leaned on the table. The emaciated old man was forced to sit as Billy glanced at the assortment of trash and containers on the table. What he didn't see between the milk carton and a fifth of whiskey was the bagged bottle of gasoline that Henry had carried back home from his abortive mission. Gasoline fumes had spread from the wet rag and wick that hung from the mouth of the bottle.

"So, answer me?" Henry said with effort. "I expected your father, not you."

"I had to tell him."

"Of course you did." The old man looked into Billy's eyes and tried to read their message. "Maybe you're a better man than your father." Suddenly he doubled over in pain.

Billy rushed to him, put his hand on his shoulder, and said, "I'll get help."

"No you won't." Henry straightened up. "Get away from me."

Billy backed off. "You're sick, Mr. Mason."

"Some men hate so much they perforate the linings of their stomachs."

"Why did you do it, sir?" The boy put his book and fossil rock on the table and seated himself across from Henry. "Was it the alcohol? Did something go click in your head?"

Henry struggled to sit up. He tried to stare Billy down. "Well, I'll be damned. You got a helluva lot of nerve, kid." Lacking enough strength to be harsher, he looked away and muttered something about evil and punishment. After several gasping breaths he managed to gaze into Billy's eyes and quote Scripture: "The Lord destroyed Sodom and Gomorrah."

Billy waited for more of an explanation. He kept looking into those hollow eyes, hoping for answers, praying for some sort of justification or anything that might help excuse the old man, even a little.

"Well, boy, did you get a good look? Did you see what you came to see?"

"I wanted you to know that I told my dad. That's why I came. I wanted to tell you first, before they came for you." Billy's eyes moistened. He looked down. "I wanted so much to like you, Mr. Mason."

With effort, Henry stood and turned his back on Billy. "Please go now."

"But I want you to tell me..."

"Go to your old man. Tell him I'll be right here waiting for him."

Billy didn't move.

"Get out of here."

The boy stood, and without another word walked through the pantry and into the October sunlight.

Minutes later Henry noticed that his gift to Billy, Andrew's plant book, and the fossil rock still rested on the table amidst the debris. He picked them up, and although pierced with pain, walked haltingly to the back door, fearful that the boy was far gone. To his surprise, Billy was sitting on the steps twisting honeysuckle vine around his fingers. At first Henry just looked and said nothing. Billy rose quickly, spun and backed off.

Stammering, Henry said, "Why... Why are you still here?"

Billy could not answer. He knew, however, that he had stayed because something was unresolved.

"Here, you forgot these." His hands trembling, the old man held out the book but lost control of the fossil. The rock dropped, hit one step then another, and fell to the ground.

Billy ignored the rock, locked his jaw and stared at Henry.

"Here, take the book," Henry said.

"It doesn't matter."

"It's yours."

"How can you burn people, but give me gifts?" Billy's visage was not unlike that of a thwarted child. With his mouth turned down, he gritted his teeth and squinted as his face flushed.

A deep sadness revealed itself in Henry's countenance, an expression far different than any Billy had seen before. The old man leaned against the rail and dangled the book in his hand. A look of beseeching kindness seemed to intersperse with that of sorrow, and Billy saw a man who was more akin to a benign Dr. Jekyll than a malevolent Mr. Hyde.

Billy stepped to the porch and reached for the book. "Thanks. I really do like it." He grasped it tightly, held it against his chest, and backed away. "I'm not sorry I climbed your cherry tree."

The old man was taken aback. Stunned for a moment, he gaped at Billy while holding his stomach. The boy misinterpreted Henry's expression, backed off, and turned to leave.

"Wait a minute!"

Billy spun around, but continued moving backward until he ran into a bushy spirea tangled with bindweed. There he stayed, his eyes focused on the gaunt, bent, belly-squeezing old man.

"Come back here." Henry's voice did not demand. It pleaded.

Stepping from the bush, Billy moved slowly toward the old man, only to stop about halfway.

"I want to show you something," Henry said.

Mason led Billy through the kitchen and, with painful effort, up the back stairs—dark, winding stairs to the second floor. The dull orange glow from the hallway light tinted the faces of man and boy as they passed the grim portrait of Grandmother Mason and stopped before the closed door to *The Room*.

"You wanted to see," said Henry as he turned the key and pushed open the door. "You wanted to know what was in here. That's why you climbed my cherry tree." He shuffled into the dark room. "Well, now you'll have your chance."

The boy hesitated.

"Come on."

Billy stepped into the room and immediately breathed stale

air and dust. He could see only a few thin threads of light that entered between the boarded-up shutters at the windows. Stopping just inside the room, he waited for his eyes to adjust to the darkness. Gradually he began to see disorder—a peculiar array of scattered objects.

Henry sat on a stool, reached down and turned on a table lamp that rested on the floor—a ship-in-the-bottle lamp with a nautical shade of discolored parchment, yellowed by age and scorched by heat. It gave little light and cast long shadows on the walls and ceiling that chilled Billy with an eerie feeling.

Billy's eyes darted about, taking in more than his mind could fathom. The bed frame was up against the wall, so bent out of shape that it was split into bizarre angles, as if someone of great strength had lifted, tossed and smashed it. Stretching from it across the floor, the mattress was in shreds, obviously pierced and slashed and bludgeoned again and again, its springs jutting out through piles of stuffing. An ax handle projected from its heavily mangled center. What might have been bed linens were torn, twisted and clinging to a broken headboard.

Dust balls shifted and drifted as Billy stepped here and there obviously fascinated by his findings.

While watching Billy, Henry made a feeble effort to stand, yet remained on the stool. He allowed his eyes to wander, except toward the battered bed. When the boy walked to the mattress, the old man locked his stare on the opposite wall.

Turning about, Billy glanced toward the upper reaches of the room where drastic temperature changes had peeled the wallpaper— discolored paper of sailboat design. Hanging from mid-ceiling was a ship's steering-wheel chandelier, draped in cobwebs.

Henry's eyes began to lack focus as time elapsed. His expression denoted meandering thoughts—recollections that tugged at his gaunt features and seemed to age him by the minute.

"This was your son's room, wasn't it?" Billy asked.

Henry did not respond, not even with flickers of awareness in his eyes.

"Are you okay, Mr. Mason?" Billy stepped close to the old man.

* * *

Blocks away in the Bannon house, Charley and Mary sat at the kitchen table, their heads hanging over their cups of coffee.

"Don't they wonder where you are?" Mary asked, distress punctuating her words. "You always said Saturday duty was all-day duty, and here you sit!"

"Captain George knows. So does the chief."

"But they don't know about him, do they? About Henry Mason?"

"Not yet. I'll take care of that."

"When? What are you waiting for? This is insane!" Mary stood and began pacing again.

"Sit down!"

"I can't."

"Let's give Billy a few more minutes."

"Maybe he's with Lori."

"No. Here's over there. I know it. I can feel it. I know how he thinks."

Mary stopped pacing and glared at her husband. "You do? Well, that's a breakthrough!"

Charley simply stared into his coffee cup.

Mary began pacing again. "I can't believe that any father—let alone a police lieutenant—would allow his son to powwow with a madman. That old lunatic might torture him or burn him or something."

"No."

"Please, Charley. Go get him before it's too late. He might get hurt."

"It won't happen. I know."

Mary stopped pacing and glowered again. "I wish you'd explain that!"

* * *

Billy watched as Henry shuffled toward a long pole with a clipper and saw blade at one end. It rested against the wall near a window. When the old man lifted it, Billy saw that a small bucket was attached at the clipper end.

Finally, Henry spoke in a whisper that was strangely ethereal, perhaps directed to himself rather than to Billy. "His cherry picker."

"Wow, how about that!" The teenager could see that the fruit-picker was contrived from a tree-pruning device. He overdid his enthusiasm in an effort to lift the old man's spirits. "That's great!"

"Even after he was gone, he still called me to the window. 'Watch me, Dad. Watch me.'"

The words puzzled Billy. But the slight smile on Henry's face gave him hope. In an effort to cultivate the mood, he quickly said, "That's cool, man. Really cool."

Henry stood with Andy's picker in hand and began to survey the scene. Finally he focused on one object then another, but still avoided the bed. When his eyes were captured by a glass-enclosed butterfly collection, Billy noticed and hurried toward it. The case hung on the north wall, unscathed, as if the perpetrator of the onslaught had not dared to touch such a fragile display.

"A blue swallowtail," Henry uttered just loud enough to reach the ears of Billy, who thought he heard a slight touch of pride in the old man's voice.

The boy was becoming less fearful of any rage, destruction, or shouts of hate and damnation. He was beginning to feel a bit of pride in himself for diverting Henry from the fury that surely had erupted in this room time and again. "Your son caught these? Wow! They're beautiful." Billy didn't know a blue swallowtail from a viceroy, but saw only one specimen that could be so named—a radiantly beautiful, iridescent blue butterfly in the center of the case.

Seconds later Billy was gazing on pots of dry earth and protruding roots. "He liked to grow things, didn't he?"

"Like his mother."

Billy felt in control, as if he were leading the old man through an obstacle course of memories, but avoiding booby traps.

Henry pointed toward an old bureau. "Andy made them." For the first time, he had uttered his son's name. Yet he kept his distance from the assemblage, even stepping back as Billy approached the statuettes.

A dozen clay figures, four and five inches high, intricately molded by patient hands, stood in thick dust on the bureau top. Guessing they were creatures of Andy's life, Billy wondered which ones gave pain and which gave happiness to the old man. Perhaps they even embodied hate and love. A woman. Was it Andy's mother? A dog. Was it his beloved pet? A boy. Perhaps his playmate. A soldier. Friend? Enemy?

What appeared to be a typewriter took Billy's attention. Centered on a grimy desk, it was thickly coated with ugly matter, perhaps at one time mold on a pasty or doughy substance. Now dry and crusty, it was blotched with blue-green. Gobs of the mush had dribbled onto the desk and hardened.

"Andy wouldn't always eat his oatmeal." The thought obviously upset Henry. His eyes darted in confusion as his lips quivered.

Billy feared a wrong turn, a trip wire, a pitfall. He attempted a rescue by pointing to a baseball bat jutting from a closet. "Hey, look at this." He reached for the bat. "Man, it's a genuine Louisville Slugger!" An Army brogan fell from the closet as the boy pulled and lifted the bat.

Henry caught sight of the shoe. It sent him plummeting into depression, anger and hate. He muttered words barely heard by Billy: "They defiled my house."

Billy looked from Henry to the brogan and back to Henry again. He sensed what had happened and damned himself for carelessness, but had no understanding of the whys and wherefores of the shoe's power. Distraction was surely the answer. And a monumental one suddenly flashed into Billy's head. The teenager lunged toward a window in the south wall, pushed up the sash, and struck the shutters with the bat. "Let's open these freakin' windows!" he yelled, praying that his attack would reap a Jekyll, not a Hyde. Swinging like a sandlot batter, he hit the shutters again, slightly dislodging them and the outside boards. He dropped the bat and pushed with his hands as his biceps bulged. Using a full-body thrust, he forced the shutters to give another inch, then stepped back to catch his breath. Seconds later he grabbed a chair and stood on it, held onto the window frame, and kicked the shutters. The teenager kicked again and again with apparent desperation until the shutters ripped open and the cross boards flew into the cherry tree, bounced from limb to limb and fell to the ground.

Billy squinted as sunlight streamed into the room from the

southeast sky—streamed in because the cherry tree had lost most of its foliage. The brightness fell freely across the dusty floor, lighting up objects that had not reflected sunlight in decades.

When the boy spun about he found Henry cowering in a far corner. He and the old man stared at each other, saying nothing as moments passed. Searching urgently for some answer or recourse, he shouted, "Come help me! Please!"

Billy attacked the second window after removing jagged pieces of glass. Using the bat, the chair, his fists and muscles, he pushed and kicked with renewed vigor as the old man approached him from behind. Henry reached around the boy and feebly pushed on the wood. Laughing loudly, the boy shouted, "That's it, Mr. Mason!" He then shoved with his shoulder until the second pair of shutters flew open, banged against the house and sent the wooden planks flying.

Boy and man looked at each other in triumph, then gazed here and there in wonder, peering through millions of tiny, bright, flashing particles of dust that swirled in the light. More cobwebs lit up, as did dust balls and thick fuzz on chests, overturned bureau drawers, scattered books and sundry items.

To Billy's amazement, the old man actually showed a sense of excitement. The look in his eyes enthralled the boy, who then raced to the back window, threw up the sash and punched and batted until the boards creaked and split. With one triumphant thrust he opened the third window and stood there in the brightness, looking down at the scattered boards, each caught in a tangle of overgrown shrubbery and vines.

A silhouette in the sunlit haze, Billy turned slowly and faced the old man. The room and all of its scattered objects were ablaze with light, a weird wonder that touched him with awe. Henry was part of the strange scene as he leaned on a window sill and gazed at his cherry tree.

Within moments, Henry turned and faced the bright room—a room transformed by fresh air and sunlight, a room so reshaped by light that it profoundly changed the old man who gazed upon it. And Billy recognized that change. Every piece and part of Andy's bedroom took on new form, altering the fragments of Henry's mind, reflecting in his eyes, and recasting the furrows of his countenance.

Billy stood still, allowing silent time to stretch.

Henry turned back to the window and the cherry tree. "Come here, Andy. I mean... I mean, Bannon. Come here. Sit on the windowsill."

The boy hesitated.

"Please?"

Billy looked at the old man, drew insight from his eyes, stepped to the window, picked up the cherry picker, thrust the bucket end into the branches of the tree, and sat on the sill.

Henry Mason's eyes moistened. "He was a good little boy. So happy. Strangers would smile at him, and I was so proud. I used to take him to the ballpark to see the A's play. And we'd take him to the zoo. He wondered why a kangaroo had a pocket. I tried to explain. He laughed. I can still hear him laugh. When Anna played songs and sang, he'd listen and smile. He liked marching bands, and all sorts of parades. He'd stand on a box and stretch his neck to watch the Mummers strut up Broad Street. Then I'd pick him up and hold him high."

Fiddling nervously with the pole, Billy knocked a few red-brown leaves from the tree.

Henry's vague smile and distant stare denoted drifting thoughts.

"What happened to your son, Mr. Mason?"

"What happened? Oh, didn't I tell you." The old man's expression changed. His eyes grew cold and the corners of his lips fell as his cheeks sank. "He died."

Chapter Twenty-Eight

Agray pin-stripped suit. A necktie. Henry hadn't worn a necktie in two decades. But he decided to dress for the occasion. Anna's favorite tie had been the red one with gray swirls. Where was it? Bottom drawer? Tie rack? Shirt drawer? His closets and dressers were in disarray, and that tie was probably buried under a tangle of clothes.

Weaker than ever, he cursed the demons that sucked away his strength. But it was important to dress. What better occasion than his arrest?

Henry tried to tie his shoe but was pulled to the floor by those demons. Stretching out, he breathed hard in an effort to relieve nausea and prevent a faint. A meager amount of blood returned to his head, enabling him to stand and stagger to the hallway. He backed down the stairs while gripping the banister. Clinging to the newel, he gathered a little strength, enabling him to walk toward the front door. He gripped the wall, made his way to the vestibule, and pulled on the doorknob.

At 2:30 p.m. Charley Bannon found Henry sitting in the doorway, his head against the doorjamb, his legs stretched onto the porch. After hurrying up the porch steps, the big cop stood looking down on Henry, who wore gray pin-striped trousers and a white shirt, unbuttoned and half tucked in. A red and gray necktie dangled from his neck.

"Why if it isn't Lieutenant Bannon," Henry whispered between gasps.

"You okay, old man?"

"No, not at all."

"I didn't think so. Be right back."

Charley returned to his car, leaned in and talked to Sergeant Brady at the wheel—a lanky, blond uniformed officer.

"Jake, I don't think we'll be going back to the station with him. He's in bad shape. Call for an ambulance." Charley stepped away from the car, only to return. "You stay here like we agreed. I still want to be alone with the old buzzard. You can cut out after the ambulance gets here. I'll ride with him."

A strange feeling—sadness, regrets of youth—permeated Charley as he glanced up at Mason House. He tried to shake it off as he hurried back to the porch where Henry was trying to lift himself.

"No!" Henry insisted when Charley reached out to assist him. The old man pulled himself up and held onto the railing. "I wanted to greet you on my feet."

"So, you're on your feet. Now don't be stubborn." Charley slipped his arm around Henry, held him tightly around the rib cage, and pulled him back down to the doorway step.

"Who the hell do you think you are?"

Charley sat next to him, stared straight ahead, and after a moment of thought asked, "Goddamn it, old man, what the hell have you been up to?"

"Watch your tongue, Bannon." Henry's voice was weak but gruff. "I haven't given you absolution yet."

"You stood for something, you know. To me, anyway."

"Humph!"

"Years ago, when you took justice into your own hands, you saved a kid who grew to thank you every night in his prayers. Why did you have to start playing judge, jury and executioner?"

"God wasn't doing his job."

"God doesn't throw Molotov cocktails."

"If you've come to arrest me, then arrest me, damn it!"

Charley hurt, from guts to gray matter.

Shrill sounds of the siren reached Mason House long before the green-and-white ambulance sped around the corner and pulled up alongside the police car. Henry didn't like the feeling of finality he experienced being hoisted, carried, and then closed inside the ambulance. Charley stayed at the old man's side. Emotionally unable to shape words, the big cop could comfort only through his presence.

Chapter Twenty-Nine

"So this is where you and Clarence hang out."

"Sometimes." Billy had never expected to sit on the curb in front of the deli with his dad, the big cop. No way. Nervously, he tossed more pebbles into the street than ever before.

"My old lady was a weak and whiny alcoholic," Charley said. "That's why I never talked about her, even when you asked. Frankly, I never wanted you to meet her. And my old man? Hell, I never really knew him. He gambled away the money that Mama didn't drink away, I know that. When I got older, I figured he must have slept around, 'cause he was never home. Anyway, I grew up angry as a hassled hornet. Mad at the world, I guess."

"Like Mr. Mason?"

"No. I never threw a bomb. I didn't have his kind of hate. It's crazy, kid, but he's the guy who patched me up. And then he goes schizo or something. Strange thing is, when he talks straight, he seems to know what he did."

"What's gonna happen to him? Is he dying?"

"The way I see it, he's sick in the head and the belly."

"So? Is he going to die?" Billy stopped tossing stones and looked at his father.

"Maybe."

Billy looked down into the gutter. Seconds passed before he said, "I gotta see Lori."

"Wait. Please. Look, Billy, about you and Lori. Mom said I should talk..."

"It's okay. You don't have to. You're not good at stuff like that anyway. You told me."

"You don't make it any easier."

Billy laughed nervously, shifted his buttocks, rubbed his sneakers in gutter grit, and started throwing pebbles again. "You can't say much anyway, Dad, after what you told me about that girl and all that other stuff." The boy immediately regretted his words. His face flushed.

"Don't throw it up to me, Billy. That's unfair. It wasn't easy for me to share all that. I told you because I didn't want you to be a stupid ass like me. Get it? Prove me wrong, and you're going to prove Mom wrong, too. She said you were the kind of guy I could be honest with."

"You can. I'm sorry."

Neither spoke for several moments.

"She's got the idea that confiding in you would bring us closer," Charley said.

"I know."

"You got anything you want to tell me?"

"I don't know. Not now, I don't think. Sometime maybe."

"That's good. I mean, that you'd come to me."

"Sure."

"I guess it's a matter of trust."

"Trust?"

"Yeah. I want to be able to trust you. And I don't want my garbage to stink up your life."

"It's okay, Dad. Really. You don't have to worry. Lori and me, we'll be all right."

"Here, I want you to have this." Charley unzipped his jacket and pulled out a notebook he had hidden against his chest. "It's got some stuff in it that I scribbled down long ago, from cases I handled." He flipped some pages. "Like this one about a guy who walked into the station and returned some baseball cards he stole. Some of it's kind of crazy stuff. Even funny. But there are lessons here. You know, about life. I don't know. Just thought you'd like to have it, not just because it teaches things, but because it's something personal from me."

"Thanks, Dad." Billy took the notebook and squeezed it nervously. "Hey, this is great. I didn't know you wrote things down like that. I'll read it all."

"Don't go wild on me, Billy."

"Dad! What are you getting at? You think I'm out gallivanting, looking for the good life?"

"No. Of course not. Anything but. You're making the most of what you've got. I know that. My God, you're always pocketing something from everything around you, whether it's from rocks, bugs, Mom's garden, Bobby's books or Mr. Mason. You reap from it all. And I'm damn proud of you. I never told you. I should have. So, now I'm telling you."

Billy tapped the notebook with his fingers, bit his lip, looked at his dad and smiled feebly.

"Your Mom, now she's special," Charley said. "She's always been the rudder that steered the family, you know." The big cop put his hand on Billy's shoulder and squeezed. "Me? I've been the stubborn ass who thought he was in charge."

Sheepishly, Billy said, "I think you're special, too, Dad."

"More like a guy stuck in a rut."

"No. What is it they say? A diamond in the rough?"

"I'll take that as a compliment. And I'll polish myself up a bit. And, now, I'm about to go on a hunt and do some real digging…"

"Digging?"

"Yeah. Digging."

Chapter Thirty

The rag and the long wick that intertwined around the neck of the bottle drew gasoline from inside, soaking the material that hung outside almost as much as that within. Fumes rose and evaporated into the room, allowing the fabric to suck up more liquid.

Gradually, the air in the kitchen held more and more gasoline vapor until it was ignited by the pilot gas-flame in the stove. The explosion shattered shelving and cabinet doors and sent china and glassware flying and smashing. The splatter of gasoline from the bottle spread fire quickly. Within seconds, flames were lapping at the wooden doors, cabinets and drawers. The old linoleum bubbled and then flared. Heavy coats of varnish and paint on the woodwork blistered, scorched and then flamed. The back stairway acted as a chimney or draft that drew smoke and fire toward the second floor. The old, wooden stairwell became a raging inferno with high-reaching flames roaring up through the narrow passage. Tongues of fire soon lapped around the doorway at the top of the steps and then spread into the second-floor hall, fed by painted walls and thick varnish on the floorboards. Within minutes, the blaze reached the upper portion of the front staircase.

Downstairs, the fire had spread to the dining room. It was feeding on the handsomely carved legs of the massive mahogany table. The heavy finish on the buffet began to crack, crinkle and blister after fire burned around the edge of the broadloom carpet and reached its legs. By the time flames had encircled the silver tea service, the shelves of the china closet were giving way to smoldering fire, collapsing one by one under the weight of the heavy willowware. Dinner plates, cups, saucers and serving dishes crashed to the floor.

Fire spread rapidly into the living room and the intense heat began to wilt the plants. The succulent leaves of the giant jades literally cooked, the thick fleshy tissue sizzling and dripping water as the leaves wilted into translucent globs and then darkened and fell to the floor. The huge leaves of the fiddleleaf figs turned brown and then smoldered into ash as the feathery ferns and palm trees blackened and shriveled. A six-foot rubber tree nodded and hung its broad oval leaves as they curled into contorted, liver-colored plummets.

The smooth finish on Anna's harpsichord began to crinkle and blister as flames lapped at its legs. Each flare-up, fed by resins in the wood, led to another as the fire moved up toward the body of the instrument. The broad surface burned from within until the flames burst through the center, drawing in oxygen that turned the entire harpsichord into a roaring torch.

After flames wrapped around the newel in the front hall, fire moved up the banister and met the blaze on the second floor where each room was already engulfed. Scattered objects in Andrew's room carried the fire to the bed and the ripped mattress where the ax handle burned like a giant candle in a flaming cake. The desk and worktable blazed and the dry oatmeal on the typewriter smoldered. Roaring, the fire spread swiftly in the dusty, long-closed bedroom because the windows, opened by Billy, fed the blaze with oxygen. It was from Andrew's room that the flames leaped outside into the gray of evening, lighting up the cherry tree, the tall privet hedge and the cemetery wall.

Seconds later the kitchen wall gave way, and the entire back of the tall Victorian house was ablaze by the time the police and the first fire company arrived. Within minutes, another volunteer company was on the scene while sirens of a third and a fourth echoed through the night. Firemen smashed windows, hacked doors with their axes, squirted heavy streams of gushing water into the house and wet down the outside walls. The towering house that for years had reached quietly skyward, dominating the landscape, was soon a gigantic torch. Flames shot well above its rooftop, lighting up the cemetery, turning the night clouds aglow, and reflected for miles.

Crowds of onlookers grew as the screaming sirens and brilliant flare in the sky drew residents from near and far. Police blockades held them back from the intersection where a maze of hoses carried water from fireplugs. Gasps and sighs of horror added to the roar each time flames flashed into the open or a section of wall collapsed.

Billy stood in the midst of the north-side crowd that had been forced up the street. He couldn't speak. Tears streamed down his quivering cheeks. His lips were parted, his head thrown back, his face and glassy eyes reflecting the red-orange glow. Lori pushed through the crowd, calling his name, but he didn't hear her. She elbowed her way, excusing herself as she bumped shoulders at left and right "Billy! Billy, I'm here!" Billy!" She reached him as a portion of the front wall collapsed sending sparks and embers flying as flames flared and roared. Wrapping her arms around him from behind, she held tightly and rested her chin on his shoulder. "My God, Billy! Oh, my God!"

* * *

Seeing his lamp aglow, Mary looked in on Billy long past bedtime. She found him still in his jeans and T-shirt, lying atop his bed, his fingers linked behind his head on the pillow.

"Are you okay?" she asked as she stepped toward him.

"I guess."

"Come on, now. Get yourself ready. You can't stay up all night."

"I hope they don't tell Mr. Mason. You don't think they'll tell him, do you? About his house?"

"Maybe not. He's a sick old man." Mary leaned over her son and pushed hair from his forehead. "Get some sleep, okay?" She smiled plaintively and tossed a kiss. After studying his face for seconds, she turned and stepped toward the door.

"Mom," he called in a whisper.

She spun around. "Yes?"

"Y'know something? Dad's an okay dude. He's really an okay dude."

Chapter Thirty-One

"Never saw such a fire," Charley said for the fifth time. "Never. Not around these parts." He leaned on the kitchen table and rubbed his temples with his fingers. "Bitch of a thing, I'll tell you. Bitch of a thing."

Mary poured more coffee into his cup.

"Just a little."

"Say when."

"Stop. That's plenty."

She sat across from him. "I've seen you upset, Charley, plenty of times. But not like this. You're downright morose."

"Well, it's a bitch of a thing."

Sunday morning was almost over. Mary and her husband had been tossing words back and forth since 10 a.m., having slept late after a short and fitful night. Billy had awakened early, despite little sleep, and had left the house in a noisy hurry, leaving his parents to fret over his behavior.

"I wish he had eaten breakfast," Mary said. "Maybe he grabbed a banana or something."

"I know where he is. He's over there staring at the ashes."

"I'm getting a little tired of Henry Mason."

"You don't understand. It's just so damn cruel. Why couldn't the old bastard's life end with trumpets blowing or something? Why this?"

Bobby thumped down the stairs and stepped into the kitchen, his cherry red backpack tugging on his shoulders. "I'm heading out."

"So soon?" his mother asked, showing dismay with a frown. "Aren't you staying for dinner? I'm fixing pot roast, your favorite."

"Sorry, Mom. Next time. Okay? I gotta hit the library. I have a paper due for Jensen's class."

"You never go back to school this early on Sunday," Mary said as she scowled at Bobby, then glanced at her husband.

Charley's mind was elsewhere. His eye's focused somewhere beyond the walls.

"I'll call tonight," Bobby said. "Okay? I want to talk to Billy, anyway." He turned and hurried off.

Mary reached across the table, took Charley's hand and squeezed it. "I can't say I blame Bobby for heading back to school early, what with the mood around here." She saw distance in Charley's eyes, lifted her eyebrows, sighed, and pulled back her hand.

Charley didn't respond to Mary's comment. Still dwelling on Mason, he said, "If the old man survives, he'll end up in prison or the nut house. I guess that infuriates me more than anything. What the fuck. I can't do anything about it."

"Hey big guy, that's one word we don't allow in this house. Keep it for the cop shop."

"Sorry."

"He did kill people. Remember?"

"And you keep reminding me!" Charley glowered.

"You're touchy as hell. I know you're upset, but don't take it out on me." Mary carried the coffeepot back to the stove, then leaned against the refrigerator and stared at her husband, first with a knowing look, then with a question in her eyes.

"Why are you looking at me that way?" he asked gruffly. "Don't answer. I know. I get the picture. Y'can't figure why I'm so fucked up over... Excuse me. I mean, messed up over this thing when I've drenched myself in bloody murders and rapes, yet played it cool at home."

"You said it, Charley. I keep thinking of old Mrs. Kelly getting stabbed, and those poor Hobbs kids getting strangled by their father."

"This is different."

"Apparently. And it's not just because of Billy, is it?"

Charley knocked over his cup, jumped, and pushed his chair back with a screech. "Ouch! Damn it!"

"Here, let me get that." Mary leaned across the table and wiped up the spill with a napkin. "Are you okay?"

Charley nodded and waved Mary off as he wrapped his handkerchief around his hand. "The things I want to say, I can't. I don't seem to know how."

"Oh?" Mary lifted her eyes, looked uncomfortable for a moment, and waited.

But Charley shifted his thoughts. "Somebody's gotta tell Mason about the fire. Things have to be settled. Property and all that."

"Is he well enough to be told?"

"Hell, I don't know. I suppose it's up to the doctors."

"Who's going to tell him?"

"Frank Matthew was the investigating officer, but I told him I'd take care of it. I mean, what the hell, the old guy has no family, unless you count his son Andy. And who the hell knows where he's hiding out."

"But you shouldn't have to..."

"Maybe I want to." Frustration showed in Charley's expression. "Not really, I guess. But in a way. I mean, I'm more family than anyone else he's got."

"You are?"

Charley was quick to divert the conversation again: "Let me tell you something that'll really scramble your noodle. Billy wants to tell him."

"What?"

"You heard me. If Mason has to be told, Billy wants to be the person to do it."

"Our Billy?"

"We don't know any other Billy, do we?"

"You must be kidding."

"No way. He wants to."

"Oh, my." Mary's whisper was almost a gasp. She lifted her fingers to her mouth.

"Did you talk to him last night?"

"Briefly."

"So did I. My freakin' mind wouldn't let me sleep. I got up and went to the bathroom, saw his light was still on, and poked my head in. He asked me who was going to tell Mason about his house, then insisted that he's the only one who could do it right. Can you believe that? He's afraid someone else'll bungle the job. Even me."

Mary was pensive and puzzled with thought. Her eyes drifted.

"This thing between Billy and Mason," Charley muttered. "It's like the old guy's still playing games with me, still holding on."

Mary grasped no meaning from Charley's words, primarily because she didn't focus on them. "Maybe he should do it."

"What?"

"Maybe Billy should do it. If he wants to, maybe he should."

Charley was taken aback. He gaped at his wife.

"I'm not sure," she went on. "But think about it. Seems to me that if a teenage boy wants to take on that kind of responsibility, it shouldn't be denied him. It's a big step in growing up. Most adults wouldn't want to do it. He must think he knows how, and he shouldn't have to carry that sort of thing, unfinished, never tested, for the rest of his life."

Charley's eyes floated here and there as he recalled the burden of obligation strapped on him by Mason.

"Take him with you," Mary continued. "He might say the right thing. Who knows?"

"But maybe it's my place."

"Why? To pay off some sort of debt?"

Charley was startled, couldn't hide his jolt, but forced himself to let the remark pass without comment.

Mary didn't take her eyes off of him. "So? Say something."

"Well, as for Billy talking to Mason... I suppose..." Charley interrupted himself. "To tell you the truth, you amaze me."

"Oh?"

"You're steering the ship, again. I told Billy you were the rudder in this family, even though I pretended to be."

Mary couldn't help but smile. Then she offered her knowing stare—the one that always churned her husband's gut.

Charley struggled, then said, "Okay. If the doctors permit it, Billy goes with me, and we stand side-by-side at Mason's bedside. How's that? Now, about that other matter." He glanced out the window, then down at the table as he twirled his fingers. "I'm not really afraid to tell you the things I dumped on Billy. Actually, my tongue keeps shaping the words. There's something inside of me that keeps pushing me, even though you've let me know again and again there's no need. I suppose I'm the one with the need. It's just that it's embarrassing. Maybe I'm ashamed. So, I keep putting it off. I never wanted you to think of me as anything but... How can I explain. When you've been playing a certain role for years, and then..."

Chapter Thirty-Two

Like many a hospital room, Henry's was a white-walled unit for two, the beds separated by a green curtain pulled around the patient when needed for such private occasions as shaving body hair or voiding into a bedpan.

Henry was incensed by the matronly, motherly, happy-talking practical nurse who insisted that he could get out of bed and sit on a bedside commode. Well aware that he couldn't, he warned her— "Keep your goddamn hands off me!"—before making a reluctant effort and being hit hard by those demons that sucked away his strength. As she guided him to the commode, he suffered nausea and a pre-faint sweat, and was suddenly jarred by an insane urgency to throw himself to the floor.

Red faced and vehement, the full-breasted practical nurse clasped her hands on Henry's shoulders and tried to hold him on the commode. She insisted, "Doctor says you can do it this way." With a sudden thrust he broke from her and threw himself on the bed as intravenous lines, wires and poles flew in all directions. "No, no, you can't do that!" the nurse yelled. "Stop it! You're breaking everything!"

The explosive incident stopped traffic in the hallway, drew a cluster of gapers to the doorway, and led to a decree from the head nurse: henceforth, a bedpan for Henry Mason.

Now stretched flat on his bed, Henry was being reattached to IV lines and wires, despite his protests. Choking and strangling, he caused frustration and impatience in a Pakistani intern assigned to push a narrow hose up his nose and down his gullet. Henry slapped the tube away twice before the intern finally succeeded. Thanks to persevering nurses, the old man was once again being fed intravenously through one arm while blood was being transfused through the other. This, his seventh transfusion, obviously would not be his last. More pints were standing by. He had arrived at the hospital having lost 40 percent of his blood.

Herman Dunn, a gregarious house painter, age 55, occupied the other bed. His lengthy spells of chitchat annoyed Henry to the extreme. Dark-eyed and pug-nosed, Herman was a broad-shouldered man with a solid jaw and little hair. His steady stream of visitors talked more than he did and irritated Henry as much as the nose tube.

Grumbling and talking to himself, Henry was alert enough to know that his much-abused stomach was the cause of his internal bleeding—inordinate bleeding that failed to stop despite heavy infusion of a new drug just released for use in the United States and being hailed as a miracle drug for ulcer victims. While physicians waited for results, two surgeons stood by for possible removal of Henry's stomach on quick notice. The catch was, the old man was too weak for an operation.

A repelling stench filled the room.

"Herman, what on earth is that horrible odor?" the painter's wife exclaimed.

"That's me!" Henry bellowed.

An hour later Herman Dunn was moved to another room, while Henry's ill-smelling flatulence spread into the hallways. The old man overheard a nurse: "My God, what are we going to do? Evacuate the whole wing?"

Another transfusion. Another. And another. Still the blood poured into his stomach and putrefied his bowels. Henry began to taste blood, sensed an oncoming eruption, and yelled in panic none too soon. Nurses began scurrying about for pans and bowls. Vomiting was unpleasant enough, let alone the disgorging of blood by violent upheavals that ripped his guts.

"My God, now it's coming out both ends of him!" exclaimed a skinny blonde to a chubby brunette as they passed each other in the bucket brigade.

For Henry, the spewing seemed to last an interminable time. But it did end, and the nurses set to work cleaning the old man, changing his hospital gown and bed linens, and checking his tubes. They could offer little comfort through medication. Strict orders called for no sedatives, other than a muscle relaxant injected into his buttocks every few hours. So they tried happy talk and pillow fluffing.

"I want to see Andrew," Henry muttered.

"Who?" asked the chubby brunette.

"My son, Andrew. I want to see him."

"How can we reach him."

Henry failed to answer.

"Mr. Mason? How can we reach your son?"

"I don't know." He turned his head away from the nurse. "Forget it."

Charley and Billy waited down the hall in the solarium, among patients and Boston ferns and checkerboards, while the nurse catered to Henry's needs.

"You know, Billy, I was thinking of asking around a little bit to see if I might find Andrew Mason," Charley said. "Maybe I can pick up a lead somewhere."

"Mr. Mason said he's dead."

"No way. Maybe in Mason's eyes he's dead. That's the way the old guy wants it, I guess. Or, at least, thinks he wants it. He might be fooling himself. Put 'em face-to-face and no telling what might happen. Could be ugly, but I doubt it. No harm in finding out, though, is there?"

The nurse signaled, and Charley stretched to relieve tension. Billy led the way to Mason's room while his father followed and milled thoughts in attempts to form appropriate sentences.

Despite the nurse's warning, the stench nearly pushed Charley and Billy back into the hallway, but they fought off their impulses, gained control and stepped toward Mason's bed.

Henry was dozing among a flood of images, feelings and sounds—movement of the gurney, bright lights, a closed curtain, whispers among hovering doctors and nurses.

Suddenly conscious of visitors, Henry opened his eyes and

rolled his head toward them. "God help me! Both of you. As if one Bannon isn't enough."

Looking over Billy's shoulder, Charley forced a smile and asked, "They fixing you up?"

"Hell no!"

Awkward silence followed as Charley shifted and Billy bit his lower lip.

"Breezy day." Charley offered some small talk. "But the sun's out."

"Mr. Mason," Billy began, "something happened to..."

"We've got some damn, lousy news for you," Charley interrupted. "I might as well spit it out fast and get it over with. Wish there was a better way." He hated the sound of his own words.

Henry showed little expression.

"You see, there was this fire..."

"Let me tell him, Dad," Billy interjected. He gulped air as he gained control of himself, then spurted words almost too fast—words that had been going around and around in his head. "Your house burned down, Mr. Mason. Your, big, wonderful house. And everyone's so sorry. That house meant a lot to us kids. It was special."

Henry didn't move except to fix his eyes on Billy.

"It's hard to explain," Billy said, "but your house was something for us kids to talk about and wonder about, to look at. It was our Halloween house, our storybook house. We let it play on our imaginations."

Charley was nonplused by Billy's words. His throat tightened as a sense of pride grew from his sudden awareness of his son's insight.

"I'll always remember it until the day I die," Billy continued as he let his heart lead his head. "Your house will always be here." The teenager touched his forehead. "It'll never go away."

Charley's pride continued to expand as he marveled at his son's sagacity.

"Thanks, Mr. Mason. Thanks for your house." Billy was so intent and sincere that his eyes and hands and body reflexes told the story as much as his words. "And thanks for taking me inside and showing me things."

Infirm as he was, the old man could feel Billy's intensity, but said nothing. He turned away and looked toward the window.

Billy wanted to say more, but Henry's reaction, or lack of it, troubled the boy and flushed away his thoughts.

Finally Henry spoke in a guttural whisper: "Is it all gone?"

"You might say that," Charley said. "Part of the north wall is still standing."

Henry kept looking toward the window. He envisioned the fire, then tried to erase the image, but it kept returning in flashes.

"Mr. Mason, I collected a few things from the ashes," Billy said. "I have a sack full. I'll clean them up and save them for you."

Henry didn't respond.

"I'll question you later about other things," Charley said. "The Philadelphia police want to talk, too. But I'll put them off."

Billy thought his father's words were untimely. He grimaced and kicked Charley's foot—not once, but twice. After a few glances at each other, the Bannons stood ill at ease waiting for whatever. Seconds of silence elapsed before they looked at one another again, this time to ask with eyes, brows and shrugs: Shall we stay or leave?

Suddenly, Henry turned his head and stared at Charley. In a tremulous voice he said, "Find Andrew for me."

The words sent a tingle through Billy's body as he recalled his father's words in the solarium. He looked at Charley with wide, questioning, beseeching eyes while nodding again and again.

"I'll try," Charley said without hesitation, although he reminded himself that he was not in the lost-persons division. "Captain Mullen has plenty on the docket for me. But I'll see what I can do."

Henry kept his red and swollen eyes on Charley, struggled to suck in air, then said, "Find him for me."

"Believe me, I'll try. Somehow I'll fit it around other things."

Billy was annoyed. He wanted no qualifications from his dad. "He'll do it, Mr. Mason. He'll find him."

This time it was Charley's turn to kick Billy. But his eyes stayed on Henry as the heel of his shoe struck the boy's ankle. "My debt is paid off, old man. If I do it, it's because I want to. Understand? Hell, you won't believe this, but I was chewing on the idea long before you spit it out. Frankly, I was hoping to shove Andy at you, like it or not."

Henry attempted to sneer, but was too weak to carry it off. "Damn right I don't believe you." Turning away once more, he struggled again to close out disturbing images. His mind's eye saw the bottle of gasoline in his kitchen. He envisioned the fire, and pictured Anna's harpsichord, then her plants—green flesh that he had nurtured through the years in a direct line from her. He gave in and permitted a view of Andy's room, but tried to purge an intrusive vision of flames lapping at his son's treasures. The ache in his heart equaled that in his belly.

The brunette nurse stepped into the room and tapped Charley's shoulder.

"I guess we have to go, old man," Charley said.

Billy added, "I'll be back, Mr. Mason. You can count on it."

As the visitors edged toward the door, Henry tried to turn his head again, but failed to find the energy. "Sorry about the stink," he muttered.

* * *

After midnight.

Charley rolled over in bed. He adjusted his pillow, pulled on the sheet, and turned toward his wife.

"Mary, are you awake?

"Hummm."

"Are you awake?"

"Well, I am now."

"You were right."

"About what?"

"I didn't know Billy. I really didn't know him."

"Uh-huh."

Charley turned his pillow, flipped over, yanked the sheet again and scrunched it under his chin. Seconds later he said, "Mary, you still awake?"

"Mmmm."

"I've got a little vacation time coming. I'm thinking of moving it up, if they let me. I could use the extra days now."

Suddenly Mary was really awake. She sat up and switched on the lamplight. "Where are we going?" she asked with a touch of sarcasm.

"Mary, listen to me. I don't have any choice. I have to look for Andy Mason. Arsonist, murderer, or whatever the old man is, he still should see his son before he dies."

"Is he going to die?"

"Death, prison, booby hatch—does it really matter? And whether he likes it or not, Andy should see his father before it's too late. Regret is sometimes worse than the hate that separates men."

Mary smiled poignantly.

Charley could not interpret her response. He looked at her and asked, "Remember what you said about Billy? How he should tell Mason about the fire if that was his calling? Well, that feeling, that need, that whatever you want to call it—it's inside of me, and it's not going to go away."

Chapter Thirty-Three

Strapped on a gurney by taut sheets, Henry was wheeled by a slim, dark-haired orderly who said nothing to him, but spoke cheerfully to nurses and others in the hallways and elevator. Two floors up, and he was pushed down another corridor, then left alone against the wall for what seemed an interminable length of time. His anxiety mounted, primarily because he was shackled, immobilized, unable to scratch an itch. Whatever the medics intended next, Henry wished they would get on with it. He sought the attention of a nurse, then an orderly, but to no avail. Panic set in, not so much because he cared what happened to him, but because he wanted it to happen faster. What seemed an hour was but 15 minutes.

All this without a cigarette to smoke.

Although it was an eternity for Henry, about 40 more minutes elapsed before he was wheeled to a monstrous machine—a scanner governed by a gray-haired, stocky man garbed in white. The technician smiled matter-of-factly and looked Henry up and down with pale blue eyes magnified by thick eyeglasses. "Here we go now," he said as he elevated Henry. "One, two, three," and he shoved the old man under the waiting eyes of the scanner. "Now drink this and keep drinking it. Don't stop." The technician poured a glass of milky white liquid and held it to Henry's lips. "Don't stop, now." Each long, breathless swallow was followed by the hum of the machine as it positioned Henry and telescoped its lenses toward his guts.

Henry was back in his room by noon, and the 15th pint of blood was attached to the IV line that entered his left arm. Despite the transfusions, blood was not adequately supplying his brain, making his hospital ordeal much more traumatic because of strange aberrations. The feelings that plagued him—the downward pull, the sapping of strength, the eerie other-world sensation—would have created fears in the strongest of men. To combat illusions, he struggled to channel his thinking. But the efforts were often too difficult. Sometimes his thoughts slipped into a strange abyss, yet at other times they traveled to memories he was too weak to avoid.

Of Andy:

"Now I lay me down to sleep, I pray thee Lord my soul to keep, if I should die before I wake..."

"Daddy, what makes snow?"

"Frozen rain."

"Miss Brown says sleet is frozen rain."

"Snow comes from water in the clouds."

"Does that mean snow is frozen clouds?"

"You might say that."

"Good night, Daddy."

"Good night, Andy."

Of summertime and playtime: *Down front at the park concert, chasing lightening bugs. Biting into a hot dog. Mustard on his T-shirt.*

Of fall and winter and school: *His lunch box. A banana and a peanut-butter sandwich. "A, B, C, D, E, F, G..." Running in the schoolyard. Climbing the jungle gym. 1 + 1 = 2 and 2 + 2 = 4 and 3 + 3 = 6 and... Drawing pictures. "This is you, Daddy, on a horse. And this is Mommy, sweeping the porch."*

Of springtime: *Under the cherry tree. Amidst a pink rain of blossoms. Blowing dandelion seeds to count the kids... "Happy birthday to you, happy birthday to you, happy birthday dear Andy, happy birthday to you."*

Visual recollections darkened, only to brighten again.

Andy chasing a yellow balloon. Laughing, laughing, and laughing again. A bee stung Andy on the cheek. He cried. Crying, crying, and crying again. Andy wore his white sailor suit.

"Mr. Mason." Dr. Otto Sherman tried to get Henry's attention. "Mr. Mason, are you awake?" Almost shoulderless, the physician was a hook-nosed, dark-eyed, thin-lipped man with a bulging belly and sagging jowls. His sparse hair was brushed tightly to his scalp.

"Andy?"

"No, Mr. Mason. It's Dr. Sherman."

"Huh?"

"It's Dr. Sherman. Can you hear me?"

"What is it?"

"We didn't get all the information we needed from the barium X-rays, so we want to try something else. We still can't tell if you have an ulcer in the opening to the duodenum, and this is vital in the event we must operate."

Henry was frustrated by his difficulty in following the doctor's words. His eyes darted as his lips quivered.

"You have more than just an ulcer problem, and that complicates things," the physician continued. "You have what we call hemorrhagic gastritis. In other words, you have general bleeding in the stomach."

"So. Get on with it."

"Well, it's required that I explain this." Dr. Sherman pulled nervously on his left ear.

"Whatever you say. So, do what you have to do. I don't need an explanation."

"We want to place a tube down your throat and into your stomach and take a look around. And we don't have time to waste."

"So, get on with it."

"Well, it's necessary that I explain the procedure. It's not pleasant, but we can't give you an anesthetic, you understand, because of your condition."

"So. You just told me."

"Just so you understand the procedure and consent to it."

"Do I have a choice?"

"I wanted you to realize..."

"So, I realize." Henry turned away from the physician and gazed toward the upper corner of the room. His stare was distant but inward.

"The procedure will be carried out by Dr. Louis Madera, a gastrointestinal specialist."

"I don't care if it's Jesus Christ!"

Henry had hours to think about the upcoming periscopic look-see into his stomach. Long before the orderly came to wheel him away again, his mind rode a roller coaster in and out of dark and light. From a frightening abyss he rose to clear consciousness, dipped again, then vacillated between now and then.

"And, flinging himself by the side of the dying monkey, he gathered him close to his breast, regardless of the blood that poured over him, and stroking tenderly the little head that had nestled so often in his bosom..."

Andy reached out to the book and put his fingers on the picture of Toby Tyler and his beloved monkey. "Why did that have to happen, Daddy? Why would anyone kill Mr. Stubbs?"

"That's what Toby asked."

"But why would anyone do that?"

"I don't have a good answer, Andy. Some people are cruel. They shouldn't be, but sometimes they are. Others are sick and can't help themselves. Anyway, Toby had to learn to live with it. Maybe it was good that he learned about death as a boy."

"Why?"

"Because he'd have to face it later. He'd have to understand."

The slim, dark-haired orderly startled Henry as he slid the gurney alongside the bed. The old man stared wildly, then focused on the brunette nurse who smiled down on him in an effort to comfort. Together, the nurse and orderly maneuvered Henry onto the gurney.

The young orderly interspersed his hallway and elevator chitchat—none of it aimed at Henry—with the humming of God Bless America, infused in him by Kate Smith's rendition, played before every Philadelphia Flyers hockey game. His mind was on hockey and his girlfriend, not on this old man. But then he didn't relate to oldness any more than his gurney passenger related to him or anyone else in the hospital. Because he was so sick, Henry allowed the agony-of-self to close out much of his surroundings. More than that, his inclination toward reclusion had not totally vanished simply because of Billy Bannon.

Henry's sharpest spurts of unadulterated thought included fearful notions that Andrew might not be found in time.

Secured in position, Henry could see little more than lights and faces glaring down on him. He saw the distorted face of Dr. Madera, the close view enlarging the physician's dark, penetrating eyes and elongating his chin and nose. As for the assisting nurse, the close-up of her mousy face turned her automatic smile into a fiendish grin.

"Don't gag, now," Dr. Madera said as the nurse made certain that Henry's legs and arms were tightly restrained—essential in this case, since the patient could not be anesthetized.

To Henry, the tube looked like a garden hose as it came at him. Inside, it felt like a lead pipe as it scraped his esophagus.

"Don't gag, now," repeated Dr. Madera.

Henry gagged and gagged again as the doctor pushed. Thick phlegm oozed up around the tube and into his mouth.

"Don't gag, now," repeated the physician as he continued to shove.

Henry surely would have pulled the "garden hose" from his mouth if he could have ruptured his restraints and freed his hands. He gagged.

"Don't do that," Dr. Madera insisted.

After the look-see was completed, Henry lay weak, limp, quiet. In time, he was wheeled back to his room, but not to stay. By dinner hour he was in the Intensive Care Unit, closely monitored.

That night, sleep sucked Henry into a dark whirlpool. Again and again he reached out to a familiar figure, only to have it turn and reveal itself as a beast—once a half man, half elephant with blood dripping from its trunk. He fought to keep himself awake. Each time he dozed he could feel the suction of the dark, whirling pit and its unearthly, echoing sound. The fight to stay awake drained his already exhausted body.

"You were hallucinating because of lack of oxygen in the brain," Dr. Sherman explained with unusual compassion the next morning as he took a chance and administered a light sedative to Henry.

Minutes later a nurse attached the 20th pint of blood to the IV line in Henry's left arm. She was a quiet-spoken woman with a gentle smile, soft features, smooth skin and amber hair, reminding Henry of his wife.

The nurse adjusted his pillow. "Are you comfortable?"

Henry failed to respond. He simply gazed at her, then far beyond her.

Anna at the harpsichord playing Sweet Mystery of Life.

Nursing Baby Andrew on a swing under the cherry tree.

Sunday noon. After church. Anna in a broad picture hat. Walking hand-in-hand with little Andy along the creek amidst the colors of spring. Bright yellow-green. Clumps of violets and buttercups.

"What's this, Mommy?"

"I think it's a windflower. Take it to Daddy. He knows."

Chapter Thirty-Four

Mid-afternoon.

On the way home from school Billy and Lori stopped to see the ashes.

The remaining portion of the north wall of Mason House was gone. So were the bulldozers. The ground was level, except for a pile at one side—a heap of ruins yet to be hauled away. Billy and Lori sat shoulder to shoulder on the curb across the street, trying to adjust to the new look. The old crooked garage was still there, along with a few broken trees and trampled bushes on the edge of the property. The charred cherry tree stood alone. Its scorched and blackened branches reached out and up like soot-covered tentacles in prayer—grabbing at nothing, sad in Billy's eyes, a dark silhouette of mourning. The boy wondered if any life remained in the tree. All he could do was hope. In dismay, he pictured the flames roaring through its branches, an image that he knew would be with him forever.

On the morning of his search through the ashes, Billy had blackened his hands on burnt bark as he searched for life. Stabbing a limb with a rusty steel rod, he had been saddened to find it soft, brittle and coarse like charcoal.

"Those lead soldiers I told you about," Billy said, "the ones I found in the ashes, the ones the heat didn't melt into funny-looking globs, I washed them clean."

"What else did you find?"

"A lot of stuff."

Lori wanted more of an answer, but she let it pass. She scanned the scene, then said, "It looks so different. All my life that house was there."

"I still see it," Billy said. "I always will."

"I keep thinking of us sneaking behind it and into the cemetery night after night."

"And trying to look through those windows."

"And you, climbing that tree." Lori squeezed Billy's hand. "I still don't understand why Mr. Mason did what he did."

"He was angry. Too angry."

"Mom says if all of us went around burning and bombing things we didn't like there'd be nothing left."

"Maybe he was alone too much, and everything got mixed up and distorted in his head. Imagine being alone day and night, haunted by your thoughts."

"He didn't have to be alone, did he?"

Billy twiddled his thumbs as he thought. "I don't know."

"What's going to happen to him?"

"If he lives?" Billy looked at Lori.

She nodded.

"I guess he'll stand trial for murder."

Lori glanced down at the gutter, then up at the garage. "Did they take away his car?"

"I don't know. I didn't look."

"Don't you want to?"

"I guess." Billy put his arm around Lori's waist, stared at the cherry tree for a moment, then looked down. "Do you think we'll ever walk back there again, behind the hedge, to hop the wall?"

"I don't know."

Billy grew tense. He pulled his arm away from Lori and pinched his lip. "We never talk about that night."

"What night?"

"You know. In the cemetery."

Lori said nothing.

"I know why we don't talk about it. If I said it was the most wonderful, beautiful, fantastic thing that ever happened to me, you'd be upset and think I didn't care, that I wanted more, that I thought you were just some loose thing to be had again, or something like that. Then again, if I said it was wrong and we should have waited, you'd feel ashamed of what we did. You'd think less of yourself for giving in. You'd think I saw you as some slut or something. In either case, you'd be wrong. Totally wrong."

"Why are we talking about this?"

"Because we have to. It was my doing. I pushed too hard. If there's any blame, it's mine. I'll always think you're the most wonderful girl in the world. I love you. As for that night... Well, I'm glad it happened and I'm sorry it happened. That's right. Glad and sorry at the same time. It really was the most fantastic thing that ever happened to me. I relive it over and over. I don't go to bed at night without reliving it. To me it was a piece of heaven on earth. But I'm sorry, too, because of the gap or silent barrier or whatever that it created between us. I'm sorry because it made you worry about my feelings toward you. Believe me, my feelings are stronger than ever. And I don't care what they say about sixteen-year-old love."

Lori wrapped her arms around Billy and held tightly until a car approached. After it passed, the teenagers scampered across the street. Billy began rooting through the remaining pile of rubble as Lori raced to the garage.

"Billy, it's still here. The Packard. It's still in the garage."

Billy heard Lori, but something in the pile of debris caught his eye. He hurried to it and tried to pull it from under burnt timbers. "Lori, it's the innards of the harpsichord! The strings! Look!"

* * *

Hours later, as Lori waited at home for her mother, she was struck by a sudden urge and dashed to the refrigerator. Within minutes she was dicing steak and tossing the pieces into a frying pan. As she seared the meat in butter, she sliced mushrooms and minced onions.

Candles burned on the dining table when Evelyn Lippincott arrived home exhausted. "The upper-ups were in from Chicago," she said before noticing the table settings in the dining room. "And Tobin was a wreck. He was on me from the start." She sighed loudly, then said, "What smells so good?" Seconds later she was peering at the candle-lit table, a platter of peas in a ring of rice, and a serving dish steaming with steak laced with sour cream. At center was a bouquet of bur-marigold weeds that had withstood the winds of October. "Oh, my!"

"Surprise!"

"Oh, honey! It's so beautiful! And I'm so hungry, too."

"Sit down before it gets cold." Lori began pouring an inexpensive Bordeaux into seldom-used goblets.

"Wine, no less!"

"I don't know why you've been keeping it. I swear, it's been in the cupboard for years." Lori set the bottle aside, sat across from her mother and smiled broadly. "There!"

"Thank you, honey. It really is beautiful."

"It was cool, Mom, doing it this way. Fixing it up special for a change. Quickies at the kitchen table get to be a bore. Someday I want to make fabulous meals for Billy night after night after night. It'll be so much fun!"

Evelyn's smile faded only a touch as she studied the glee in her daughter's expression. She knew only too well the feelings stirring in Lori. Her lips parted, but she held back.

"Don't, Mother. Don't say it, whatever it is. Just because you and dad couldn't make it doesn't mean..."

"Hold it! Now you're the one who shouldn't voice unnecessary words. Let's neither of us spoil this beautiful meal."

Lori glanced from the pea platter to the beef. She quickly shifted the conversation: "You know, Mom, I've been thinking of quitting the cheerleader squad and giving more time to the poetry society and the chemistry club."

"Why? Are you having an identity problem?"

"Well, it's just that I want to be so many things for Billy. He's into all kinds of stuff, and I don't want to be far behind." She glanced around the table again. "Sure, I want to fix nice meals for him, but I also want to be somebody."

"But you are, honey. Don't give up cheerleading if you like it. You can still dabble in poetry or whatever."

"I'm so afraid of disappointing him."

* * *

Billy and his mother ate in the kitchen, without Charley. The big cop was busy catching up on paper work and reassigning duties after Henry Mason's arrest was made official. Arriving at dessert time, he pushed into the kitchen through the back door, grunted hello, then asked, "What's that filthy contraption leaning against the garage door?"

"It's mine," Billy answered as Mary looked from father to son.

"What the hell is it?"

"It's the inside of a harpsichord. I want to clean it up and do something with it."

"Henry Mason's harpsichord?"

"Yeah."

Charley stepped to the stove, lifted a lid, and sniffed the ham and cabbage. "And just what do you plan to do with it?"

"I don't know. Something."

* * *

That night in bed Billy lay awake seeing images of Mason House, the cherry tree, the fire, the Packard, the wall, the cemetery, the tombstone, Lori. He twisted and turned as sensual feelings permeated his body. He fantasized.

Chapter Thirty-Five

Dawn. Three days after Henry Mason's arrest.

Rising earlier than usual, Charley brewed his own coffee and was drinking his third cup by the time sleepy-eyed Mary stepped into the kitchen, still in her nightgown and bathrobe. As she focused on her husband, the day's first rays of sunlight turned the kitchen aglow with bright orange-yellow patches on the west wall.

"Must have been those sparrows on the window sill," Mary said, holding back a yawn.

"Huh?" As usual, Charley was buried in his newspaper.

"The chirping birds must have stirred your juices."

"No. I woke early and couldn't fall back. If I'm taking time off, I gotta handle it right with the chief, get things up to snuff, and spread the jobs around. My mind wouldn't let me rest." Turning a page, Charley scanned the editorials, then mumbled "Goddamn" as he started to read letters to the editor. "I can't believe this stuff."

"I hope you made enough coffee for me." Mary grabbed her favorite mug and picked up the pot.

"Finish it up. I've had enough." He kept reading. "Holy shit, what's with these people, anyway? You should read these letters."

Mary poured coffee and sat across from her husband, her elbows on the table and her mug in both hands. "You had trouble falling off right away last night, didn't you? I figured you were still upset."

"The arrest didn't upset me. Actually the old man cracked a smile as I read him his rights, then asked me to smuggle in a fifth of rye and a pack of Camels. It's the damn television news that gets to me, more than anything. I shouldn't watch that eleven o'clock garbage before I go to bed."

"How else could they play it? An old recluse from a spooky house that burned to the ground is arrested for fire-bombing porno shops and gay bars. Not only that, he's arrested while bleeding to death in the hospital. Come on Charley! Could anything please the news hounds more? Talk about lurid stuff!"

"Well, they've stirred up the citizenry. These letters make me want to puke. Listen to this. 'Dear Editor, Henry Mason deserves a slow death in prison, so I hope they patch up his stomach. Temporarily, that is.' And get this one. 'Those doctors should stop wasting time and money trying to cure a murderer. Let the old guy bleed to death.' Here's another. And another. Don't these people have anything to do but spit venom?"

"I guess they don't like old men who throw bombs."

"Oh God, here's one from the other camp. 'Dear Editor, Henry Mason deserves an award for helping to rid the world of perverts.' Assholes to the left and right. Where are the level-headed people in the middle?"

"They don't write letters to the editor."

"Here's one that tugs at the gut. 'My son Jason died in the Black Tulip fire. He was only 18, a brilliant art student who had his whole life to live. Henry Mason should live to be punished.'"

* * *

Two young resident physicians turned their heads as the woman pushed her way into the hospital. Dressed in a black suit designed by Lacroix of Paris, she was a well-groomed woman in her late forties with a profile not unlike that of certain royal heirs and sovereigns with aquiline noses and receding chins. The sharp, staccato hammering of her high heels on the masonry floor of the lobby denoted anger almost as much as the expression on her face. Her head was held high with pride, as usual, but her lips were tight and her chin was firm with tension. She hurried toward the information desk, argued vehemently with the petite blonde receptionist whom she overpowered, and took off down the hallway, dodging others as she rushed toward the elevators. Her heels struck even louder and faster than before.

Minutes later she circled a nurses station on the third floor, looked up and down the quiet corridors, and then pushed through swinging doors into the west wing. She glanced at the ICU sign above the door to the Intensive Care Unit and, without hesitation, entered the restricted area.

Patients in the ICU were in walled cubicles that fanned out from a central control station replete with monitors and other equipment. Three nurses were absorbed working in the unit when the seething woman-in-black bounded in and glanced about. Two were with patients, taking temperatures and pulse rates, while the third—a freckle-faced little redhead—was busy marking medical charts at the circular desk just inside the hallway.

"Wait, you can't go in there!" the redhead insisted, after looking up from her work.

The woman ignored the nurse, darted around patient-care equipment, and hurried from bed to bed before the redhead reached her, yelled "Stop!" and grabbed her arm.

"Don't you dare touch me!" the woman yelled as she broke loose.

"You can't do this!" the redhead shouted as the other nurses sped to her aid. "If you're a relative you have to check in. If not, you're not permitted here."

The woman sighted Henry in a cubicle on the north side. She raced toward him, threw herself against his bed and pounded his legs with her fists. Seconds later she struck his belly and chest as she screamed, "Murderer! You murderer, murderer, murderer!" The nurses tried to pull her away, but her rage, fueled by hate, more than doubled her strength. "Murderer!" she yelled again as she tugged at Henry's right leg until she pulled it from the bed.

"Get away from me!" Henry wheezed in an attempted scream. "Goddamn!" He kicked and pushed feebly.

"Murderer!" the woman screamed once more as she leaped at the pole holding the patient's 25th transfusion of blood. The pole crashed and spurted blood over the bed linens, the floor and two of the nurses, not to mention Henry and his attacker. The IV line, needle and all, was ripped from Henry's flesh. He twitched, writhed in pain, and pulled the other IV line—the feeding tube—with him as he struggled with the woman and tumbled from the bed. The second pole fell and the bottle spilled across the bed as the wires to his heart monitor were torn from the wall.

While the two dark-haired nurses struggled with the woman, the redhead raced to the circular desk and called the Security Office.

By the time the security guards reached the ICU, the woman was subdued, partly through efforts of the nurses and an orderly, partly because her fury had waned. She was emotionally drained.

Soon doctors joined nurses in bringing a semblance of order to the ICU. The woman sat on a straight-back chair against the wall, her face buried in her hands. She cried deep, hysterical sobs. A resident physician attended to her while others worked to patch up Henry.

"I know that woman," one nurse whispered to another. "She's that horse lady from the Main Line."

Hours later, when the little redhead was going off duty, she stopped at the first-floor security desk and asked Officer Harry Withers about the woman.

"Don't you know her?" the portly, bald officer asked from behind his desk. "That's Mrs. Frederick J. Evans, the third. Lives in Radnor, I think. Her husband's chairman of the board at Morton and Morton. She's a tennis freak and a big wheel at the Devon Horse Show. Gets her picture in the paper all the time. Her daughter burned to death in the Black Tulip fire."

Chapter Thirty-Six

October's coldest day, so far.

The low temperatures were unexpected. Weathermen on TV channels 3, 6 and 10 had each predicted that a southern flow of air would block an oncoming cold front from Canada. They were wrong.

Billy and Lori carried their schoolbooks as they walked along the cemetery wall, bucking stiff winds as leaves, twigs and dust swirled about them. "Ouch!" Billy exclaimed when hit on the cheek by an acorn.

"What is it?" Lori asked.

"I got stung by a flying nut!" Billy protested as he raised the collar on his zipper jacket.

Now and again the teenagers braved the wind to glance up at fast-moving clouds that raced across the sky—clouds that allowed sunlight to splash fleetingly on the pavement. Beyond the wall, tombstones seemed to pulsate as they flashed on and off, looming bright, shrinking dark.

Billy and Lori walked arm-in-arm, pondering their summer nights in the cemetery.

"So, we could go to your house," Billy said meekly. This was not a new suggestion on his part. It had popped out of his mouth a few times before.

"Billy! Why do you do that? You know I want to. But you know how my mom feels."

"We don't do anything really bad."

"That doesn't matter. I still feel guilty. She asks questions, and it's so hard to look her in the eyes, even if we haven't done anything. Let's face it, she just doesn't want us in the house when she's not there. It was a big concession on her part to let us watch television together when she's home. If she knew the way we were touching, she'd kill us."

"I think adults forget what it's like to feel like we do at our age."

"I think Mom remembers what it was like, and that's the trouble."

"Y'know, it's really not fair."

"Y'mean my mom?" Lori pulled her arm from his.

"No, no, no. I mean in general. It's not fair that human beings, young like us, have to feel this way, can't do what's natural, have to wait years, and all that stuff. Of course there's plenty of 'em going at it mighty strong, like Becky Kittridge and Rusty Kirk. Y'know damn well what's going on there."

Billy grabbed Lori and linked arms with her again. A moment later they stopped on Mason's land and glanced about.

"They took the last pile away," Billy commented.

"The garage is still there."

"Let's go behind it for a quick kiss."

"It's too cold."

"Come on. Just a quicky."

They scampered by the blackened cherry tree and across the scorched earth. Behind the garage they embraced. Billy kissed Lori about the neck and ears, then on the lips. He slipped his hands under her jacket.

Later, shivering and yearning for warmth, they peeked from behind the garage, then began to race toward the sidewalk. But Billy stopped suddenly for a quick detour. He ran to the garage door for a look, then caught up with Lori.

"You like that car, don't you?" she asked, rhetorically.

"Oh, jeeze, it's cool. Really cool. I'd love to sit behind that wheel, with you next to me, and ride a twisting road through the fields, into the woods and up and down the hills. Can't you just feel it?"

Lori smiled and kissed Billy on the nape of his neck, nearly erasing his thoughts of the Packard and inflaming his already aroused libido. She took his arm and quickly sensed his tension.

As they walked arm-in-arm once more, Billy felt frustrated and kept reflecting on the arousals that burdened him each day—whether on a bus or trolley car, or while daydreaming in the library or school auditorium, or even while eating in the cafeteria. Fresh in his mind was today's English class in which Miss Bloomfield had rambled on about Moby Dick while he fantasized. "Is there something wrong?" she had asked him, seeing him still in his seat after class. "No," he had replied, before standing and hurrying toward the hallway, holding his books in front of his fly.

"Mom works so hard," Lori said. "And she tries her best to make things work between her and me. She messes up. But she tries."

"The way I see it, you don't feel guilty because of what we do. You feel guilty because of what you believe she thinks we do. If that makes any sense."

"Maybe." Lori tightened her grip on Billy's arm. "You know what I worry about most?"

"Oh shoot. Here we go again."

"About losing you."

"How did I guess. I told you, that's stupid! It won't happen."

"I can't help how I feel."

"It's not rational."

"Maybe not. But I wake up sometimes in the middle of the night. And I have this awful fear. It was real bad after that night in the cemetery when we... Well, you know. But it also happens when we go pretty far and I cut you off and you look so hurt. It's almost like I'm damned if I do and damned if I don't. So then I worry that I could lose you either way. If I stop it, or if I let it happen."

"*You* don't stop it. We stop it together."

"We do?"

Together, they walked up the steps of the Lippincott house. Billy embraced Lori, but kept it short, aware of her nosy neighbors. After she slipped into the house and closed him out, he stayed at the door with his nose against the glass, peering in and making funny faces. Lori hung her jacket on the newel post, returned to the door, smiled comically, then waved. But Billy didn't leave. He tugged on the knob until she opened the door.

"What do you want?"

"Let me stand just inside the door for a minute. It won't be the same as coming into the house."

"It won't?"

"Not exactly."

"Yes it will."

"I'll keep my heels on the threshold, so it won't be like I'm in the living room. At least not all the way in."

"You're being silly!"

"Please?" Billy pushed his way in, then stood with his back against the door. "See? I'm hardly inside."

"What if Mom comes home early?"

"She never does, and you know it." Billy wrapped his arms around her and kissed her. He moved his lips here and there about her neck. "Oh, Lori." Holding tightly, he kissed her on the lips again. His heartbeat raced, as did Lori's.

"You better leave," Lori said. But she didn't let go. In fact, she held more tightly.

"Oh, God," he whispered.

"Please, Billy."

* * *

Not relieved and highly keyed, Billy jogged faster and faster as he raced toward home. Almost as if punishing himself, he increased his speed, turning his jog into a run. He didn't pause, even to catch his breath, until he leaned against the curbside sycamore tree in front of his house.

Hearing her son enter, Mary Bannon stepped from the kitchen in time to see him dash up the stairs. "Billy?"

"Yeah, it's me."

"You all right?"

"Yeah, of course I'm all right. Why wouldn't I be?" Billy's words were sharp and quick. "Gotta use the john."

Mary heard the bathroom door close, stood for a moment at the foot of the stairs, then returned to the kitchen where she chopped vegetables and prepared a meat loaf. When dinner was well underway, she wiped her hands on a towel, tossed it over her shoulder, returned to the stairs and called, "Billy? We need ketchup. Do you mind running to the store?" Hearing nothing, she mounted the stairs, saw that the bathroom door was still closed, and asked, "Billy? Why are you still in there? Are you okay?"

"I'll be right out."

Chapter Thirty-Seven

A warm evening for late October. Just past sunset.
Charley slowed his car on the tree-lined street as he searched. He pressed down on the brake pedal when he thought he saw 124 on a white clapboard house, a Dutch colonial heavy with shrubbery. Allowing the car to coast, he then increased the speed and drove to the next intersection. After a U-turn, the car inched past the house again. Although the digits were draped in hemlock, Charley was certain this time that the number was 124. He drove around the block, then parked his car directly across from the house and studied it careful. Lights burned downstairs. No vehicles were visible. The macadam driveway led to a basket and backboard of regulation height. That translated to children. Probably teenage boys.

Stepping from his car, Charley strolled across the street and followed a flagstone walkway to a solid white door with a brass knocker.

Inside the house, Frank Manley, a fabric-dye specialist for the Middletown Carpet Company, slept in his reclining chair near the fireplace. Short, bald and bulging at the midriff, he was deep in his third snooze since his heavy dinner of steak and potatoes. His first rude awaking had come from Lily's screechy shouts from upstairs: "The boys need sneakers. I'll drive them to the mall if you don't need the car." The pat-pat-pat of the basketball then faded away within Frank until he was zapped again: "Tell the boys to come in and change! I'm not going to the mall with them all sweaty like that!" His wife's high-pitched squeak had irritated Frank for the past dozen years.

"Christ almighty!" he had muttered, before forcing his chair upright and finding his left foot asleep—a foot that he dragged across the crowded living room (called "eclectic" by Lily) to the driveway side, where he tried to shake away the pins and needles while opening the window. "Get in here! Your mother wants you!"

Later and vaguely, somewhere in half sleep, he had heard the commotion of Junior and Teddy running up and down steps to the accompaniment of Lily's shrill voice.

Now, Frank was alone in the house and at peace. Dreaming about football and beer, he was awakened again, startled by the ringing of the doorbell. "Goddamnit, what now!" He tried to gather his wits and guess the time. Rubbing his eyes, he struggled to his feet as the bell rang again. "I'm coming. I'm coming. Hold onto your friggin britches." Surely it was an insurance salesman or those Watch Tower people, he told himself. Actually, Frank was annoyed with life—same job since graduation, same grass to mow, same arguments with Lily, same friends for poker on Friday nights.

He hesitated, then switched on the porch light and opened the door to find a big man in a navy suit.

"Is this the Manley residence?"

"Yes." Frank was but half awake.

"I'm police Lieutenant Charles Bannon." Charley pulled his hand from his inside coat pocket and flashed his badge. "Are you Frank Manley?"

"Yes. Yes, I'm Frank Manley."

"Wonder if I could have a word with you?"

Frank was still trying to gather his senses. The word "police" helped a bit, for it was something like a splash of cold water. "Right. Sure. Yeah. Come on in." His thoughts raced as he tried to figure what crime he had committed, what trouble Teddy had caused, what car Lily had smashed, what girl Junior had seduced.

"May I sit down?"

Frank curbed his desire to be abrasive. "Well, yeah, I guess. Here. Here, why don't you use this?" Frank offered his recliner, then tripped over his own feet as he headed for the couch. He sat across the coffee table from Charley. "Now, tell me, what can I do for you?"

"I believe you know Andrew Mason?"

Still struggling to control his irritability, Frank gave too much thought to the question, leaned forward, then asked, "You mean Andy, from over the big house near the cemetery? The one that burned down?" He sat on the edge of the cushion.

"Yeah."

"Years ago. I haven't seen him since... well, I bet it's been twenty years. His old man's in trouble, right? I read about it."

"Yes, he's in trouble."

"So, what are you telling me? This has something to do with that?"

"In a way."

"Yeah?"

"The old guy's sick. He might not make it. So, he wants to see his son."

Frank ran his fingers through his hair. "Jeeze, man, I don't know. To tell you the truth, I don't know what happened to Andy. We really didn't see much of each other after high school."

"Why's that?"

"Well, he went off to Penn State and I went off to Lehigh. Then there was the Korean thing. He went. I stayed home with asthma. After the war, we didn't see much of each other."

"Was there a reason for that?"

"Hell, I don't know. I mean, we'd talk. You know, small talk when we'd meet on the street." Frank's mind seemed to drift. "Nice guy, he was. I always liked Andy." Relaxing somewhat, he finally leaned back and crossed his legs. "So tell me, why'd you come to me? I don't get it."

"I had to start somewhere. The old man doesn't remember many names. I found you in a high-school yearbook, pictured next to Andy here and there. It didn't take much to figure you knew each other."

"Ah, yeah. The Experimenters Club!" Little by little Frank was waking up. In fact, his eyes suddenly brightened with memory. "We were both members of the Experimenters Club. Great fun. When your club is called Experimenters you can experiment with just about anything, and we sure did. Andy got us into mixing pollen and turning yellow and red four-o'clocks into striped ones. Soon we were messing with more than flowers. You know, like the pretty little things that wandered the hallways. Farty Fartrum, the principal disbanded the club. Andy knew things, but kept his mouth shut. He was a right kinda guy."

"Oh?"

"Sort of quiet. Never took offense. But could win his points. He had a way about him. The guys liked him. So did the chicks."

Charley shifted, then focused on Frank's eyes. "But what about later? Where'd he go? What happened to him?"

"Like I was saying, I didn't see much of him."

"Can you remember anything that might help me? What were his habits? What kind of places did he frequent? What did he like to do?"

Frank took a cigarette from a silver box on the table. "Have one?"

"No thanks." Charley shook his head, then pinched his chin. "You hear anyone say anything about him? You know, good or bad? Anything? I don't care how trivial, it might help. For me, it could be a lead, even if you don't see it that way. Know what I mean?"

"Damn. I don't think I can help you." Frank sat forward again. He ran his forefinger across his teeth until his eyes lit up again. "Hey, I do remember something. Thought it was strange at the time. Then brushed it off."

"What's that?"

Frank lit his cigarette, puffed twice, then took a deep drag and released the smoke slowly through his mouth and nose. "You talk to anybody else? You talk to Larry Malvern yet?"

"No. Who's this Larry?"

"You should talk to him. Larry was much closer to Andy than I was. They hung together, even after Korea. So close we used to call them queer for each other."

"Were they?"

"Hell no! A joke man! Just a joke. But like I was saying, this funny thing happened when we were at the Redwood drinking beer." Frank suddenly lifted his brows and interrupted himself: "Hey, can I get you a brew? I got some premium stuff on ice."

"No thanks."

"You sure?"

Charley shook his head. "So, go on. You were at the Redwood."

"Yeah. I was single in those days, and we'd hit the Redwood on Wednesday nights. That was Wildwood Night, and they'd have this guy at the piano who could really tickle the ivories. Straw hat. Striped shirt. Suspenders. And he'd play the old favorites like *Sweet Sixteen* and *Old Mill Stream* and stuff like that. Anyway, Larry and I and Bobby Hopkins were in a booth clicking our mugs and pouring a few when in comes Andy and these two dudes. Never saw them before. Well, Andy just ignores us. Like we weren't even there. And this is Larry Malvern sitting over here, you know? Larry, his bosom buddy. Get me? And it's like he doesn't even see him. But he sees him all right. Anyway, these guys go to the bar, and Andy looks kind of nervous, because of us, I think." Frank drew in smoke again, then exhaled slowly. "Sure I can't get you a beer?"

"I'm on duty," Charley lied. "I can't. Really."

"Well, like I was saying, Andy's uptight as hell. And Larry, now, he's not gonna be snubbed by his old sidekick, you know? So he goes right up to them, and Andy acts surprised. Introduces the two dudes, all right, but they don't stay. Andy leaves, and the other two follow. It was like Andy was ashamed, or something."

"Where would I find this Larry Malvern?"

Frank drew hard on his cigarette, held the smoke in his lungs, and let it out a little at a time. "Over on Grayson Avenue. But you better call first. He's still single, still moving fast. Got a bit of traffic in and out of his place." A smile touched Frank's lips, and a little envy showed in his eyes.

Chapter Thirty-Eight

"That's nice."

"Mmmm."

"You like that, huh, Baby?"

"Uh-huh."

"And this."

"Come on, now. Don't do that."

"How about this?"

"Mmmm. That's good."

"You are delicious, you know that?"

"Hey, that tickles! Larry, stop it! Stop it, I say!"

"How's this?"

"That's better."

The room was dark. Only a touch of light from a streetlamp shone beneath a pulled shade at a window open but a few inches. Tap, tap, tap, the shade flapped in a breeze that cooled the warm apartment. The only other sound, besides the whispery voices and the sighs, groans, gasps and grunts, was the hum of a refrigerator in an adjoining kitchenette. The numbers and hands on a luminous clock glowed greenish white on the nightstand beside the bed.

"Oh, Larry!"

"How's that feel?"

"Keep it up. Don't stop."

The telephone rang, echoing loud through the dark room. Larry tried to ignore the ringing, hoping it would stop. But it continued and began to play havoc with his mind.

The ringing stopped.

"It's gone, Larry. It's just us now."

Within seconds, he recovered.

When it was over they lay limp in each other's arms, breathing heavily, the weight of his body increased by his total surrender. Minutes passed before Baby said, "You're too heavy on me, Honey."

Larry turned over, then reached for the lamp. Light filled the room, reflecting on an array of bright colors as it bounced off posters and paintings, a wall rug depicting a red and yellow rooster, a nude statue of a nymph wearing a green derby, and an elk's head above the bed with Baby's pink panties and bra hanging from the antlers. Larry had allowed the bedroom to grow day by day, much as his life, haphazardly. Skis stood in a corner. Running shoes projected from under his bed. This was his fun-time room, and, without a doubt, it reflected fun. His apartment living room differed from his playroom in terms of tidiness, but not come-on. Masculine-suave, it was smooth, sleek, modern, manly, brown-and-beige. Its carpeting was fluffy and soft, and so were the cushions on the square sectional pieces. Low lights, a well-supplied bar, and a large cactus in a brown-and-white Mexican bowl added to the ambience.

Larry was handsome, even-featured and blue-eyed. He was a 48-year-old youngster who touched up the gray at his temples. His body was trim and muscular, and he worked to keep it that way. He was well tanned by the summer sun, but his nakedness exposed a band of pale flesh from his bathing suit.

"Why don't you go shower?" he suggested. "And then I'll buy you some supper. You want steak at the Ale House or lobster at Mariner's Inn?" He really wasn't in the mood to take her anywhere.

"Let me think about it," Baby said with a coy smile and a kittenish wiggle. A five-foot-four, well-proportioned brunette with big dark eyes and long false-eyelashes, Baby owned one of those perfect faces molded by her nose doctor. She grabbed a tissue and wiped away the sticky from both of them, then bit his ear and giggled as he yelled "Ouch!" After tickling his ribs, she ran from the bed as he whacked her across the buttocks. Her well-rounded rump flowed smoothly to solid thighs that Larry treasured—at least for this month.

Baby disappeared, only to pop back through the doorway, bat her lashes and giggle again.

"Get going, damn it, or you won't get steak or lobster." He forced a broad grin and winked.

"Okeydokey, Poopsydoopsy!" She stuck out her tongue.

Larry pushed himself from the bed, stretched and grunted, squeezed his backside to make certain it wasn't flabby, then pulled a fresh towel from his bureau and followed Baby to the bathroom.

* * *

Overdressed in yellow satin that twisted tightly about her torso, Baby toyed with her rhinestone necklace and chewed breath-freshening gum while standing near the cactus waiting for Larry to tighten his belt and slip into his Italian shoes.

"Lobster!" she exclaimed. "I want to suck those little, fleshy pieces out of the claws and right into my mouth." She lifted her forefinger toward the cactus as if tempted to touch, only to pull it back.

"I told you before, you're supposed to use that little fork and dip the pieces in butter," Larry instructed.

The door-knocking started seconds before Larry walked into the living room dressed in fitted trousers and a silky cream-colored shirt, embroidered with a black monogram and open at the neck deep enough to display a bronze medallion between his well-developed pecs.

Waiting for Larry to respond to the knocking, Baby struck an impatient pose near the cactus, then tested the sharpness of the spines with her little finger.

"Be right with you!" Larry flexed his muscles, checked his fly, then pulled open the door. "Yeah? What is it?"

"Larry Malvern?"

"That's my handle."

"I'm Police Lieutenant Charles Bannon. Wonder if I might have a word with you?"

Larry looked Charley up and down. "I didn't do it, man," he said, cracking a crooked smile.

"It's about Andrew Mason."

Larry's eyes widened. "Andy Mason?" He shook his head, slowly, then more rapidly. "Hell no, I don't want to talk about him."

Charley flashed his badge.

"Look," Larry said. "We're on our way out. We're late for dinner."

"Mr. Malvern, if you could give me a few minutes, I'd appreciate it. I've been trying all day to reach you. And I'm pushed for time, or I wouldn't have come this time of night."

"Jeeese..."

"I could insist, you know?"

"Well. Okay, come on in." Larry backed up. "To tell you the truth, Lieutenant, I really don't want to talk about Andy. He's a sore spot in my life. Whatever he's done, I'm sorry, but I don't want to know about it. I just don't want to get into the act."

"Oh, he didn't commit any crime that I know of. I'm simply trying to find him."

"Well, I helped another guy try to find him once, and lived to rue the day."

"A few minutes?"

"What do you want to do, tell him about his old man? Take it from me, he wouldn't want to know."

"Henry Mason is sick and wants..."

Larry interrupted: "The way I hear it, he's more than sick."

"He wants to see his son."

"Goddamn, wouldn't you know! Stupid old goat waits until he's dying."

"We don't know that he's dying."

Baby meandered around the room, touching everything she could reach, especially the soft and the smooth.

"Look, Lieutenant. Yes, I knew Andy. We were friends. But that was a long time ago. I don't know where he is, and I don't much care."

Larry had yet to offer a seat to the big cop, and Charley shifted from foot to foot as he questioned, "But you helped someone else find him?"

"Years ago."

"If you could give me Andy's last address..."

"And be shit on again!"

"May I sit down?"

Larry turned to Baby and suggested, "Why don't you go into the bedroom and play with my barbells or something?" Then he nodded to Charley and pointed to a gathering of soft sectional pieces not far from the bar. "Do you want a drink?"

"No thanks."

Baby pouted. Annoyed that Larry ignored her pout, she took her time leaving the room, looking back twice with disdain.

Larry stretched, expanded his chest, leaned on the bar and said, "This is a bitch for me, man. I mean, it isn't easy."

"Try."

"I work at not thinking about old friends, even relatives, my old man or my old lady. I substitute work and pleasure in quick succession. Gratification, but no involvement. That's me. If that seems like a shitty existence, you can blame them. All of them. Including Andrew Mason." Larry glanced at his wristwatch. "To tell you the truth, Lieutenant, I need a few stiff drinks if I'm going to take this on. Sure you won't join me?"

Charley shook his head as Baby appeared at the other end of the room, leaning against the doorframe. "Larry," she whined. "Don't forget me."

Larry glanced at her, forced a smile, looked back and Charley and asked, "Did you know him?"

"Who?"

"Andy."

"Yes, but not really."

"What's that supposed to mean?"

"We hung with different crowds. Very different. I did odd jobs for his father, but he kept Andy and me at a distance from each other."

"But you know what he was like?"

"Not really."

Larry motioned to Baby, forcefully tossing his hand twice. After another pout, she slipped away again.

"To tell you the truth, Lieutenant, I can't do this," Larry said. "Not right now. I just can't." He leaned on the bar, stared directly into Charley's eyes, bit his lower lip and shook his head. "Not simply because of my anxious friend in there. But because I just couldn't sort it out for you right now, even if I had the time. And tootsydoll, here, she's chafing at the bit to suck on some lobster claws. I'll try tomorrow, if you insist, alone, after about six martinis."

"Why not just give me that address now?"

"No. I promised."

Charley looked puzzled. "Who?"

"Him."

"Andy?"

"You got it. I promised, and it was a big one."

"But I don't understand. When?"

"When he left. When he took off for whatever."

"But I thought you didn't care."

Larry glanced away, pondered the thought, then looked back at Charley. "I don't. At least I don't want to. Let's say I try not to. Okay?"

Charley said nothing, but sensed a great deal. He pushed himself to his feet and waited.

Larry studied the big cop for a moment, then asked, "Do you get into Philly?"

"I can."

"Do you know Watson's Pub?"

"Doc Watson's?"

"Eleventh near Locust. I work near there."

"My older son hangs there sometimes."

"Meet me there. Late afternoon. About four. I'll break away early."

Chapter Thirty-Nine

Larry was drinking his fourth martini by the time Charley walked into the pub and took a stool next to him at the bar. "Let's grab a booth," Larry suggested as he swung around quickly. He stepped across to the other side of the narrow barroom—a tavern reflecting the days of Sherlock Holmes.

Dr. Watson's Pub catered to college-agers and a goodly splattering of others during late night hours when standing room crowds pushed to and fro on all three levels. But not so now. Larry and Charley were among the early, after-work drinkers who spoiled their dinners with salted nuts and little fish-shaped pretzels. Few patrons hugged the bar and several booths were empty, as Larry had hoped.

Spreading his elbows on the table, Larry hung his head and looked into his martini as he said, "Get yourself a drink."

"I will." Charley slid into the booth and glanced about for a waitress. He was not only off duty, but now far out of his territory.

"If you want to catch up with me in one gulp, Barry makes a sneaky wang-banger called a Born Loser that'll do it every time. Secret recipe."

"I'll stick to beer."

"Suit yourself."

"So tell me..."

"Andrew Mason," Larry interrupted. "Dear old Andy, and the case of how-the-hell-did-you-screw-up. I can't tell you much, but I got plenty of gut feelings. So whatever I give you, man, y'gotta weigh it for what it's worth."

"I'll take anything."

"Humph! The man says 'anything.' So, anything it is."

Charley turned to the sandy-haired little barmaid and asked for a bottle of Light.

"Well, let's see now. Anything, anything, anything. Andy and I played ball together, captured tadpoles together, trapped pigeons together, skinny-dipped together, ate pizza together, and sneaked beers together."

"And after Korea?"

Larry finished his martini in one gulp, flushed, wiped his lips, looked down again and said nothing for a lengthy moment.

"Is that hard for you?" Charley asked. "I mean, the Korean thing, and what happened afterward, and all that. Is it tough turf?"

"Naaaa. Not really. Not any more." He wiped his lips again. "I came home from Korea, out of it all. Lost. I couldn't settle in. My true and trusting girlfriend was shacking up with some creepy weasel that turned her on. My folks had split and didn't want my troubles. My old lady moved in with some dude in Atlantic City, and my old man fell apart. He couldn't keep his business together. I told them all to go to hell."

"Sorry."

"Hey, that's the way the bubble bursts or cookie crumbles or whatever. On top of everything, I couldn't find a job. All I had was my old buddy, Andy, who lectured me night after night. He kept feeding me a platter of Pollyanna stew that made me upchuck. Y'gotta understand. I didn't want to think. No way! I just wanted to keep doing things, one after the other, quickly, to smother everything else, fill time, keep me from thinking. So, I'm still at it, Lieutenant. Involvements? Hell, no, I don't want 'em."

"I'm not asking for anything more than information." Charley was aware that alcohol was opening up Larry. He also suspected that Larry needed to unload.

"Those goddamn lectures," Larry mumbled. He motioned for another martini. Then a strange, painful smile crossed his face. "Who the hell am I kidding? I didn't really mean it when I told Andy to shove it. He knew I'd be back for more. I'd call and say, 'Let's go to a Phillies game,' or 'Meet me at the Redwood for a couple brews.' It was my only way of touching base with sanity."

"So, Andy didn't make you upchuck? Is that what you're saying?"

"Well, I learned how to fake a gag or retch. In fact, I can still hawk a big one. You know, Lieutenant, a guy can get so far away from the mainstream that he begins to think his frenzied beating of the drum is really life. He's gotta reach out and grab something or someone sometime. So I used to grab Andy just in time. Before it was too late. He was my tie to reality, to some sort of solid substance."

"But for you it was thanks, Andy, but no thanks, is that it?"

"Some of us are quick to spit out the pill. I guess I just didn't want the cure. But I think he saw something underneath my mask. So, he'd wait. And I'd come back."

Charley had not expected such an outpouring after yesterday's encounter. But this was not last night's macho man. This was a bleeding Larry Malvern, a drifting soul with no Andy to grab.

"What's your name, Lieutenant? I didn't catch it last night."

"You can call me Charley, if you like."

Larry's eyes were glassy from alcohol. He slurred his words as he said, "Charley, is it. I like that. Charley. Well, I'll tell you, Charley, th... the way I figure it now, I screw around 'cause it would hurt a lot more if I didn't. Call it avoidance of pain, if you like. A quick cure that fades fast if you don't fast feed it."

"Without Andy, no surcease? Is that it?"

"No up and down. No off and on. Just on and on and on." Larry sipped his fresh martini, then stared at the glass after interlocking his hands around the stem.

Charley had learned patience. Long ago he had discovered how easy it was to alienate by pushing. So he had no intention of hurrying Larry. And he decided to steer with restraint.

Larry was quiet and pensive. In time he said, "Andy was a perfect balance between a saint and a rake. A good guy with a touch of the devil. I hated him for being so sane, but I loved 'im. Then somethin' happened. When a guy gets burned he changes. I don't know what he's like today."

The big cop finished his beer, glanced about, then held the bottle high for the bartender to see.

"Then there was that night at the Redwood, when Andy came in with those two creeps." Larry's words were sluggish and intoned with resentment. "He snubbed me, and it was like he clobbered me with a club and sta... stabbed me in the gut at the same time. Shit. I didn't know I needed crutches until they were gone." Gulping his drink, Larry burned his throat and strangled until tears wet his flushed cheeks.

Charley waited as Larry reeled and struggled to recover.

"I wen't'is house the nex-day." Larry wiped his face with his handkerchief. "I don't think Andy wanted t'let me in, but I jus stood there til he did. I followed 'im to the kitchen where 'is father was fixin' some lunch. I 'member, Andy poured me a Coke, and I talked to his ole man. Somethin' strange. Right away I knew somethin' strange was goin'on. Uptight, both of 'em. An'... an', I don' know, but somethin' strange. I could feel it." Larry's words trailed off to nothing.

Charley weighed his words carefully and used a sympathetic tone when he said, "I know how you can sense those sort of things. I guess it made you uncomfortable. Can you tell me more?"

"Oh, there's more, all right. Those two creeps—the ones from the Redwood—they come down in their bathrobes. It's noon, and they're jus gettin' up, mindja. Andy's dad walks right out of the kitchen, leavin' his lunch on the table. And my ole buddy, he tenses up and turns 'is back while these two turkeys go about helpin' themselves to anything, like they own the place. It's like I'm not even there, til I show my chip and start shovin' this one jerk around. Ole buddy Andy... he tells me t'get out."

"Did you?"

"Wasn't stayin' where I wasn't wanted." Larry tried to suck a drop from his empty glass.

Charley sensed that Larry's heavy dose of martinis and his disturbing memories had not only altered him mentally and physically, but had nearly obliterated his surroundings by putting him in a never, never land—a state always dreaded and avoided, but probably needed. "You were saying?"

"Those creeps," Larry muttered. "They had somethin' on Andy, an' they moved in an' took over."

Charley waited patiently.

"The old man." Larry's words were but a whisper. "Did I tell y'?

He finally blew things apart." Quiet and thoughtful, Larry stared at his empty glass.

"Waitress!" Charley called. "Bring us some coffee. Black."

* * *

An hour later they sat in Charley's car, parked in an underground municipal lot. Dim light from overhead barely reflected on their faces.

"Andy... oh he comes to me, all right," Larry said, "after he gets thrown out on his ass. Never saw him look so bad, like he's drained dry by blood-suckers. He tells me he's pullin' out for good. I jus listen, y'know, an' then let 'im go without tryin't'stop 'im."

"Why?"

"Can't answer that. I was so goddamned pissed, I guess."

"But you heard from him?"

"Yeah, he writes me. Says I'm to be his only tie with the past. Well, time changes things, y'know? I start feelin' sorry for the bastard. So, I write 'im a letter."

"Can you give me that address?' With his left hand resting on the steering wheel, Charley turned and looked at Larry, but couldn't gain eye contact.

"It was long ago." Larry dropped his head, stared at the car floor, and added a wistful tone to his words. Sobered but a trifle, he began to reveal sorrow and hurt more than resentment as he said, "He's not there now. I don't know where he is."

"But that address might lead me to another."

Larry's mind seemed to wonder. "This creep—the one I shoved around Mason's kitchen—he comes lookin' for me. Finally finds me one night at the Redwood. Says he has to find Andy. I give 'im that address."

"Why did you do that?"

"Fuck, I don't know. He said he had t'make up for past crimes, or something like that. Calls it life or death, or some damn thing. Whatever. Who the hell knows? So, I gave it to 'im. And then Andy comes down on me like I raped his mother. I get this fuckin' letter you wouldn't believe. Rips me all t' hell."

"You still have it?"

"Chrisno." Larry finally looked at Charley. His eyes were deeply troubled. "Tore it int'little pieces an' flushed it down the john. An' Andy, he changes his address. Haven't heard a thing since. Been twenty years at least."

Charley's tone was far less amiable as he said, "Look here, Larry. I want that address. You hear me?"

Maybe it was the alcohol. Whatever, Larry failed to react to the big cop's change in temper and simply said, "Sure would like to help you, but I don' have it anymore."

"Think hard. Can you remember part of it? Any part of it?"

"Can't say I do."

"The city, town, whatever?"

"Dryden."

"Dryden what?"

"Little burg in New York State."

"And that's all you remember?"

"Yeah. Dryden." Larry suddenly opened the car door. "Oh, shit. I don't feel so good."

"You gonna get sick? Here." Charley was quick to grip Larry's shoulders. "Bend that way." He attempted to turn him. "Put your legs outside the car and hang your head between them. Go on."

Larry complied and immediately began to gag. "Oh, God!" He disgorged again and again, spewing sour-smelling vomit on the concrete floor and his shoes. Minutes later he was dry-heaving, bringing up nothing with each retch but viscous strings of phlegm. "Here. Take this." Charley offered his handkerchief.

"Oh, God. Thanks, man." Larry wiped mucus from his lips and chin. "Sorry 'bout this."

"I'll drive you home."

"My car's in the Jefferson lot."

"Leave it there. You're not driving."

"You're not either. Not yet, anyway." Larry wiped his shoes, looked about, then tossed the handkerchief under the car. "I wannabe sure of myself before I get jostled." He pulled in his feet, leaned back, and with his nose in the air and his mouth open he breathed heavily.

Charley waited patiently, then quietly asked, "What's the name of the guy you pushed around in Mason's kitchen, the one who came after you for Andy's address? Where can I reach him?"

"Timoth..." Larry continued to inhale through his mouth, deeply and often. "Timothy Wood. That's Timothy all the way. Not Tim. He wants it full blown. It's gotta be Timothy."

"Is he still in the area?"

"Gimme a second." Larry continued to pump air for a lengthy moment, then sat forward and struggled to compose himself. "I don't think we ever got rid of the bastard. Saw 'im 'bout a year ago sellin' pottery and sand candles at Headhouse Square. I got this guy figured by the creeps he hangs with. Got a feeling about what happened in Korea. But it doesn't add up. It jus doesn't. I knew Andy too well. I've seen 'im in action too many times."

"Can you describe this Timothy Wood?"

Larry seemed oblivious of Charley's question. "My old lady really screwed me. I wanted..." Tears welled in his eyes as his thoughts wandered. "My old man runs a gas station. I go out of my way not to pass it."

"You okay?"

"If only..."

"Hey, Larry, are you with me?"

"What's that?"

"About this guy Wood. What's he look like?"

"Andy won't come back. No way."

"About Wood? Tell me about Wood?"

Larry turned, looked at the big cop, and smiled. "You're all right, Charley, y'know that? You're an all right guy."

232

Chapter Forty

Mary turned from the sink, dried her hands, and stepped to the open cellar door. "Billy! What in the world are you doing down there? And at this hour? Did you forget that it's Saturday?"

"I'm fixing something."

After a brief hesitation, Mary stepped down to the landing in the cellar way. "What do I smell?"

"Paint."

Billy stood at the workbench, toiling over the innards of Mason's harpsichord.

"Do you realize the time?" Mary asked. "Your father's not even up yet." Step by step she lowered herself into the cellar—an unfinished basement, but neatly kept, with whitewashed walls and a well-built workbench fronting a vast collection of tools on wallboard hooks.

"I woke up early." Fervently held by his earnest efforts, Billy used a steady hand as he continued to paint the strings and the harp-shaped frame. He had yet to turn and look at his mother. "Couldn't get this thing off my mind."

"What is that?" She stared over his shoulder. "Part of the harpsichord? You're painting it gold?"

"And then I'm going to mount it on black and frame it."

"What on earth for?"

"I don't know. Maybe Lori and I will hang it in our house someday."

"And maybe you won't!"

"Well, to tell you the truth, I'd like to give it to Mr. Mason's son, if dad finds him. It was his mom's harpsichord. So, that's really why I'm messing with it."

Mary's expression changed from one of reproach to one of approval. Billy turned just in time to see a reflection of pride in his mother's eyes. She parted her lips as if about to express her feelings, but simply smiled warmly and turned away. As she mounted the steps she wondered what words could best express her pleasure in recognizing Billy's benevolent traits. As she approached the landing she looked back and said, "You've grown into quite a man, Billy." She knew immediately that her words were inadequate.

"So you like my idea," said Billy as he returned to painting the strings.

"Not just that. I like a lot of what I've seen in you in recent months."

Billy dropped his brush and turned. His expression revealed slight puzzlement.

Mary continued toward the kitchen.

"Wait!" he called.

"What is it?" She turned and stepped down.

"It's about Dad, and why he's doing what he's doing."

"Oh, I know why. It's not just for Mr. Mason. It's for himself and for you. I've put most of the pieces together, Billy."

* * *

Saturday breakfast had ended, and Billy had lined up most of Mason's lead soldiers on the kitchen table. The arrowhead plant, hanging in the window, captured sunlight, its fresh leaves reflecting brilliant yellow-green. Shade from the tangled vine tempered the glare on the table top, and some soldiers cast more shadow than others as they stood among splattered light.

Billy had spent tedious time sorting properly shaped soldiers from those deformed by the fire. Most had survived the flames as originally cast, although they needed touch-up. Standing by was Billy's set of oil paints and brushes. After scrubbing each soldier, the boy had been able to arrange the troops by nationality, despite the discoloration of many. American revolutionaries were in pairs next to the British redcoats. Italians and Ethiopians faced each other on the other side of the table. In between stood American Indians, bunched into a war party. Still soiled with soot, the Chinese and Japanese waited in a nearby box.

Billy was standing at the table examining the bow and arrow on an Indian when his father stepped into the kitchen and asked, "Where's you mother?"

"She took some clothes down to the washing machine."

"On Saturday?"

"I dirtied up a lot of stuff."

"I think it's about time you stayed away from those ashes." Charley started toward the cellar steps.

"Wait, Dad."

"What is it?"

Billy returned the Indian to the table and stepped toward his father. "You think they'd let me into the Intensive Care Unit if I explained that Mr. Mason doesn't have any relatives around these parts."

"I don't know, son. It might be better if you stay away. We had to station a man in the hallway after that Lesbos group pushed its way in." Charley took a long look at Billy's plaintive eyes, then added, "I'll tell you what. We'll go over there together. Okay?" He started toward the cellar again.

"Dad."

"Yeah?" Charley turned back.

"You're not like those other cops."

"Other cops?"

"Well, yeah. Some of them. I mean, it's like you're not so... so... so hard or something."

"Hard?" Charley smiled. "You mean I'm an old softy? Is that what you're saying? You didn't used to think so."

"You're different." Billy looked embarrassed. He returned to his soldiers.

Charley walked to his son's side. "I've always had feelings, Billy, but maybe I just never showed them enough. Other policemen have feelings, too. I suppose we all get a little cynical. Some of the guys grow elephants' hides to protect themselves. As

235

for me, I'm a little late growing up, I guess. You're way ahead of me, boy." He rumpled Billy's hair, then walked to the cellar way. "Mary! I'm going to the station for a bit."

"Why today?" she yelled above the sound of the washing machine. "I thought you were on leave."

"I won't be long. I gotta check on a couple things."

* * *

Thoughts interfered with Charley's concentration as he drove toward Police Headquarters. Suddenly aware of his heavy foot, he caught himself and reduced speed, but couldn't stem his anxiety. He kept hearing Larry Malvern: *Stupid old goat waits until he's dying.* Not until his shoulder ached did Charley become aware of his rigid right arm. He made a deliberate effort to relax. But Malvern's words didn't stop: *I got plenty of gut feelings... gut feelings... gut feelings.*

The big cop saw little, except in his mind's eye, as he raced from the parking lot into a backdoor of the brick and concrete building. *... Got a feeling about what happened in Korea... in Korea... in Korea. But it doesn't add up... add up.* Passing doorways at his left and right, he hurried along the corridor to the steady beat of Larry's words: *They had somethin' on Andy... moved in an' took over... took over... took over... took over... took over.*

Up front near the main entrance, Charley called "Yo, Joe, how y'doing?" to the desk sergeant, then knocked on a smoke-glass door marked Captain F. Mullin. Without waiting for a response, he opened the door and stepped inside.

"Working Saturdays, eh Chief?"

"I'm short-handed. And you're not helping things, you know, taking quick leave like this." Frank Mullin sat with his feet on his desk, twirling tissue paper into rabbit ears. "What the hell are you doing here? I thought your wild goose would have led you to Punxsutawney by now." Too short for a police chief of stature, Mullin was a round-faced, bald, bubble-nosed man of 60 years, a good-natured bully who grumbled and shouted with a flicker of fun in his eyes. His men liked him.

The captain's office was an ugly mixture of stained oak and black metal bookshelves stacked with police manuals and racy paperbacks. His desk was a massive block of oak that held two telephones, an intercom, family pictures and piles of paper work. An elaborate police radio system was on the wall behind his swivel chair.

"Smitty still haunts the joints around South and Second Streets, doesn't he?" Charley asked. "I could use his input. I'm looking for a guy who used to peddle sand candles near the Headhouse."

"I know he drinks at Dickens. Tosses darts there every Thursday night."

"Is he in?"

"He's with Carney, checking on a burglary at Bond's Shopping Center."

"What else you got going?"

"Some weirdo knifed an Upper Darby High School girl on the tracks near Fairfax and Hillcrest. And some skirt-chaser over on Grayson Avenue committed suicide. I'll tell you, it's been a busy Saturday so far."

Charley reached to a high shelf and pulled an atlas from among manuals and Police Academy textbooks. He flipped pages to a map of New York State. "Can I borrow this for a minute?"

"Take it."

Scanning the map, Charley found Dryden—a tiny dot, just outside of Ithaca. "Who was that guy on the Philadelphia force who helped us check out the gay bars when we were looking for Patsy Donohue? I think I could use him."

"You mean Berny Howard. Lieutenant Bernard Howard."

"Another thing." Charley closed the atlas, held it under his arm, and stepped to the desk. "I'd like to add a couple more days to my time off."

"You gotta be kidding!" Mullin pulled his feet from his desk and sharpened his stare.

"I got plenty of vacation time coming. Hell, I won't be using half of it. Look, it's important. Okay? When have I ever asked anything like this before?"

Mullin rubbed his chin as he mused. "Well, maybe. But only if Lazarus agrees to cover for you."

"He will," Charley said as he hurried toward the door. "So, it's a done deal." He grabbed the door handle, then spun around and asked, "What were you saying about Grayson Avenue?"

"A guy in the Grayson Apartments hanged himself in the fire stairwell. Used an extension cord looped around an upper railing. Cleaning lady found him dangling there, naked as a mole-rat. She hit her head on his bare feet as she came up the steps. Her scream shook up the whole joint. The guy was a bachelor with a reputation. Let's see, name was Malvern. Larry Malvern."

Charley stared in disbelief. His lips stayed parted as he gazed at Mullin and tried to accept what he had just heard.

The captain leaned forward and looked hard at Charley. "What the hell's wrong?"

"Jesus!"

"What is it?"

"Holy shit!"

"Charley, what is it? You know this guy or something?"

"Oh, God."

"Will you cut the crap and tell me, damn it!"

"Yeah, I knew him. For a few hours. Truth is, I think I helped kill him."

* * *

Charley sat on the couch in the living room as Mary prepared dinner. He fiddled with an ebony elephant that, among other things, decorated the coffee table in the modest room of contemporary furniture and accents of highly polished wood. After fingering it for several seconds, he placed it next to a brass bowl of strawflowers, only to pick it up again. He was toying with it when Billy dashed by, only to stop and turn.

"Dad! What's wrong?"

"Do I show it that easily?" Charley returned the elephant to the table for the sixth time.

"You never sit there. Not before dinner. Besides, you have a funny look on your face."

"Come here. Sit across from me."

Using one foot, then the other, Billy pushed a hassock close to the coffee table, then sat on it with his knees spread wide. "What happened? Is it Mr. Mason."

"No, it's not Mr. Mason." Charley gathered his thoughts, then said, "You know, Billy, I've seen some upsetting things in my life. When you're a cop, you can't avoid it. But even some of the blood and gore didn't upset me as much as this guy who killed himself early this morning. And I didn't especially like the guy. Not at first, anyway. But when his defenses slipped, I could see his humanity. Maybe I felt sorry for him. I don't know."

"Who was he?"

"A guy who was running away from himself."

"I don't understand."

"Oh, I guess he was kicked in the butt too many times, and he didn't want to remember. Funny thing is, I figured he needed to remember."

Billy still looked puzzled. "You knew this guy?"

"I was with him last night. Funny thing about suicide, you figure you could have said something or done something to stop it. And it eats at you. It gnaws at you even more if you figure you said something or did something that pushed him into it."

"You think you did that?"

"I told Kathy Smothers not to blame herself when her boy Teddy shot himself. Told Mrs. Callahan the same thing when her husband took an overdose. But I can't seem to tell myself that." Charley picked up the ebony elephant and rubbed his finger up and down the trunk. "This fellow. He was Andy Mason's friend. They had a falling out after Korea. Last night in bed, I kept thinking of the day I might bring Andy here. Figured the two of them could meet. I kept getting this image of them suddenly recognizing each other, smiling, running at each other, embracing."

"Might not have happened anyway, Dad."

"Might not."

Chapter Forty-One

Billy was in his room studying chemistry.

Mary had turned off the television and was reading a magazine in the living room. Nearly two hours had passed since she finished stacking the dinner dishes.

Shades were drawn in the kitchen where the telephone cord stretched from the wall to Charley. Before him, on the table, were several scraps of paper and a half-empty cup of lukewarm coffee.

"Who did you say you are?" The male voice was sharp, articulate and of middle pitch.

"Lieutenant Bannon. Upper Darby Police."

"Upper Darby?"

"Look, this is nothing official. I'm just looking for information."

"Well, I don't think I can help you."

"The name Andrew Mason means nothing to you? Is that what you're saying?"

"No, I didn't say that, did I? It's just that I don't know who you are or what you want. And why did you come to me? What do you figure me for, exactly?"

"Mr. Wood, I really don't figure you for much of anything, right now. So, please. Don't get your defenses up. I'm simply hoping you'll be helpful. I need to find Andrew Mason."

"Even if I knew his whereabouts, I wouldn't tell some stranger over the telephone. You say you're a police lieutenant, but I have no way of knowing. And even if you are, why should I give you information about anybody? I'm sorry, but I'm going to hang up this phone."

"Wait! Henry Mason's dying. He wants to see his son. Please. I'll come see you if necessary."

"No, don't bother. I won't be here."

"I know you wrote to Andrew Mason, or at least tried to."

Timothy Wood failed to respond, but stayed on the line.

"Mr. Wood, are you there?"

"Yes."

"If you could simply give me the last address you have, it might help."

"Look, you caught me in the middle of something. I don't have time for this." After a long sigh, Wood continued, "If it's what you say, and the mad bomber needs to see his son, I'm sorry. I really am. But I don't have anything that would help you."

Charley thought he recognized a conciliatory tone. "Why don't you let me decide that?"

Any softening of manner evaporated when Wood said, "Now you're pushing, and I don't like to be pushed."

"I know a few things about you, Mr. Wood." Charley was immediately annoyed with himself and wished he could retrieve his words. He had promised himself not to tread in that direction.

"Oh, I see. You've made some sort of prejudgment, is that it?" Wood's words were cool and cutting.

"I'm sorry. I didn't mean it the way it sounded."

"Yes you did. If you know me as you say, then you know I run a respectable business. Good night, Mr. Policeman, or whoever you are."

"Damnit," Charley mumbled after hearing the click.

Within minutes, Mary stepped into the kitchen to find Charley bent over his notes and coffee cup. She saw that he was deeply reflective, soberly pensive. "You okay?" she asked while standing behind his chair and placing her arms around him. She hugged him, then kissed his ear. "Tell me about it."

"I messed up. At one point I thought I made contact, but I lost it. He's defensive as hell. Maybe he has reason to be."

"So, when are you heading north?" Mary asked as she rubbed his shoulders.

"I can't tomorrow. Too many things to do first. And I gotta talk to this guy again. In person. Eye contact is the only answer, and I'm not sure of that now. I hope I didn't push him into a corner."

"I thought you said you couldn't wait, that Mason's time was running out."

"Time is running out, and I shouldn't delay, but I'll have to chance it. I know they can't keep giving blood. They're going to operate, I'm sure. And that's going to kill the old guy."

Mary sat next to her husband.

Charley pushed away the papers and gazed into his cup. "I hate what he did. I hate him for doing it. But I think I'm beginning to figure out what triggered his distorted sense of justice."

Mary waited for more, but it didn't come. She tried to offer strength through her silence and a firm touch, as she did so often when Charley was troubled or vulnerable. In time, she said, "Sometimes I want more from you than I dare ask."

His eye's questioned her meaning.

"But I've always been grateful for what you've given me," she added.

Gazing intently at her, Charley shook his head as if to insist that she had it backwards. "Hey, who's giving whom the transfusion right now." He leaned over and kissed her. "You're my strength, kiddo, and because of it, I can unload. I can tell you that I feel remorse."

"Remorse?"

"And I can't shake it off, no matter how many times I try. I keep telling myself that Larry Malvern's death wasn't my fault. It wasn't, was it?"

"Well, now, let me see. I think I'll quote someone dear to my heart. His name's Charley, and he has often said, 'It's never anyone's fault but the person who does it.' Face it, Charley, if this Larry what's-his-name hadn't killed himself now, he would have done it later."

"He exposed his guts to me. He remembered what he wanted to forget. Maybe he just couldn't take the pain."

"You can't convince me that he was able to escape painful thoughts every waking and sleeping hour, except for this one night with you. Come on, now!" She took his hand and waited as his mind wandered.

"And then there's Mason. I can't help but wonder if I'm going to bring him more pain. I don't know where all of this is leading. I don't know what I'll be bringing to his bedside, if I bring anything."

"So, it's a gamble."

"Sometimes I think maybe I should leave well enough alone. But that wouldn't work either. I could never live with myself, not because the promise would be unfulfilled, but because I might deny him his final happiness, maybe his only happiness as an old man. Of course, I suppose some would say that a man who commits heinous crimes should be deprived of any happiness."

"Like I said, it's a gamble. But it's a gamble you're going to take. I know you, Charley."

"And then there's Andrew Mason. Maybe he should be left alone. I keep wondering if his life should remain untouched. Maybe we're opening up something that shouldn't be opened."

"But you have to do it, right? Isn't that what you're saying?"

Charley nodded his head. "Some wives would be angry if their husbands used vacation time like this."

"Well, I'm not up for Disney World or Bermuda or Paris right now. But you owe me. I'll hold you to it."

Thump, thump, thump came Billy, thumping down the stairs. He did a quick detour to the kitchen, shouted "I won't be late," and headed for the front door.

"Wait!" his mother called. "Where are you going?"

"To Lori's."

"This late?"

"My homework's done. We're just gonna watch a video tape."

"Is Mrs. Lippincott home?"

"Yeah. Sure. See yuh." Billy slammed the door.

Mary stood. "How about a hot cup of coffee?" She went to the sink and poured water. "You know, Charley, you've become Billy's hero. He really looks up to you now."

"I think I owe Henry Mason another debt."

As the coffee brewed, Mary returned to her husband and massaged his shoulders. "Tell you what, big guy. Let's go to bed early."

Charley leaned back and looked up at her. "That's the best offer I've had in a long time." He smiled. "I love you. Did I ever tell you that?"

"A couple of times."

Chapter Forty-Two

Charley moved quickly while others strolled along the streets of Old City, Philadelphia, the restored area of quaint shops, restaurants, and brick townhouses dating back to Colonial times. He hurried across cobblestones and Belgian blocks and followed brick sidewalks in search of the Rose Root Gift Shoppe.

Old City, with its aura of pre-revolution, was rife with lamplights, shiny brass knockers, white stone steps, wrought-iron railings, footscrapers, and shutters in muted shades of blue, green and yellow ocher. Houses declared their age with historic markers riveted to refurbished brick walls. Iron gates sometimes led to small enclosed gardens.

The Rose Root Gift Shoppe was appropriately fitted to the period. Its display windows were divided into small panes of glass and a suitable lamplight adorned its Colonial doorway.

Charley stepped out of the sunlight and into the gift shop where amber glass lanterns reflected light on a vast collection of objects of glass, china, wax, metal and polished wood. Moving slowly, he examined stained-glass butterflies and copper twirling-bird mobiles while surreptitiously eying his surroundings. The shopkeepers were busy with customers, so Charley occupied himself with porcelain figurines and music boxes. While examining African woodcarvings, he gained a better view of a tall, slender, middle-aged male behind the cash register. A salt-and-pepper Vandyke beard, high cheekbones and a turquoise turtleneck stayed in his mind as he fingered decanters, elaborate bottle openers and corkscrews. When the bar tools carried his thoughts to Larry Malvern, he moved quickly to pewter pots.

Charley was toying with a small gold cat when his peripheral vision picked up Vandyke's partner, a boyish sort, far older than his looks but much younger than his associate. Apparently his hormones offered little facial hair to his peachy-cream flesh. Blue-eyed and dimpled, he smiled a lot as he glanced from person to person.

Two customers left, leaving only three—a young couple and an elderly woman.

After browsing among glass dogs and cats, Charley turned toward an arrangement of lotus pods when he saw Vandyke approaching. He spun away quickly and stepped toward the sand candles.

"May I help you with anything?"

"Oh, hi. These are interesting."

"We make them by pouring wax into molds of wet sand."

"Wow. Yeah. I like the way you combine them with driftwood and rocks."

"Is there any particular one that catches your fancy?"

"Truth is, I'm just looking." Charley smiled as he glanced into the gray-green eyes of the bearded man. "Are you the proprietor?"

"Yes. Why do you ask?"

Charley reacted to the man's searching gaze, looked away and said, "Well, you have such a wonderful collection of things."

"I have a junior partner. We work together. Actually, we make some of the things ourselves. Perhaps you've noticed these rose roots. We gather and clean them, then stain and polish them." He lifted a root. "This is a particularly nice one, don't you think?" He handed it to Charley.

Charley recognized Vandyke's voice from his telephone conversation with Timothy Wood. He felt somewhat uncomfortable for not having identified himself as yet. "Yes," he said, holding the root in both hands. "An interesting shape."

"It reminds me of a bird with its wings and tail spread on the ground, pushing. Except for this piece over here."

"It reminds me of a man, climbing, crawling, trying to escape."

"I don't really see that."

Charley returned the root to its place among others, and Vandyke glanced about for customers, but all were gone. Baby face was arranging abalone shells.

"You're Timothy Wood, aren't you?" Charley asked abruptly.

Vandyke was taken aback. "Why do you ask?"

"I'm Lieutenant Bannon. We spoke on the phone last night."

Anger immediately flared in Wood's eyes. His faced reddened. "What are you doing here? What do you want? I thought I told you..."

"Take it easy."

"Take it easy! Why are you spying? Why did you lead me on? Why didn't you identify yourself?"

"I intended to explain who I was. You had customers. So I waited."

"And talked about rose roots and sand candles! What were you waiting to see? Whether I wiggled my ass, is that it?"

"Now, wait. I didn't intend..."

"This is harassment! You get the hell out of here!"

Baby Face perked his ears, stepped away from the abalone shells, lost all signs of a smile, watched and listened.

Instead of leaving, Charley walked toward the rear of the shop, infuriating Wood, who stood glaring at the big cop for seconds before following.

"Give me a minute," Charley insisted as Wood approached him. "I've got to know some things. Time is running out. I need to shorten my hunt as much as possible. And if and when I meet Andy, I've got to be well armed. The more I know, the better I can organize myself and say the right things. I don't want to lose before I start."

Wood attempted to control himself.

"Look, I need your help." Charley had trouble effecting the beseeching look of a puppy dog, but he tried. He suspected that Wood's past relationship with police had much to do with his mistrust and defensiveness. So he struggled to conjure up the softest Bannon in his repertoire.

Wood looked back at Baby Face, then studied Charley's expression. "You're not going to give up, are you?"

"You got it right, Mr. Wood."

"Frankly, I hope you do find him. I certainly don't want to stand in your way."

"Then give me some clues. A piece of an address. Anything."

"It's not something I can unravel easily."

"Some streets or numbers. I'm not looking for details of your relationship with him, or anything like that."

"I guess I can give you what I remember. But it may not lead you anywhere."

"Hey. Anything." Charley flipped open a note pad and tested his pen.

"First it was Lake Road, Dryden, New York. Don't recall the number, but it had the letter B next to it. I figured it for a second-floor apartment in a private house. When he moved, I traced that through the post office to an Evergreen address, still Dryden. I don't know if it was road, street or lane. Evergreen something. It's been a long time ago. I didn't keep a written record. Tossed out everything after his third move. He cut himself clean. I figured he moved to another town. I wrote once more, hoping they'd forward my letter. Never got an answer."

Charley recognized a bit of slippage in Wood's flippancy. In fact, he detected a touch of sadness. Looking up from his notes, he asked, "Just out of curiosity, Mr. Wood, why did you keep writing?"

"Now you're treading in the wrong direction."

Charley shrugged his shoulders. "Then forget it."

"Ahhh, it's okay, I guess." Wood pondered the thought. "To tell you the truth, Lieutenant, I wanted to apologize for being a jerk and causing trouble. Dear ol' Private Mason, my good wartime buddy, didn't deserve what I laid on him. He was a first-rate guy." Wood glanced toward Baby Face, who had moved within earshot and feigned busywork. Then he looked at Charley and said, "You know, we all do things when younger that we wouldn't do when older. It took me a long time to figure myself out, let alone understand my actions."

"What actions?"

"No you don't." Wood's expression soured.

"You're so touchy."

"That's right. When it comes to Mason, I'm defensive as hell, and I get emotionally worked up. You touched a sensitive cord, Lieutenant. You see, I was never allowed to finish what I started, to correct what needed to be fixed, to say I was sorry. And that's not easy to live with. It eats at a guy."

Charley saw that Wood had slipped again into a softer more responsive mood. "You sound like you might like to talk about it."

"Don't kid yourself, Lieutenant. But since you opened up an old wound, I will say this: It was never my intent to hurt Mason or blackmail him in any way. And you can tell him that if you ever find him."

"I'll do that."

"After Korea, I pushed myself into his life. I handled the whole thing wrong."

Charley waited for more, but it didn't come. He finally said, "Well, I'll check things out in Dryden."

"If I were you I'd check the plant nurseries. Knowing Mason, he's probably hanging around with rhododendrons or tiger lilies."

"Okay, I'll check out the lilies." Charley kept staring at Wood, wondering how such a man could have knocked over the first domino.

Wood stared back. "I know what you're thinking."

"No. I don't think so."

"Do you realize what it was like for someone like me in those days after Korea? Ah, the nineteen-fifties. I was angry with the world. And I was angry with myself for what I was. Then I flaunted it like a cripple who shoves his mangled limbs under everybody's nose."

"You're way off base. I was thinking of a long line of misfortune, from a fleeing son to fire and death."

Wood looked puzzled. Then his eyes widened as his expression suddenly awoke to a revelation. Within seconds, the impact transformed his visage to one of shock.

"I know you read the papers, Mr. Wood. What were your words last night? Mad bomber?"

"The old man. My God. But I didn't make the connection. I didn't see myself as a player."

An elderly woman with blue-white hair entered the shop and began fingering the rose roots. Baby Face hurried toward her.

"Let's go back here," Wood suggested. He led Charley into the storeroom and down a narrow passage between shelves stacked with boxes. After gathering his thoughts, he said, "Do you know what it's like in a small Midwestern town for someone like me? A guy doesn't dare come out of the closet. He grows up scared and guilty as hell. He's a freak in his own eyes. So then he joins the Army, and suddenly he's thrust into a crazy, abnormal existence. Things happen. And when he gets out, there's no going back to that town in the middle of Iowa. He heads for a big city where he thinks he can lose himself and maybe seek his kind. But if he can't adjust... If he's just an overgrown kid from Iowa, immature for twenty-three, not worldly... Well, he's a strange animal on the loose. He doesn't fit yet. He tries to take what he wants or needs. And if he has no money, and he needs a stopover before he settles in... Well, he uses a friend, if he has any."

"Andy Mason?"

Wood nodded.

"Is he...?"

"No, I don't think so."

Wood looked Charley up and down and smiled wryly. "You're pretty good, Lieutenant. Do they have those new sensitivity courses in your outfit? Did they teach you to choke on the word faggot and swallow it instead of spitting it out?"

Charley looked down.

"Not yet, eh?" Wood snickered. "Well, maybe by the eighties, the nineties, the turn of the century."

"Who knows what the eighties will bring."

"You know, I'd like to tell you that you had no right to wake me from my blissful sleep. But maybe you did."

"Blissful?"

"I came to peace with myself long ago." Wood walked toward the salesroom. "Come on, I'll introduce you to my partner."

Charley followed

"Danny, come meet Lieutenant... What is it again?"

"Bannon."

"Oh, yes. Come meet Lieutenant Bannon."

Baby Face was back at the abalone display, for the blue-haired woman had left. He looked up, stepped toward Charley and smiled.

"Hi," was Charley's quick greeting as he nodded, then headed toward the door.

Wood stepped behind Danny, wrapped his arms around him and whispered, "It's okay. I'll tell you all about it. It happened a long time ago."

Chapter Forty-Three

Lori's sticky hands moved quickly as she tried to make room at the kitchen table for her next creation. Her mother stood in the doorway watching, wanting to help, a frown of dismay on her face.

"Please let me do a few things, Lori."

"No, Mom! This has got to be special. I have to do every bit of it myself, so I can tell Billy I did it all, and hope that he believes me. You have to tell him, too. He'll believe you."

"He knows you can cook."

"Not like this."

"You've made beautiful meals for me, without all this fuss."

"This is different."

The Lippincott kitchen—an attractive combination of pea green walls, cafe curtains and copper appointments—was now a nightmare. Flour had spilled to the floor, sticky bowls filled the sink, and a little bit of everything crowded the table and counter space—cake tins, eggshells, lemon rind, a colander of noodles, deboned chicken and a pile of bones, pasty globs, pots, a dozen spice containers and a few olives that got away, among other things.

But by some miracle, the almond pie-cake was finished and its sweet aroma filled the house. And the first casserole was in the oven, just beginning to add a new aroma. This was a massive undertaking, far beyond Lori's usual efforts—even fancy efforts—for her mom and herself. Billy was coming to dinner.

Evelyn Lippincott had not expected to be cut out of all

preparations. She felt that her idea had gotten out-of-hand. It was an idea that had surprised her daughter, resulted in kisses and hugs of thanks, and sent Lori into a frenzy of buoyant activity.

"Yesterday it was all talk of this profession or that profession. How you wanted to be this shining star and keep up with Billy intellectually. Then I mention having him over here for dinner, and suddenly its gourmet domesticity a la grandiose. Maybe you're trying too hard to please him."

"I like to please him. Besides, if Dad doesn't come through and I can't go to college because of money, I better know how to cook."

"I'm sorry I talk about money so much. I shouldn't."

"It's okay."

"You'll go to college even if your father reneges. It won't be Princeton. But you'll go, even if you have to start at Community College. I don't work extra hours for nothing."

"Ouch! I burnt myself! Mom! Let's not talk about those things now. Tell you what. You can get out the candles for me. The white ones."

"At least let me set the table. We'll use the good Irish linen."

"Okay, okay." Lori consented because the kitchen had gotten ahead of her. She wiped her hands on her well-stained apron, sighed, looked about for a clean pot, then glanced at the stove clock. "I told him seven thirty. He's going to the hospital first to give Mr. Mason the soldiers. Dr. Sherman gave him permission."

Evelyn frowned.

"Don't say it, Mom. You want me to burn myself again?"

"A murderer is a murderer," Evelyn muttered under her breath.

"I heard you. Billy separates the man from the deed."

"You can't do that. A man is made up of his deeds."

"Billy thinks differently."

"Oh, yes. Billy's a kind and generous boy, but his mind wanders into strange levels of thinking. Sometimes you parrot him too much. You do have a mind of your own, you know."

"Ouch! Mom!"

"Sorry."

* * *

252

In the hospital ICU by special permission, Billy had lined up the lead soldiers on the bed table—a table that swung over the bed and now stretched in front of the patient. Redcoats, bluecoats, yellowcoats, browncoats—all in marching formation. Billy had researched the colors in book after book. He had touched up the guns with silver, gold and black paint. Feathers in Native American headdresses were bright with a gamut of colors—true colors of the tribes, thanks to three volumes on Indians found in the local library.

The patient, his head propped up slightly, gazed without a trace of smile or frown. Utterly emaciated, Henry kept his hollow eyes on the troops as Billy stood perplexed, anxious and uncertain.

"Mr. Mason?" Billy paused and watched. "Mr. Mason?"

The boy was so proud. His eyes were intense. He kept looking for response in the old man—any response, even the slightest turn of the lips. Feeling awkward and uneasy as time passed, he began to rearrange the soldiers. He marched the battalion of British redcoats to the edge of the table.

"They used to march like this, in straight files. Then they'd line up like this for battle. And the Americans would shoot them."

Henry grunted.

Billy lifted his head suddenly and stared at the old man. He saw a big tear roll from the patient's left eye.

"This is..." Henry's lips quivered as he tried to speak. His voice was but a whisper. "This is the... the most wonderful..."

"Yes?"

"The most wonderful gift anyone has ever given me."

Billy sucked in his lips as he struggled to contain himself.

Henry reached for the boy's hand.

* * *

Billy arrived home late to find a squashed pumpkin splattered at the front door, its pieces scattered here and there on the steps. He stared for an instant as a sickening feelings permeated his body, then slipped on a wad of slimly seeds as he tried to enter the house. After cleaning his foot on the threshold, he stepped into the living room and yelled, "Yo, Mom! Who tossed the damn pumpkin?" Mom?"

"I'm in the kitchen."

Billy found his mother alone at the kitchen table polishing silverware. "Where's Dad?"

Mary looked at her watch. "Well, about now, I'd say he's somewhere north of Scranton. Maybe across the New York State line."

"He left?"

"Hours ago."

"There's pumpkin slime out front."

"I know. How was your dinner?"

"Unbelievable! You can't imagine! Lori outdid herself. And you know something? Her mom's really not a bad dude."

"Dude?"

"Whatever. She's okay. But Mom, you should've seen this cake or pie or whatever it was. Made of almonds. Real moist like. It was great." Billy quieted as he tried to read his mother's expression. Pointing over his shoulder, he asked, "But what about that? That pumpkin mess?"

"Will you clean it up for me?"

"Yeah. Sure. But..."

"You also got a couple nasty phone calls."

"I did?"

"Some pretty vile words. I hung up both times."

"You mean obscene stuff?"

Mary nodded as she continued to shine the silver. "Maybe you talk about Mr. Mason too much. At school, maybe?" She looked up from her polishing.

Billy's expression of concern grew to a look of panic. "No way! Just to friends."

"Maybe the wrong people hear the wrong remarks."

"I don't know about that, Mom. That creep, Marty Shoemaker, comes up to me wearing a 'Burn Baby Burn' T-shirt and says, 'Great guy that Mason for burning those queers.' But I tell 'im to get lost"

"I don't like that term, Billy."

"Just quoting."

"The caller was at the other end of the spectrum. Called you a f'in' pig for befriending a f'in' killer."

"Christ almighty!"

"Hey!"

"Damn it, Mom, the worst sort of person deserves some kindness when he's dying or going to the gallows. Doesn't he? He's a human being! Besides, I don't think Mr. Mason's mind tells him he's a killer. He was..."

"You needn't repeat yourself, Billy." She mocked him: "'He was obsessed with punishing. Blinded by his obscssion.'"

"Well, it's true."

"Maybe you're a bit obsessed. Ever think of that?"

Billy stiffened his jaw, but said nothing.

"Which reminds me," Mary continued, "I put away those psychology books you had strewn all over the place. I hope you don't mind, but I read your underlinings."

"So?" His look was defensive.

"There's something I have to know, Billy."

The boy raised his eyebrows.

"Tell me the truth now," Mary said. "If Mr. Mason should recover by some miracle, what do you want to see happen?"

"To him?"

"Yes, to him."

"He should be tried, convicted if guilty, and punished if... if..."

"If?"

"How do they say it? If... if of sound mind, or something like that. Jeeze, Mom, what did you expect me to say? That he should live happily ever after? I'm not a screwball idiot! Don't you think I know it's best if he dies? Don't you think Dad knows? How do you think it makes me feel? How do you think it makes Dad feel?"

Proud yet nearly dumbfounded, Mary said nothing as she gazed on her 16-year-old boychild. How was it, she thought, that an old man of evil deeds had brought together father and son?

Chapter Forty-Four

An Ithaca morning.

Beth was serene as she sat alone on the rooftop porch at Willard Straight Hall, Cornell's massive student union, a building of gray stone on a steep slope, a building of arches, spacious rooms, lobbies displaying handsome murals, and dining halls decked with Ivy League crests.

The rooftop porch was among Beth's favorite places, especially before the noontime students arrived to fill the chairs and crowd the tables. The morning was sunny. Breezes swept in from the west, and Beth's eyes drifted over the Ithaca valley, over rooftops and the hills beyond, over clusters of autumn yellows and reds mixed with dark evergreens. In the distance, on South Hill, the modern-day buildings of Ithaca College were glowing reflectors of the sun.

Beth's tweed jacket was open at the bottom, spread apart by her rounded belly. Her hands folded over her baby, she sat quietly and talked gently to her unborn child: "It's got to be a special day, Little One. This has got to be the most wonderful birthday of John's life. Your daddy likes roast pork, so we'll have a beautiful feast, cooked apples and all. His music. His mums and bittersweet. Pumpkins and gourds and corn and all the things of autumn. He loves the fall. But then your daddy loves all the seasons."

An English sparrow captured Beth's attention as it perched nearby on a rail, fluttered to a table, feasted on crumbs, looked up at her, tipped its head and chirped. When the sparrow took flight, Beth followed it with her eyes, smiled and blew a kiss. "Goodbye little bird."

The more the breeze tossed Beth's hair and chilled her cheeks, the more radiant she felt, the more excited about God's gifts to her, about the vastness, the fullness, the beauty that she felt was hers. She wished that somehow she could wrap it all up and give the bundle to John for his birthday. But surely parts and pieces had to be presented on this special day—her feelings of joy, even her fearful hopes born of her love.

Beth fancied herself breathing in the entire valley that stretched before her, holding it within her bosom, making it part of her. The fuller she was, the fuller she could make John.

"He's special, just like you're special, Little One." She tapped her belly as she inhaled deeply.

How remarkable, how creative, how magical to mesh the seeder of flowering beauty with the artist. Brushing her colorful oils of imagination, Beth permitted fanciful images of germination, blending blossom and baby. She smiled as she remembered her mother's words: "A gardener! You must be kidding!"

"Tulips and baby, daisies and baby," Beth uttered in a singsong whisper.

Again her mother's words intruded: "Don't get married too young. Wait. But don't wait too long."

Beth looked up at the sky as she locked her hands over the baby again and reflected on her mother's lesson that love doesn't bloom uncultivated like a "lily in a field of weeds." She kept smiling as her mother's words reverberated: "You just don't wait, hope, and expect it to happen. Work at it. But don't marry a man too much older than yourself."

Pregnant at forty!

"Oh, Mama, I've got to tell you how it feels to carry his baby."

* * *

An Ithaca evening.

A warm October evening was such a perfect time to wander in Sapsucker Woods, twisting and turning on pathways through thickets of nature and across wetlands that bordered a woodsy pond. Because Indian Summer persisted, John was able to fulfill a promise postponed from September. He was grateful that bright leaves still clustered on many a tree and that migrating ducks and geese still stopped and rippled the waters on their way south. It was not too late in the season to hear the lingering summer birds. John chose evening, as he always did, because it offered a blending of sounds—the final calls of the daylight songbirds and the beginning chatter of the night creatures. This was a two-way time of transition—summer to winter, day to night.

For an artist who painted nature and a gardener who worshiped everything from skunk cabbage to primroses, Sapsucker Woods at sunset was an evening in Eden.

"Let's talk about the baby's name again," Beth suggested as they followed the path into deep woods. "This seems a proper place to pick a name, don't you think?" She smiled warmly as she looked into her husband's eyes. "I don't know what you have against John. I like John. It's a good name. If he's a boy, why shouldn't he be a junior?"

"It's such a common name."

"But it's your name."

"We'll call her Elizabeth." John took Beth's hand and guided her with unusual care among protruding roots. Beth's fullness and radiance pleased John, who was more than solicitous for her welfare. Sometimes he gave so much attention to her needs that she would burst into laughter and proclaim, "My God, John, I'm not an invalid!"

"And if it's not a girl?" Beth asked.

"Aloysius or Alphonso."

"Don't be silly. But that's an idea. Let's start with A, then go on to B, and so on. How about Alfred or Allen?"

"I prefer Algernon."

"No you don't! Stop it now! This is serious." Silently, she played with the letter A, then said, "I think I've got it. Andrew. How about Andrew? It's a good name. It has a strong and wholesome quality. What do you think, John? Do you like Andrew?"

"Look at this. It's some kind of tree fungus."

"You didn't answer me. What about Andrew?"

John squatted and examined the fungus on a rotting tree stump. "Look at this, Beth."

"John!"

"It's an okay name, I guess."

"Does that mean you approve?"

"Like I said. It's okay."

"Well, that's about as much enthusiasm as you've given me for any name."

"Come on, let's go. Look ahead. Up there. That's a sapsucker, I think."

Sapsucker Woods was a Cornell bird sanctuary. Its trails wound about trees and underbrush, then changed to narrow boardwalks over swamps. The pond stretched from its northern boundary. Near the water's edge stood the University's Laboratory of Ornithology, a ranch-type building with wide picture windows facing the pond and tall grasses and reeds. Trees on the meandering banks leaned toward the smooth water, broken here and there by the V-ripples of mallards, wood ducks, and an occasional muskrat.

"Watch that rock!" John warned. He guided Beth by the elbow. When they reached the elevated planks over the wetlands, he was quick to take her arm and lift. Then he held her tightly from behind and kissed the back of her neck.

The evening song of the hermit thrush charmed John and Beth with its flute-like sounds. They stood still as a slight breeze stirred the leaves and carried the melody. It faded, giving way to the pure fluting and descending spirals of a migrating veery paused on its way south.

"Then it's agreed," Beth said. "If it's a boy, its Andrew. If it's a girl, well, maybe Elizabeth. We'll see."

John said nothing. Confounded by the irony, he could feel the beating of his heart, but refused to be distracted from his concentration on Beth. Behind her, but close, he carefully watched each of her steps as she walked the boards. He was prepared to grab her in an instant if necessary.

The last of the day's sunlight turned the tops of the trees into torches of flaming color, but as quickly as they blazed, they darkened, and a chill fell over the woods. From the high grass at the pond came the sound of a distant banjo, a bobolink singing its last song of the day.

"Remember when we first came here?" John asked. "It was spring, and you kept kneeling to look inside the pitcher plants to see if they caught any bugs."

"And I fell head first into the mire, with my feet up here on the boards. I couldn't get up, and you kept laughing at me."

"But I pulled you out."

"After you made me suffer."

"You looked so cute with your butt in the air."

"Ooooh!"

"Your pretty blouse was all spotted with mud."

"So was my face."

"But I kissed you anyway."

"I wanted to go home. But you insisted I stay."

"Just to see the skunk cabbage."

Autumn had yellowed and thinned the underbrush and waterweeds, but the insects remained abundant, buzzing and chirping as the evening darkened. Deep dusk had settled over the pond by the time John and Beth finished their walk and stood gazing at the water as the peepers and frogs awakened. A sandpiper's lilting call echoed across the wetlands.

John put his arm around Beth as their eyes lost sight of detail. He whispered, "You've given me a wonderful birthday."

"Have I? I wanted to so very much."

"Dinner was scrumptious, the cake beautiful, and I love my scooter."

"Do you?" She squeezed him.

"Bright red, no less. I guess you want everyone to see me coming. I just hope it can put-put its way up Buffalo hill."

"I asked the man at the cycle shop, and he guaranteed it."

"Now tell me, how did you afford such an extravagant gift?"

"Mom helped me a little. But to tell you the truth, I've been keeping a secret. I sold one of my paintings to Dr. Morse in the entomology department."

"You're kidding! Which one?"

"The sunflowers with the big bee. It was the bee that got him, I think."

"But I love that painting. It's better than Van Gogh's."

"I'll paint another, especially for you." She kissed him on the cheek.

A chill wind turned John and his pregnant wife away from the pond. As they walked arm-in-arm, he whispered, "Coming here was special, too. A perfect cap on a super birthday."

"But your day's not over, John."

* * *

An Ithaca night.

Near to him. Near to her. Naked.

"Turn off the light, John."

"No. I want to see you."

"Please?"

"Why? I want to see you."

"I look funny."

"You're beautiful."

"No, John. Not with this big belly."

"Oh, yes. Beautiful, beautiful, beautiful."

"Oh, silly. I don't like you to see me this way." Beth pulled the sheet to her breasts and smiled at the ceiling.

John stayed propped on one elbow as he smiled down on her and repeated, "Beautiful, beautiful, beautiful."

She looked into his eyes, feasting on them with a deep, warm gaze as he reached across and held himself above her with his strong, muscular arms. She grasped his firm biceps, then his shoulders, and pulled him down until their lips met.

Seconds later he turned her onto her side. She reached for the light and switched it off. "Please?" she asked while cuddling close to him. The room was dark but for a dim glow from beyond the doorway.

John put his nose against hers and whispered, "You sure it's okay? You know, what with the baby?

"Yes, yes, it's okay."

"You sure?"

"Of course I'm sure. Silly man. How many times must I tell you?"

Outside, the winds of autumn bared more branches and the

leaves fluttered like nighttime butterflies in the glow of the streetlamps. Lights in the windows of boardinghouses on each side of Buffalo Street silhouetted Cornell students at their studies.

And when the passion was spent, John held tightly in the afterglow.

"I love you, John."

"And I love you."

"I hope the baby looks just like you. A beautiful, healthy boy. With your eyes, your chin, your hair, your nose, your..."

"Let's just hope the baby's healthy." John ran his fingers through her hair, then slipped away from her and lay on his back, at peace in the darkness.

"My mother lost her second baby," Beth said quietly, almost distantly. "A little boy." Her mind carried her to far-off visions, then brought her back. "That's why Mom frets about me so much."

"Why do you think of that right now?"

"I don't know."

"You're not worried are you?"

"Not really."

"You saw Dr. Hutton again last week."

"I know."

John placed his hand on her belly and felt the baby move.

"My father came home one night and decided to free his conscience. Strange. His urgent need came suddenly after months of guilt. So he told my mother about his affair with his skinny, little flirt of a secretary. My mother cried all night. The next day he rushed her to the hospital."

"Damn it, Beth, how come you never told me?" John froze, for he couldn't believe his question. Never before had he asked even a trifle about his wife's bygone days. He wanted to take back his words, but couldn't, so he waited for her recriminating remarks about his secret past.

Stillness owned the room for a long moment.

Beth swallowed her thoughts of countercharge with difficulty. "This is your birthday, John. I'm not going to spoil it."

Chapter Forty-Five

When the season was ripe—nippy at night, sunny at day, dry and pungent with Canadian breeze—the splendor of late October spread from the northwest over Canandaigua Lake southeast to Keuka and the vast vineyards, east to the shores of Seneca, then to Cayuga's silver waters, Ithaca and the gardens of Cornell.

Even at mid-afternoon, temperatures in the shade chilled John, chasing him to the warmth of sunlight in the rose beds on the Cornell Plantations. As he raked autumn leaves and twigs from a garden patch he caught sight of a man watching him from afar, standing in the shade of a shedding maple. At first he thought little of it, but the man stayed and stared. Finally the stranger was gone, and John gained comfort and raked with vigor.

Sugar content in the maples and weather conditions had mixed just right this fall to turn many of the trees fiery red-orange, contrasting with the russet oaks and the yellow elms. Even as late as this, a few blooms in the Plantations' rose gardens had fought off the cold nights and held themselves proudly, giving scattered bursts of pink, yellow and red. John saw something special in an autumn rose, even if the tips of its petals were brown. He would sometimes gaze on one, allowing it to free him of other thoughts.

John knelt near his wheelbarrow and spread leave-and-peat mulch around the roots of his rose bushes. When he stood and reached for his shovel, he saw the man again, this time standing on the far side of the flower beds, staring at him. Dressed in a heavy brown tweed, the big man slipped his hands into his pockets and struck a casual pose.

After a moment of puzzlement, John went about his business, shoveling from the wheelbarrow, until he realized that the man had stepped closer and continued to stare. He stood still, one hand on his shovel, and gazed hard at the man for several seconds, then returned to his work.

Minutes later, John noticed that the stranger was much closer, and again he stared back, this time tossing his shovel into the wheelbarrow without breaking eye contact with the man. Something familiar about the intruder's appearance startled John, but he couldn't figure out what it was. He tried to place the man, but couldn't.

"Hello!" the stranger called as he neared.

"Hi!" John answered.

"Nice day."

"Sure is."

"Mulching your roses, I see."

"It's that time."

"What variety is that one?"

"It's a new hybrid, tagged only with a number. A beauty, isn't it?"

"I see you prune all but a few bloomers."

"Don't have the heart to cut some. Not yet, anyway."

"Have a minute to talk?" Charley Bannon asked as he rounded a bed of pruned bushes, their stubby stems only inches above the mulch.

John started to answer, then hesitated as uneasiness plagued him.

"Do you mind?" Charley asked.

"Got a lot of work. Got these beds to cover." John turned toward his wheelbarrow, but was compelled to look back.

"Give me a minute."

"Do I know you from somewhere?"

Stepping closer, Charley ignored the question and asked one of his own: "Andrew Mason, isn't it?"

Fear and disbelief struck John. He had not heard anyone say his true name in more than 20 years.

"Don't get upset, Mason. It's okay. Really."

"Sorry, but you have the wrong guy. I don't know any Andrew Mason." John betrayed himself with an awe-struck look of terror. Fear and shock not only showed in his eyes, they distorted his entire expression.

"Look, I don't mean any trouble."

"Trouble? I don't know what you're talking about. Like I said, I'm not the guy you want."

"Please listen to me. This isn't about you. It's your father. He's ill. Very ill. And he wants to see you."

"My father's dead. As I said, I don't know any Andrew Mason." John began to turn away, only to look back, frown in thought, and stare. He keep his eyes on Charley, and suddenly he saw the boy of years past behind the facade of today's man. "Oh my God," he mumbled.

"What's that?"

"I have work to do." John turned toward the wheelbarrow and grabbed his shovel.

"Your father might die. And he knows it. He wants you with him."

John began to shovel mulch, but he couldn't concentrate, lost his balance, misfired, and tossed the shovelful of leaves and peat moss onto the grass pathway near Charley. He looked up at the big man, leaned on his shovel, then asked, "Why did you come here?"

"I told you."

"So you're still my father's errand boy."

"I chose this errand. There's a sick old man back there who needs to see his son before he dies. Only you can give him the peace he needs before..." Charley's words trailed off to nothing.

"I have a new life, Banning."

"The name's Bannon."

"Whatever. I have a new life. I'm a different person. I don't want to remember." Andrew gestured and glanced over his garden plots as if they represented his world of today. "Besides, my father doesn't want anything to do with me."

"He does now."

"Well, it's too late. Please go and leave me."

"I can't do that."

Andrew walked toward the north end of the garden plots, as if he wanted a moment of escape to clear his head and gather his thoughts. He headed for a cluster of shrubs. Charley waited, then followed. He was close behind when Andrew stopped, spun and asked, "What the hell did my father have on you anyway? What kind of a weak, mealy-mouthed creep were you that you let him push you around that way?"

"I'll tell you, if you tell me." Charley's words were clear, strong, straightforward.

"What the hell are you talking about?" Andrew backed off. "Tell you what?"

"The parts I don't know."

"What parts?"

"I think you know."

"Damn! I don't owe you a single word! You hear me?" Andrew turned and walked among the trees toward Fall Creek.

"I know why you left," Charley said as he caught up to Andrew and walked at his side. "I know about Korea," he continued, pretending he knew more than he did. "I know about Timothy Wood. I know what happened in your father's house."

Andrew could barely tolerate his fear as he thought of Beth. He stopped under a blight-stricken elm marked for cutting, sighed, gave up all pretense, and humbled himself as he pleaded: "Please, you don't understand. I have a wife who doesn't know. And she's pregnant with our first child. Please go, forget we ever talked, leave me alone. Look, I'm begging."

"May I call you Andy?"

"Call me anything, but please go." He wiped his dirty hands on his overalls and leaned against the dying tree. Sickened by desperation, he feared irrationally that he might lose everything his new life had wrought.

"I told you I meant no harm, Andy. Please believe me. If I can't convince you, I'll get the hell out of here, and that'll be it. Honest. That's a promise. But hear me out. Okay?"

"No, you don't understand, Bannon. It's impossible."

"Call me Charley, please."

Andrew walked on and on, and then on some more. The big cop followed, up a hill, down a hill, over fresh grass from cool autumn rains, through thickets and into groves and dells. Not until they reached Forest Home Road and a cluster of cottages did they look at each other and ask silent questions.

Later, on a dirt path along Fall Creek, they had no choice but to walk single file. It was here, as Andrew led the way, that he spoke again: "I don't know what you know, or what you may have found out. But whatever, you couldn't possibly understand. Only I know the truth, because it's inside of me and nowhere else."

They looked down at their feet as they stepped carefully on hardened mud and protruding rocks that formed the narrow pass among trees and underbrush between Forest Home Road and the creek.

"I could never explain it to my wife. So I have no choice. I couldn't go, even if I wanted."

"I can't accept that."

"How did you find me?" Andrew asked as they passed a stone footbridge and neared the rushing water that roared its way into Beebe Lake.

"Larry Malvern."

"Bastard."

"He's dead."

Andrew was staggered. He looked into Charley face, parted his lips, but couldn't speak.

"He killed himself," Charley said matter-of-factly. "Hanged himself in a stairwell at his apartment. An unhappy guy, trying to cover up with fun. He didn't want to think about his mother, or his father, or you. He didn't want to think about you. I opened up all the wounds, and neither you nor anyone else was around to heal them. We both helped kill him. But it was more your fault than mine."

Andrew stopped walking and leaned against a young oak. "My God."

Charley was aware that in his effort to spew it all fast, he had been harsh—severely harsh. He looked at Andrew and saw eyes terrified by horror.

"My God," Andrew repeated.

"I'm sorry."

Andrew stayed against the tree. His expression failed to change.

"I really am sorry." Charley knew his words were not enough. In an attempt to cut the pain, he launched an explanation of his trail-tracking efforts, hoping it would divert attention and smother Andrew with other thoughts. He told of pursuing leads from

Manley to Malvern to Wood to Mrs. McIlhenney, the Dryden landlady who knew that Cornell flowers and trees played a role in John Smith's life.

Lifting his eyes, Andrew gazed into the tree branches. First he wanted to pray for help, then to convince himself that the nightmare would end when he awoke. In time he spoke, sadly, slowly: "Why did you say that I helped kill Larry?"

"I shouldn't have been so blunt."

"But you were. So?"

"I'm sharing some of the guilt. I guess I wanted to unload it. That was wrong, since I don't know everything."

"You're right. You don't know everything. And you're not really answering me."

"Well, hell, don't expect me to unravel your relationship with Larry Malvern. I will say one thing, though. I have a feeling you didn't fully understand his attachment to you. And I suspect Larry didn't understand it himself."

Andrew said nothing. He stayed against the tree, almost motionless. Thoughts of Larry and old times mixed with flashing images of his pregnant wife. His trauma tightened his stomach and throat as nausea moved upward from his gut. He closed his eyes for a lengthy moment, and when he opened them, he hurried toward the lake as if to seek breathing space. Charley followed, watched keenly and tried to interpret every move. He fell behind as a group of five male students in jeans and jackets strolled between them, laughing, joking, swinging their books. Not until Andrew was halfway along the south side of the lake did Charley catch up with him.

"My father," Andrew said, almost whispering as if afraid to hear himself. "Tell me about my father." He slowed his pace, knowing that the closer he came to Triphammer Falls and the Hydraulic Laboratory the more students he would encounter.

"To tell you the truth, Andy, I don't know where to begin. I know there's a lot I have to explain. I even practiced the words, but they've escape me. Oh, man, this isn't good."

"That bad, eh?"

"Yeah. It's bad, all right."

"You said he was dying?"

"It's not just that." Charley gathered his wits and decided to toss the words fast. "He's under arrest for burning and killing. There, I said it, and I'm sorry. I'm supposed to hate him like the others do, I guess. Some think he's a freakin' lunatic. Others call him the worst kind of murderer. I don't know what I feel, but I just want to give him something before..."

"He killed someone?" Andrew interrupted.

"Don't say anything. Just listen. Let me back up, okay?" Charley breathed deeply as he looked into Andrew's anguished face. "Your father withdrew from life a long time ago. Maybe you can figure out why."

Andrew backed away and turned. He walked to the edge of Beebe Lake and allowed his eyes to scan the water and the trees on the north shore. Then he looked toward the women's dormitories but was barely conscious of them. Questions flooded his mind, but he asked none.

Charley stepped close to Andrew and said, "Being shut up like that, away from all, he began to see things strangely. I'm sure his whole thinking process became distorted." The big cop was aware that he was interpreting. Yet he knew of no other way to explain things than to offer them from his own perspective. "Your father wanted to avenge. So he would sneak out at night and throw firebombs at gay bars and porno shops. Maybe you know why."

"Holy shit."

"In light of all that, and whatever happened before, surely you can realize what it would mean to him to know that you're living a decent life, married, and about to be a father. Why not take your wife to him?"

"Oh, my God!"

"Do you hate him?"

"I never hated him."

"He's bleeding, not only in the stomach, but in the heart."

Andrew stood motionless for several seconds, then turned and walked quickly along the edge of the water. He stopped suddenly, as if aware that he was racing for no purpose. Obviously perplexed, he spun around and tread back, more conscious of each step. When within earshot of Charley, he asked, "What's it to you, anyway? I mean, why are you into this? I don't get it. I don't understand."

"I'm a cop following a trail."

"A cop?" Andrew's eyes flared.

"Yeah, a police detective. But I'm not on a case. I'm up here doing my own thing."

"Your own thing?"

"Well, I'm not out to arrest anyone. Your dad, now, he's already in custody. So, I'm trying to bandage some wounds."

"I still don't understand."

"Your father gave me a break a long time ago. You might say I'm still repaying him. But, then again, that's not quite true. Truth is, I don't owe him anything. Not any more. The debt was settled years ago." Charley picked up a flat stone and skimmed it across the water.

"So, go on."

"I guess I'm doing it because of how I feel about him and the life he made possible for me. It's a long story. I'm not ashamed to tell you." Charley picked up another stone and skimmed the surface of the lake. Then another, and another.

"So, tell me."

"Oh, I will. Believe me, I will." Charley decided to gamble. "But first, why don't you straighten me out about Korea and Timothy Wood?" The big cop trusted that his next few words would not only crack the shell but would spill the yolk. "You don't want me to see only through Wood's eyes, do you? You don't want me to have a distorted view, do you?"

Andrew's jaw fell. He could keep his eyes on Charley only briefly. Turning away, he pictured painful scenes that tightened his gut.

Charley tried to fashion a know-it-all expression, the kind that suggested unsavory knowledge, in hopes that Andrew would gaze at him again. But he couldn't hold the look long enough.

Besides, Andrew's next glance was brief because he envisioned the worst—a licentious tale of a gay libertine. Anger and frustration raged within him as he turned away from Charley and began to retrace his steps along the edge of Beebe, his eyes on the island near the mouth of the lake. He stopped again and transfixed his stare on the rippling water. Time passed painfully for him. The sun was low in the sky before he began to form phrases in his mind—difficult phrases depicting fragments of his past.

"Are you okay?" Charley asked as he approached.

"Of course not."

"Can I help?"

Andrew began to explain. His words came slowly at first. His eyes were glassy and distant, not long aimed at Charley, but quickly turned toward the water. "It was the summer of the hills and mountains. Wet. It was so wet, and the rain pushed mud down the slopes. The Commies increased their artillery fire. Our attacks were usually small probes into the hills, and we were often driven back, sometimes separated. At times it seemed the mortar and artillery fire would never stop." Andrew paused. He kept his eyes on the water.

Charley nervously picked on a fingernail as he waited. He said nothing, fearful of saying the wrong thing. His keen insight told him that Andrew was caught up in throat-tightening images.

Moments later, Andrew shook his head, breathed deeply and said, "I was tired, always so tired. Do you know what it's like to always be so tired? The nights were the worst. I'll never forget the nights. We would crouch and crawl our way up a muddy, slippery, rocky slope in the darkness and then..."

Chapter Forty-Six

The battle of the peaks, summer-fall, 1952.

United Nations and Communist forces were separated by as much as 10 miles at some points, yet at others were only 50 yards apart. Battle positions often ran along ridge lines that offered lookout posts. Intense fighting aimed at possession of the high mountains, each named by the troops who struggled up their slopes and fought bitterly to hold them: Bunker Hill, Big Nori, Kelly Hill, Old Baldy, Arrowhead Hill, Bloody Ridge, Whitehorse Hill, Sniper Ridge, Triangle Hill, Finger Ridge, Capitol Hill, Heartbreak Ridge.

Even reconnaissance patrols met heavy attacks and mortar and artillery blasts as the Communists fired up their determination to resist any U.N. thrusts northward.

Andrew Mason, Timothy Wood, Gregory Johnson and Joe Mancini were with the 25th U.S. Infantry Division, one link in a zigzagging line of a million men who faced each other and stretched across the peninsula just south of the 38th parallel. It was this division of U.S. soldiers and a Turkish brigade whose agonizing hand-to-hand combat led to the taking of Heartbreak Ridge.

But after thrust upon thrust, somewhere and sometime in the darkness of night, Mason, Wood, Johnson and Mancini became separated from the others and found themselves down a muddy slope, hiding in a thicket of pine, the night sky all about them exploding with gunfire. They were disoriented, unsure of their whereabouts after a series of turns, after slipping and sliding in torrential rain and running wide swings around clusters of rocks and stubby trees. Only Wood and Mancini had held onto their weapons, but each had little ammunition. The combat fatigues of all four oozed with water and mud. The men huddled together, clinging to each other as the night breeze sent chilling shivers through their aching flesh and bones. They shared the warmth of their weary bodies as they slept together on a wet bed of mud and pine needles.

But total exhaustion was not enough to prevent Mason—so youthful, even boyish—from waking now and again and yearning for his father's house. How clearly he saw it reaching toward the heavens on a moonlit night, the clouds racing high above its rooftops. How he craved the womb that was his room—the womb that cradled him and held his treasures. How he wished to sit in his window and fish for cherries.

Mason was deep in slumber when the Korean dawn brought a thin, hazy band of light to the jagged horizon. Mancini shook him and whispered, "Get up!"

The morning was quiet and heavy with drizzle. The eyes of the four men darted here and there as quicker heartbeats replaced the slower beats of slumber. No one else was in sight—friend or foe. They looked at each other, spoke little, and crouched as they moved from their thicket.

Mancini was a small-boned, dark-eyed, third-generation Italian-American with a quick wit that boosted morale. A native of Newark, N.J., he was the first to brush off adversity and often smiled widely, displaying bright teeth that contrasted with his olive-tone skin.

"You know something, Mancini, I've never been with a woman," Mason whispered. "Y'know what I mean. That way."

"Y'mean you never got laid, is that what you're saying? Hey, a guy doesn't admit that unless he thinks he's gonna die. Snap out of it, will you? You ain't gonna die."

Wood was close enough not to miss a word, and he stayed close and kept his eyes on Mason. A young version of the Philadelphia gift-shop owner, he was tall, thin and clean-shaven, having not yet considered a Vandyke beard. His unblemished skin was pulled tightly over his high cheekbones, and his clear-cut features and gray-green eyes contributed to a smooth yet bony and hollowed kind of handsomeness. Sandy hair showed from under his helmet. Out-of-place in war, he was lost from that small town in the Midwest. His eyes were unsettled, often searching. He seemed to yearn for attention, friendship, meaning in relationships, but was often too defensive to relate fully to the other men, except for Mason.

Johnson led the way as the foursome moved stealthfully. A tall, solemn-faced farmboy of only 19, Johnson hailed from rural Minnesota and owned muscles formed by years of lifting bales of hay from dawn to dusk. He was suited to the Korean countryside and found strength to trudge through wild terrain whether it was muddy or dry, denuded or thick with underbrush. A long-faced blond, he was sad-eyed, partly because his bushy eyebrows sloped downward toward his cheeks. His Adam's apple was large and protruding, his ear lobes long.

"Slow up, damn it!" Mason said after gulping air. Trailing the pack, he was softer and thinner then the Andrew Mason of decades later. Although handsome in most eyes, he was not yet as muscular as the Cornell gardens would someday make him. He showed no touch of the crow's-feet that future years in the summer sun would give him. Six-foot-one, he was almost tomorrow's Billy Bannon, but taller with lighter hair. Perhaps he was close to the Billy Bannon who would emerge after four years of college, his cranium spread, his face marked with greater intellect. At first resented by some because he was college educated, Mason grew to be well liked by his fellow soldiers. He hated military life, but he made friends.

The deep gray sky made it difficult for the foursome to tell east from west, north from south. They trudged down a slope, clinging to rocks and trees when the going was steep. In time, they reached a valley and a small plot of trampled grain—not rice, but what looked like millet, once cultivated in the rough terrain.

"This way," Johnson said as he pointed.

Ahead they saw the remains of a stone and mud fence that had previously protected a house and courtyard. Barely apparent were vestiges of chicken coops and storehouses. Only the large stones that had marked the corners of the house remained.

Mancini and Mason kneeled on the wet earth, along what might have been a pathway leading to the homestead, and pulled radishes from the well-soaked soil—large, white, overgrown, woody radishes, once part of a garden patch, perhaps seeded from a previous season. Wood and Johnson joined in the digging and pulling. Soon all four sat on the ground, brushed away as much dirt as possible from the roots, and munched quickly on the tough radishes as they worried about lack of shelter from the enemy. They neither spoke nor looked at each other as they ate and ignored the grit they cracked between their teeth.

The four men feared their surroundings, not knowing if they were in enemy territory or safely behind their own battle lines. They fled from the radish patch and raced toward a pass between ridges, hoping they were heading south. Within a half-hour, they reached a small patch of basswood and birch along a narrow stream in the lowlands between hills. They stopped, looked about, knelt, then cupped water in their hands and drank. Uncertain of their next moves, they worried and waited for they-didn't-know-what. Mason sat against a birch tree, gripped his knees with his arms, bent forward and buried his head.

Wood squatted nearby and asked, "Are you okay?"

Mason grunted.

"You sure?"

Mason lifted his head, but didn't look at Wood. "My mother. She's dead, you know. She used to play the harpsichord. When I was a boy, I'd sit beside her. She'd take my fingers and put them on the keys."

Mancini stood by the stream, but gazed at nothing. Johnson stretched out among the trees and closed his eyes.

But the foursome felt it unwise to rest long.

Hours later, after wandering far and eating roots, berries and fern tops, they finally neared some sort of a homestead that appeared converted to a military outpost. They kept their distance and stayed well hidden behind a hill and in a thicket of brush.

Mason moved his foot and crunched dried stalks and seedpods.

"Shush!" Johnson whispered.

Movement of guards in and out of the gateway sent fear surging through each of them when they recognized the markings of North Korean troops. They remained frozen, fearful of moving backward or forward, and kept their eyes on the compound of stone, wood, mud plaster and straw. When they had gathered their wits, they slipped away, again following vegetated lowlands between hills.

On the second night they slept in another patch of pine. The drizzle had stopped, but the cool night breeze forced them to huddle again, seeking the warmth of each other's bodies. As before, Wood rolled close to Mason.

Not until late afternoon of the next day, amidst brightness of the week's first sunshine, did they sight a homestead that appeared deserted but almost intact. It rested on a narrow plane among overgrown, weed-filled gardens. With care, and bending their shoulders toward the ground, the four Americans hurried down a slope and through high grass and thorny brush toward the mud and rock fence and an open gate. Wood and Mancini cocked their rifles and held them tightly. Mason pushed himself faster then his legs could carry, and he fell forward, sprawling into a clump of wild Manchurian peonies. Wood came to his aid instead of staying alert to possible danger and concentrating on his forward movement and loaded weapon. Mancini and Johnson were too intent to notice.

"I'm okay," Mason complained, annoyed by Wood's solicitude. He pulled his arm away from Wood's grasp, kicked himself loose from the peonies, struggled to his feet and trudged on.

Wood stood still for an instant, watched Mason, then quickly caught up with the others.

The homestead ahead was apparently the last of several that had once clustered together, forming a small village whose inhabitants shared a common well. Beyond it lay the remains of other houses and courtyards, so smashed and pillaged, then rained upon, as to be seen only as lumps of earth and vegetation among high grass and weeds. The pattern emerged to the men as they neared.

His rifle raised and thrust forward, Mancini was the first to step through the gateway of the homestead—a typical rural Korean property, built around a courtyard, with worksheds and stalls forming two walls, the house and gateway-fence completing the rectangle. He was followed by Johnson and Mason, with Wood bringing up the rear. Still fearful and alert for trouble, the men moved slowly and cautiously through the courtyard, their eyes darting left and right as they tread stealthily toward the house. At their sides were stalls, work bins and implement sheds, empty chicken coops and a cow shed—but no cow. These American soldiers knew, only too well, that in times past, the courtyard had been busy with children at play, with men honing their tools, with women mending clothes and chopping vegetables. It was here that grain had been dried and threshed.

"What a waste," Johnson muttered, his mind badgered with thoughts of Minnesota farms, his father's fields of grain, his mother's dinners of abundant homegrown foods—thoughts that too often bedeviled his brain.

The color and texture of rural Korean houses—the brown tones of wood, mud and thatch—usually merged with the landscape. This house was no exception. Its roof was thick, having been covered with shocks of overlapping rice-straw thatch time and again, year after year. Eaves extended three feet from the walls, providing shade from the summer sun. Heavy timber on a base of rock and mud supported walls of woven reeds plastered with a mixture of mud and rice straw.

Mancini was first to approach the door of latticed wood covered with light-filtering paper. With the others standing close behind him, but to the sides in caution, he reached out slowly and opened the door. Shock of surprise and fear sent electricity through his body, and he could feel his hair rise. Wood, Mason and Johnson jumped uncontrollably, startled by the face that peered from the darkness. An old, gray-haired Korean man stood hunched inside the door, staring at them with scared eyes and fright distorting his wrinkled features. Neither he nor the four intruders moved as silent messages passed among them.

Mason looked deep into the old, ruddy, yellow-brown, weatherworn face—a gaunt face with high cheekbones.

Johnson was the first to step forward. He smiled, then instinctively reached out with his hand. The old man didn't offer his hand, but he smiled broadly and bowed. He was obviously relieved. So were the U.S. soldiers, but their relief was tempered with wariness. They watched the Korean bow again and back deeper into the house, and they let minutes pass before stepping to the doorway. Johnson stretched out his arms and stopped the others, then squatted and took off his muddy brogans.

"Take off your shoes," he said. "Korean floors are for eating and sleeping."

Mason was quick to comply, followed by Mancini and Wood. Their socks were nearly worn away. Their toes protruded. As each man stepped into the house he cautiously glanced left and right.

"It could be booby-trapped," Wood whispered.

"I don't think so," Johnson said as he glanced about and watched the movements of the old man. "Grandpa was left behind to die when the family fled. That's the way I see it."

The house was simple inside, like most rural Korean homes. Its mud floors and walls were covered with oiled paper, and it contained few furnishings, some wooden planks, and several wooden chests, bound in brass. Much like the outside, the inside displayed little color. But the grain of the wood and the soft texture of paper gave warmth. The air was heavy with the smell of garlic.

Johnson tried to communicate with the old man, using a few words of Japanese and Korean splattered amidst his English. He had little success, except to learn the Korean's name.

When Kim bowed again and backed toward the kitchen, the four men followed, still cautious, suspicious of what lay behind the lattice door. As Kim pushed open the sliding panel, Mancini tightened his grip on his weapon. But the old man simply smiled again and stepped down onto the earthen floor of the kitchen. The GIs stretched their necks, but saw only a crude stove—iron kettles in a covered fireplace of stones and mud—and an old wooden cabinet next to a few earthenware crocks. The fireplace was built along the inner wall to supply warmth to the rest of the house in winter.

Kim took four wooden bowls and a ladle from the cabinet and spooned kimchi from one of the crocks. Each time he filled a bowl, he handed it to one of the GIs who were crowded into the small doorway and watching his every move. The smell of garlic increased as each man took his bowl. The four Americans knew about kimchi, but only Mancini had ever eaten it before. A unique part of the Korean diet, kimchi was an unbelievably pungent pickle dish containing Chinese cabbage, long white radishes, red peppers and plenty of garlic. Kim's crock of kimchi had been aging for weeks and was a wicked blow to the American palate.

"Wow!" Mancini exclaimed as he pushed some into his mouth with his fingers. He flushed and wiped his forehead.

Aware of Korean custom, the hungry Americans knew that the old man would have offered rice if it had been available. They gathered together on the floor in the adjoining room and ate without wincing, despite burning throats, runny noses, and heavy sweat on their brows and the backs of their necks. The Korean sat cross-legged near the Americans and watched.

"Good!" Johnson said, smiling and nodding at Kim.

The other three soldiers followed suit, all tipping their heads and forcing grins.

"It reminds me of sauerkraut, only stronger and hotter," Mason remarked.

"My mom used to cook up the best kraut with pork," Johnson said, his eyes staring distantly, plaintively. "I loved that smell. Sometimes I smell it in my dreams."

"You can't smell a dream or dream of a smell," Wood said.

"I can."

"Sometimes I think I smell my sister," Mancini said.

"Your sister?" Wood questioned.

"Yeah. Her perfume. This real sweet smelling perfume. And then I see her. All dressed up for a date or something."

"Funny about smells," Mason said. "They can bring back so many memories. Like freshly cut grass. This neighborhood kid used to cut our grass, and I'd get this funny feeling. I didn't like it. I still get it when I smell cut grass."

"Why didn't you cut your own grass?" Johnson asked.

"That's the point. I did. Up until this kid comes along. My old man puts him to work around the house and tells me to go get a paper route."

"Maybe so you could make some money," Mancini said.

"I don't know about that."

"Smell of hay reminds me of my favorite cows," Johnson said pensively.

"You had favorites?" Mancini asked.

"Yeah. 'Specially old Marigold, a Holstein with a dried up utter. Nice old gal with big eyes. I wouldn't let my father send her to slaughter."

Kim nodded and seemed to give astute attention to each man as he spoke, yet had little or no understanding of the words. When the bowls were empty, he opened the chests and took out sleeping pads, knowing that the men were tired. Johnson, who took a special liking to the old man, hurried to his aid and rolled the pads onto the floor. As Mason, Wood and Mancini stretched out, Johnson sat upright on his pad near the Korean and tried to converse. Kim kept smiling, then suddenly lifted his tattered shirt, turned his back, and displayed a series of scars up and down his backbone.

"Holy shoot!" Johnson exclaimed, thinking the old man had been tortured. "They did this to you?"

Kim continued to use expression and movement in an effort to explain, smiling all the while.

Johnson finally realized that Kim was proudly showing him acupuncture and burn scars, results of treatment for an aching back in which parchment had been twisted into the needle holes and set afire. Unsure how to react, Johnson smiled and frowned at the same time, then tried to learn about the old man's family and others who may have lived in the compound. Using all sorts of gestures and a few Korean words, he asked if they were still alive. Had they fled? Were they captured? But the old Korean kept pointing to his infirmities—a crooked knee, a split elbow, a missing toe.

Questioning with his eyes, Johnson asked, "Where did they all go?" He used his hands to express children at play. He outlined the shape of a woman. He pointed in all directions.

"Yo, Johnson," Mason called without lifting his head. "Cut it, man. He doesn't want to talk about those things. They hurt too much."

"You think?"

"Shit, yeah. Don't you get it? He's escaping by showing you that stuff. Let 'im tell you about his broken bones."

The old man took a stub of dark wax from his pocket and drew pictures on the floor paper.

"Good, good," Johnson said. "That's a chicken and that's a pot.

But this? A spider? No, it's a scorpion. He repeated the word slowly: "Scor—pee—on."

Kim nodded as if he knew the word, then drew arrows from the scorpion to the chicken to the pot. Holding his belly, he grimaced, and as if drinking a toast, lifted his hands to his mouth and mocked a long swallow.

"I don't understand," Johnson muttered as he shook his head.

Kim kept trying to explain, but the 18-year-old American just didn't understand. Finally the Korean gave up and pointed to a small wall-hanging depicting waterfowl, perhaps ducks, woven into a mat of rice straw. Johnson smiled, but wondered about the truth and depth of the message.

Soon the old man fell victim to his plight. The escapes no longer held. He had no more infirmities to show, nothing more to display. Sitting stoically, he tried to hold back his anguish, but Johnson saw the struggle in his eyes. When his tears welled, Kim lowered his head to shadow his brow, as if to save face. But Johnson knew.

Mason had listened to all. He had opened his eyes and watched, finally propping his elbow and lifting his head. Mancini also lay awake. Only Wood slept.

Later, after sunset, Johnson whispered to Mason: "I wish we could do something for the old man. Maybe we could hunt and find him a couple pheasants. He won't get by the winter. He doesn't have any rice, and he's too old to hunt. His garden will die off, and he won't have any vegetables for kimchi."

Chapter Forty-Seven

Mason dreamed of giant vegetables pushing their way up through the Korean soil. Blood ran as the earth cracked, and the vegetables reached upward, twisting and grabbing at each other. They tore at green flesh and squeezed deformed buds until puss spurted.

In the morning, Mason awoke startled and found Johnson standing at the door polishing his rifle. The old Korean sat cross-legged nearby. Mancini lay on his side, his eyes open. Wood stirred.

"What's happening?" Mason asked.

"Let's get us a couple of those ring-necked pheasants," Johnson urged. "Test our aim. Get the old man some meat. And feed ourselves."

Mancini sat up, yawned widely, grunted and stretched.

Wood opened his eyes.

"We'll split into pairs," Johnson suggested.

Mancini frowned and said, "We only got two guns."

"So, one for each pair," Johnson said. "We'll cover two areas. But nobody goes alone."

"I don't like it," Wood said.

"There's a big patch of high weeds and grass to the north, just this side of some scrubby pines. On the south side there's woodland with a lot of underbrush. We're bound to find pheasant. Maybe even a wild boar."

"You don't know what the hell we'll find out there," Wood said. "Maybe a couple North Koreans."

"Goddamnit, Wood, we gotta eat!" Johnson protested. "What

the hell y'gonna live on? We'll get so fuckin' weak we'll never find our way. Besides, the old man needs some meat."

Kim smiled and nodded, even though he failed to understand. His eyes moved from one man to another as he listened to the strange foreign words.

Johnson glanced at Kim, then looked at the others. "Face it. They left him here with his pot of kimchi 'cause he was too old to travel."

"But Koreans respect the elderly," Mason said. "It seems strange they..."

"Maybe they didn't have a choice," Mancini interrupted.

When ready to leave, Johnson tried to explain to Kim that they would return. The old man nodded and smiled, but his eyes were heavy with sadness.

Orange sunlight of morning cast long shadows in the courtyard as it warmed the brown tones. The sun's rays streamed from above the hills, brightening the tops of ridges that contrasted with the dark chasms. The slopes took on patterns and textures, deep indentations and brilliant highlights that were softened by distance and morning haze. The clumps and clusters of trees and brush were set aglow as an orange hue tinted the green, beige and umber. The countryside was quiet but for the calls of the birds.

Mason carried Wood's weapon as the pair raced north into high grass. They pushed on, finding the weeds and wild flowers thick and thorny. Insects jumped, flew and retreated as the two soldiers moved deeper into the thicket of intertwined brush and stubby, gnarled pines.

"I keep seeing his face," Mason said.

"Who's that?"

"The old Korean man. Mr. Kim. He's got the kind of face that sticks with you, know what I mean? I keep seeing him. His smile. It's like it's always in my head." Mason scratched the back of his neck, brushing away an insect. "The old guy must hurt something awful deep inside, yet he's warmhearted and generous. Now, my dad, he didn't always show what he really was. A good man, but kinda strict. Real God-fearing type. You towed the line with him, but you knew he loved you. I guess he gave me more than I ever realized. God, I hope I get to see him again." Looking at Wood, Mason asked, "You never talk about your folks, do you?"

"No. I guess I don't."

"Do you think about them?"

"Sometimes. But I try not to."

"Why's that?"

Wood's prickly body language and facial expressions revealed a touch of rancor.

"Sorry I asked," Mason said under his breath.

The two GIs pushed on, but no pheasants came into view. They were far from the house when Wood grabbed Mason by the shoulder and in a hushed voice of panic exclaimed, "Look! Look, back there! The house!"

Mason turned and immediately threw himself to the ground, burying himself in the weeds. Wood flopped next to him. They watched a band of about a dozen men move into the homestead. The intruders appeared to be rough and ragged North Koreans in torn and tattered uniforms, perhaps lost from their brigade. Mason guessed them to be pilfering deserters on the hunt, certainly no part of any organized mission.

"Thank God for the tall weeds," whispered Mason, who was even more grateful for the distance that stretched between them and the homestead. He worried that Johnson and Mancini might be unaware of the intrusion since they had pushed south, deep into high brush and a densely wooded thicket. "Shit, I hope our guys don't start back too soon."

"Y'better hope they don't fire on any fuckin' bird or beast," Wood uttered in hushed but nervous words. "You can be dead sure those bastards'll hear it."

Keeping their eyes on the house, Wood and Mason stayed on their stomachs for minute after minute, moving little except to brush away insects or shift to relieve pressure. Thoughts swam widely in Mason's head as he tried to think of what he might do to alert his friends if they headed toward the compound.

More minutes.

A half-hour.

Forty minutes.

Fifty.

An hour. And Mason and Wood still stayed on their bellies. No sign of Mancini or Johnson.

Mason thought of home again. But the thoughts were like desperate efforts to grab a piece of this and a piece that—the tall Victorian house, his mother's plants, his room, coffee at the big kitchen table, the cemetery wall, the cherry tree, the messages in his father's eyes. Never before Korea had he realized how much it all meant to him. Strange, but not so strange, to think of home at such a moment. It seemed the images flashed when peril loomed.

But the thoughts were wiped away when the North Koreans meandered out through the gateway, looked about, and then headed south where Mancini and Johnson hunted. Mason and Wood agonized in fear for their friends. They stayed prone, but soon began to crawl toward the house. Minutes later they ran through the high weeds, crouched, Mason holding the rifle. In the courtyard they found overturned bins, as if the intruders had searched, perhaps for food.

This time they didn't remove their shoes.

Inside the house, Mason and Wood looked for Kim. The sliding, lattice door to the kitchen was open, so they hurried to the doorway and gazed down at the earthen floor. There was Kim, stretched on his belly, his hands gripping his empty kimchi crock, the lid at his side, the floor sucking up blood that oozed from his neck and chest. Mason threw himself next to the old Korean man and felt for a heartbeat. Kim was dead. Looking up at Wood in horror, Mason tried to speak, but couldn't. His face was distorted by sorrow. Wood just stared, his mouth open, his eyes fixed on the body.

Seconds later, Mason turned the body over, closed the old man's fear-frozen eyes, and folded his gnarled hands over the bayonet wounds in his chest. His neck had been slit.

"They killed him," Mason whispered as his sadness cut deep. He thought about Johnson, the 19-year-old boy who had taken such a liking to Kim. "They stole the old man's kimchi and killed him." Mason had seen killing before and often, but this was different. This was the aged Korean who had taken him and his friends in and given them kimchi—Mr. Kim, who had smiled, nodded and bowed to them, who had shown them his scars, had tried to avoid the truth, had lost his family.

"We're not going to make it, you know," Wood said in sputtering words that seemed to choke from his throat in panic.

"We're not going to make it."

"Cut it out, man!"

"We're not."

"Okay, okay, maybe we're not. So let's tell ourselves it doesn't matter. That we don't care."

"Oh, shit!"

"Say it, damn it! Say it! We don't give a fuck! We don't give a fuck! Come on, damn it! Say it!"

Wood put his hand over Mason's mouth as he glanced about in sudden overwhelming fear. "Are you nuts! Stop it!" The fatalistic stare in Mason's eyes alarmed Wood more than anything, for his buddy had been his bulwark. A new kind of desperation within him suddenly changed things, reversing roles. He was now the one demanding surcease: "Snap out of it, Mason. Oh God! Come on! Snap out of it!"

Mason ripped away Wood's hand and pushed him. The two men stood a few feet apart staring at each other, hyperventilating through open mouths. It took more than seconds for them to gain control and ease their breathing. Mason was the first to focus more clearly on their plight. "We have to find Johnson and Mancini before we bury the old man."

"No. I'm not going out there."

"We don't have a choice."

"If something happened to them, it'll happen to us."

"If something did happen, we can't leave them out there."

"No. I won't go."

"Okay. To tell you the truth, I don't give a goddamn what you do. I'm going out there." Mason stepped up from the kitchen into the other room where he glanced about for the rifle. He saw it propped against the wall near the door. "Why don't you dig some fuckin' radishes while I'm gone."

"You're wrong about me."

"What's that supposed to mean?"

"I'm no more a coward than you are. I just don't think we should fuck up what's left of this deal. It's just you and me now, y'know? Just you and me. They're gone, man. So forget about them."

"Dig the goddamn radishes, and I'll do what I have to do."

Mason grabbed the rifle and hurried out through the doorway.

"Don't go. Please don't go." Wood hurried to the doorway and stopped. He stood there, hating himself as much as he hated the world.

Mason looked back but once, then sprinted south.

The sun was high over the hills now, and the orange glow was gone. No breeze stirred the grass or leaves. The day was bright and still.

Mason disappeared into the southern thicket.

A dozen or more ducks flew overhead, directly above the homestead, then south toward Mason, their deep nasal quacks echoing through the valley as a stray goral, an Asian goat-antelope, ventured from the highlands, only to turn and head back into the hills.

Wood was racked with guilt as he ferociously dug and pulled vegetables from among weeds in the hard earth of Kim's garden patch. He captured a salamander, held it by its tail, then let it go.

By the time Mason returned, the sun was almost overhead and Wood was back inside the house lying next to a small pile of radishes and greens. Mason stood in the doorway, trembling, his face ghostly white. His cheeks twitched as his lips quivered. Wood sat up, then stood. He knew immediately that his friend was in a state of shock. Saying nothing, he watched Mason move to a corner of the room, slide down the wall and sit hunched.

"Mason! Say something."

Mason shivered uncontrollably. He folded his arms across his chest in an effort to control the shaking. His glassy eyes told Wood that he had seen horror of some sort. Each time he tried to spread his quivering lips, no words came, and Wood realized that his friend was emotionally unable to speak.

In time, Wood decided to chance a question: "What is it?"

Mason failed to respond. He didn't even focus on his fellow GI when Wood kneeled before him in search of sparks of awareness in his eyes.

"Tell me what's wrong!" Wood suspected the worse and wanted to comfort his friend, but didn't know how. He yearned to reach out and touch him and soothe Mason's quivering flesh, but didn't dare. "Where are they? Tell me! What happened?" Pushing himself to his feet, he slowly backed away, all the time studying his friend's painful expression.

Mason's eyes still stared afar, his body still shook. Unable to control his shivers, he again tightened his arms across his chest, this time gripping his shoulders.

"My God," muttered Wood when he saw that Mason's hands were heavy with dirt, his fingernails split, black and bloody. He backed away again, then paced aimlessly before sitting on the floor across the room. Dropping his head, he stared between his legs.

Neither man spoke as minute gave way to minute.

The sun had moved to the western sky by the time Mason stood and went to the kitchen, lifted the old man, and carried him out of the house. There in the center of the courtyard he laid him upon the earth and looked down on him. A moment later he glanced about, then hurried to the toolsheds and hunted until he found a shovel. His eyes intent, Mason spaded the earth as if possessed. He struggled to dig a shallow grave, sweating as he heaved the soil with anger.

Wood watched from the doorway, then stepped toward Mason as if to help, but was motioned away.

Breathing heavily, Mason walked to the door, shoved Wood out of the way, went into the house and returned with the kimchi crock and placed it atop the grave. Using the colored wax, he wrote on the crock: "Here lies Kim, who shared his kimchi."

At sunset, the two soldiers said nothing to each other as they chewed raw vegetables.

That night Mason's shivers returned as the temperature dipped. Again he seemed powerless to control his body. He curled into a tight fetal position, holding fast to his knees with his arms.

Wood was afraid to ask more questions about Johnson and Mancini. He lay next to Mason. In time he curled up tightly, put his arms around him, tried to warm him and ease the shivers. They stayed wrapped together as the night grew late, but they did not sleep. Finally Mason relaxed and stretched out somewhat, not so much by choice, but involuntarily from pure need. It was as if he had to escape the shivery trauma or be consumed or ravaged.

"Remember how Johnson would talk about the farm," Mason said in slow, quiet words, "about how he used to whistle old Swedish melodies while loading bales of hay, about the wheat fields when the wind blew and the grain looked like a rolling ocean of gold." Mason's voice was strange and distant. He spoke as if compelled to remember, as if pushed by painful recollections. "He was just a big kid, and he wanted to go home for his sister's wedding. He wanted to hold his baby brother again." Mason swallowed hard and tried to wet the lips of his dry mouth. "The guys in the barracks used to kid him about his big ears. Remember? He'd laugh and kid right back." Then an unnatural whisper moved up from Mason's larynx: "The Commies cut off his ears." For a moment he was quiet and breathed in quick, short gulps. "They cut off his ears and stuffed them into his mouth." Tears rolled from Mason's eyes.

Wood didn't want to hear any more, and he tightened his hold on his friend. "Don't, please," he whispered.

But Mason went on: "I buried him. Not deep, but I tried. With my bayonet and my hands. The roots. The goddamn roots were in the way. Oh God. Help me. They cut him apart. I buried the pieces."

"Shush." Wood put a hand on Mason's cheek, felt moisture and wiped away a few tears.

"Then I found Mancini's head, and I buried it. That's all I could find. His head. That's all."

"Stop it!" Wood couldn't take it. His saliva turned bitter and his heart seemed to pound heavier with each of Mason's words. "Stop it! Please stop it!"

"Mancini wanted to taste his mother's linguine again. Linguine and meatballs. Well, he's not going to. No more fuckin' meatballs! Do you hear that God? Are you listening? No more fuckin' meatballs!"

"Stop it!" Wood shook his friend, then tightened his arms around him.

The night was among the coolest of the season as a Manchurian high pushed south. Outside, clear air opened the sky to millions of stars. The moon was full and bright enough to cast shadows in the courtyard.

Time passed.

The moon moved across the sky.

"It's all over for us, man," Wood whispered. "Isn't it? You said so yourself."

"What I said was, tell yourself you don't care."

"How do you do that?"

"Try."

"Okay. I don't care."

"Good."

Wood moved his hands here and there about his friend's slender body. Mason didn't flinch, needing anything that eased the pain and gave comfort, anything that might help him forget. The desire for human touch was strong. Wood sought the gratification he craved. He unbuckled and unbuttoned, fingered flesh and fondled. Mason submitted. They used each other.

The episode went unmentioned the next day.

Mason and Wood remained in Kim's house for three more days, each night escaping by using each other.

Chapter Forty-Eight

Andrew stepped back from Beebe Lake, lifted his head, and breathed deeply in an effort to gather strength from the autumn air. A breeze cooled his moist eyes. Without looking at Charley, he began to walk east toward the mouth of the lake where water tumbled over rocks in Fall Creek before spreading into the wide, placid pool. He kept his head high despite his sadness and apprehension. Charley followed at a distance until Andrew stopped and gazed deeply into the autumn trees that stood half naked, half in brilliant dress. Then, with Charley at his side, Andrew spoke again:

"When I came home, I was lost. I tried to find a job, but there wasn't much for a political science graduate with no experience except ground fighting in Korea. My father was kind. But his patience filled me with guilt. Finally I found myself a job as a clerk in an insurance company. It wasn't much, but at least I could hold up my head.

"It took me time to learn to mix. I just didn't feel like talking much to old friends, except with Larry, and maybe that was because he had problems. My dreams were nightmares, and I had to work hard at trying to forget. The struggle not to think about Korea seemed to sap my strength."

"Let's sit," Charley suggested. "Over here." He pointed to a large, flat rock. "Come on. I don't know about your knees, but mine aren't what they used to be."

Andrew glanced at Charley, then looked away. He stepped

toward the sizable hunk of smooth stone, hesitated, then sat, but remained silent for seconds after Charley joined him.

In time, the big cop made an effort to spur Andrew into continuing his hurtful discourse. "So, after you settled in with your dad?"

"I worked a lot in his garden. Maybe it was partly an escape, but it kept me going. It seemed I had to work with my hands because my head wasn't ready for much." Andrew looked down between his knees and tried to control the bounce in his nervous feet. "But little by little I put the pieces together. Thank God Larry had problems. Poor, crazy guy. Strange how we used each other. I guess I liked his dependency on me. I needed him because his problems diverted me from my own. By telling him how to live I began to teach myself. He thought I was so strong. Crazy fool.

"Then they came. I'm not sure what year it was. Two or three years after the war I suppose. It was fall, like this. I know it was fall because the cherry tree was dropping its leaves. When I answered the door I felt this horrible, agonizing pull on my mind and body. I was brought face to face with the worst part of my life and all of its ugly images. I didn't want to remember, but Wood's face made me remember.

"'Hey, old buddy, look who's here to see you!' he said. I just stood there with my mouth open, unable to invite him and his friend into the house. It seemed he didn't belong in my father's house. He was of a different world and a different time. And I was no longer the person he knew in Korea. That was a different Andrew Mason.

"I remember his words so clearly. Even today they reverberate through my head. 'Aren't you going to invite us in, Mason?' That's what he said. Those words, they still cut deep and send a shiver up my spine. It's a moment that thrusts itself into my dreams even now, after so many years. I couldn't speak. I remember glancing to see if my father was near, even though I knew he wasn't home. Finally, I stepped back. But I felt sick as Wood and his friend walked in. They pranced around the living room looking at my mother's plants and gushing about this and that. And I felt sicker. They didn't belong there.

"Wood's friend was Peter Scott, a pale, skinny thing with icy blue eyes who laughed at just about everything with one of those nervous laughs that was half giggle. He was younger than Wood. Always wore tight pullovers that showed his ribs. He was into faded jeans, wide belts and big brass buckles. Wood called him Scotty. I got to hate the name Scotty. Over and over it was Scotty this and Scotty that. Oh, look at this, Scotty. Feel this, Scotty. Taste this, Scotty.

"Wood asked if he and Scotty could stay a few days while they tried to find work in the city. Said they were out of cash and didn't know anyone else. I tried to give them reasons why they couldn't stay, but my excuses were feeble, and Wood showed annoyance. He kept telling me that we were bosom buddies, that we owed each other something, that we were bound by what happened in Korea. I tried to convince myself that I was over-reacting, that these were just two human beings who weren't to be feared, that what happened over there was just some strange thing that happened in war.

"I told them they could stay. I knew my father would be home any minute, and I didn't want any unusual or revealing give-and-take to occur in front of him. Besides, I thought maybe I did owe Wood something in some odd way—a debt of a sort after two years of hell together. But mainly, I guess I was scared. Oh God I didn't want them there. But I just didn't know how to get out of the icky muck or whatever it was.

"My father didn't like them from the start and sensed that Wood had some sort of weird hold on me. And he particularly didn't like the way they took over and helped themselves. They kept late hours and slept until noon. They ate what they wanted, when they wanted. After three days I asked them to leave, but Wood confronted me with what happened between us in Korea. I wanted to kill him.

"At first, I tried to make it work. Even drank beer with them at the Redwood. But each time I asked them to leave I was laughed away. I recognized blackmail even though it was never mentioned.

"Late one night, when they were in the kitchen drinking beer, I came down the back stairs and asked them to keep quiet. They were drunk, and Wood asked me to sit on his lap. I just stared at them, and they both laughed. Then Wood said, 'Why don't you stop pretending, Mason? You know what you are. Give in. I remember, and I'm sure you remember.' I think I would have killed him then and there if I could have. But I turned and went up the stairs. My father was standing in the hallway in his pajamas, a strange look on his face. I'm not sure what he heard or thought, but he questioned me with his eyes, and I know I showed guilt. I looked away from him and said, 'I'll tell them to leave tomorrow.' It had been seven days, and this was the seventh night. I'd been sleeping in the guestroom since they came. As I headed there, my father stopped me and said, 'If you don't, I will. I want them out of my house. They're only here because you said one was a friend who helped you during the war. But I think you're wrong. Timothy Wood is no friend and you know it. Maybe tomorrow you'll tell me the truth.'

"I couldn't sleep. I felt weak, unmanly, humiliated, disgraced before my father. But I would have taken almost any kind of abuse to keep Dad from knowing what happened in Korea. I even wondered if I would kill myself if he found out. Strange the kind of horrible thoughts you get at night sometimes. You lay awake, and the thoughts get worse as they go round and round and pull you down. That night I lay awake for hours, and just like the night before, I could hear them in the big bed in my room. I knew. I had known for several night. The sweat was heavy on my forehead and under my arms. I hated like I had never hated before. I got out of bed and walked quietly into the hallway, barefoot, only in my briefs. For a moment I stood before the door to my room, then I opened it and switched on the light. I saw them together, but they didn't care. They looked up and laughed, then they went on. Then they looked up again and laughed. 'Join us,' Wood said. I told them to get the fuck out. I didn't want to yell because of Dad, but I kept telling them over and over. 'Get out! Get out! Get out!' I remember calling them leeches and blood suckers. And they kept laughing. I tried to control myself, and then begged, 'Please. Please go.'

"Finally, Wood looked serious and said, 'Come over here, and we'll talk about it.' Like a fool I stepped closer and they grabbed me and started laughing again as they pulled down my shorts. They threw me on the bed and tried to use me. They acted like it was all in fun, some big joke. I was about to break away when the door opened and my father stood there looking at us. Never will I forget his look of horror and disgust. What he saw tore him apart. He was a man I had never seen before. His face seemed to swell up like it was going to explode. He couldn't look on us, but he did. I knew he would never forget. I knew that the image would always stay with him, that he would be tormented the rest of his life, that he would think my nights in Korea were like that. I'm sure he's never been the same. And I guess I'm not really surprised at what you've told me happened to him. I tried to explain, but there was no way. He shouted and ordered me to leave his house. He refused to see me, talk to me. Even years later I wrote to him, but my letters always came back. I was dead in his eyes.

"That night, Wood kept apologizing. 'It was all in fun,' he said. For years he tried to say he was sorry. But I wouldn't let him.

"I went to Larry. It seemed I had to tell someone I was leaving. I guess I wanted one connection with the past, just in case." Andrew viewed Larry Malvern as alive. It was as if he were oblivious to Charley's ugly story of Larry. But suddenly he felt a weakening sweat sap his strength as his throat filled. "My God, he's dead." Still, he couldn't grasp the truth of it. He stood and walked to the edge of the lake. There he stayed for moment after moment, now and then pushing his fingers through his hair. He picked up a pebble and tossed it into the water. "Larry's dead." He watched the ripples, kept gazing into the water long after the little circles of waves disappeared, and he found a reflection of the past.

Charley waited at the rock, giving Andrew time alone. But after minutes passed, he also stepped toward the lake, yet said nothing.

"I remember how Larry used to sneak up behind me and pull out my shirttail," Andrew reminisced aloud. "Funny thing to remember, eh? He used to shout for me, 'Hey, Andy-o-buddy-o!' I'd stick my head out the window and ask, 'So, what's your problem this time?' Crazy guy. We had good times. Real good times. Poor Larry." Andrew looked toward the sky and yelled, "Oh, shit!" Then he closed his eyes and said, "It shouldn't have happened. It doesn't make any sense."

Charley wanted to say something, but couldn't find the words. He simply waited and watched.

Andrew was quiet for several minutes, then said, "I'm John Smith, and I don't like it when Andrew's ghosts come back to haunt me. John

Smith was born here. This is my place, my life. I can't go back. You don't understand how hard I've struggled to close out the past."

"But maybe you'll never really be free of it," Charley said. "Maybe there's only one way to free yourself."

Andrew turned his head and looked at Charley. "I can't. I can't go back. I could never face him."

"Your father was wrong. Why don't you forgive him?"

"Has he forgiven me?"

"Maybe."

"I doubt it. How could he shake off that image? No, he couldn't really forgive me. Anyway, I don't feel forgiven."

"He asked to see you."

"I don't know that I could face him even if he said he forgave me. Besides, I have a wife. A pregnant wife. And she doesn't know."

"Does she love you."

"Yes."

"You know that?"

"Yes. Without question. I've never been more sure of anything."

"Then don't be afraid."

"You don't understand."

"Maybe you're more afraid of yourself."

"What do you mean?"

Charley didn't answer. He simply stared with eyes that asked questions.

Andrew turned away.

"I owe you a story about my past. I promised you an explanation. But first I want to tell you about my son, Billy, and about your father's house."

"I see that house in my mind's eye again and again," Andrew said in a wistful tone. "It's an image I can't seem to erase. That, and visions of my room, my window, and the cherry tree."

Charley's next words were stuck in his larynx. He struggled, then said, "I have some more bad news. The house, well, it burned. It's gone."

Andrew stared at Charley in disbelief. He said nothing. His lips began to quiver, then his eyes welled with tears.

Chapter Forty-Nine

Andrew and Beth sat across from each other at the polished pine table in the dining area of their airy and arty apartment. The only light that edged their silhouettes was an early evening glow from outside. Both heads hung, their eyes staring into empty coffee cups. Neither husband nor wife sought the gaze of the other, and Andrew welcomed the darkness. He had been talking for nearly two hours. Beth was still listening, trying to take in all of his words and fit them together, almost afraid to speak. An open envelope and a two-page letter lay on the table between her hands.

"I never wanted to tell you all this," Andrew said. "I figured that even if you played the part of the understanding wife, even if you said you could live with the thoughts or wipe the slate clean or just forget the whole thing, I'd know that the images would always be there. There'd be times when you'd picture it all, and you couldn't shake it off completely. And then there'd be me—my knowledge that you knew, my constant fear that it bothered you, perhaps that you were haunted by the images. How could I ever be sure? So, now you know, and I can't do anything about those fears. They're just going to be, I suppose.

"That steel strongbox that you wondered about. It contains a few pieces of my past life. Strange, I wanted to cut off everything, every trace of the past. But I couldn't completely. For some reason I had to hold onto that one box of memories, even though I opened it only once in two decades. I guess I feared the time might come when for some reason I'd have to prove who I really was. My birth certificate. My college transcript. But some crazy things, too. Like a little bird book that my mother gave me. Even the stripes from my Army uniform. One of my toy soldiers, and even a silly picture of Larry Malvern sticking out his tongue. More than that, I kept some pictures of my mom and dad. I don't think I could ever take the hurt of looking at them. I've been afraid to. Maybe that's why I've never opened the box, except to hide that letter. Timothy Wood's last letter."

Andrew was suddenly quiet, as if his thoughts had clogged his throat.

Seconds later he said, "My mother was killed in a car crash when I was a teenager. Smashed between two trucks in an eight-car pileup. I've never really gotten over it. Dad had such a hard time trying to tell me. I went to my room, and I wouldn't come out. He suffered. I never realized how much he loved her until the years passed and I looked back on how he treated her. Always like a very special lady. He adored her. I can still see him offering his arm to her on Sunday morning and walking her off to church. She was very pretty, my mother.

"Then Dad put all of his hopes in me, his only son, a piece of my mother that he still had left."

Andrew pushed back his chair and turned away. Then he stood and looked everywhere but at his wife, almost as if hunting for an escape. Suddenly, with a surge of courage and hope, he spun toward Beth and looked at her. But her eyes were still down, and his hope dimmed. He wanted to plead, but couldn't, knowing it would be wrong. He didn't want her pity or sympathy; he wanted her acceptance.

"Why did you keep this letter?" Beth asked.

"I'm not sure."

"I think I know."

Andrew simply stared at his wife.

"You wanted some kind of proof in case you got found out," she said. "You wanted to be able to toss it on the table in front of somebody. As it turned out, that somebody is me."

Andrew flinched, but said nothing.

"This guy Wood kowtows to the extreme in saying he's sorry, sorry, sorry. He insists he knows you're not of his ilk. And he gives you every possible out, every possible excuse for what happened in

Korea." Beth looked down at the letter. "What's he say here? You were like young sailors at sea, starved of affection. Or prisoners behind bars." Beth looked up, then down again. "Then there's this whole paragraph on arrested adolescence. Two Boy Scouts in a pup tent? My God! Was your adolescence arrested, John or Andrew or whoever you are?" She stood and walked away.

Andrew couldn't read his wife, couldn't sense the meaning of her tone, her inflections. He watched her enter the bedroom. Sickness and shame overwhelmed him. Emotionally overwrought, he hurried to the door and left the apartment, taking two steps at a time as he raced toward the street.

Not fully aware of where he walked, Andrew let his legs take him up the hill while his thoughts spun in misery. A sad figure in the dusk of evening, he trudged on, his head down, his body racked with distress. Mental and physical hurts merged, and he saw himself stripped of his life.

A few Cornell students passed him as he pushed on through autumn leaves on the cracked sidewalk, unaware of his surroundings. He remembered yesterday, his excited wife, bubbling with laughter and fun as she kept him out of the bedroom while she hid his birthday present. How happy she was, simply because of a day in the life of her husband. He could barely swallow.

Evening grew darker.

Lights went on in the upper rooms of the big, old rooming houses as students settled in to study.

Andrew disappeared somewhere in Collegetown—the cluster of shops, restaurants and taverns outside the gates of Cornell.

Four hours later, Andrew was still on a barstool where he had been for more than three hours. He was slumped over the bar, sucking on his eighth bottle of beer. A few students drank at the bar, but it wasn't crowded. Others sat at tables in the dimly lighted tavern of dark wood, Cornell banners and fraternity crests. Someone put hands on Andrew's shoulders, startling him from unhappy thoughts. He turned and saw Beth.

"No wonder you looked so strange when I picked the name Andrew for our baby," she whispered into his ear. "You didn't know I was psychic, did you?" Speaking even more softly, she whispered into his other ear. "Timothy Wood is right. I know you too well. I've looked into your eyes too many times. I've held you in my arms and felt the right messages. I've slept with you." She kissed his cheek. "I decided to bake you another birthday cake. Chocolate this time, instead of vanilla, because you really like chocolate better. Don't you?"

Chapter Fifty

"What's wrong with you?" Mary Bannon said in frustration. She stood at the front door, ready to leave the house. "Settle yourself. And stop running up and down the stairs."

"I need Bob's dolly so I can cart my gift," Billy said. "It's not in the basement where it should be. It's not in the garage, the attic, or his closet."

"I think he took it to school. Call him."

"On a Saturday morning! You gotta be kidding!"

"Well then, I don't know, Billy. You'll have to figure out something else, I guess."

"Where are you going?"

"To the mall with Martha Greene."

"I need something to wrap it in."

"Don't you dare use that blue tablecloth. Like I said, there's not a thing wrong with it."

"It's old. You never use it."

"Billy!"

"Jeeze, Mom."

"Wrap it in gift paper like you're supposed to."

"It's too awkward and heavy. Like I said, it'll tear. I need something strong."

"Well, not my tablecloth." She glowered at him. "Now, I have to go. And I want to find that tablecloth in the closet when I get back. And calm down. Mr. Mason's son's not going to disappear. I suspect he'll be there most of the afternoon. Now, call your brother.

He has no right to sleep this late. And ask him if he's coming for dinner tomorrow." On her way out, she muttered, "We never see him. He might as well live in another country."

Seconds later, Billy was hanging on the kitchen telephone listening to a dormitory student at Temple University hoot like an owl, laugh, clear his throat, and then say, "Fourth floor, Johnson Hall."

"Would you knock on room four-forty and get Bobby Bannon to the phone, please."

"Last night was a party night, dude. You want me to wake him?"

"Yeah. He's my brother. It's important."

"Hold on."

Minutes later a hoarse and sleepy voice said, "This better be good, Billy."

"I need your dolly, and I can't find it anywhere."

"You need my what?"

"Your dolly. You know, that thing you push and pull stuff around on."

"Is that why you got me out of bed? I don't believe this. It's here. I used it when I changed rooms. Remember?"

"Can you bring it home?"

"When."

"Now."

"You gotta be kidding! We're heading up to North Jersey for the Rutgers game. What do you need it for, anyway?"

"Forget it."

Seconds later Billy was on the phone with Clarence: "Your little brother still got that wagon? You know, the old one with the wooden slats on the sides?"

"It's in the cellar, I think."

"Can I borrow it? I need it something bad."

"What for?"

"To carry that thing I was telling you about."

"It's only got three wheels. One came off."

"Can you fix it?"

"If I can find the wheel."

"Find it, please. Then call me. I need it right away. I could use you, too."

After hanging up, Billy immediately dialed again.

"Hello."

"Lori, I need something to wrap this thing in. Before you come over, find something for me, will you? Paper won't do. Some kinda tough material. But a nice color, y'know? Hunt through your mom's stuff. And see if you can pick up a big bow somewhere. It's gotta be big. And make sure the colors go."

After a moment of silence, Lori asked, "Are you finished?"

"Ah, Lori, please."

* * *

One o'clock. Mary had yet to return. Lori was in Billy's bedroom looking into his microscope. "Oooh, what funny-looking things, especially the wiggly ones with hairs."

"It's water from the swamp over by the causeway," said Billy as he continued to examine the curtain Lori brought from her attic. "Gray isn't exactly what I had in mind. But it'll have to do."

"That's not gray. It's a decorator shade of blue."

"Whatever."

"Put the big yellow bow against it and it'll come alive." Lori backed away from the microscope and turned toward Billy.

"Yeah, that's not bad." Billy tossed the ribbon aside, laughed and gyrated as he whipped the curtain around and around, then grabbed Lori and wrapped the blue-gray material around her and himself. He kissed her—long and fervently. They quickly fought their way out of the curtain and rolled onto the bed. They lay there, kissing, touching, feeling. Time moved fast and Billy fretted about his mother's upcoming return. But he passed off the thought in the heat of the moment.

Although they stayed fully clothed, both teenagers felt the beating of torrid impulses that pushed them on until Lori feared the point beyond. Tears filled her eyes.

Billy's emotions raged and he bit her lip.

Lori winced.

Billy pulled away and sat on the side of the bed. "Damn it!"

Lori sat up. She looked at him and smiled weakly. "You know what our folks say about being alone in the house."

"I've been so worked up. This is such a special day. I guess I was too keyed up."

Lori held him tightly around the waist.

"I can't believe we're trying to play it like in the nineteen forties or something," Billy said. "I'm beginning to wonder if they were all so pure back then anyway. Damn, they all must have been a bunch of sexless freaks or something."

Lori squeezed him. "Come on, now. We've been doing okay."

"Well, we better move. Mom might show up. And Clarence'll be here soon. With the wagon, I hope."

* * *

The package was big. It extended far outside the wagon. Clarence guided it while Billy pulled. Lori led the way and watched for bumps in the sidewalk. Where sycamore roots lifted the concrete, the threesome would steer the wagon onto the street, maneuvering carefully.

As they crossed a busy intersection, a car full of glaring teenagers slowed, then picked up speed. One of the boys yelled, "Whatcha got there, Clarence, a big yellow ribbon for your empty head?" Clarence responded with a one-finger salute.

"That looks like your father," Lori said as they approached the hospital, a massive structure of concrete and glass.

"Where?" Billy asked.

"Over there. On that bench. Near the main entrance."

"Oh, yeah. What's he doing there? I thought he'd be up in the room."

As the threesome guided the wagon to a stop near the big cop's feet, Billy looked at his father and asked, "Why aren't you with him?"

"I thought it was better if he went up alone. It wouldn't be right for me to intrude. They gotta do it their own way, know what I mean?" Charley glanced at the package. "You don't intend to take that up there, do you?"

"Why not? You can clear the way, can't you?"

"That big thing? Wagon and all? No. Listen. Why don't you

wait here awhile. Give them some time. Then go up alone, and maybe bring him down. I'll stay here with Lori and Clarence." Charley glanced at Billy's companions and nodded warmly.

Clarence stood awkwardly, his thumbs tucked under his belt, his long fingers hanging over his jeans. Always a touch uncomfortable with Billy's dad, he offered a crooked and somewhat feeble smile and stared at the ground like a shy youngster.

Lori, on the other hand, was quick to sit on the bench beside Charley and start conversation while Billy pondered his plight.

Chapter Fifty-One

Andrew and Beth entered the ICU and spoke to the head nurse. She pointed, and they walked slowly to the old man's bed. The feelings within Andrew were beyond sorting. He was a tangled mass of emotion. His trepidation, his trauma involved all of his functions, all of his life from boyhood up.

Henry was rawboned, his flesh a pale shade of putty, his cheeks drawn inward. He was still attached to tubes and wires and surrounded by bottles of fluid and plastic bags of blood. His eyes were closed.

Andrew looked at him, but failed to speak in fear of releasing tears. Beth held his hand as they waited at the bedside. Finally, the son reached out and placed his hand on the wrinkled, cold hand of his father.

Henry opened his eyes and simply stared at Andrew without uttering a word or seeming to recognize. Within moments, however, recognition revealed itself ever so slightly in his gaze. He kept his eyes on Andrew as if afraid to lose the vision should he close them or look away. In time he asked, "Andy?"

"Yes, Dad, it's me."

Henry took hold of his son's hand and squeezed as tightly as he could. He was too weak to lift his head, but appeared to try. Andrew understood, leaned down and kissed him. He knew that his father was dying, having learned from the doctors that the new drug, just okayed by the FDA, had stopped the bleeding only briefly. The only recourse now was an operation, unlikely to be successful.

Andrew's words were soft, broken, uneven: "I... I love you, Dad." He leaned over again and held tightly to his father.

The old man struggled to lift his arms, then held onto Andrew with all of his strength. He wouldn't let go.

Beth stepped back and wiped her eyes with her handkerchief. She stood quietly watching.

In time, Andrew pulled away and smiled down at his father. "Thank you, Dad, for asking me to come."

The old man kept looking at his son. "You have your mother's eyes," he said in a husky whisper, "just like when you were a little boy."

Andrew tried to smile.

"I wanted you to come long ago," Henry said. "I've always wanted you."

Tears streamed down Andrew's face. He was unable to express the things he wanted to say.

"I have your soldiers here," Henry whispered in a voice barely audible. "In that box over there."

Andrew pushed hair from his father's forehead. Then he said, "I brought you something." He put his hand behind Beth and pulled her close. "This is my wife, Beth."

Warmth showed in the old man's eyes as he looked at the woman next to his son.

Andrew took his father's hand and placed it on Beth's belly. "Your grandchild."

Henry's face was touched by peace. Tears moistened his deep-set eyes. But suddenly, in fear and panic, he started rambling incoherently about money and banks and stocks and lawyers and a crazy mishmash that upset Andrew.

"Please, Dad."

"But you don't understand. I have money in five banks." Henry struggled to raise his whispery, gravelly voice. "I have stock in three corporations."

"Stop it, Dad. I don't want your money."

"Then I won't give it to you. I'll give it to little Henry."

"Little Henry?" Andrew questioned.

Beth looked perplexed.

The old man tried to reach for Beth's belly. "Little Henry."

Beth grinned and said, "Or little Henrietta."

The old man smiled.

Andrew laughed and cried at the same time.

"You get that damn Charley Bannon to get me a lawyer," Henry whispered. "Right away. Hear me? Right away." Suddenly his eyes seemed to focus afar as if some movement had caught his attention.

Andrew and Beth turned to see a young man standing in the entranceway.

"Hello. I'm Billy. Billy Bannon."

* * *

Andrew spoke to Billy as he, Beth and the boy exited the main doors of the hospital: "You father is very special, you know."

Billy nodded.

"And he thinks your very special, too," Andrew continued. "My father must be hated by so many people." The words came hard. And the next words came even harder: "I hope he dies on the operating table." His voice quivered. "Better than in prison."

As Andrew, Beth and Billy approached the bench, Charley and Lori stood to greet them. Clarence scrambled clumsily to his feet from a curbstone under an old oak. He walked toward the others in his usual ungainly way as Billy began the introductions.

"You know my father. And this is Lori, my girlfriend. And that's Clarence, my friend. This is Mr. and Mrs. Andrew Mason."

Beth was somewhat taken aback, for it was the first time she had been called Mrs. Mason. "Please call me Beth," she said.

"My father wants to see you right away," Andrew said, looking at Charley.

The big cop started toward the hospital entrance.

"He's so different," Lori whispered to Billy. "Your dad. He's really changed."

"I know," Billy said. "Yo, Dad, aren't you going to wait for the unveiling?"

Charley turned and faced the others.

Billy smiled broadly at Andrew. "This is for you," he said as he took hold of the giant package.

Lori pulled off the yellow ribbon, Billy folded back the blue-gray curtain, and Clarence gawked. All stood silent for seconds.

"Wow," Andrew said. "It's like a harp of gold and white on a night sky. The strings seem to radiate." He glanced at Billy. "You made this for me?"

Billy stood proudly next to his creation, still smiling broadly.

"Touched by the angels," said Beth, the artist, with a strong look of appreciation. "And the heavy white frame brings it alive."

"It's from the inner workings of your mother's harpsichord," Billy explained. "I rescued the pieces from the fire."

Emotional feelings surged within Andrew. He pictured his mother playing at the harpsichord and he heard her soft, melodic words: "Ah sweet mystery of life at last I found thee..."

Chapter Fifty-Two

Henry Mason died on the operating table at 10:40 a.m. on October 27. He was buried alongside his wife in the cemetery that adjoined his property.

FROM THE LAST WILL AND TESTAMENT
OF HENRY JAMES MASON:

...and to William Lee Bannon I leave my 1942 Packard and my cherry tree and the property on which it grows.

Chapter Fifty-Three

Early spring.

Each day Billy checked his property, sometimes with Lori, who dreamed of the house they would someday build next to the cherry tree. Each day Billy looked for life among the old, charred limbs.

Time and again he worried, especially when the buds of other trees began to swell. How dark, how naked was his tree.

Then, on a sunny day in early April, he saw that swollen buds had split to expose soft pink petals. Henry Mason's legacy was alive. A radiant smile spread across Billy's face. He was buoyed by joy, and ran all the way home, bursting to shout the good news.